PERISHING HILL

LELIA A PIET

"Some things you carry around because you can't put them down.

Some things you carry because if you don't, the storm will."

— — FROM THE DUNE DWELLER LOG BOOK
SEPTEMBER 1964

When tragedy struck,
    Friendships unraveled, hearts ran amok.
    A shame no one stayed in touch,
    Especially when you all shared so much.

From long past comes a knock once more.
    Although, please, no slamming the door.
    Let's take time to get reacquainted
    and give notice to memories tainted.
    By the seaside, we'll clear the air,
    All the while waving goodbye to despair.
    Dust off your secrets kept,
    As we remember those for whom we've wept.

Make no mistake, your presence is expected
    And excuses for absence will be rejected.

.   .   .

Recall your friends from Perishing Hill,
    Then prove that you cherish them still.

A fabulous weekend by the sea awaits,
    A reunion to tempt even reluctant fates.

No RSVP necessary. Instructions attached.

one

THE FERRY

Carmen

The low thump of the radio's bass keeps rhythm with the beat of a rising headache as Gabe maneuvers the car along highway NC-12. He watches the road ahead, yawning while I work to stifle one of my own. Is it any wonder? Neither of us got much sleep last night, wrestling with the anxiety of what this summons holds. At least there are signs of civilization along the route now— a store here, a church there; oh look, an Outer Banks souvenir shop. The earlier portion of the trip was all two-lane highways, flanked by thick, overgrown forest on each side and caution signs posted to warn drivers of crossing foxes and bears.

White feathery clouds flit across the bright blue sky outside the windshield as if racing to escape. Escape from what? Unlike us, they're running away from the ocean while we make our way ever closer on this cool, crisp first weekend of November. Who goes to the beach this late in the year, anyway? It's North Carolina, for goodness' sake, not the Caribbean.

A long, dark hair snakes across Gabe's shoulder—no doubt one of mine. I reach to pluck it from his white shirt, crack the passenger window, and toss it into the wind, welcoming the rush of air on my face.

"What's your navigation app say now? How much farther?" Gabe asks, clenching the tattered leather and wood-grain steering wheel.

"The map is showing another ten miles to Hatteras Landing and then...," I pinch two fingers to expand the map screen. "I can't tell after that. The invitation didn't have an address for the vacation house, only the ferry terminal." The invitation didn't have much information at all, actually. We each received our own email invites—one for Gabe Torres, another for Carmen Torres—the same juvenile rhyme, the same lack of detail. What the host made quite clear, however, was the importance of meeting our guide aboard a ferry departing from Hatteras Landing Marina at 2 PM sharp.

Nerves grow more tender the farther we get from our home in Norfolk. Anticipation of what to expect, of who to expect, continues to poke at our normally calm demeanors. Gabe and I rarely fight, yet we've had two blow-outs already along the route.

Gabe releases his left grip to prop his elbow on the armrest of the driver's door, then leans his head on closed fist. Bored concentration? Agitation? Sullen? It's hard to guess where Gabe's mind is these days. More and more, I am witnessing what I believe to be signs of depression—the dark circles under his eyes from lack of sleep, his frequent irritability, his decline in appetite, that dull look in his eyes. Though each time I broach, he shuts me down. We are at mid-life age. Perhaps those are the thoughts behind his drawn expression, the reason why his usual spirit seems lackluster? Maybe.

I slump back into the seat, staring out at the two-lane highway stretching the length of the Outer Banks. Instead of dense forest, we are now flanked by water and sand dunes, though we do come upon clusters of towering vacation homes perched roadside to overlook the ocean. Will our host be waiting for us in one of these gargantuan monstrosities? Moreover, why is this host demanding our presence, and who else, if anyone, has been summoned?

"Did it say anything more?" Gabe asks as if reading my thoughts.

"You mean the invitation?"

"Yeah, 'course. What else would I be talking about?"

"Let's not get snappy again; you know I don't know any more than you do. We both received the same e-vite. The question is, who else is on the guest list? There has to be more than just the two of us," I say. How many times have we been over this? Since receiving the cryptic poem, we've played out this same conversation repeatedly, yet haven't gotten any further in ideals than we are at this late moment. It's tedious as well as unproductive. "Let's just get there and find out."

"It specifically mentioned the neighborhood, Perishing Hill—it hasn't been Perishing Hill in over twenty years, not since they finally renamed it. And then that comment about 'for those we've wept,' I mean, what the hell?" Gabe scoots around in the bucket seat, straightening his back. "God, my ass hurts."

"Please, don't start again." I close my eyes and tap the pads of my fingers along my pounding forehead.

"If you don't want to do this—and I've said multiple times I have no desire to participate in this weekend getaway—then why are we about to get on this ferry for Ocracoke?"

"Because, Gabe," I release the breath I've been holding in a huff. "Because we don't know who sent that invitation or what that person knows."

Terry

"The woman at the information counter said we can park the car here for the weekend," Yvonne says as she throws open the driver's door.

Watching her slip underneath the steering wheel to sit, I ask, "What do you mean park the car for the weekend? I thought we were taking the ferry across to Ocracoke."

"We are."

I tilt my head, raising eyebrows in question of her latest riddle.

"Make sure you get everything you'll need for the weekend. We're not on the vehicle ferry to the island. Evidently, our host contracted the express service ferry to take our group over to Ocracoke."

"Group? How many of us are there?"

"The woman didn't say."

Yvonne pushes the button to cut the ignition, then reaches to flip the lever, releasing the trunk hatch. "Do I need to grab the luggage, or are you done with your work notes?"

"No. I'll get it," I say. "Give me a minute to finish up this email to Phil. The bereaved of Mrs. Jensen have collectively decided on a different selection again for the deceased woman's funeral attire."

"And Phil doesn't know how to change a damn dress? Don't be ridiculous, Terrance Marshall. You're procrastinating, and we both know it."

"I'm not exercising tactics of delay, Yvonne." Although there is some truth to my wife's accusation. "Honestly, this family has revised decisions on every last detail of this funeral. Flowers, casket, hairstyle, accompaniments—you name it. Phil has his hands full."

Yvonne twists in her seat to face me. "I understand this isn't the best time to take a long weekend, but we didn't have a choice on the timing, Terry." She flips the visor down to check the mirror, smoothing her eyebrows with a fingertip, patting down a stray hair that has sprung from earlier placement.

"We didn't have to come." I hear the distinct note of whining in my baritone and work to correct it. Neither of us wants to be here. The difference is that Yvonne understands our attendance for what it is, while I hem and haw. "Simply because someone sends out an invitation doesn't mean we're required to attend." I snap the laptop closed and file it into my carryall. "One can politely decline and move on with life."

Yvonne grabs her handbag from the backseat and begins the

act of rummaging inside the deep cavern. "Well, this didn't sound like a polite request for attendance," she says, searching the depths of the bag. "Besides, we're here now, and the lady inside said the guide will meet us at the ferry station on Ocracoke, then escort us to our final location."

She pulls a lipstick tube from her bag and looks back at the mirror to apply the deep red shade. She rubs her upper and bottom lips together, smacks a couple of times, then checks her work in the reflection. "And," Yvonne adds, capping the tube once more, "if we don't hurry, we'll miss this ferry. The woman said someone contracted the express service specifically for our party. Something about how the service doesn't run this particular ferry after Labor Day—not that it matters."

"So, we're not going to have transportation all weekend? Why don't we take the vehicle transport ferry instead?"

"It's pulling out now." Yvonne reaches across my lap to open the glove compartment. "And there won't be another one until after four, which would make us late." She retrieves her weapon and slides the handgun inside her purse.

"You're packing this weekend?"

"I don't know these people," she says, stepping out of the vehicle, tossing her purse onto her shoulder.

Outside the car, I move to the trunk to haul out our weekend luggage, the scent of salty sea water attacking my nostrils.

Yvonne's long legs carry her to my side. She takes her small suitcase from my hold and begins wheeling it across the parking lot. I hurriedly pull my bag from the trunk—I've no choice but to follow, as if I've had a choice in this weekend at all.

Griff

The process strikes me as something symphony-like. Not that I've ever been to such a shindig, but the steps to the ferrying process are nothing less than orchestrated and must be performed as instructed. Skipper waves my way. He's seen me watching from aboard the express passenger ferry. I toss back the greeting, wishing I were on the vehicle transport, lounging back in the bottom compartment, shooting the breeze with the guys I've known most of my life. That's a job for you, and we all have work to do. Right now, mine involves taking this pack of old neighbors to meet their host for the weekend ahead.

Manning the information counter inside the ferry terminal, Gina alerts me each time one of the couples checks in. She's to let the couples know they should board the express ferry with their belongings and that someone will guide them to their accommodations once they reach the island, nothing more, nothing less. The host wants to deliver intentions to everyone at the same time. Seems a bit on the dramatic side if you ask me. 'Course no one did, so.... This host has some bulging pockets, but my opinion is not what I'm being paid for.

The vehicle ferry makes its way toward Pamlico Sound, the same path we'll follow once all the couples have boarded. Got some thoughts as well about taking out this ferry for only four couples rather than putting them all on the vehicle ferry. But again, money moves mountains, or in this case, ferries. Ordinarily, this particular ferry is dry-docked, doesn't even run after Labor Day because it's huge, not enough passengers to justify it. Tourists don't have much use for us once the summer's done, and there aren't many of us residents in Ocracoke.

These last twenty years or so, I've called Ocracoke home, me and about seven hundred and fifty other folks. We welcome visitors throughout the year, but the majority of them hit us up March through September. A few trickle in through October, though rarely do we see them after Halloween. No one wants to be in Ocracoke during the winter months, although I stay plenty busy with or without visitors. Lots of repairs and handiwork to be done while the island is gearing up for the next season.

Most of my time is spent overseeing a good portion of the vacation rentals on the island. It's good money, a good schedule, and I work solo, which is how I prefer it. Until recently, I've been taking care of other people's homes, but now I have one of my own, Dune Dweller. Just wrapped up the renovations on her. Season being over and all, it never occurred to me I'd get a rental on my property this year. But this particular renter found me. Deal fell right into my lap. Not calling it kismet or some such horseshit. Let's just say, after all these years, the connection between the person holding the checkbook and me... it ain't luck.

Wind's picking up. I check the skies for signs of coming weather. Don't know if any of these folks have bothered to take a look at the forecast, but from what I saw, it ain't looking good this weekend. This storm blowing in done snuck up on us.

The ferry crew and I were just discussing the incoming weathermaker with Skipper. It initially came through the Gulf and took a hit on Florida. Was supposed to keep moving through the middle of the country but got pushed east by a front. So yeah, we know it's coming, but we sure as hell weren't expecting it.

Doubt this one will be that bad, though. Did most of its damage down south, so now it'll just come tool about up here, create havoc—flooding stretches of NC-12, shutting down local businesses. Most of us 'round these parts are used to these systems rushing in, hurrying out, but the visitors aren't. That's why we don't normally rent out our vacation homes in the off-season. Liability and all that. This renter didn't give two thoughts 'bout liability. Cash up front and extra for my troubles. But to be part of this weekend, I'd have done it for nothing.

The Host

This weekend has been in the works for a lifetime, so what will a few minutes longer hurt? Patience is wearing thin now, however. While it may be an exaggeration to claim I've planned this my whole life, the fact that I've been seeking answers to these questions throughout all my walking, talking years is not.

The ferry has left Hatteras Landing and is currently making its way to the Silver Lake terminal on the island of Ocracoke.

Everything is ready and set for their long-awaited arrival. I suppose I could have been the one to escort the group, the one to welcome them to Dune Dweller.

The thing is, I want the moment of connection to be a theatrical one. I'm looking for the truth, and perhaps holding the element of surprise will keep the members of the party from coming up with falsehoods. I mean, really, is it too much to ask for the truth? Seriously? Because for as long as I can remember, I've never received an honest answer—and from family, no less. Isn't family supposed to give you the truth, not force you to gather eight strangers in hopes of finally obtaining answers that should have been readily shared long ago?

Griff is due to video call any moment now. Photos of the guests are not what I seek, however. I've done the research and accumulated all the knowledge I could via the internet and social media. Appearances are just that: what other people wish to reveal about themselves, not who they really are behind the false veneers. That's what this weekend is about—stripping back the pretenses and unveiling the secrets of the past.

I'm hoping Griff will be able to provide video footage of the guests, yet remain unaware of being surveilled, before they are welcomed into the doors of Dune Dweller. For instance, how will they act knowing this weekend has to do with their connected pasts while oblivious as to the identity of their host? Does this gathering make them nervous? Are they excited about their impending reunion? Have they already begun the celebration, having run into an old friend on the ferry ride to Ocracoke?

Willing the video call from Griff, the tablet in front of me continues to display a solid black screen, my unyielding impatience clawing at the calm exterior I'm trying to convey. And then, there it is. I press the green button to accept the video call. The screen brightens, Griff in the forefront, behind him views of the open water, Pamlico Sound, on a beautiful, cloudless afternoon. Griff holds his phone at arm's length with one hand as he reaches to tug at the corner of his eye, blinking rapidly. I nod in approval, and Griff begins to descend the stairs into the ferry's cabin.

The camera angle flips from Griff's face to the seating area of the enclosed space. Windows line each side of the boat with pairs of blue bucket seats running the length of the ferry. Down the center aisle are tables split by a partition, three seats on each side of the tables. Heads are visible, but not much more from this vantage point. Because I charted this ferry for my guests, every head I see should be arriving at Dune Dweller within the hour. Griff will need to get closer for me to understand who I am viewing, but I can't readily convey this request. Prior to setting off to retrieve our guests, I instructed him that we would not be making conversation on this call. Discretion is a must, and Griff has proved good at following instructions.

At the back of the passenger compartment, he walks the aisle toward the unmanned beverage bar (I did not pay extra for this service), stopping next to a couple seated by the window as if to check his phone. The woman turns from the window to see who is shadowing her peripheral vision. Carmen Torres. Teacher at East Tanger Middle School, eighth-grade English. Next to her is Gabriel Torres, prefers Gabe, a financial clerk for the comptroller's office of Norfolk City, Virginia. From research, I know the pair are in their early to mid-fifties, as are the other guests. Carmen and Gabe both have dark hair and eyes, though Gabe is graying significantly throughout his full head of hair and neatly trimmed goatee.

Carmen smiles politely as Griff continues to move forward. I've asked Griff, if possible, not to let the guests know who he is until the ferry arrives at the dropping point, Silver Lake Harbor in Ocracoke Village.

Griff proceeds in the direction of the empty beverage bar. He must swivel because now I am viewing the main cabin once more. He zooms in on another woman, this one seated alone. Yvonne Marshall, wife of Terrence (prefers Terry) Marshall, but where is he? I do hope she hasn't made the trip solo. Yvonne is a homemaker officially, although she helps Terry out regularly at the Marshalls' funeral home, offering condolences, arranging schedules for the bereaved to follow. Yvonne looks up at Griff. Is she trying to get his attention? Has he been standing there too long? Her dark, rich complexion is one of the loveliest I've ever seen. Though I know her age, she does not portray the advanced years.

Griff's forward movement suddenly halts. She's speaking to him.

"I'm sorry. Were you talking to me?" I hear him ask Yvonne Marshall.

"I was asking if you were waiting for the restroom."

"No, no. Just walking the boat, stretching my legs."

"Oh, good. It's my husband. He's in there. Poor thing gets seasick just looking at the water."

"That's unfortunate," Griff says to her.

"Is there another way on and off the island? Can you drive from somewhere, fly maybe?"

"We have a small airport on the island for private and chartered flights. It doesn't get much use this time of year, though. Most people stick with the ferry. Aren't any roads, bridges, or underwater tunnels to the island."

"Do you happen to know how long this ride over to Ocracoke takes?" Yvonne asks.

"Right 'bout an hour or so. Think they call it an even seventy minutes."

"Excellent." She takes a breath. "So, it won't be much longer then. I should probably look into getting something for motion sickness on our way back to the mainland. There is a pharmacy on the island, right?"

"Mmmm, yeah," he says. "Probably should sit where he can see the horizon, your husband. Helps with the motion sickness," Griff offers, taking a step forward and walking on. As he steps away, I see Yvonne look toward the bathroom once more, then back down at her phone.

Griff's stride continues as I wait for the next couple to come into view. As he rounds a corner, I spy the crowns of two more heads huddling together as if in whisper. Griff's motion halts once more. The camera view flips back to Griff's face. I see him grimace, a finger punching at the screen. I can only hope that to the onlookers, he appears to be taking a picture of the ferry's cabin. It seems he's back in control as the camera angle flips again to take in the next couple, Frank Alan and his wife Kathryn Caron—the Carrickferguses. This couple was by far the most difficult to locate due to the fact that they do not use the Carrick-fergus moniker. With a last name like that, I'd probably consider using my middle name as a surname, too.

I half expected not to recognize Kathryn, but she has applied the full coat of glamour she wears on air every evening. I understand news anchors must wear heavy makeup for their broadcasts, but I assumed this woman's face would want a break from all the cake-y cosmetics she must apply daily.

Frank is exactly what I expected, no different than his profile photo on the real estate website he maintains. From the information I've gathered, Frank is highly sought after in his field. This man is one who uses benches, buses, and billboards to display his face/person to drum up business—seemingly quite proud of his mug, by the way. Even though I don't know him personally yet, the pink polo with the collar upturned suits him somehow.

Griff continues to stroll. From what he has presented to me, the guests have not determined his identity on this special charter boat, nor have they run upon one another and had time to postulate the reason for their summons. Except for the fact that the Perkins are missing at the moment—though I know they are aboard, as Griff texted when the couple boarded the ferry—it's just as I planned, just as I wanted. My guests have no idea why they have been assembled or who has beckoned them.

Kathryn

Thank goodness that strange man is making his way down the

aisle and up the stairs. He was taking pictures of the ferry with his phone, but I'd almost swear he recognized me and was covertly trying to photograph his proof of proximity when he brags to friends and family later. I don't mind. It comes with the job, and after all these years, I've grown numb to it.

My concern at the moment is the woman across the room studying her phone. She looks terribly familiar to me, but I can't place her. I'd chide myself about age, not paying better attention to others, about the fading of my memory. But really, how can anyone fault me for not having the ability to recall all of my acquaintances over the years? Working as a high-profile news anchor in a large media market makes it impossible to keep track of everyone I meet. Because people see me daily and hear snippets from my life (and some of those don't even hold true), viewers think we have some sort of bond, that I should know them as they know me.

"Frank," I whisper around my open compact. "Frank." I should probably have his hearing checked.

"What?" He asks, his voice too loud, abrupt. Startled maybe?

I scoot farther back in this uncomfortable, god-awful seat. An errant wave slams into the side of the boat and knocks me from my position again. Who designed this monster of sea travel? Good thing I don't suffer from motion sickness. Green is not a good color for me, not to mention it's not feasible to wear the color when working in front of green screens. Come to think of it, I don't think I own anything green. I need to ask my stylist about that.

Stay on script, Kathryn.

"Do we know her?"

"Know who?" Frank asks, turning his entire upper body in the direction I've motioned. So much for discretion.

"God, Frank, really?" I snap the compact shut and toss it into my purse, digging inside the bag for effect in case the woman looks up and wonders what man is speaking so forcefully.

"Really, what? You ask me if we know someone, but I'm not

supposed to look at who it is you are asking me about. Besides, she's facing the other way. She can't see me."

"Could you be more obvious?" A hissing sound escapes, capping off the question. Sometimes that man... he sends me right over the edge. "She might not be looking, but someone else may be watching us."

"Forgive me, Kathryn. You're the one who wanted to sit inside the boat. It may be a big ferry, but there aren't many places to be inconspicuous down here in the bowels of this vessel." Frank's features screw in displeasure—not a good look for him. "What is that smell?"

"Sea air and it's wreaking havoc on my hair. Trust me, it's much better down here than up there in the wind where we'd be completely exposed to everyone."

"I simply don't understand why we're doing this. And how are we going to figure out who sent the invitation if all we're going to do is hide?"

"We're not concealing ourselves the whole weekend, but we need to figure out who is behind this so we can make a plan."

"Plan what? We don't even know why we're here."

"It's something to do with our time living in Perishing Hill. We know that much."

"That was over twenty years ago. I barely recall living in that neighborhood."

"Well, it seems someone remembers, and we need to get in front of it before that bit of history leaks. It could destroy our professional entities, Frank, and we've worked too hard to get where we are to have it unravel. We need to be smart about this, know what we're dealing with here, get ahead of it."

Frank makes a move to stand. "Where are you going?" I tug his hand to halt him.

"We can't very well figure out who she is if all we see is the back of her head. I'm going to take a look."

"Try not to be seen."

"Yes, Kathryn. Calm down already."

Frank shakes free of my grasp, runs his hands over the front of his pants to smooth away any wrinkles, and walks the length of the aisle toward the unmanned beverage area. To anyone watching, Frank appears to be searching for someone to help him at the counter. He casually turns to get a better look at the familiar woman, her head down, scrolling through something on the phone in her hands. Frank turns back to the counter, taps it twice with the palm of his hand, then returns to sit beside me in these god-awful accommodations.

"I couldn't tell anything. Looks like she's watching the restrooms. Maybe she's with someone who is in one of the bathrooms?" Frank muses quietly.

"Or maybe she's the one who is demanding our attendance in Ocracoke this weekend."

"Didn't you say something earlier about a guide meeting us at the ferry dock in Ocracoke?" Frank asks.

"That's what the woman at the Hatteras terminal desk said. I suppose that person could be on the ferry with us, but I haven't seen anyone who fits the bill. Have you?"

"That woolly man, the strange ferry worker wandering the vessel, maybe?"

Frank is good at getting accurate reads on people, better than me. "I suppose he could be our guide, but he was taking pictures of the ferry. Come to think of it though, why would one of the ferry employees be taking pictures of the cabin?"

Frank tilts his head as he lifts his perfectly groomed eyebrows in question. "Or was he taking pictures of us?"

Patrick

A bug flies straight into my face and lodges itself between my front teeth. "Jesus—" I spit, swiping at my mouth, catching the blasphemy. "Mary and Joseph, amen," I add to correct my lack of reverence. It happens to the best of us. Pastors too. We're not perfect, although we are often mistaken for it.

It's breezy up here on the deck of the ferry, but I prefer the open air to the claustrophobic confines of the cabin below. Melanie isn't keen about being out here, but she's sacrificing her happiness to stay by my side. That act alone states the magnitude of our current situation. Ordinarily, Melanie does what Melanie wants, regardless of my thoughts or feelings on the matter.

Next to me, Melanie shivers, rubs her arms. I remove my windbreaker and place it around her shoulders. Why in Sam Hill would anyone propose a seaside weekend getaway during November? We're heading to a remote island where the only activities are beaching and fishing. The only other thing I could find on the internet about this place was the tidbit about it being home to Blackbeard during his final days.

Here comes that strange fellow again. He disappeared for a bit, but looks like he's stepped back up on deck to watch us pull into Ocracoke. The unruly hair blows wildly. The man reaches into his pocket, pulls out a rubber band, grabs his hair, and secures it back into what Melanie would call a make-do ponytail. Out of the corner of my eye, I catch her also watching him. Of course, knowing Melanie as I do, she's not thinking about the man's hair—most likely, it's his cock she's picturing. I leave her to it and move to stand next to the man at the railing.

"You live on the island, or are you visiting as well?" I ask him.

The man stands straight, appearing flustered that I've approached him. He returns to his position, leaning forward, resting both arms on the ferry rail. "Yep, all year round."

"Are there a lot of residents in Ocracoke?"

"A few. 'Round a thousand, thereabouts."

"You must know all your neighbors, then?"

"Pert' near, yeah."

Talk about a man of few words. But those in my profession learn to pull it out of people, the conversation, the truth, the lies, questionable desires, and motives.

"I was under the impression this ferry had been reserved for a private group of guests?" I ask the man, digging for more information from anyone who might know something about why we're here.

The man pushes himself from the railing, standing at least six-foot-two, three, I'd say. His eyes squint in the glare of the late afternoon sun coming off the water.

"You're right about that," is all the man says—then, "Griff Munson." He offers a hand. I take it, shaking to our meeting. "Patrick Perkins." I turn, nodding toward Melanie, "My wife, Melanie Perkins."

Melanie nods, smiling through pleasantries. "Nice to meet you, ma'am." At least Griff isn't gruff—ha! He has manners, which is something you don't get much of from people anymore.

two

THE REUNION

Yvonne

Terry emerges from the restroom looking peaked or putrid—think we'll go with both—and plops down beside me.

"You okay, babe?"

"It had to be a boat," he says, using a tissue to blot the corners of his mouth.

"The vehicle ferry most likely would have had the same effect on you, honey."

Looking as if he might be sick again, I watch as my husband wipes the sweat from his brow and asks, "Have you seen anybody we know yet? Been able to determine why our presence for attendance in this full weekend soiree has been deemed necessary?"

I pass over the bottle of water we purchased at the ferry landing. "Nothing. No one. It's weird. I assumed we would have recognized someone by now. I did, however, talk to a ferry worker who lives on the island about other modes of transportation to Ocracoke. He was too young to be anyone we knew from our old Perishing Hill neighborhood, though."

"Did he say if there is another way to get back across when we're done with this farcical charade—all for the sake of recall?"

"No, I'm afraid you're out of luck. He did say the ride was right around an hour, so it shouldn't be much longer."

"The state of my physical well-being is most grateful to hear this pertinent information." Terry reaches for the water bottle I've set out for him. He swallows and brings a hand to his mouth, looking as if he might be ill again.

"Let's head upstairs. The fresh air will do you well, and we're almost there. We can watch the docking process, see if we recognize anyone up there," I suggest, squeezing his hand in comfort.

"Sounds like a good idea. Seasickness or not, I'd feel better if we could get an idea of the purpose behind this required participation. Perhaps even the person bidding it so?"

Gabe

Carmen leans forward over the railing of the express shuttle. I join her to look out over the water at the shoreline in the distance. Her long hair blows furiously around her face.

"Hey," she says, tucking the strands behind her ears. We watch in silence as the ferry approaches the Silver Lake terminal on the island of Ocracoke. "Not much longer now," Carmen adds.

"What are we going to do when we get there?" I hear the edge in my voice and work to smooth away the tension. "We still have no idea who wants us here and why."

"Someone will be at the terminal to meet us. There has to be because we have no further instructions on where to go or what to do upon arrival." Carmen has always been the optimistic one. "Surely, all of our questions will be answered once we get there." She rubs my arm to quell my anxiety. Carmen may be keeping up the appearance of a calm demeanor for my benefit, but I know underneath it, she is as concerned as I am about how this weekend will play out.

The sun is slowly beginning its descent into the horizon, the warmth of the day slipping away with it. Voices carry in the wind.

I glance over my shoulder to see who is in conversation behind us, then twist back to view Pamlico Sound just as fast.

"I'm pretty sure we have our first clue," I whisper to Carmen.

She inches closer, shoulder to shoulder. "Who?"

Another subtle peek, to be certain. "A man and woman."

"That tells me nothing, Gabe. Can't you be more specific?"

"I know. I know. Hang on." I straighten my back, holding onto the railing as I turn to face the other side of the passenger ferry. "It looks like a couple we knew from Perishing Hill."

"Well, no shit, Gabe. We had that much figured out." Carmen swivels to view the couple. "Yep." She turns back so we stand face to face rather than looking in the direction of the couple.

"What?"

"It's the Carrickferguses."

"You're kidding me." This is going to be worse than we thought.

"Nope," Carmen answers, then "And here comes the...."

Melanie

"Carmen! Gabe! My gosh, how wonderful to see you both," I wave, raising my voice to carry over the noise of the vessel cutting through the water. I'm hoping my actions convey a sincere sentiment rather than the dreaded doom I feel at discovering the pair have also been solicited for the mystery weekend.

"Melanie! I can't believe it's actually you." Carmen approaches, arms outstretched for the perfunctory greeting of two old, disconnected friends. "And Patrick," Carmen addresses my husband. "You two look great," she proclaims.

Gabe arrives at Carmen's side, offering a hand to Patrick, pumping firmly in salutation, then pulling me into a brief hug.

Patrick returns the greetings and pleasantries while I switch on the demeanor I reserve for playing the part of the pastor's wife, gushing over how wonderful the two appear to be since we last saw one another. Carmen's expression changes at something she spies over my shoulder. I turn to see what has taken her attention from our conversation.

"Is that..." I begin, but can't get their names out before Carmen steps around me.

"Yvonne! Terry!" Carmen says, "It's been ages. How are you two?" Carmen takes Yvonne into an embrace as well, then Terry.

The sound of the ferry's engine rumbles in a low growl as it pulls toward the terminal on the island of Ocracoke. The six of us huddle together against the wind, exchanging the polite words old friends speak to one another after a long absence. A shrill voice rings over the noise of the shuttle's engine, cutting through the wind.

"Well, isn't this a good-looking gang here!" Our party turns in unison to find—the remaining couple of our Perishing Hill gang —the Carrickferguses approaching.

Kathryn

"Well, paint me surprised," I shout to the group of people I haven't seen in over twenty-some-odd years. "What are you all doing here?"

"Same as you, Kathy, if I had to hazard a guess," says Patrick. He always had such a direct manner about him. I could never tell if Patrick was being matter-of-fact or flat-out rude.

"Maybe you all know, but that question remains to be answered for us as of yet," I reply. "What I can tell you with certainty is that I no longer go by Kathy. It's Kathryn now—not Kate, or Kat, or Kathy. Just Kathryn."

"Kathryn it is," Carmen gushes, leaning in for a superficial hug. "How wonderful it is to see our Carrickfergus friends again. And you two look great." She steps back to Gabe's side.

"About that," I start. (It's really best to get these housekeeping issues out in the open on the front side of a situation, I always say.) "I now use Kathryn Caron, and Frank goes by Frank Alan.

We use our middle names as our professional monikers these days.”

“Hmm,” Terry purrs in his rich baritone. “A bit unusual, but nevertheless, now that all the formalities have been addressed,” he nods in Frank’s direction. “Nice to see you.” He then offers the same nod of recognition to Patrick and Gabe before continuing. “Shall we talk about why we’ve all been gathered together for this weekend of unexplained frivolity and rehashing memories of antiquated friendships?”

That man’s voice is as slow and smooth—deliciously deep and soothing—as it was all those years ago. I hardly mind his tedious versions of getting to the point. His skill would prove a prominent selling feature at the funeral home, I think. Who wouldn’t want to listen to him speak over their dead loved one? Funny, I don’t remember him being so muscular and toned back in the day. Yes, Terry has most assuredly been hitting the gym. Not a good sign for Yvonne. When men start taking care of themselves this late in the years, it means one thing. Affair. Inarguably, he’s a good prospect for some lustful, amorous woman out there. But my mind has wandered again...

Pulling my gaze from Terry, I find Gabe watching me with that scrutinizing intensity he hasn’t lost over the years. The dark crescents under Gabe’s eyes prompt wonder at what is stealing the man’s sleep. Trouble with Carmen? It’s amazing these two are still together. I would not have bet on them lasting this long. The pair was never terribly affectionate with one another. Then again, you never know what goes on behind a bedroom door, do you?

Stay on track, Kathryn.

“I am curious why this journey has been laid out before us. Did you all get the invitation?” I toss out the inquisition to the group, hoping for some insight into the mysterious summons we’ve seemingly all received.

“We got a poem,” Patrick says.

“I would hardly call it a poem, maybe a children’s rhyme.” Melanie contradicts her husband.

Yvonne's eyes flit over the members of the group. "We got the invite, of course—that's why we're here. But I assumed one of you was behind it. Who else would know about our gang's old friendship from a neighborhood we all moved away from over twenty years ago?"

"Only Shane and Amber," Carmen says.

My back stiffens in response to the spoken reference.

The comment rattles Patrick as well. Shuffling weight between two feet and huffing, Patrick snips, "Well, we know they're not the ones behind this forced gathering."

"Sorry to put you out there, Patty," Gabe snaps. "Did they take you away from the car lot this weekend?" I'd forgotten how at odds these two always were. "There'll be other days to sell a car, but right now, we need to get to the bottom of this game that someone is playing with us so that we can return to our lives."

"I'm aware of what we need to do, Gabe," Patrick spits back. "And I'm no longer a car salesman." Patrick runs a hand through his hair and steps back toward the ferry rail, adding, "You need to calm down, man."

Melanie takes Patrick's wrist, pulling him back into the huddle. "Patrick is a pastor now. Pastor Patrick Perkins." She rubs the inside of Patrick's arm.

An affectionate move, but Melanie's not fooling me. Twenty years may have come and gone without any contact from the couple, but Melanie and Patrick have never had a touchy-feely, loving relationship. For mercy's sake, Melanie didn't even take Patrick's last name when they got married, and it didn't have anything to do with some lofty career-building tactic. Melanie has always been an attractive woman who receives a lot of attention— welcomed attention, I might clarify—from men and women. As much as I hate to admit it, I find myself enamored with her looks. If I had given the word all those years ago, I, too, would have been one of Melanie's marks, but I'm too well-known for such a scandal to break out.

"A pastor, wow," Carmen says. "That makes you the pastor's wife, eh, Melanie?"

Melanie tilts her head to one side. "Indeed, it does, Carmen. What about you? You still teaching the kiddos?"

"I am. Eighth grade English and Spanish."

"That makes sense, given your ethnic background," I say.

"Please don't be catty this weekend, Kate. Sorry, Kathryn," Carmen says. "We all need to be on the same page with the outcome of this weekend."

"And what outcome are we looking for?" Frank asks.

Terry pulls air into his lungs, expanding his broad chest, then lets out a long, heavy sigh. "The one where we all leave this island without breaking the pact we made over twenty years ago."

three

DUNE DWELLER

Gabe

That strange fellow lurking about the passenger ferry turns out to be our guide. Griff Munson. As usual, Carmen was right not to worry over the 'what next' and 'how' that often take up space in my thoughts. That's where we differ. Whatever the situation, Carmen carries blind faith that it will work its way out, whereas I constantly worry over the details and need the plan laid out in front of me before taking the first step.

Loaded and seated on a ten-passenger luxury golf cart, our crew now waits for Griff while he informs the young man in the golf cart behind us to collect our bags and deliver them to the weekend rental. Carmen cinches the belt on her jacket tighter, preparing for the breezy ride, as she gives me a sideways eye roll that says, 'What in the hell have we gotten ourselves into?'

Once he had officially introduced himself to our group, the burly man escorted us off the ferry, then explained he would take care of our luggage and get us to our accommodations for the weekend.

"It can't be too far," I assure her in a whisper, hoping I'm right, given the sun's sinking position on the horizon. "It's a small island."

Griff zooms the cart along the narrow roadways, delivering a brief history of the town. Though it isn't evident this time of year, Griff says the island is bustling during the summer season. People come from everywhere to enjoy the beaches and unplug from the rest of the world. There are several shops and mom-and-pop restaurants along the thoroughfare. We strain to hear Griff's monologue over the friendly toot-toots of passing drivers—everyone seems to know one another.

"Approximately one thousand O'cokers reside on the island, but come season, tourists pad that number to the tune of eight thousand plus."

While I appreciate Griff's shared knowledge of the island, it appears the others have little to no interest. Their expressions reveal weary resentment and little respect for the man's knowledge of his hometown. I find it interesting that the island's two hundred K-12 school children just received their new school after a horrendous hurricane took it out two years prior and that from tip to tip, the island is only sixteen miles long. I'm a numbers guy, but the others huff, fold arms over their chests, and scroll furiously through cell phones while complaining about spotty service.

"You all are the first group I've had in the house since I finished the remodel," Griff informs us.

Frank leans forward, raising his voice over the noise of the wind and the cart's engine. "How long have you had the house, Griff?"

"'Round a year and a half now."

"Must have been a big remodel," Frank weighs up, letting the rest of us know this is his line of expertise.

"Yeah, bit of a mess it was." Griff signals a left turn. "Not anymore, though. Size of the place was the biggest issue."

"And it's on the beach?" Yvonne asks, raising her voice to be heard from the vehicle's third row.

"Yes, ma'am," Griff answers. "Only house on the island to be on the east side. Most of that strip is the Cape Hatteras National Seashore. Because of some old permitting laws, we were able to get this house up and running for renters. But if you're not a fan of the ocean, don't worry; there's a hot tub for your use."

Yvonne looks to Terry, giving her husband a look I can't read. Terry responds with a slight shake of his head. From behind them, I wonder what their unspoken exchange is about, what Yvonne is thinking at this moment. Yvonne was always the fun one. Impulsive and fearless, unconcerned about what others thought of her. I envy that.

"How'd you manage all that? House in a national park and all?" Frank asks, skepticism thick in his voice.

"Like I said, old permitting screw-up that worked to our benefit. Gotta know the right people, or at least know someone who knows someone."

The conversation is cut short by a loud crackling noise coming from the front of the golf cart. Someone is summoning our driver on the walkie-talkie attached to his belt. Given the noise of the drive in the open-air vehicle and our position at the back, I can't make out anything that is said except the standard 'over' and 'copy' phrases used in this type of communication.

Griff ends his conversation and makes a fast right, throwing us into an unannounced shift of weight. I use the back of the seat in front of me to right myself straight once more and see Griff guide the cart down a long, narrow driveway.

Out the front windshield in the distance, I see a three-story, yellow house adorned with aqua-blue shutters. It sports three levels of white decking and lattice adornments, with a widow's walk topping it off. The house is bright and cheery and would appear gaudy, situated atop a different landscape. The loud pairing of colors is fitting for a beach house—a party and good times waiting to be had inside the home. However, the solo structure strikes me as odd, somewhat out of place, plopped in the middle of the natural landscape. Nothing but dunes and an endless stretch of sand surrounds it.

"There she is," Griff says proudly. "Dune Dweller. Think I

probably would have gone with a different name, but I didn't want to disrespect the previous owner's history with the house."

The house is perched on stilts. A look *underneath* the house reveals towering dunes on the oceanside of Dune Dweller, leading me to wonder if this is perhaps how the house came to be named.

"What are we looking at here, Griff? Four, five bedrooms?" Frank probes as Griff slows the cart's speed to traverse the rough gravel drive.

"Eight," Griff replies. "And five of those eight are primary rooms. Six full baths and one half." Instead of pulling up to the house and parking underneath the structure, Griff brings the cart to a halt about a football field back. He slips out from under the driver's wheel as he says, "Don't worry about waiting for your bags. I'll bring them in once they arrive. First, you all need to get inside, have a tour of the house, find your rooms." Griff turns to lead the group toward the entryway.

"And will we be meeting this host soon?" Patrick lobs.

"Yep," Griff says, hurrying ahead.

Hands resting on hips, Patrick shakes his head, mumbling to Melanie words the rest of us can't hear.

The air prickles with electric anticipation—more likely dreaded trepidation, I'd say. From what I've gathered, the others don't know any more than Carmen and I have been able to deduce. And here we are, finally, collectively waiting with bated breath as if our demanding unknown host is going to descend one of the many staircases cascading the house's facade. But to learn more, we must follow through with this game. We gather our personal items, readying to follow our guide as we take in the scenery: the house, the surroundings, the lack of any other structures nearby.

"The houses we passed on our way here, are they rentals or private homes?" Terry asks.

"Most of the island residents live inland, away from the sound and the seashore. The ones you're speaking of are indeed rentals," Griff returns. "But nobody rents out this time of year."

"You did?" Kathryn presses.

"Yes, ma'am, I did. What can I say? Got lucky. It was a good deal. You do what you gotta do, am I right?" Griff removes the key from the golf cart and heads toward Dune Dweller. His long strides leave the rest of us looking to one another for confirmation that we are all in agreement to go forward with this.

And then, without words, the decision is made as our aging group follows Griff toward the house. The spring in our steps has softened somewhat. We are no longer thirty and as nimble or spry as we once were, all those years ago. Dancing, drinking, stumbling to our respective homes in Perishing Hill after a long night of foolish antics. All of us, now having breached our fifties, follow like school children without hesitation or protest, eager to please, or rather keen to learn. Or perhaps, anxious to squelch out the past—for good this time.

Yvonne

The climb up the outdoor staircase has left most of us breathless and thankful someone else will be hauling up our luggage. A bell fixed to the door knob jingles as Griff opens the entryway. Griff politely holds the door for our group while I tuck my hand inside my bag, feeling for the presence of my gun. Never have I been fond of surprises, and I refuse to be caught off guard while I follow this beast of a man into his cavern of unknowns. The last one inside, I follow Terry through the threshold. Griff reaches to secure the door behind me, "After you, ma'am."

"Yvonne," I remind Griff, stepping past him to join the others.

Once inside Dune Dweller, my apprehension ebbs. While the facade is garish and bold and difficult to miss from the road, the inside is dazzling and contemporary, furnished with current trendy finishes. The effect is cozy, safe, and inviting. Reconciling Griff's rugged appearance with the elegant sophistication of the open room in front of me is not forthcoming. This guy knows his stuff; it's impressive, really. There's no other way to say it.

"Obviously, we're on the bottom level here. Can't call it the basement, but I like to think of it as such. Made it into a game room, if you will—been referring to it as the recreation room. There's a wet bar over here, fully stocked by your host," Griff explains, pointing to the far corner. The area gleams with stainless steel, mirrors, and glassware. "Got your pool table." Griff motions to the middle of the room as if we can't see the large piece set center stage. "I haven't stocked all the games for future renters yet," he says, looking toward the built-in bookshelf, "but according to your host, it's not an issue. Activities have already been planned and sorted for the weekend."

The eight of us stand quietly, dutifully listening to details laid out by this odd, disheveled man who gives us an extra moment to take it all in. Or is he perhaps stalling?

I look around the room, sparkling and unmarred by prior guests. The practical off-white tile, water and sand-friendly, has been laid with the knowledge of beach outings to come. Two rows of recessed lighting stretch the room's length, illuminating from above.

"The hot tub is through that door and down one flight of stairs." Griff points, indicating the sliding doors at the far end of the room. I walk in that direction to take in the view, noting the sea just beyond the tops of the sand dunes practically butted up against the house. "That's the easiest exit for the hot tub as well as the beach. Got the tub covered right now due to weather, but if you all want to take a soak, just let me know. The cover on that thing is weighted and pretty heavy, but I'm happy to remove it for you."

"Back down that hallway is the laundry area," Griff says, nodding, clearing his throat, rubbing the back of his neck.

"Okay, then, let's head on upstairs. I'll show you the other two floors. Bedrooms are all located on the second floor. You all can choose your rooms after the tour." Griff leads our group toward an obscured hallway behind the bar area, then up the staircase.

Tromping up the stairs behind Griff, we bypass the midlevel floor, heading to the top. The staircase spits us out into an open room boasting a full wall of floor-to-ceiling windows on the east side of the room and a wall of mirrors on the west side. The optics fool the mind into believing the ocean surrounds a person on all sides of the dwelling. This floor's foundation is done in faux-oak laminate flooring, unlike the bottom level, which was laid in unremarkable tile. The exception, however, is the kitchen, which has been laid in white square tile to match the cabinetry. Stainless steel appliances butting up against flint gray Corian work surfaces break up the pristine white kitchen.

The other area of the open space has been allotted as a sitting area, laid out in front of the wall of windows. Two sofas face one another, and a long rectangular table splits the space between them. Club chairs cap off the ends of the table, creating a cozy conversation area.

I watch the actions of the others while Griff explains the current tide schedule, the King Tide forecast for the weekend. Carmen eyes the man suspiciously, her brow wrinkling in skepticism. Gabe stands beside her, taking in Griff's every word just in case there's a pop quiz afterward. He always was a nerdy bird.

Having given us time to digest the layout of the room, Griff continues the tour information once more. "Got your dining room table over there, big sitting room in that corner, and sunroom off the living room back there. Obviously, there's your kitchen," Griff waves an arm to the ocean side of the room. "Fridge is stocked per your host's instructions. Go ahead, make yourselves at home. I'm here to answer questions, but I don't tend bar or cook—so you all are on your own there."

No one speaks, no one moves, waiting for Griff to continue. Kathryn breaks through the awkward and drawn-out silence. "Am I to understand we must fend for ourselves, then?" Kathryn throws her hands up with a grunt of exasperation. "We were lured here with the promise of a 'fabulous weekend by the sea,' and now we have to cook and clean and play guess the mystery host." Kathryn turns, stepping toward the wall of windows to view the ocean beyond. Frank hurries to her side. Heads together in whispers, the rest of our group peels off into spousal pairs.

"What do you think we should do?" Terry says, his voice barely above a murmur.

I shake my head and sigh. "I don't know. I mean, we're here now, and that trip sucked."

"You got that right. Maybe we stay for the night, and then we'll get out of here tomorrow."

"Yeah, the only thing I want to know at this point is who is behind this weekend," I whisper, turning back to face the caretaker. Guide? Dune Dweller's owner? Creepy ass, man?

A crackling noise sounds as someone speaks from the walkie-talkie on Griff's belt. He doesn't bother to reply but rather twists at the knob on top of the thing, rotating it back and forth. Griff stuffs his hands into his pockets and rotates a bit in the direction of the hallway on this floor.

"Wait. What's back there? You haven't shown us that part of the house," I ask Griff, folding arms across my middle. Something feels off, and if we're going to be spending the weekend here, I want to know what we're all up against.

Griff turns his head toward the back hallway, almost as if he's willing someone to emerge.

Frank jumps in, "Is someone else here? If there's someone else back there, we need to know."

"It's just a couple more bedrooms, but your host has placed you all in rooms on the second level." Griff's lower lip juts out as he nods. "We can head there if you want to check out your digs. Freshen up? Your bags have arrived. You'll want a moment to get settled," Griff twists to begin his descent.

"Now, hold up a minute," Patrick says, halting the group's migration to the lower levels. "When exactly are we going to meet this host you keep speaking about?"

Terry steps up to join Patrick in support of this inquiry.

"Don't know nothing 'bout the agenda for the weekend. Alls I was told was to pick up the guests, give the tour, and show the group to their rooms."

Terry places hands on hips. "Well, you must have a name. You don't just rent out your home to someone without having a name."

"I'm not here to make introductions, sir." Griff reaches up, tugging at the corner of his left eye. I've noticed him perform this nervous tic a few times now.

I move to stand by my husband's side, take his hand, hurrying to Terry's defense. "Okay, yeah, sure, but you have obviously met this mystery host. You must have a name. You rented out your house to this person."

"Yes, ma'am. You are correct. I do know your host, but it ain't my place to reveal their identity."

A loud, staticky sound punctuates Griff's sentence. We watch as he unclips the mechanism from his belt and lifts it to his mouth. "On my way. Over and out," he says, turning to head down the staircase.

We look at one another, shrugging in frustration, features twisting, and shaking our heads, everyone decides to follow. What other choice do we have?

four

ALYCE FISCHER

Alyce

Apprehension nips at the nerve endings just underneath my skin. "No nails," I lecture the mirrored reflection, running the palm of my hand up my neck. Claw marks do not portray confidence. "And, no turning back now." Every detail of this weekend has been planned—no need for stress. I try seeing myself in the reflection as the group will view me when I introduce myself, when I explain the purpose of the weekend ahead. I'm not even half their age, I think, tilting my head, contemplating the all-cream pantsuit. Initially, I thought the outfit conveyed confidence, maturity, sophistication. Does it? I shake my head. White would be better, but then it's November, and there are just too many opinions on the color after Labor Day for me to feel comfortable with that look.

"Maybe I should have put my hair up with this outfit," I suggest to my image, pulling my hair up and off my shoulders. A long side braid, maybe? No. I drop my hair and lift my hand to take care of the itch, steadily crawling up the center of my chest.

Stop it.

Competence, will they see competence? Yes, that's what you need to project. Do you see competence, Alyce?

"No. No, I do not," I relay to my likeness. "Why are you so concerned about these people?" Shaking my head, I turn away from the mirror, pace the room, muster the courage to call the guests from their quarters for cocktail hour. It is next on the agenda. Time to begin. Am I ready? Are they ready? Will they trust me? Would I?

Ironic is the term that best fits this moment. Engaging with a room full of middle-aged adults is nothing for me. Up until I went away to college, I'd experienced little social contact with peers my age. Homeschooling and tutors left little opportunity for friends, birthday parties, sleepovers, and the like. I never gave it much thought. My network of comrades consisted of those sixty-five and older. Occasions to engage with other children my age were few to non-existent, not that it bothered me. I had the most adoring grandparents and never felt a lack of necessities, love, or even friendship. Never did I question having friends who were fifty to sixty years my senior.

From infancy, my grandparents, Rosey and Pops, made sure I had all I needed to thrive, and thrive I did, though not in the manner most children make strides. Of course, my grandparents had raised a child previously—my mother—and knew what needed to be done. Still, they were wildly underprepared to be parents again when I came along, and by that time, they had no desire to prepare school lunches and afternoon snacks. After years of public service, retirement awaited them. Rosey and Pops found a way to live out their dreams while seeing to my well-being.

The pair dragged me with them all over the world while they ticked exotic locales off their bucket list. Cruises, safaris, pilgrimages, I went everywhere they went and can thereby say I'm the most well-traveled twenty-four-year-old I know. (And now that I have recently wrapped up my master's degree, I actually do know a fair number of twenty-somethings.) Functioning alongside members of my generation on a daily basis these last years of college, I have deduced that my maturity level and wisdom measure far beyond the years of my peer group. And though my upbringing may have been unconventional, I can say with genuine confidence that I am your typical young woman on the brink of beginning my adult life.

That said, the transition from my grandparents' care to college life was quite an adjustment for me. My childhood was full of flattering remarks and praise. I had naively come to expect such comments, not realizing they were typically reserved or withheld in most situations. I was accustomed to hearing all the usual compliments from my grandparents' acquaintances. "How well-behaved you are, young lady." "What a precocious child you are, dear." "How well-mannered this girl is!" "Isn't she stunning!" The praise was something I strived for and knew precisely how to achieve. After some time, I became well-versed in dealing with the older generations but had little to share with kids my age. Of course I didn't anticipate such complimentary phrases from my peers. Still, the new phase of adulthood took a bit of getting used to.

I twist back to the mirror and address my image. "You're more than capable of hosting a weekend getaway for this group of old friends." Feeling less than confident, I sigh deeply in response, but now that my guests have arrived, it's time to face them. "This is simply another cocktail hour, Alyce. You've done a hundred of them."

On the dresser across the room, my phone vibrates. I leave the mirror to check the message. It's Jude. If all goes well, his ferry will arrive in twenty to thirty minutes. I was hoping he'd be here for moral support. I could claim this is about me and not him, but it is about both of us. We can't marry until I have the answers I've long awaited. Once I have them, I will finally understand who I am, where I came from. Then, I will be whole and ready to give myself to Jude.

My future husband has been so supportive already that it seems terribly unfair for me to be upset with him for his lack of punctuality. I had hoped he would be on the express ferry with the other guests, but Jude has been working in Wilmington,

North Carolina, all week and is coming into Ocracoke via the Cedar Island ferry. The poor guy has had a hideous time getting here. I do feel bad putting him through all this, all the tedious travel, spending the weekend with strangers. But on the other hand, I can hardly wait until he gets here and can't stand the thought of not having him by my side. Once we're through this reunion of sorts, though, we'll be ready to make wedding plans. I'm beyond ready for us to make our commitment so that we can finally be husband and wife.

Though I agreed to become Mrs. Jude Saches—and yes, I intend to take his last name, unlike both of our Generation X mothers who kept their maiden names because it was the trend of the time—I did so with the stipulation that I carry out this weekend prior to our nuptials. Jude readily agreed to do whatever it took to make me say I do. And I will, after this weekend is off the books, of course.

Jude and I have shared everything about ourselves with each other. Everything except our families, that is. We met while attending school at Duke University—me finishing the first year of my master's program, Jude in his final term before heading out to an internship. We had more in common than either of us could have imagined. The meet-cute (I adore that phrase) was at a coffee shop. Jude grabbed the last packet of artificial sweetener just as I reached for it. We learned neither of us uses a full packet, so we agreed to split it, and our story began. But here's the real miracle of our tale. We weren't even on or near campus when we met. Heck, we weren't even in Durham at the time of our meeting.

I traveled to Virginia on one of my free weekends to search for information on my family's history. My trip was not producing the facts I sought, which led me to a cafe for coffee and Wi-Fi. Jude was in town to see some old friends. Imagine our surprise when we learned both of us were heading back to Duke at the conclusion of our visits. The two of us could not believe we were attending the same university. Since that meeting, our love story has been a whirlwind.

The early months of our relationship were spent separated by a state line. Only a couple hundred miles, but I'd never had a long-distance relationship and didn't know anyone who had success with this type of love affair. Nevertheless, we wanted to give it a go, and I'm so grateful we did. Jude is my person, and I am ever so ready to marry him. I just have to get through this weekend first, and then we plan to tell our families. Rather, I should say, we plan to introduce one another to our prospective families.

That last statement doesn't scream confidence to someone looking in on our commitment to one another, but I will not doubt our intentions or our love for each other. Jude and I have our reasons for not bringing our families into our relationship just yet. Namely, because we're quite certain both sides will try and find a way to talk us out of what we want, especially when they learn we've never lived in the same city together.

The bits of our history we've shared with one another are only experiences. Of course, we've shared minute details. Jude has told me how controlling his father can be, and I've informed Jude of Rosey's dominant behavior. But that is it. I mean, yes, I've told Jude my grandfather has passed on, and he's explained that his parents are married yet not terribly affectionate with one another, but not much more than that. There will be plenty of time in our future together to get to know one another's families, but precious little time when it is only the two of us to think of.

Jude asked me to marry him while we were on spring break this past March. It was spontaneous and impulsive—Jude popping out of the ocean, wide-eyed and giddy, "Let's get married!" I didn't even have to think about it. I've never wanted anything more.

We thought then of relaying the news to our families, but I squelched that too. I wanted to wait until I had the details of our proposed nuptials ironed out because I wanted to be the one to plan them. My grandmother has always believed her way is the very best way—the only way, really—and she gets more adamant about getting her way with every passing birthday. I want this wedding to be about what Jude and I want, where we want, and when we want. And if I can get everything planned prior to filling my aging grandmother in on my intentions, then she will have to accept them as is. Rosey may have recently celebrated her eighty-fifth, but no one would ever know it, particularly when it comes to confidence, competence, and conviction levels. I could use a bit of all that right now. Because right now...it's time to meet my guests.

five

COCKTAIL HOUR

Kathryn

That prickle starts at the top of my spine, the one I get when I sense things aren't as they should be—the same one that rears up when a news story takes a wrong turn, the kind you can't stop. Of course, Frank and I have already relayed our unease concerning this weekend, but this is different. Something doesn't feel right, and I am rarely wrong about these things. Frank claims he doesn't make big decisions without asking for one of my readings—'What do you think, Kathryn? What does your gut say?' It's a gift that has boosted my career. But right now, I'm not sure I like what it's relaying.

"Something is off here, Frank." I pull a blouse from my bag and secure it to a hanger from the closet. "The old gang? All of us gathered here? Why? Who would want to bring us together now, after all these years?"

"Didn't we just have this conversation?" Frank asks absently, walking the perimeter of our room, eyes upward, examining the ceiling.

"Sorry to disturb you as you critique the craftsmanship of this garish beach box on stilts." I slam my suitcase shut, pulling the zipper secure.

Frank turns to face me before lowering his voice to a whisper. "I'm not working here. I'm looking for hidden cameras."

"No! Do you think? In our bedroom? Seriously?" My heart races in response. "I am a public persona, Frank. I can't have my private life played out on some social media app or, God forbid, some artificial intelligence composed in my likeness."

"Why do you think I'm taking this precaution, Kathryn?"

"Are you finding anything suspicious? I'll help." I lift my view to the ceiling, pacing the room. "What am I looking for?"

"No, it's okay. I don't see anything of concern. Come sit down and try to relax. I think it's all clear in here, but keep your eyes open when in the common areas. There may be cameras hidden throughout the living spaces. A lot of the vacation rentals install them."

I plop onto the bed. It squeaks. Fabulous. "We've barely been here an hour, and all I can think of is getting out of this house."

Frank sits next to me on the bed, resting his hand on my thigh. "What did you think of Griff?"

"He knows more than he's letting on—that's what I think."

"I agree," Frank says, lifting his wrist to check the time. "We're supposed to be back out there in five."

I huff with more flair than necessary, though I couldn't care less who hears it. "We may as well have been kidnapped. This is ridiculous. I have absolutely no desire to fulfill this mystery host's inane...." A knock sounds from the bedroom door, sending a jolt through my body, snatching away my last thought.

"Hello. Griff here," the burly man calls from the other side of our closed door.

Frank yells, "We already got all our luggage," then adds, "Thanks." Frank turns so I can see his lips move in silence as he mouths, "Do you think he heard us?"

I shake my head no, keeping words and thoughts safely to myself.

The rapping continues. Frank pushes himself to stand, heading to answer the door. On the other side, the large man, who looks to have found a comb to run through his hair since we last saw him, announces, "It's time for cocktail hour. Your host is requesting your presence in the recreation room."

Frank turns to look at me, "Recreation room? Remind me."

"On the bottom floor," Griff answers glibly. "First room on the tour."

Frank nods, checks his watch again. "Looks like we still have a couple of minutes. Anything else?"

"No, sir. I was charged to round up the guests, and here I am," Griff says, turning to leave. "See you downstairs."

Frank closes the door as rapping begins down the hall. He turns back to address me. "Well, you ready to meet this host?"

Carmen

Gabe touches my elbow to get my attention. "White wine or something stronger?"

"'I'd prefer something stronger, but we need to keep our wits about us."

"Agreed," Gabe says, reaching for glasses then pouring drinks. He hands over my wine, surveys the room, and sips the beer he's poured for himself. I follow Gabe's gaze across the room. It's strange looking at these old neighbors, almost as if I'm looking at the after picture when I've only known them from their 'before shots.' I wonder what Gabe and I must look like to them after twenty years gone.

Kathryn and Frank have planted themselves next to the pool table. Frank runs a bony hand over the felt, listening as Kathryn speaks softly to him. She's spiked up her pixie cut, applied a deep magenta shade of lipstick, and added a pair of knee-high boots to go with the wrap dress she wears.

Melanie and Patrick have positioned themselves next to the sliding glass door, their backs to the rest of us as they stare out over the top of the dunes. Though we haven't hit the evening hours, the sun is all but gone, the last dregs of daylight slipping away. The pair won't have much longer to use the view as an excuse to shut out the rest of us. Knowing Patrick—having known Patrick previously—he'll find some other way to dismiss us. Patrick always considered himself above the company of this group.

Leaning in for only Gabe to hear, I speak in our native tongue, "You think he wears a clerical collar?" Patrick was sporting an outdated windbreaker earlier, so I couldn't get a good look. "It'd probably get him a free coffee or something, right? Maybe a donut?"

Gabe chuckles, quietly answering back in Spanish. "If he were a priest, I would say yes. He'd never miss that opportunity. But nah, Patrick is a pastor, preacher, whatever you want to call him, and they don't wear those collars."

I turn my attention back to the center of the room, finding tiny details I missed earlier, admiring Griff's handiwork.

We hear them descending the stairs before we know who to expect. The couples turn in unison to learn Yvonne and Terry are the last to join us for cocktail hour. Yvonne holds Terry's arm, speaking quietly in his ear as the two round the corner from the hidden staircase and approach the bar area, their faces twisted in wary expressions.

"You all get unpacked and settled in?" I ask, hoping to break the tension, sipping from my wine glass.

"I guess you could call it that," Yvonne answers for the couple. Looking at her, I can't believe I've forgotten how beautiful she is. Her gorgeous dark complexion, wide eyes, and high cheekbones. "You guys?"

I nod as Gabe asks the pair if he can pour them anything—gin and tonic for Terry, a glass of red for Yvonne. Gabe presents them with drinks. I motion to cheers but quickly pull my glass back, thinking the other couples might view this action as rude.

Instead, I turn to ask the room. "Should we make a toast?"

Patrick turns from viewing the dunes outside, shoving his free hand into the pocket of his pants (Gabe was right—no collar).

"And who exactly would we be toasting?" Patrick slams back the remainder of his cocktail.

"Pour you another, Patty?" Gabe has now assumed the bartender position for our cocktail hour. Like days long gone, we all seem to be slipping into our old roles.

Melanie turns to face the group. She's changed into a low-cut silk blouse and faux leather pants. Age has not mellowed Melanie's penchant for provocative attire, but exactly who is here for her to entice? Griff?

"Thanks. I'll take care of it," Patrick replies, then checks to see if Melanie would like a refill as well.

Melanie ignores Patrick, instead addressing Gabe. "Gabe, what a doll you are. Yes, I'll take another," she says, hurrying ahead of her husband to the bar, holding her empty glass out for Gabe to take. Frank and Kathryn shuffle toward the group reluctantly.

"I guess we could go around the circle and tell what we've each been doing these last twenty-odd years." Melanie fingers a lock of hair, tossing it to fall behind her shoulder. "What's that called, Carmen? You're the teacher. Show and tell, is it?"

"I can think of nothing more that I would NOT like to participate in than that," Kathryn drawls.

"No need for bitchiness, Kathryn. We're all in misery," Yvonne tosses back.

"I'll drink to that." Kathryn holds her glass in the air.

Frank backs his wife. "Cheers."He holds his glass out to gesture a clink.

The group falls silent—sipping, mulling, sulking. In the quiet stillness, footsteps sound from above. Eight heads look up in unison. The tread grows louder, closer. It sounds as if someone is descending the stairs.

"Could be Griff," Terry says.

"Nope," Gabe responds. "Griff's footfall would be a lot heavier than that."

Behind us, a bell jingles. Wind whips through the room,

blowing over a lamp, banging an open door against the wall. The group turns to see Griff, his arms full of firewood, hurrying inside, closing and latching the door behind him.

"Wind's building up out there," he says, carrying the logs across the room.

Patrick steps forward, following the caretaker. "What are you doing with all that wood? I didn't see a fireplace."

"There's not. Got a fire pit on the back deck here—one of those new smokeless ones, keeps everything contained. Host thought you all might want to roast marshmallows or something later," Griff explains, nodding at Patrick in thanks for the assist, then stepping through the open patio door.

"What in the hell?" Frank looks at Kathryn. "A campfire?"

"We'll be holding hands and telling our deepest secrets before you know it," Yvonne jokes.

Kathryn drains her martini, signaling Gabe for another. "I've no intentions of doing that."

"And why not, Kate—I mean, Kathryn?" I ask. "Don't think we can keep a secret? Oh, I forgot. That's you."

"Don't start with me, Carmen. There's already too much going on here."

We watch through glass doors as Griff stacks the wood on the outside deck, then steps back into the room. "Yep, it's really crankin' up out there. Good thing you all got here when you did."

"What exactly is that supposed to mean, and where the fuck is this host?" Patrick's tone takes a turn. Melanie cuts her eyes at her husband and drinks from her glass.

"Didn't think preachers used that word," Frank says.

"You're correct, Frank. Lost myself there for a minute. I apologize," Patrick says to the group, then addresses Griff. "But where is this person? We've been on this island for almost two hours, and not one hint has been uttered as to why we've been summoned."

"I'm right here. Welcome." A female voice floats into the room from the direction of the stairwell.

We turn to see a young woman enter from the dark hallway. As she steps into view, I blink to adjust my vision. It can't be. I twist to view the expressions of Yvonne, and Melanie, and Kathryn, right before Kathryn falls dramatically into Frank's arms.

Yvonne

Terry hurries to assist Frank, who is struggling to keep Kathryn upright. Frank always was slight, but now he seems to be shrinking with age. Carmen stands behind the bar next to Gabe, frozen in disbelief. Melanie rushes to Kathryn's side as if she's some medical professional readying to administer aid, her risque blouse gaping open. Nice to see the years haven't changed Melanie's dress for sexcess code.

"I'm fine, I'm fine," Kathryn insists. "I've got it."

The young woman steps toward the bar, concern marking her familiar features.

"Are you sure? I can send Griff to find a doctor," she says, catching Griff's eye as he watches the theatrical scene play out.

"That won't be necessary," Kathryn says. "Really, I simply lost my footing," she adds, though we all know she's lying. The eight of us might not have been in the same room for the last twenty years, but we still know the tactics, the telltale signs that we each used (and apparently we still use) for personal manipulation.

The young woman nods, then moves to put more distance between herself and the group. "If you insist," she says apprehensively.

The room and its guests righted, Griff steps back outside to complete his work. Kathryn, upright and stable, Terry steps back to my side. I rub the length of his arm, surprised to find gooseflesh. He's seen it too. Judging from the looks the others wear, they too, are thinking the same thing we are.

Patrick, Mr. I'll Handle This, steps forward to stand directly in front of the woman, planting feet wide, hands on hips. It's his show now. "Who exactly are you, and why are we all here?"

"Perhaps we should share a drink to the weekend, and then I'll tell you all you wish to know," the young woman says. "Gabe, would you mind pouring me a Sauvignon Blanc?" The brief statement stuns our group of age-old friends—would I still call us friends? Yes? No? And yet, the fact we all stand here together, mouths agape and wondering about the identity of this young lady (who knows more about us than we do about her) lumps all of us into some sort of alliance once more.

"Of course," Gabe stammers, thrown as are the rest of us that she has called him by name.

The host steps to the center of the room. Everything about this woman suggests sophistication and a privileged upbringing. She's dressed head to toe in off-white, her long, thick, shiny brown hair cascading down her back. As she turns, the lighting overhead catches the glimmer of the dainty gold accessories on her neck, wrist, and ears. The overall look is understated and mature in a way that defies this woman's age.

She raises her glass. "To a weekend of enlightenment."

Terry

"It is high time you did some explaining, young lady." Patrick was never known for an abundance of patience.

"Yes, Mr. Perkins, it is indeed," the young woman agrees.

"Then let's start with your name, since you seem to know all of ours. I think it only fair you extend the same courtesy."

"My name is Alyce. Alyce Fischer." Alyce sips from her glass, then turns to place it on the ledge of the pool table behind her. As she twists back to face our group, Alyce folds her arms over her midsection in a manner that suggests, 'Fine, we'll do this if that's what you'd like.' The body language is not wasted on this crowd. Although her mannerisms emit an air of wisdom far beyond the young years of this woman (girl?)—she can't be more than twenty-five—there is an edge to her voice that betrays her attempt to appear at ease and in charge.

I step away from the group, pulling Yvonne to my side, separating us from the others a bit. No need to wonder what the others are thinking—their faces all project the same incredulous expression.

"Okay, Alyce Fischer," Patrick begins. "Why bring us all together? Answer that one."

"I appreciate that you all have many questions. I, too, have several, but we have the whole weekend to get to know one another."

"Um, we're leaving tomorrow," Yvonne says. She grabs my hand to show we are in solidarity. "Terry and I were just discussing this in our room. While we appreciate your hospitality and thank you for including us, we've decided that whatever this is,"—Yvonne circles her hand in front of her—"we aren't interested in being a part of it. Respectfully, of course."

"And we aren't interested either," Kathryn hurriedly adds, having regained her equilibrium and senses after the fainting spell. Frank eyes Kathryn in question but says nothing to contradict his wife.

"Let's give Alyce the opportunity to speak," Carmen says. "I'm sure she has her reasons for bringing all of us here, and we'll never learn them if we keep taking jabs at this lovely young lady."

"Carmen makes a good point," I say to the group, then turn my attention to Alyce. "Alyce, I've done a fair amount of work with people in my time...."

"Living or expired?" Patrick snidely interrupts.

I ignore Patrick's derisive comment. "And I find that fear is the biggest motivator in our lives."

"Christ!" Patrick spouts, stomping his foot as the group gawks in disbelief at our resident pastor. "Almighty God," he adds quickly—a bit too quickly. "Give our friends and our host the courageous strength to speak the truth," Patrick continues in disingenuous prayer, covering his blasphemous blunder.

"Amen," Frank quips, though he nor any of our group members were ever particularly religious in our younger years. Still, the rest of us follow suit with the affirmation. Regardless of whether or not it was an actual prayer, we're all reluctant to piss off our great maker should we need him later on in the evening.

I continue. "As I was saying, fear has been used as a form of motivation, as a manipulator, since mankind began." Yvonne lays a hand on my wrist, her method of letting me know I'm veering off track. She'll often say, 'This isn't one of your eulogies, Terry.' Though at this moment, I understand there is no reason to say more about the matter.

I change paths. "Alyce, why have you brought us here?"

The question makes the rest of my cohorts antsy with anticipation.

"Well," Alyce begins, lacing her long, elegant fingers, then extends her left hand. "I'm getting married."

"Not to be patronizing, but I fail to see how your engagement has anything to do with us," Melanie states, cutting off Patrick before he can make his next biting remark.

"I never had the opportunity to know my parents," Alyce says.

"Again," Patrick starts.

This time, it's Carmen shutting out Patrick's next barb before he can continue berating the woman. "How can we help? Do we know your parents?"

Never one to be outdone, Kathryn jumps in. "Oh, honey, how awful for you." She always was one to make everything a competition, that is, until she wasn't winning. "So then, just tell us who they are, and we'll tell you everything we know. Of course, that is, if we know them."

"I appreciate that, especially considering I've exhausted all the usual tactics: questions, research, archives. My fiancé and I are very much excited about getting married. However, I feel that until I know more about my past, I can't possibly step into my future."

"Poor guy," Patrick mumbles.

"Excuse me," Alyce replies. Judging from the look crossing her features, this event isn't going as she planned.

The sliding glass door flies open. Griff ducks inside, brushing the hair from his eyes as he quickly slides the door closed against the howl of the wind.

"Alyce?"

"Yes, Griff."

"Thought I'd let you know your fiancé just arrived."

"I thought you were going to pick him up from the ferry terminal?" Alyce questions, her eyes glazing with alarm.

"The ferry got in early. He caught a ride to the house with one of the locals."

"Where is he now?" Their conversation continues while the rest of us look on.

"He went to change. Said to let you know he'd be down in a few."

"Thank you, Griff."

The big ring of keys hanging from his belt jangles as Griff saunters through the middle of the room, heading toward the staircase. Listening as he trudges up the stairs, we wait for what will happen next.

"You were saying, Ms. Fischer?" Patrick asks, eager to get back on topic.

"This weekend has not started as smoothly as I had hoped. But I'm determined not to waste this opportunity to finally have the chance to know all I can about my family. From the little information I've obtained, I understand that you all were quite close with my parents. Neighbors, as a matter of fact. Pershing Hill."

Next to me, I feel Yvonne tense at the mention of our old address.

Kathryn reaches for her martini, sips, then says, "It wasn't Pershing, sweetheart. It was Perishing Hill, and if it didn't hold up to its name...."

"Hush," Patrick snaps.

"Don't hush my wife," Frank jumps to Kathryn's defense. "It was Perishing Hill. That damned developer and his extra 'i' screwed all of us."

"But it is Pershing now, correct?" Alyce asks for confirmation.

"Not that it matters, but yes, the lawsuit that was brought resulted in the renaming of the neighborhood. It was all worked out in the end," I relay.

"But not before we all lost money on the resale of our homes," Kathryn says, her bitter feelings on the matter oozing forth.

Gabe, observing from behind the bar, finally speaks out. "I don't remember anyone from our old neighborhood with a daughter your age. What are your parents' names, and where are they that you can't confront them about their past?"

"Excellent question, Gabe, my man," Patrick spouts. "But I wouldn't get my hopes up for an answer from that one. It's clear," he jabs a finger in Alyce's direction, "that little girl only wants to keep the eight of us in the dark."

Melanie shakes her head at her husband's horrendous manners but says nothing to the contrary.

"I've barely had a chance to speak," Alyce says in her defense. "I'm not trying to keep my intentions from anyone. In fact, it's just the opposite. I want to learn as much as possible about all of you, my parents, your time spent together. I'm happy to answer any and all of your questions, but we've barely gotten started on our weekend together, and already you've stated your resolve to leave."

Carmen asks, "What were your parents' names? Let's start there."

"Shane and Amber Thompson."

After all these years, hearing their names is like receiving a fist to the midsection, though I'm not sure any of us are surprised, given the girl's resemblance to her parents. Still, how can this be?

Kathryn looks to be sliding down the side of the bar again.

Frank grabs an elbow and takes the martini. "That's not possible," he claims, holding firmly to Kathryn, a tuft of her hair now out of place, giving her a bird-like appearance.

Yvonne studies the young woman. "You can't be their daughter. One, she would be...."

"Twenty-four," Alyce states matter-of-factly.

"Okay," Yvonne says. Behind her eyes, I can tell my wife is mentally calculating the years.

The faces of our former neighbors all register the recognition of truth in Alyce's claim.

"Of course," Carmen says. "Yes, Amber and Shane had a little girl. I babysat for that sweet child, but her name was not Alyce. And then, you said your last name is Fischer, not Thompson."

The facial expressions around the circle appear almost hopeful with the revelation.

Alyce breathes deeply, then runs two fingers the length of her long hair, smoothing the pieces around her face, dragging a lock behind her shoulder. "You did know them." Her eyes glisten with hope.

"Yes, but how is it possible you are their daughter? Their child went to live with Amber's mother," Carmen relays. Now that Carmen says it, the moments of that painful time race into my recall.

"Rosey Fischer," Alyce states. Her proclamation elicits a collective gasp from the group.

"That child's name was Elizabeth." Yvonne makes one last attempt at disproving this young lady's claim.

"Elizabeth Alyce Fischer-Thompson," Alyce says. Then, "My grandmother officially changed my name after my parents were killed."

Six

JUDE ARRIVES

Carmen

And just like that, the reason we've all been wrangled into this weekend has been revealed. I step toward Alyce. This young woman is Amber's daughter? Of course she is; I see it in the periphery of my memory. On some level, we all knew the moment she showed her face tonight.

Alyce, standing here before us, emphasizes the years gone by, all the life we've lived that Amber and Shane never had the opportunity to experience. The thought of Amber's daughter growing up without her mother weighed on me in the years that followed the death of my friend. But like most things not part of immediate life, I'd forgotten about the little girl, though, every now and then, she popped to mind, I'd type her name into an internet search engine with no success. As an educator of young people, it was difficult to imagine anyone in Alyce's generation without a social media presence, and now I know why. Rosey altered the girl's identity. But why? It wasn't a secret Rosey took her granddaughter to raise, but I had no idea she changed the child's name.

"Why did Rosey feel the need to change your name?" I ask Alyce, thinking of my old friend, remembering the numerous conversations we shared about Amber's responsibility to give her baby the perfect name. It was not a decision she wanted to make lightly. Amber was convinced the name had to be right in order to give her baby girl a proper start in the world. With the right name, her child would surely flourish.

"We have more important issues to address here than this girl's name, Carmen." Patrick shifts his weight between feet, clearly uncomfortable with this new knowledge. Patrick hasn't lost his abrasive personality, though I think the loss would behoove him, given his new profession. Automotive sales may have allowed for such a character trait, but for those of the cloth, it seems Patrick's brusque nature would be a flawed attribute.

Terry tries to calm the situation. "Patrick, Alyce deserves the opportunity to speak her peace. Explain to us why she has chosen this particular method to obtain the answers she seeks before you…."

"Do you hear yourself, Terry?" Patrick throws his hands up in the air, huffing, shaking his head. "Good grief, all these damn words you use, jumbling up and muddying this conversation."

"Conversation?" Terry snaps. "Is that what you call this, Patty? Allow me to clarify this for you. A conversation is when one person allows another person who is engaged with said first person…."

"Jesus, I can't with this group. And I'm not Patty," he tosses out before turning to Melanie. "Get your stuff together. We're getting out of here."

"Mr. Perkins, if you allow me to finish, I'd be happy to have Griff assist you and Mrs. Perkins back to the ferry terminal. I assure you my intent was not to frustrate, humiliate, or issue a reprimand to any one of you with my extended invite. I've one agenda, and that is to get to know my parents finally."

Kathryn, standing solidly on her own once more, folds arms across her middle. "So why not confront your grandmother with these questions? She would know your parents far better than any of us would, particularly your mother."

Alyce lowers her gaze as she picks at her cuticles, inhaling deeply to give herself a moment to come up with an answer to such a reasonable question. When it becomes clear Alyce has no answer for Kathryn's query, I share the explanation with the group.

"Because when Amber passed away, she and Rosey were estranged." A few of us knew, a few of us didn't. It wasn't like we all shared all our private details with every group member. Amber and I were both teachers, albeit we taught different grade levels—middle school for me and high school for Amber—we were employed by the same school system. The two of us had a lot in common and, therefore, shared more with one another than we did with the other neighbors. I watch Alyce for her reaction to the revelation, and judging from the look that passes over her features, I believe Alyce wasn't aware of this information.

"Rosey forbade the mention of my parents' names," Alyce begins by way of explanation to Kathryn's question and my declaration. "After they died, Rosey's mission was to erase any and all reminders of my parents. I did try to explain on several occasions how important knowing them was to me, but I have yet to get through to my grandmother—twenty-three years after the fact. As well, I'm certain Rosey also prohibited my grandfather, Pops, from sharing the information with me. After Pops died last year, I realized they both intended to take the information to their graves."

"I understand your predicament, but this is not our problem," Frank says, then looks to Kathryn. "Would you like to leave with Patrick and Melanie?"

Kathryn nods. "Yes, let's call this."

"Wait, why not just spend the night?" I try to reason with my former neighbors. "I think we should help Alyce. Surely, one night and a few anecdotes aren't too much to ask from us. We knew Amber and Shane, but Alyce was robbed of that opportunity."

Patrick refuses to be reasonable. "She wasn't robbed of anything. I mean, yes, she lost her mother and father, but her damn grandmother should be handling this. As far as I'm concerned, this is a domestic disturbance that has nothing to do with us."

Patrick takes Melanie's arm, turning the two of them from our view to whisper in his wife's ear as we wait for their exit. Whether the group members decide to stay or go, I've decided that I want to help Alyce. I've no qualms Gabe will want to do the same. It's the least we can do for the daughter of our old friends.

Alyce's face changes suddenly as I open my mouth, ready to deliver my intentions. A smile spreads across her features, lighting up her eyes. The euphoria is hard to miss. The others all wear puzzled expressions, but having spent all my career working with teenagers, I know the look of love well. I follow Alyce's gaze to the back hallway and see a young man exit the staircase. He, too, wears the unmistakable grin of a man in love.

"Hi," Alyce says, holding out a hand for the young man to take as he moves to stand beside her.

Alyce's fiancé bends to kiss her hello, then turns to face the strangers taking in their private reunion. He's handsome—a square jawline under blue eyes. Brown hair tops his chiseled physique. The young man surveys our small gang, smiling, waiting for introductions to begin, but the smile abruptly falls away as his gaze shifts.

"Dad?"

"Jude? What in the hell are you doing here?"

Frank

"Surely, to God, this is a sick nightmare," I say. "Nothing else makes sense."

"What the hell is going on here?" Kathryn demands.

"Isn't it obvious?" Yvonne quips. "Looks like Patty and Mel are getting a new daughter-in-law."

"Wait, this boy is your son?" Kathryn asks Melanie.

Melanie nods, though not convincingly.

Alyce appears to be as confused as the rest of our party, and the look on her fiancé's face reveals this is as much of a surprise to him as it is to the rest of us. Everyone in this room, as a matter of fact, is stupefied. Of course, none of us would have known this man to be the Perkins' son or that he and Alyce are engaged, but Patrick and Melanie should know their boy is getting married. At the very least, they would know the name of the woman their son was in a relationship with, wouldn't they?

"How is it possible you all are caught unawares?" Gabe asks. "Surely, this can't be the first time you all have met? And then there's the name thing—I can't understand how you wouldn't have figured this out prior to tonight."

"Gabe, my man, not everything is black and white like the ledgers you work with," I explain. Gabe would be wise to proceed with caution at this junction. Patrick was a loose cannon before he found out his son was marrying the daughter of an old nemesis. Nothing good can come from this unexpected divulgence. I glance at Kathryn. It's unlike my wife to remain speechless, even if this event is getting wilder and more out of control with each moment.

Patrick moves to confront his son. Hands on hips, no regard for privacy or feelings, he begins. "You mean to tell me you're engaged to this girl? Do you know who she is? Who her family is? We haven't even heard you speak one word about this girl. How can you be engaged to someone we've never met, much less approved?"

"I don't need your permission or approval to marry anyone, Dad. I'm a grown man, and just because you're the preacher man doesn't mean everything you say is gospel."

Melanie steps between father and son. "This is not the time or the place to have this conversation, guys." She places a hand on Jude's cheek, squeezing his arm in greeting. I get the sense this isn't the first time Melanie has had to intervene between these two.

"Hi, Mom. Did you meet Alyce?" Jude turns his gaze on his fiancée.

"I have now," Melanie says. "Oh, Judey, you really should have done this as a family rather than making a whole weekend of it."

"That's my fault," Alyce hurries to say. "Jude knew I was planning this weekend and has been so supportive, but he had no idea who was on the guest list."

Feeling a bit uncomfortable witnessing this private moment, I ask the others, "Should we leave, you think?"

Kathryn nods while Terry and Yvonne look at each other, their heads bobbing in agreement. Carmen tells Gabe she wants to stay; perhaps she can help smooth things over if the conversation goes badly.

Terry, Yvonne, Kathryn, and I head toward the back staircase but halt as Alyce hurries to say, "Please don't go. We still have so much to talk about. Even more now."

Across the room, Patrick paces, Melanie looks out at the dunes, and Jude holds tightly to Alyce's hand.

Patrick saunters back to where Jude, Melanie, and Alyce stand. Face red with rage, he jabs his pointer finger in Melanie's direction. "This is all your fault."

"My fault? How the hell do you suppose this is my fault? I didn't know Jude asked Alyce to marry him. Allow me to remind you: I, too, just met Alyce," Melanie says.

"How did you meet our son?" Patrick narrows his gaze at Alyce as he begins his interrogation.

"In a coffee shop," Alyce replies.

"This is unnecessary, Dad. If you have questions about our relationship, I'll answer them, but you leave Alyce out of this."

"You want to marry this girl, but I'm supposed to leave her out of a family discussion?" Patrick's voice rises with each word he speaks.

Jude drops Alyce's hand. "This doesn't sound like a discussion to me. It sounds like we're about to be on the receiving end of one of your sermons."

Patrick raises a hand, rearing back. As he brings it forward, Jude catches Patrick's wrist and throws his father's arm backward. "Really? I'm no longer a child, Dad, and I will not freely allow you to hit me anymore."

Patrick eases backward, using the hand he planned to strike with to rub the back of his neck. "Forgive me. I've let my temper get the best of me. However, I need to understand what is going on here. So I'm going to ask a few questions now."

Jude slides his arm protectively around Alyce's waist. The four speak amongst themselves, the exchange calm for the time being.

The six of us wait, watch, listen, and sip from our cocktails, exchanging looks, whispers, and thoughts about whether to go.

Kathryn whispers, "Well, since we're all here, I want to see what happens."

"You're just being nosey," Gabe retorts. "This isn't any of our business."

"Of course it's our business. The girl brought us here," I say in defense of my wife.

Yvonne shakes her head, offering, "It's obvious Alyce didn't know her fiancé's parents were part of her guest list. I'm with Kathryn on this. I want to know what's going on."

Carmen chimes in. "And we still don't know exactly what Alyce knows about her parents, or Rosey, for that matter."

"What do you mean, Rosey?" Kathryn asks.

Carmen offers a sad smile. "According to Amber, Rosey was less than accepting of Shane and their child, Alyce, as we know her now. As far as I can remember, Rosey hadn't even met Elizabeth, or rather Alyce, when Amber and Shane died. When Alyce was born, Amber hadn't seen her mother in a number of years. Amber never wanted to say much on the matter, but I could tell she was more than bothered by the estrangement. It bothered her that her baby wouldn't have ties to her grandparents, that her child would grow up without them."

"Giving birth to a child and not having the support of your family, particularly your mother, would be difficult," Yvonne says. "Our three children—I say, children, they're all grown now—are so close to both sets of their grandparents. I can't imagine them growing up without extended family."

"So we're staying?" Terry asks his wife.

"We are," Yvonne confirms.

"Us too, I guess," Kathryn states, then adds, "for now."

Carmen tilts her head at Gabe and says, "So are we."

In the end, without Griff or transportation, there is nothing else for us to do than stay and see this through—at least for the night. We turn our attention back to the scene playing out in the center of the recreation room. Patrick's hands fly, keeping time with his words. Melanie protectively stands on one side of Jude while Alyce takes the other. Patrick insists that someone explain to him how Alyce could not have known he and Melanie are her fiancé's parents.

"And exactly how long have the two of you been engaged? How long have you been keeping this from us, Jude?" Patrick lobs.

"Dad, stop. Look, I had every intention of telling you. We wanted to tell the two families together, but it was important to Alyce to get through this weekend before we told either of our families about us."

Patrick shakes his head in disbelief. "So you're telling me Alyce's family has no idea about this either?"

"I am. And as for the name, I dropped the hyphen."

"You did what?"

"I dropped the hyphen a couple of years ago. I didn't want to be Jude Saches-Perkins, so I dropped the Perkins. See, there's no way Alyce would have known you two were my parents when she sent those invitations."

As we continue to watch the happenings across the room,

Gabe whispers, "Is it common for people to use a name different than the one given at birth?"

Kathryn pops a vodka-soaked olive into her mouth and chews, then says quietly, "I did a fluff piece on that very story for the news station. It's this generation. They don't like their names, so they change them. No regard for their parents or family traditions. To them, it's no different than getting a tattoo."

"Shush," Yvonne silences the pair as the foursome in the middle of the room appears to be coming to some sort of truce.

"Mr. and Mrs. Perkins, I want you both to know how sorry I am about this. I had no idea this would create such chaos. When I extended the invitation to share this weekend, I had no ill intentions. All I was looking to accomplish was to speak with people who knew and spent time with my parents. To find someone who might be able to tell me what kind of people they were, what they liked and disliked, how they spent their free time."

Melanie nods, though Patrick doesn't appear convinced by Alyce's avowal. Nevertheless, it seems the evening is moving forward.

SEVEN

JUST THE TWO OF US

Alyce

Jude follows me into the bedroom on the top floor of Dune Dweller—the owner's suite, Griff called it. I have been affectionately referring to it as the love bubble because this was to be our little sanctuary for the weekend, just Jude and me. Peering out the window at the ocean, arms crossing my middle, I breathe deeply, trying to make sense of what just happened downstairs. Behind me, I hear Jude tap on his phone, mumble about the poor service, and toss it onto the bed, then the noise of his footsteps approaching me.

Jude grabs my waist and spins me into his arms, bringing his lips to mine in a long, deep kiss. God, how I've missed him. We hold one another close, my head resting on the spot between his neck and collarbone, but only for a moment. There is much to be done before dinner.

"That did NOT go as planned." I pull away and walk to the closet, examining the contents for something dinner-appropriate.

"Maybe not, but now you know the people you're dealing with." Jude tries for optimism.

"I thought I knew who I was dealing with prior to ever

sending out the invitation. How could you not tell me about your father, Jude?"

"Now, let's be fair, Alyce. We both agreed."

"I know, I know. But just now, meeting him for the first time... I mean, you've said a few things, but I was not prepared for that. God, I looked like an idiot—some child playing tea party with her dolls."

Jude's suitcase lies open in the center of the bed, clothes scattered in haste as he changed earlier. Anger swells in the center of my chest. I begin throwing his clothes back inside the suitcase, packing him up for his transfer to another bedroom. It's been four long weeks since we've seen one another.

"What are you doing?"

"Packing your things."

"Alyce, don't."

"You can't possibly think your father is going to greenlight our sleeping in the same room, much less the same bed."

"My father doesn't dictate my life. I'm a grown man."

"Maybe this was a mistake. I'm not sure we thought this through properly."

"Wait a sec, Ally. We agreed from the beginning that we wanted our relationship to be about us. Before introducing our families into the equation, we wanted to know one another. Remember? Because we both have these overbearing relatives?"

I recall perfectly how we came to that conclusion, but I can't help feeling as if Jude has held something back from me.

A noise in the hallway steals my attention—a scuff on the other side of the door, now silence. "Did you hear that?" I whisper to Jude.

He nods in response and eases toward the door. Leaning in, his eyes narrow as he points at the hallway and mouths, "Someone is out there. Listening to us."

"Fine," I mouth back, my heart racing with fury and resentment. If that's what my guests want, to eavesdrop, well, have at it.

We'll make sure they have something to gossip about—they're welcome to take notes.

I continue to question Jude where we left off in our private conversation, my nerve endings inflamed, tingling with electricity. "When we met in that coffee shop in Norfolk, you never mentioned that's where your family was from, where you grew up. You just said you were visiting friends. Come to think of it, you told me you grew up somewhere else. Something small—what was it?"

"Carrollton, Virginia."

"So, what—you lied?"

"No, I didn't lie. My parents moved to Carrollton after Dad became a pastor—small town, small church. It's not like he's some devout Christian divinely charged with delivering the Almighty's gospel. It was the only church that would take him. Mom continued to commute to Norfolk for her job, but I had no choice other than to live and go to school in Carrollton."

"Why have you never told me this?"

"We made a pact, no past, only future. It was your idea, Alyce." Jude looks over his shoulder at the closed door. "Both our families had such twisted backgrounds, and we were so frustrated by their histories that neither of us wanted to try to explain them to the other."

"I know. You're right. Heck, I don't even know mine to tell you about them." I plop onto the bed. "I was hoping to learn all about them this weekend," I say louder than necessary for the eavesdropper's sake. "But do you have any idea how embarrassing that was down there just now? My God, all those people I brought here and then to have them witness that introduction to your parents, I don't know how I can face them again. This was a huge mistake."

Jude moves to sit beside me on the bed. "Don't say that, honey." He takes my hand. "It's not a mistake to want to know the people who gave you life." And then he kisses me again, and I know we will move forward with this weekend, that together we can make anything happen. "You and I are going to start our own life, regardless of what happens this weekend," Jude whispers only for me, running his finger along my cheek.

"I know, and I can't wait," I breathe into his ear, then twist to look Jude in the eyes. "But here's the thing," I use my full voice. "You saw how your parents reacted to the 'nuptial news.' I have a terrible feeling that Rosey's reaction will put your dad's to shame; she's never considered my needs or desires, only how others will perceive our family. Just wait until she finds out you're the son of one of my parents' long-lost party group."

"Do you know how weird that sounds? My father, Pastor Patrick Perkins, part of a party group?" Jude returns in his full-volume baritone. "The man doesn't believe in fun. I'm not sure he even knows the meaning of the word, party."

"Has he always been like that?"

"Unfortunately," he mumbles.

I look toward the door, leaning in to whisper in Jude's ear. "I think whoever was out there left."

Jude nods in agreement. "Guess they heard all they needed to hear," he says, twisting to take both of my hands in his. "Please promise you won't hold my father's pious and horrendous behavior against me."

"You know I would never do that. I want to be your wife. That said, however, you need to gather your things and move to another room."

"And why would I do that?"

"Because your parents are here, and it's obvious from your dad's behavior that he does not approve of our union. I can hardly see him approving of our sleeping together out of wedlock. Need I remind you? We need to keep the peace for this weekend to work out as planned."

"Those other people can bow to my dad's whims, not us. Right now, I only have a few minutes with you before Griff starts corralling everyone for dinner."

Jude pulls me close, taking me into his arms. The inner angst and stress melt away. He leans his head to the side, moving closer, slowly planting kisses up my neck. In this moment, it almost seems possible that the past can meet the future without everything shattering.

eight

LOAD 'EM UP HAUL 'EM OUT

Griff

They've changed for dinner, piled into the borrowed van, and now sit quietly awaiting further instructions. I maneuver the vehicle down the long chert lane away from Dune Dweller and onto NC-12. Won't take us any time to get there, longer to get these folks loaded up than to transport them to the restaurant. Good thing, too, 'cause all the cologne they've doused on themselves could choke a horse. Window rolled down, and fresh air circulating throughout the cabin ain't helping one iota. Even the Christmas tree freshener dangling from the rearview mirror looks to be shriveling under the odorous pressure.

"How long to the restaurant, Griff?" A male voice asks from the back of the passenger van.

"Not far. 'Bout a five-minute drive," I answer, pulling at the corner of my left eye.

Being one of the few caretakers of the many rental properties on the island, the question of where to eat is one I'm often asked, and I'm never at a lack of suggestions. That said, I'm rarely asked to join a group for dinner after making that recommendation. In all the years I've been taking care of vacation homes, I've never had a host so insistent that I be a part of their group. I tossed out every excuse I could come up with, but short of Alyce forgetting she has invited me to join their meal, I'm gonna have to sit down with this god-awful gang for dinner tonight.

If we were having the meal at Dune Dweller, it'd be a different story; it's my house, after all. Even suggested to Alyce it might be a better idea to stay home tonight—everybody and their grandmother will be out this evening, knowing we got a big storm blowing in this weekend. Alyce wouldn't have it. Said she had this weekend all planned out, and things were already going sideways as it was. So we're off to the Red Lion Pub, where Deborah is expecting the eleven of us for dinner.

Deborah and I have known each other for as long as I can remember. Unlike me, Deborah is a true native, a real O'coker, and knew my grandfather from his days as the ferry operator. After high school, my mother left the island for the mainland, where she met and married my father. When my family made trips to the island, I used to hang out with Deborah and her friends. They were a few years older than me, but nevertheless, they included me in whatever mischief they were up to. Never forgot Deborah for making sure I didn't feel left out. Got to the point I lived for our trips to Ocracoke as I got older. It was the only place I ever seemed to fit in. So, now, when I get asked for dinner suggestions, Deborah's place, The Red Lion Pub, is always one of the first I mention.

Inside the forty-plus-year-old establishment, the sharp tings of silverware and the buzz of laughter and conversations amongst diners welcome us into the dimly lit pub. The scent of malt vinegar mingles with the smell of stale beer and old cooking oil. Deborah touches a tabletop and nods before making her way toward the front door to greet us.

"Hey there, Griff," Deborah says. Like her father before her, Deborah inherited the pub from her dad. Been about five years now since Deb took over, and every day since, she has threatened to remodel but never gets any further into the project than issuing the warning.

"Deb," I nod hello, reaching to turn down the walkie-talkie so as not to disturb the other diners.

"This your group?" She asks.

"Yep, this here is all of 'em, ten total."

"You're sitting with them tonight, aren't you?" Deb wipes the outside covers of menus, making sure they're clean for the next guests.

"Not if I can get out of it."

"I hear that. You got all your properties ready for the storm?" One thing about O'cokers, they love to chat about the weather. Can't help it; weather dictates how the folks living on this island go about their days, living out here in the ocean, twenty-three miles offshore.

"Yeah, I got everything secured before this group came over today. Knew they were going to keep me busy, so.... Hey, I saw where the ferry altered the night route for the high school football team. Your David playing? He doing okay? Liking that new school they finally got built?"

"He is. Thanks for asking, Griff. As a matter of fact, he's playing up in Norfolk tonight, up there near your old stomping grounds."

"Is he really?"

"Yep, they're in the playoffs."

"Well, good for him. I'm rooting for him."

"Thanks, Griff," Deb says as Alyce finds her way to the hostess desk to stand next to me.

After introductions, Deborah asks Alyce for confirmation on the headcount as she gathers the necessary paraphernalia for the evening meal. Smells coming from the kitchen tell me tonight's special is the barley and malt smoked cod and salmon fish pie. It's a fall/winter staple at the Red Lion, one the locals look forward to, though I doubt any of this group will order it.

"Folks, if you'll follow me," Deborah shouts over the heads to get the group's attention. "I've got you all set up in the backroom. You'll have plenty of privacy there."

She leads the ten of them through the dining room; Alyce and her guests follow dutifully. They must be hungry because they've bucked and scoffed at every other request made of them. The prissy little lady with the short haircut sniffs the air, making a face at her preppy husband—Frank, I'm pretty sure. Preacher man still looks to have a stick up his ass. Seems he can't get past the fact his son is marrying Alyce. The mother, what was it? Oh yeah, Melanie, she's good-looking. Can't quite figure out what she's doing with the preacher, but hey, not my gig.

Deborah weaves in and out amongst the tables, speaking to the diners in the joint as she goes. I hang back, hoping Alyce is content that I have gotten them all here in a timely, safe manner and will leave me be for a bit while they eat and jaw at one another.

But no.

In the private room at the back of the restaurant, Alyce waves her hand, motioning for me to come and join them. Deborah has arranged the tables so that they all connect in a U shape, making it possible for all the group members to see one another and participate in the conversation should they wish to do so. As I mosey that way—nodding and speaking to several of the diners, eyeing a nice spot set off from the others—I understand Alyce is making a place for me near the middle of the U. When I booked this group for dinner, I told Deborah I'd probably be taking my regular stool at the end of the bar. That spot suits me just fine, but from the looks of it, I won't be getting any peace or quiet with my dinner tonight. I reach up, tugging at the left corner of my eye as I make my way over to take the seat next to Alyce.

nine

DINE AND WHINE

Melanie

The size of these menus is ridiculous. I can barely get it all the way open without encroaching on someone else's space—nor can I see over the top of it unless I bother to lower it into my lap. "Pickled eggs? Potted Beef? Where are we?" I ask Patrick, sitting on my left.

"Purgatory."

I glance around the table, noting the seats we've chosen. Thankfully, our host has not gone to the trouble of preparing a seating chart for this horseshoe-trough-thing we are planted around. Facing the main dining room, Carmen is directly across from me on the other side of the table. Gabe is by her side, of course, and next to him is Kathryn, and then Frank is at the end of that side of the U. Terry sits at the end of the other side next to Yvonne, who, poor thing, is positioned next to my cantankerous husband. Next to me on the right at the head of the table, Jude leans into Alyce's ear—if he gets any closer, he'll be sitting in her lap. Alyce giggles as he fawns over her, then clamps her lips shut in a closed smile, gazing adoringly at my son. Across the way, I catch Carmen watching me. I raise my eyebrows in question. What? Carmen pulls her menu up to cover the bottom half of her face, twisting to the left where our caretaker is situated. Did she just give Griff a look? What was that about?

"What kind of food is this?" Patrick lobs to no one in particular.

Terry looks up from the menu in his hands, maneuvering his torso to the right so as to address Patrick. "If you're speaking about the origin of culture for this cuisine, then the appropriate response to your inquiry would be British. It's British cuisine."

Patrick gives Terry a contemptuous look. "Jesu...cheese and crackers, man. Do you ever sit back and listen to yourself, Terry?"

Taking a cue from Terry, I ignore my husband's atrocious behavior. Patrick has done nothing except alienate the two of us from the rest of the group since we set foot on Ocracoke. It's terribly ironic that my only ally at the moment is my hellish husband—I can't recall the last time we agreed or worked together to find a solution to any problem, big or small. Of course, there's my son, but now he has a fiancée. I can hardly claim Jude to be a trusted confidant with this latest stunt he's pulled. How is it possible: number one, for me not to have known my only child is in a serious relationship, and number two, that this little twit, Alyce, coerced us into attending a weekend with three couples from our distant past? What's worse is that Alyce is the daughter of Shane and Amber.

I'd have preferred to have some say-so in his decision of who to wed—a bit of motherly advice goes a long way—and it would not have been Alyce Thompson-Fischer or whatever the hell her name is. Jude has too much potential to throw it away on this ridiculous 'I'm so posh and refined' little girl. Jude has barely pulled himself up the bottom rung of the career ladder yet. At the very least, I must push this wedding date further out—not that either of them has yet to share such details. And the ring she's wearing—my God. There is no telling how long it will take him to pay off that rock.

Patrick elbows my side, poking me in the ribs. "What are you eating?"

"The fish and chips look safe," I say, glancing at my menu, spouting the first thing I spy. Food is the last thing on my mind right now.

Obviously, the two of them are serious, right? Just look at the way she rubs a long, lean finger down Jude's arm, back and forth and back and forth. I mean, is there any possibility Jude and Alyce haven't slept together yet? It's doubtful, right? Look at her. She's stunning. Not beautiful, no, but stunning, quite unique. She has a sensuality about her that is almost uncomfortable, really. I can see Jude's appeal, though—physically, that is. He's a hot-blooded young male. It's to be expected. But does she need to be so controlling, so conniving, so bewitching?

"Think I'll just stick to a burger. Can't mess that up," Patrick says, slamming his menu shut with the finality of his decision.

Jude

"Oh! You know what I want?" Alyce asks suddenly.

"You can have anything you want, baby." I pull her closer, kissing her cheek. "Let me guess. You're getting the smoked fish pot pie."

"Eww, no. I'm not talking about food."

"Excellent. I can't wait to hear this. Do tell."

Alyce laughs, wearing a smile that gets me every time I see it. "Jude, behave." She brings her lips to my ear. "Your parents are watching."

"Giggle again. It's turning me on." I wiggle my eyebrows, hoping to make her laugh again.

"Jude!" Alyce slaps at my arm, her lips stretching high and wide under a playful gaze.

I pull myself away and try to think of food. I need to eat. Alyce stocked the bar at Dune Dweller with a bourbon I hadn't had before, but one that I can say I now know well. I was able to get Alyce to loosen up a bit, too. Coaxing her out of our room after that showdown with my dad earlier wasn't easy, but Alyce isn't a quitter—one more thing to love about my girl.

Seated on my other side, Mom leans in, addressing Alyce and me. "What are you two love birds up to over here?" She rubs my upper arm, working her way down, then back up again.

"Going over the menu, determining if there is something we might like to share," I say.

Mom continues stroking my arm. I pat her hand to acknowledge the insecure vibes she's throwing off. "Did you decide on dinner?" I shift full attention to my mother as Alyce makes conversation with Carmen and Gabe.

"I might just have a side salad. Too much going on to have an appetite," she answers, resting back in her chair. "Alyce seems sweet," Mom switches topics seamlessly, causally accepting the wine the server just placed before her and sipping. "How long have you two been seeing one another?"

I squeeze Alyce's hand to get her attention. She twists, accepting my invitation to be part of this conversation with my mom. "Mom's asking how long we've been dating," I explain.

Alyce smiles that smile, the one that makes my heart swell. "A year and a half now," Alyce tells Mom.

"Oh, wow. So, that's quite a while, then. I thought this was a new relationship," Mom says, sipping from her glass.

Knowing my mother as I do, I know exactly what she is saying without directly delivering the specific words. She's pissed I didn't inform her about Alyce. Mom would have been fine with Alyce had I told her about our relationship before letting my father in on the information. To make matters worse, though, Mom ended up learning about Alyce and me, along with everyone else. "I'm sorry, Mom. We've had a lot going on with school, internships, interviews, and jobs. It wasn't intentional."

"Please don't take it personally, Mrs. Perkins. Jude and I have barely had time to see one another, much less tell our families."

"Melanie, dear, please, call me Melanie. Just not Mrs. Perkins."

"Mom uses Saches or Saches-Perkins," I inform Alyce.

Mom sips her wine again and adds, "I only answer to Mrs. Perkins at Patrick's church."

It suddenly dawns on me that Alyce and I were in the middle of a conversation when Mom broke in earlier. I turn attention from my mother to face my fiancée. "Tell me what it is you want. You said you had something in mind that wasn't dinner." I wink to end the statement, show Alyce I haven't let go of the idea of having her all to myself again later. She catches my furtive implication, offering a sly smile of her own.

"Well, this sounds interesting," Mom lets me know she is still very much a part of our conversation, regardless of where my attention lies.

"I want a picture of the group to commemorate the weekend," Alyce says. "We can get Deborah to take it, don't you think?"

Dad leans over Mom. "What are you all talking about over here?"

Mom drains her remaining wine. "Alyce wants to get a picture of the group."

"A picture of what?" Dad asks.

Alyce speaks to my father. "I want to get a photograph of the whole group—so we can remember the evening."

"That's what's wrong with this generation," Dad says, swirling the vodka over the ice in his drink. "You see the world through the lens of your phone. Everything's picked over, cleaned up, touched up, and glossified. Every last move captured in time, documented, to portray the only vision you want the world to see, not the truth. God, no. Never the truth. Nothing is ever genuine. It's all fake. Phony. Filtered."

"Jesus, Dad, knock it off."

"Don't you take the lord's name in vain," Dad says, raising his voice, attracting the attention of the others around the U-shaped table as well as the pub patrons sitting nearby.

"Why? You do it all the time," I fire back. I know better than to start this right now, right here, with Alyce and all these other folks looking on.

Dad scoots his chair back from the table. The loud, screeching noise cuts through the dining room. Mom grabs Dad's wrist, yanking him back into his seat, whispering, gesturing wildly.

"Looks like someone hasn't lost that famous temper," Kathryn says through her smirk.

Mom jumps to our defense. "This is a personal family conversation, Kathryn. Just because you don't have a family and aren't familiar with the concept of privacy does not give you the privilege of commenting on our affairs."

Kathryn throws her head back, laughing maniacally. "Affairs," she continues her wicked laughter. "That's so true. You're right. I forgot I was never allowed to talk about your affairs."

"You really want to go there, Katy?"

"It's Kathryn," she says, tilting her head in a taunting manner. "And, I think we have more important things to keep to ourselves than past or current affairs."

Yvonne

"Ladies," I try. Someone needs to get these two under control, and since none of the others seem willing to do it, I will. "This is not the time or place for this conversation."

"How boringly cliché of you, Yvonne," Kathryn drawls.

"Let's just get through dinner—we haven't even ordered food yet. When we get back to Dune Dweller, you all can hash, rehash, slash, and slaughter for all I care," I say, tossing Terry a worried glance. How will we ever get through this weekend without another member of our group going down? This is one of the many reasons we broke up in the first place. "Can we try to hold it together through dinner, try not to embarrass ourselves or our hostess, if for nothing other than nourishment?"

Deborah, our greeter/server/bartender/manager (she's not going to have to cook, too, I hope), stands patiently in the middle of the U-shaped setup, holding a small notebook and pen. As the gang clamps down on the squabbling, Deborah speaks quietly to Griff. "Tony's at the bar. He wanted me to ask you to stop by, talk about the incoming weather."

Griff nods in reply, taking a hard roll from the bread basket.

"Folks, if you're ready to order, we can go ahead and get started."

I lean into Terry's side, whispering, questioning. "Weather? Did I miss something?" Terry shrugs, looking back at his menu before making his final dinner selection. We've all been so busy eavesdropping on each other, chiming in on one another's conversations, I don't know that any of us have selected entrées yet.

Frank speaks up to say he's ready, allowing the rest of us time to make decisions. In turn, we all name a dish we have settled on, wrangle the oversized menus, and pass them over. Another round of drinks is ordered, and Deborah leaves the group to tear ourselves apart once more.

As Deborah takes exit, I jump in quickly, hoping to reroute the last volatile topic. "Griff, what is this weather we're hearing about?"

Griff, obviously not expecting to take part in the evening's discussions, chokes back a hunk of bread he just bit off. He washes it down with iced tea, clears his throat. "Got a storm brewing."

Terry takes the baton, trying again. "We haven't heard any broadcasts suggesting that weather would be a factor this weekend, nor anything about the prediction of a storm brewing in the vicinity. Is there some meteorological event we should be aware of?"

Elbows propped on the tabletop, Griff clears his throat again, places a finger to his left eye, pulls, and says, "Yeah, well, we got one rolling in. Usually, they come off the ocean—those are the ones that get all the attention and broadcast time. No, this one's coming off the mainland. Looks to be pretty nasty. Course, here on the island, a storm is a storm, and it generally ends up flooding us out for a couple of days."

Patrick takes over. "Floods you out? What the hell is this man talking about? I thought we were all leaving tomorrow. How are we supposed to get out of here if the roads are flooded? Did you know about this, Jude? Alyce, you put this shindig together. Did you know this? Is this part of your plan? To get us here and hold us captive?"

Another round of drinks arrives, and just in time. Deborah and her aide deliver the cocktails accordingly, slipping away quickly. Who could blame them? I would take leave if I could.

"Alyce did not plan to kidnap you, Dad," Jude says to his father. That poor boy. How can this incredibly polite, well-mannered young man be Patrick Perkins' son?

"I assure you, I had no ulterior motives, Mr. Perkins. I only learned of the potential weather issues earlier today."

Murmurs fly around the table, couples speaking amongst themselves. Plans made earlier in the evening are falling away, leaving the need for new ones to be outlined.

"Then you had time to warn us, inform us, before we all drove an obscene amount of hours and got locked away on this island, in that... that house," Patrick thunders.

"I swear I think I saw flames shoot out of that man," I whisper to Terry.

Terry responds with a shake of his head, then tries his hand at de-escalating the tirade. "So, Griff, will we be able to take leave of the island tomorrow morning, or should we be preparing for a more intense...?"

"Stop with the lengthy, wordy bullshit," Frank grows irritable as well. "Can we get off this island tomorrow or not, Griff?"

"I can answer that," says an unfamiliar voice behind me. The faces of our group on the other side of the U display shock, confusion, and puzzlement.

I twist to understand why the others are gawking. "Holy shit. Is that?"

Across the table, Carmen answers, "Rosey Fischer."

ten

MEET ROSEY FISCHER

Rosey

"Well, I never imagined I'd be in the presence of this gang again," I say, announcing my arrival. From the looks of the faces gathered around the table setting, it's obvious they, too, never fathomed such a reunion. "But I must admit, never in my most twisted of notions did I dream my granddaughter would be sitting amongst the likes of you all." All the time and energy I've put into raising this young woman, presenting Alyce to dignitaries and politicians, teaching her the tactics of diplomacy and the best practices for entertaining distinguished guests, only to now find her seated around a table with society's mediocre dregs at best. I come to a halt behind Alyce, placing a hand on her shoulder and squeezing. Her body tenses under my touch.

That TV persona (what's her name—Kate) is whispering loudly to her gem of a man, his upturned collar standing tall, rising into the hair at the nape of his neck. "She hasn't lost any of her charm, has she?" Kate asks no one in particular.

"You're correct, Kate. I have not. I've only perfected it with age."

"Nice to see you admit your faults, Rosey. And it's Kathryn, by the way. No more Kate," she announces, then slurps loudly from her martini.

"What you call faults, Kathryn, are assets in the eyes of others, and you should be careful who you insult."

A server approaches the table, a tray of water glasses in hand. As she doles out beverages, I relay the need for an extra chair and place setting. I look at the rugged man situated next to Alyce and let him know I would appreciate sitting next to my kin. He tries to leave, saying there is a seat at the bar, but Alyce insists the man stay. The shuffling of chairs and bodies, drinks, and silverware commences until finally we are all settled.

"No hello, no kiss for your grandmother?" I ask Alyce. Other than protesting the man stay put, Alyce has done little more than sit rigid, mouth agape. I've no idea what Alyce has planned or intends to accomplish with this group, but I am here to make sure whatever it is remains within acceptable parameters.

"I," Alyce begins, stammers, then, "I'm just surprised to see you here, is all."

"I bet so, since you were so careful not to mention anything about such an outing as this." The waitperson arrives with my place setting. I inform the woman, "I'd like a Maker's Mark old-fashioned on the rocks." Back to Alyce, I continue our discussion. "We spoke only yesterday, and I certainly don't recall you saying anything about your new friends."

The young man sitting next to Alyce leans around my granddaughter, extending his hand, shooting it straight out in front of him. "Hello, Mrs. Fischer. It's so nice to meet you. Alyce speaks of you often."

"Well, I wish I could say the same for you, young mister, but Alyce hasn't breathed a word of your existence to me."

"Welcome to the party." Ah, if it isn't Patrick Perkins interrupting... I should have guessed.

I ignore him and continue. "Are you somebody I should know?" I ask the young man.

Seated beside Melanie, who keeps her focus on the wine in her hand, Pat persists with his drivel. "We had no idea who Alyce was either until this little soiree."

"Still the prophet of doom, huh, Patrick?"

"As I recall, nobody ever accused you of being named for your *rosy* outlook on life," Patrick tosses back. I always could count on that man for a good spar.

"Dad," the young man says as if to chastise Patrick.

"Your son?" I ask Pat.

"Yeah, and from what we all learned earlier this evening, he's to be your grandson-in-law in the near future." I wasn't sure what I would find when I finally made my way to the island, but it most assuredly was not a groom-to-be for my granddaughter.

"Elizabeth Alyce Fischer, is this true? Is this young..."

"Jude Saches, ma'am. Pleasure," he says, sticking that hand back in my face again. At least his nails are groomed and clean.

"Saches-Perkins," Patrick says, emphasizing the Perkins.

"I told you I dropped the Perkins, Dad."

"Now, folks, I think we should all take a moment to breathe, to let this new information we have all received tonight settle in," Terry says, with that smooth, deep baritone of his. "Each of us has had an extensive day of travel, of postulating and theorizing, of reacquainting."

"Ah, Terry. It's nice to see you haven't lost your flair with words. How's the funeral business?" Out of the whole crew, Terry and Yvonne were always the most level-headed and mature couple. A few quirks, yes, but still by far the most grounded of the bunch.

"They're dying to meet him, don'tchya know," Melanie answers the question I posed for Terry, cackling over her juvenile attempt at humor.

"Can I get you another glass of wine, dear?" I ask. Melanie offers a half-lipped snarl while keeping her thoughts quiet.

"Rosey," Alyce finds her voice. "How did you know where we were? And how did you get here?"

"The same as all of you, I suspect. The long, long two-lane highway, the ferry."

"Yes, but…"

"You mean, how did I know? Don't question my tactics, Alyce. Especially not when you have decided to obscure so many important pieces of your life—one I'm still funding, I might add."

"Okay, but I still…"

"If you must know, I arrived on the last ferry. The islanders are quite friendly and informative folks. Seems everyone knows everyone here." The brawny man sitting on my right grunts in agreement, nodding. "A nice gentleman from the ferry drove me to a house he called Dune Dweller. From there, the man radioed someone who told us that the caretaker of the house had borrowed his passenger van to transport you all to dinner at the Red Lion Pub. Does that satisfy your inquiry? If so, I have a few questions of my own now—starting with this ridiculous engagement announcement. How is it possible you have agreed to marry this young man without my ever having met him?"

The young man, Jude, leans around Alyce once more. "Please don't be upset with Alyce, Mrs. Fischer. We haven't told anybody about our engagement. My parents only found out a couple of hours ago."

"And yet still well before I became aware of this betrothal," I can barely contain my anger. Alyce's deceit has hurt me far more than I intend to show this squirrelly troop.

"This is the most messed-up situation we've ever been a part of," Kathryn announces. Beside her, Frank nods emphatically, that collar jabbing furiously at his drooping earlobes.

"I doubt that," Melanie spouts.

Multiple arguments and heated exchanges break out around the table. The gentleman seated on my right looks physically uncomfortable, taking in the actions of this group of old neighbors. It's clear my grandchild has taken on far more than she can handle.

"What were you thinking?" I ask Alyce as we sit amid the chaos.

Alyce pulls herself closer to the table, propping both elbows and steepling fingers. She turns her gaze on me, though I can hardly call it such, as all I see in her eyes at the moment is contempt. "I was thinking I might get the people who used to know my parents to tell me about them, since you have been hell-bent on keeping any details about them to yourself. You even made Pops promise not to talk to me about them."

"Well, that's ridiculous. Whoever gave you that notion?"

"Pops, that's who. He told me it was best not to talk about them, that the topic upset you, that you didn't want any of us talking about the dead."

"And that's somehow wrong? I was trying to be respectful of the deceased," I explain.

"Oh, give it up, Rosey. You have never allowed me the privilege of knowing either of them. My mother was your daughter. I would think you would want to remember her, to keep her memory alive, that you would want me to know her."

"This newfound insolence of yours is off-putting, Elizabeth Alyce."

A voice rises above the mayhem. "I can tell you why Rosey doesn't want you to know your parents."

"Who said that?" I ask, scanning the guests around the U-shaped table. The faces of the others whip to view the one who has spoken.

"I did. Nice to see you again, Rosey."

"Wish I could say the same for you, Gabe." My patience for this charade is long gone. Beside Gabe, Carmen watches the happenings with wide eyes. "Carmen," I acknowledge. Carmen nods her greeting but remains silent.

Alyce's focus is on Gabe. She believes Gabe will give her the information she seeks. Not if I can help it, he won't.

Without a doubt, this entire shindig needs to come to a swift close.

eleven

CONDITIONS DETERIORATE

Gabe

"She shut you down," Carmen says, her voice hushed. We stand outside the Red Lion's front door, waiting for Griff to unlock the van. The evening has grown cool. An occasional gust of wind charges the still night air.

"Rosey always did have some sort of agenda, and if something didn't play out the way she saw fit, Rosey found a way to get rid of it," I reply, toeing the gravel parking lot.

"Careful, Gabe. You're sounding bitter," Carmen warns. She's caught the edge in my voice. Earlier in the evening, we agreed it would be best to stay neutral this weekend, show no emotion, keep out of the fray.

"Where is Rosey anyway?"

"She was talking with that woman in the restaurant, Deborah."

We follow the group to wait beside our borrowed transportation while Griff finishes up inside the restaurant—something about islanders and weather and everyone chipping in to make sure all O'cokers stay safe. If nothing else, there's a real sense of community on this island. The realization gives me pause as it dawns on me that Carmen and I have never experienced that feeling of belonging in any of our life situations.

Patrick digs at his teeth with the toothpick he grabbed on the way out the door. He holds it between his lips at the corner of his mouth. "What is all this weather nonsense these people keep talking about?"

Carmen shrugs. Frank shakes his head.

"I tried to pull the weather up on my phone, but the service here is intermittent at best," I say.

"We did a piece on the storm at the station this week," Kathryn says. "A storm hit the west coast of Florida a day or two ago—a hurricane, but I don't recall it being a big one. We didn't have any follow-up segments covering any damage or destruction from it. It can't be that severe. I'm not sure what all the fuss is about."

"That's right. I remember hearing that myself," Yvonne says. "Only a Cat One, as I recall. The forecasters said it would be a rain event by the time it reached Norfolk. I didn't think about it extending out here to Ocracoke, but I guess it would stand to reason."

Patrick shoves his hands deep into the pockets of his pants, rocking back on his heels, speaking around the toothpick. "Yeah, well, the way these folks are acting, you'd think a tsunami was headed to wipe out this whole island."

Alyce and Jude step closer, joining the conversation. "Griff explained to me earlier," Alyce says, "that these types of storms end up washing out the roadways. Everyone knows to hunker down and stay safe until it blows over. Then they have a group that treks out to survey the damage and report back to the rest."

"Kind of envy that simplicity, that camaraderie," Terry muses.

"Well, we're still leaving tomorrow," Kathryn says snippily.

"And no one has said you can't," I tell her. "But if the roads are flooded, and the ferries aren't running, I don't know if we have much of a choice."

"Who said the ferries won't run?" Patrick bows up, readying

for another round of 'I'm gonna whip somebody's ass.' Always was his favorite game.

"Calm down, Pat," Melanie commands. "We're not going anywhere without Jude."

"And I'm staying with Alyce to see this weekend through," Jude informs the group.

Patrick stomps forward, bringing himself nose to nose with his son. His pointer finger makes contact with the center of Jude's chest. "Honor your mother and father -Exodus 20:12. It's the fifth commandment, and by God, you will." Patrick backs away abruptly as Griff and Rosey approach.

"Load 'em up," Griff says.

Carmen

We climb back into the twelve-passenger van, awkwardly crawling and stooping our way through the bucket seats. Griff closes Rosey into the front passenger space, secures all the doors, then proceeds to the driver's position. I watch as he nudges the gear shift, seeming to have a bit of trouble, but gets it into posi-tion and twists the key in the ignition. Apprehension engulfs the passenger compartment as Griff guides the transit van along the dark island roads. Earlier, we held to the agenda—cocktail hour, meet the host, dinner—but now the group has no idea what Alyce has planned for the remainder of the evening. At the front of the van, Rosey and Griff are in deep conversation, though I can't make out what they are saying, given the many side conversa-tions in the cramped compartment. Instead, I stare out the windows and mull over the happenings thus far.

Taking in the sights of the landscape and structures we pass on our way home proves impossible, given the cloud cover skirting to and fro, obscuring the moonlight. It's almost as if the island has secrets to keep as well. Only eight hours ago, we were racking our consciousness for who might have put this reunion together and why. Both of those questions may have been answered earlier in the evening, but I believe there is more to this gathering than is being said.

Understandably, Alyce wants to know her parents: how they lived, what they liked to do, who their friends were. I don't begrudge her seeking that information, though it seems Rosey does. Alyce is of an age where she can handle such details, cope with the loss of people she never knew. Perhaps not the particulars of their deaths, but still, why would Rosey want to keep Alyce in the dark about her mother, Rosey's own daughter? Rosey quickly changed the subject when Gabe announced he was willing to provide Alyce with whatever he could regarding the girl's queries. Then again, in Rosey's defense, the server had shown back up at that very moment to deliver the appetizers and salads. But even after the business of consuming the evening meal was complete, the topic of conversation never found its way back to Amber and Shane.

Somewhere inside the vehicle, a phone rings. Hands pat pockets and dig through handbags, everyone searching to determine if the noise is some outside source summoning them. The racket extinguishes, and a booming male voice speaks—Griff's phone.

"Hey, Charles," we hear from our seat-belted positions. The compartment is still and silent, listening for Griff to say more. "It is?" More silence. Griff glances down briefly, then reaches to his middle. "Yep. It was off again. This walkie-talkie's on/off button's been sticking on me. Sorry, man. What's up?" Again, we all wait without words, wondering what information Griff is gleaning. "You think? It's not too late?" Griff asks, then grows quiet, listening. Silence bloats the inside van compartment, making it obvious we're all invested in whatever conversation it is that Griff is having.

"Yeah," he answers. "Okay, if you think it's possible. Give me a sec. I'll ask."

Griff twists slightly in his seat, speaking to Alyce. "Charles says the lighthouse ghost tour isn't likely to happen tomorrow, not with the storm heading in. Wants to know if you would like to do it tonight instead?"

"Really?" Alyce practically squeals. "Oh, let's do it. I was afraid we would have to cancel."

Next to Alyce, Jude asks, "Cancel what, honey?"

"Yes, do what, Alyce?" Patrick jumps in. "I think I speak for the group when I say we are all done with surprises for today."

I should help this poor girl out. "Patrick, give Alyce a chance to speak before you start berating her." Amber's daughter has thus far proven herself to be a strong, intelligent young woman, but she is no match for Patrick's vitriol should he decide to start again.

Alyce speaks quickly to appease Patrick or perhaps cut him off from further insults and criticism. After tonight, Alyce may very well have to rethink her decision to marry Patrick's son. "As part of the weekend festivities—a bonding excursion, if you will —I asked Griff to arrange a private ghost tour at the lighthouse for the group. The tour is very popular with visitors throughout the tourist season, but during the winter months, it isn't offered. I obviously want to follow through with the tour, and I would love it if you all would participate, but if not, I understand."

Jude takes Alyce's hand, saying, "You and I will do it. Griff can take the others back to the house if they wish. Then you and I take the tour." Jude twists to view the others in the cabin. "If any of you want to join us, Alyce and I welcome you."

"We'll go," I say before I can talk myself out of it. Gabe gives me a questioning look, but I know he will go along without push-back. Besides, it'll be good for us to get a bit of exercise after the greasy meal we just consumed.

"Thank you, Carmen," Alyce says, then addresses Griff. "Tell him yes, Griff. There will be a few of us in attendance tonight. Oh, and thank him."

"Now, wait a minute," Kathryn says, yanking her safety belt as she pulls herself away from her seat and twists to address me. "We are not going to let you all go traipsing off with Alyce while we all return to the house alone."

"You want to go ghost hunting, Kathryn?" Yvonne cackles. "Seems your name isn't the only thing you've changed."

"What? And you're okay with Carmen and Gabe filling Alyce in on all the details of her parents and all the times we shared together? There's no telling what they'll say, and I, for one, want to be there to monitor that conversation." Kathryn's voice grows more shrill as she speaks.

"Paranoid much, Kathryn?" I ask. I refuse to sit here and let Kathryn dictate what is said and done this weekend. I genuinely feel for Alyce and sympathize with her desire for familial knowledge.

"She's not paranoid, Carmen." Frank jumps to his wife's defense. "Kathryn has always been careful and is only looking out for everyone's best interest. Besides, you and Gabe back there are always speaking in another language so that the rest of us won't know what y'all are talking about. If you ask me, it's you two who are acting paranoid and suspicious."

Melanie, who has been uncharacteristically quiet for the ride, adds to the discussion. "I had no idea you could be so chivalrous, Frank. But I will say this. I agree with Kathryn. We either all go, or no one goes."

The van erupts in arguments between the couples. Though I started this upheaval, I remain silent, watching the happenings and listening to the contentious group.

Alyce places her face in open palms, shaking her head back and forth. She is in over her head. Next to Alyce, Jude rubs his hand up and down his fiancée's back, speaking softly in her ear. Alyce is much too young to handle the dynamics of this clan. For that matter, it seems even Patrick's son, who knows what he's dealing with, is overwhelmed by all the bickering. Watching them makes me think of Amber and Shane, all the times we shared. We weren't much older than Alyce and Jude are now. Each one of us was in the early years of our careers—newly married, some with a child or even three. We were all at that place in our lives where we had recently experienced the uncomfortable epiphany that we had become the adults in the room. No longer the kids.

A loud whistle sounds throughout the van. On Rosey's instruction to get our attention, Griff calls us down.

Rosey turns from her front-row position to face us in the back. "What in the hell has gotten into you all?"

"Don't you go cursing at me, Rosey Fischer," Patrick shouts, leaning forward in his seat.

"Oh, Patrick, don't throw your righteous bullshit at me," Rosey tosses back. "Now, all of you need to get a grip on whatever this crazy is because it seems to me we're about to go ghost hunting."

twelve

LET THE TOUR COMMENCE

Kathryn

The sound of gravel crunching under the wheels of the passenger van announces our arrival at the Ocracoke Lighthouse. Griff maneuvers the vehicle to a stop in the makeshift parking area cordoned off the side of the small road. Once more, we stoop and scoot our way out of the van—easier said than done in a wrap dress and heeled boots—awaiting further instructions, acclimating to the chill of the evening, the darkness of the night. The inky black sky has swallowed the moon at the moment, leaving little illumination to enhance our vision. The wind whooshes then stills just as quickly as it blew in.

Griff saunters around the front of the van, motioning for us to follow. He marches the troop over a long walkway, bordered by railings on both sides, toward the base of the lighthouse. The clomping of shoes traversing the composite decking of the boardwalk echoes through the night air. As if the handrails flanking the boardwalk aren't enough, another fence, a decorative white picket, runs the length of the path to the lighthouse on the right. The barriers prevent access to several structures deemed as the lighthouse keeper's quarters. On our left, a rustling noise warns of some unknown animal's presence. From the other end of the walkway, a man hurries toward Griff. The closer the man gets, the more apparent the size discrepancy becomes. Next to Griff's large stature, this man appears childlike. He meets our group in the middle of the long pathway. The two speak in hushed voices while we wait obediently as if we're students on a school field trip.

"I wish someone would have mentioned we might go traipsing through cemeteries and haunted mansions after dinner," I say to Frank, holding down the front flap of my dress to keep it from blowing open in the wind. "I'd have changed into jeans before we left for the restaurant."

"At least the full chill of winter hasn't set in. Mid-fifties may not be balmy, but we're not freezing our asses off either," Frank says to me, then leans in to whisper. "Take a look at Melanie in that silk blouse. She's obviously regretting that outfit. I can hear her teeth chattering all the way back here." Melanie does look even more miserable than I feel, but we all appear uncomfortable if you ask me. Certainly, we are all out of our element.

"Did you happen to see the look Terry and Rosey exchanged at dinner?" I whisper, finally having a moment of privacy with my husband. "Was it my imagination, or did they look as if they knew each other better than the two of them let on?"

"I thought so, too. What do you think is going on there?"

My opportunity to answer falls away as Griff delivers details for the next steps of this tour. The other man stands at Griff's side.

"Folks, this here's Charles MacDougal. He maintains the Ocracoke lighthouse—gives the ghost tour, climbing tour, and the like. Anyway, Charles is going to take it from here."

Griff steps away, moving to position himself at the back of the group.

"Hello there, folks." The small man throws up a hand in greeting. "Like Griff said, I'm Charles, and I watch over our lighthouse. Now, if at any point you have questions, well, I'd rather you keep 'em to yourself. I'm happy to answer them, but not till after the tour is complete. I know. I know," he says, nodding and shaking his head at the same time. "Visitors are always claiming they'll forget their question. But you know what? If that question is important enough, you'll remember it. And hey, I might even answer it during the tour."

From the front of the group, a hand shoots up.

"Yes, ma'am?" Charles acknowledges reluctantly.

Alyce's voice floats through the night sky. "Before we get started, I just wanted to say thank you for doing this, Charles. I understand this tour is not typically given to private groups out of season, so again, thank you."

"Yes, ma'am," Charles nods. "Now let's get started."

Another hand rises and waves from the center of the pack. Charles nods in that direction to acknowledge the question, this time from Melanie, her arms wrapped tightly around her midsection. "Who lives in that house on the other side of these fences?" Melanie's words are disjointed, a staccato effect caused by the clicking of her teeth.

"That would be part of the lighthouse keeper's accommodations," Charles states matter-of-factly, turning quickly to continue before having to acknowledge another inquiry. But he's not fast enough.

"So the current lighthouse keeper lives there now?" Patrick asks.

"No, sir, we don't have a keeper any longer. The lighthouse is now part of the National Park Service. As such, it is unmanned these days."

"But there's a light on in the big house over there," Melanie manages to relay her observation despite her teeth knocking together.

Charles turns, looking in the direction of the house.

Patrick points, directing Charles' view. "See on the second floor, there? Third window from the left."

The rest of our group turns to see the sight for ourselves, witnessing the faint flicker of a light coming from the home.

"Ah, it seems our friends are eager for guests tonight."

Charles' voice takes on an eerie tone, a slight curve of his mouth. "It's not often we have evening visitors on the grounds. Seems you all have piqued some curiosity."

"How ridiculously fake is that voice he's using?" I whisper to Frank. Frank—lips pursed, eyes narrowed—nods his agreement.

"What are you saying?" Patrick challenges the guide. "That's some sort of phantom in the window? Looks to me like someone switching a flashlight on and off."

"Dad, let the man do what he so graciously left his warm, safe home to come and do for us tonight," Jude says.

Patrick bows up to return the chastising comment, but Charles returns to his spiel before Patrick can speak.

"As you can see for yourselves, our old spirit friends enjoy having company. They're anxious tonight as we have been without visitors these last couple of months. Some locals have noted our specters are also more restless around periods when we have a storm blowing in—got a double whammy for you all tonight. You all are in for a treat." Alyce claps giddily as I shake my head ever so slightly at Frank, wondering why we are appeasing a child. But I know perfectly well why we're here and that we have no other choice in the matter.

"Speaking of ghosts, our most famous ghost is Blackbeard, of course," Charles continues, his voice rising and falling with well-rehearsed tension."But our lighthouse is where most of the apparitions on the island like to converge. The energy of this place attracts the island's many spirits, welcomes them. The old light-house keeper often makes an appearance, a host, if you will. He's always described by those who view him to be wearing black pants with gray stripes. You'll recognize him by the full, heavy beard covering his face and his long hair pulled back with a piece of twine. Another of our more prominent entities is the daughter of Aaron Burr. Theodosia Burr Alston passed on after the ship she was sailing on sank off our coast during a storm, a storm very much like the one we are expecting this weekend."

"'Bout time for the man with a hook for a hand to show up,"

Patrick says, his voice thick with sarcasm. "What about that slender man? He here too?"

Charles ignores the interruption. "Theodosia roams our grounds in a long white gown, leaving a trail of water in her wake. Folks note the seaweed dripping from her hair and the musky scent that her specter often leaves behind. Now there are those who claim they've seen her specter all along the east coast, roaming the beaches, looking, searching for a ship to take her home."

I give Frank an eye roll. He shakes his head at me as we turn to trek onward once more. The group follows Charles across the boardwalk. We halt as Charles comes to a full stop in front of a door at the base of the lighthouse. Charles turns to face the tall, white, cylindrical structure and points overhead. High above us, the revolving lighthouse beam sweeps the night sky.

"The Ocracoke lighthouse is two hundred years old. It is the second oldest working lighthouse in America." Charles speaks in a slow, measured cadence—doing his best to sound otherworldly. The effect may work on youngsters or the naive at heart but does little to frighten this hardened gang.

"It stands seventy-five feet high, which is short by lighthouse standards. However, the Ocracoke lighthouse had a different job back in the late 1800s than the other Outer Banks' lighthouses."

Patrick steps forward, hands on hips. "Are we going to stand outside and listen to this mumbo jumbo, or are we going to tour the damn lighthouse?"

Gabe comes to Charles' defense. "Give it a rest, Pat. You got somewhere you need to be?"

"I'm just saying we don't need the entire two-hundred-year history of the Ocracoke Lighthouse at this hour on a windy Friday night. Perhaps we could just get on with this—and somewhere warmer, for God's sake. Melanie's going to lose a tooth over here."

"Just a couple more facts, and we're headed inside the lighthouse structure," Charles assures Patrick. "Now, where was I?"

Charles appears to be scanning his memory for the last facts offered, then begins again.

"Our Ocracoke lighthouse has been through a series of changes over its two hundred years in existence and still continues to be of great use to the island. Today, the light is maintained by the U.S. Coast Guard, which brings me to the climb. We will be climbing the lighthouse this evening, but we will not be touring the lantern room as the light is functional." For emphasis, Charles points upward again at the light illuminating the sky. "The damage to your vision from such an intense light source would be significant. Okay, then. And we're off."

"Charles, I apologize for interrupting," Yvonne says from the middle of the congregation. "I hate to do this to you, but I desperately need a restroom. Had I known we were making this detour, I would have gone before we left the pub."

"That's quite all right, ma'am. When nature calls..., am I right?" Charles looks to Griff and throws off a quick, knowing nod. "You got it from here, dude? I'll run this lady..."

"Oh, and me too," Rosey says, stepping away from the group.

"You two aren't going without me," Terry says. "I'll go along as well to make sure you both get back to the group safely."

"As you wish," Charles says. "Anyone else?"

With his charges in tow, Charles starts back down the boardwalk as the rest of us look on. "We'll be back d'rectly, folks," he shouts into the night sky.

Alyce

Rosey, Yvonne, and Terry follow Charles back toward the parking lot. I can't hold a full bladder against Yvonne, of course not. Had we known before we left The Red Lion, we all would have prepped appropriately for this activity. But Jude's parents... their unrelenting questions without any regard for rules are an altogether different kind of rude—Charles made his instructions for the tour clear from the beginning.

Watching these people, I wonder how much time my parents spent with this group during their last years of life. Did my parents share in the likenesses, characteristics, perhaps some of the philosophies of this group, each of whom has done little but display manner-challenged, high-maintenance, ego-driven personalities? Whatever those answers may be, observation has clearly revealed that the remaining members have not kept in close contact throughout the many years gone by. But, were any of them ever close, or have they always bickered like this?

From what I've been able to decipher, Carmen held my mother's confidence. But that could be Carmen's biased recollections or simply because they shared the same profession. As a young girl, I often fantasized about the lives of my parents, but the few fantasies I had been holding have been fully dispelled by the likes of these people.

Regardless of feelings, misunderstandings, or ill-prepared plans, the tour resumes with Griff as our newly appointed guide.

"Okey dokey, let's get moving," Griff directs.

"Now wait a minute," Patrick bellows. "What in the hell is this, and why are we even bothering if our tour guide has left the scene? All of a sudden, Griff's qualified to conduct this ridiculous performance? I couldn't care less about touring some fake haunted lighthouse. If we DON'T have a guide, I DON'T see the point."

"Well, Alyce wants to take the tour, Patrick, and we collectively decided that if one went, we all went," Melanie relays. She tosses me a smile that claims she's being thoughtful of my desires, although there's no sincerity behind it.

In return, I offer what I hope is a smile of genuine gratitude and turn my attention to the others. Carmen, Gabe, Frank, and Kathryn huddle close, warding off the wind. They mumble in agreement, talking over one another about going through with the tour: it'll be fun, I'm sure Griff will do a great job, it could be interesting—you never know what you're going to learn.

"If I could interject here," Griff begins, "I'm more than qualified to..."

"Great," Patrick spouts. "What pearl of wisdom do you have for us now, Griff?"

"Mr. Perkins, why not let Griff finish what he was saying?" I ask, careful not to sound judgmental or accusing. "I think it's the polite thing to do in this situation."

"Thank you, Alyce," Griff nods. "Like I started to say, back when I first moved to the island permanently, I volunteered around the lighthouse, helped out with the guests while the tour was going on. After hearing it over and over, the information became second nature, and I was able to fill in when needed. It wasn't really my thing though—found I preferred taking care of rental homes. What I'm saying is I know this tour like the back of my hand if you all want to continue."

Jude steps forward, holding firmly to my hand. "Let's do this, Griff."

I offer Jude a warm smile, then one for Griff. "Yes, let's get this started, Griff. Thank you for taking over and seeing this through."

Griff turns, leading the way to the door at the base of the lighthouse. We follow obediently, waiting for more details and history about the lighthouse. Griff remains quiet, his back to us. Was he telling the truth about having given this presentation in the past? Is he nervous, perhaps? But just as I think to break the silence, Griff's booming voice cuts through the night air.

"Ocracoke is a small island, just a bit under nine square miles, but we have over eighty cemeteries. That number doesn't include the dozens of sailors and castaways who have washed ashore and been buried underneath the dunes. No wonder our island has so many specters and wild accounts of paranormal activity. It is said by some that there are more specters on Ocracoke Island than there are living, breathing souls." Griff's voice has slipped into the eerie cadence Charles used earlier. It must be something that is expected of the tour guide—gives the experience a bit more flair.

Out of the corner of my eye, I see Jude's father lean toward

Melanie's ear. "This is bullshit," I hear him whisper loudly. Jude must have heard as well. I see him give his father a disapproving look.

"Charles spoke to you all about Blackbeard, Theodosia, and the lighthouse keeper, but he didn't mention the burning ship we often see off our coastline. Screams of the passengers can be heard ashore as the blazing vessel makes its way northeast, always northeast—no matter the weather, wind, or current."

Griff turns to face the door to the lighthouse, retrieving a bulky ring of keys from his pocket. We wait as he searches for the required key.

"Who?"

I scan the faces of our group to determine who has spoken.

"Who?"

Kathryn twists and turns. "Who the hell said that?" Heads turn, eyes widen, searching the night.

"Who?"

"I just asked that question," Kathryn shrills. "What is this? I don't like this, Frank, not one bit."

Griff looks up from his key ring.

"Who?"

"Ah, you all are hearing the call of the Great Horned Owl," Griff explains. "If you continue to listen, the hoots will take on a stutter-like sound, a quick series of hoots—hoo-HOO-hoo-hoo."

"It sounds so human," I say to the others, then laugh at my paranoia. "The ghost stories have already set to work on me, I guess." Jude pulls me to him, keeping his arm over my shoulder.

Griff turns back to the door, inserts a key, and twists. The door swings open with great effort, creaking loudly over the wind. A flash of light illuminates the sky in the distance. A rumble of thunder follows. "Looks like we'd better get a move on. Could be a precursor to this storm rolling our way," Griff says as he disappears into the dark depths of the lighthouse.

thirteen

UP, UP, AND...

Carmen

Inside the round walls of the lighthouse structure, the cool, damp air of the evening sends a chill over my body, the musty smell tickling my nostrils. I walk the periphery of the room, running my hand over the cool brick. Small lights mounted every few yards produce little to no illumination. In the center of the space is a spiral staircase, twisting, twisting, up and out of sight. An unfamiliar whooshing noise sounds from above. I may have been the first to sign up for this escapade, but in truth, this type of thing is not something I am comfortable with. Reverence should be practiced for the dead, not hunting them down, seeking them out for our entertainment.

"Carmen." Inside the dimly lit space, I hear my name but can't place who has called out for me. As I open my mouth to answer, my hand hits an intricate spiderweb. The sticky threads cling between my fingers. I try flinging away the web, plucking it off with my other hand. It is impossible to see if I have removed the web, but I no longer feel it underneath my fingernails. Still, a shudder runs through me as I try to shake off the incident.

"Carmen," I hear again. I turn quickly to identify who calls out, losing my balance, the lighthouse wall catching my fall. "Carmen, are you okay?" It's Jude asking, approaching.

I nod to affirm that I am here, that I am fine. Am I? The prospect of this activity is terribly uncomfortable. Jude takes my elbow, guiding me to his side as Alyce looks our way and smiles reassuringly. My eyes finally adjust, and as the scene comes into focus, I stand with the group at the base of the staircase. Griff delivers safety instructions, explaining the dangers of the narrow steps, the twisting.

"Ordinarily, we'd go over the many parts of a lighthouse," Griff says. "How it is laid out and whatnot, but for the sake of time, we'll just hit on a couple of the many areas you will notice on your way to the top.

"Like Charles said, we won't be going inside the lantern room as the light is functioning. We will, however, visit the widow's walk, which is where you will find the door leading to the lantern room. No need to worry that you might accidentally open the door and blind yourself. Precautions have been put into place, and that door is secure, as are the others on the way up. You will need to take care when traversing the walkway around the lantern room. Although there is a protective railing, the decking is narrow and approximately seventy feet from the ground.

"There are eighty-six stairs. We're going to make three tour stops on our way to the top, and then we'll head back down to conclude the tour. As we ascend, I suggest you go slow, hold firmly to the handrail, and remember to breathe..."

"Regular expert you are, Griff," Patrick spews sarcastically. The group ignores him, waiting instead for further direction from our substitute guide.

"There are landings every few steps. Take a moment at those spots as needed, then start again. This is not a race.

"Our first tour stop on the way to the top will be the watch room. Next, we'll visit the service room. We'll talk about the purpose of these rooms and the spirits who frequent them as we come to those areas. And finally, we'll make our way to the

widow's walk, where, hopefully, the moon and clouds will coop-
erate in providing you all with a beautiful three-hundred-and-
sixty-degree view of our island, the sound, and the ocean."

Griff goes on to explain that those having issues with heights,
depth perception, or vertigo should exercise caution and remain
at the base while the others make the climb.

"Should we wait for Yvonne and the others?" Jude asks.

"Charles doesn't have much longer to spend with us. He has
other obligations this evening," Griff says. "I hate to say it, but if
you all want to make it to the top and back down, we don't have
time to wait on the others. If they make it back in time, Charles
will bring them up."

"Rosey won't be able to complete this climb," Alyce shares.
"She has inner ear issues that throw off her balance."

"We should probably go ahead, don't you think?" Melanie
asks for consensus.

"I think we should get this ridiculous activity over with,"
Patrick says.

The remaining group members ignore Patrick's outburst as
Kathryn announces, "Well, I'm not ascending that tiny little staircase in this dress and heels."

"I'll stay with you," Frank declares, drawing Kathryn by his
side, slipping his arm over her shoulders protectively. The two of
them step aside as the rest of us start toward the winding staircase.

Patrick leads the way. Melanie, Alyce, and Jude follow. I take
my place behind the four of them and reach behind me for Gabe.
Swiveling left and right, I check the surroundings. Where has he
gotten to?

"Wait. Where's Gabe?" I turn, searching the base level of the
lighthouse. Though my eyes are now fully adjusted to the dark, I
can't find Gabe anywhere within the area. It is only Frank and
Kathryn left standing by the entry door.

"Gabe," I call. I look to Griff, who is the last one on the staircase behind me. "Have you seen him?"

"Naw, Ms. Carmen, nope. Come to think of it, I haven't seen

him since we were all outside," Griff says. He hurries back down the few steps he's traversed, then toward the doorway, opening it to the night sky. The wind rushes through the entry, chilling the quarters at the foundation level.

"Gabe! Gabe, you out here?" Griff's booming baritone cuts through the dark night. If Gabe were nearby, he would hear Griff's call.

"Maybe he went to find the others—decided he needed the restroom?" Frank muses.

"Gabe would have told me if that were the case," I say, trying to withhold the panic rising from the bottom of my stomach.

"I'm sure there's a reasonable explanation," Kathryn tries to soothe my anxiety. She's right—right? It's not as if some ticked-off apparition abducted Gabe.

"He did say something about needing a restroom earlier," I inform the others. "That must be where he went. Besides, Gabe isn't a big fan of heights, started when he was a child." As I speak this truth, the burn in my core subsides. Gabe is terrified of heights. He most likely slipped out when no one was paying attention. "Gabe probably wouldn't be interested in going to the top anyway."

"You sure, Ms. Carmen?"

"Yes, let's go," I tell Griff. The more I think about it, the more sense it makes that Gabe ducked out without telling me. He probably thought I would back out of the tour if he did. Since I was the first to speak up for the event, Gabe must have figured I really wanted to go through with the activity. And Gabe doesn't just have a thing about heights; Gabe has an irrational, inconsolable paranoia of heights.

As a child, Gabe overheard a spiritual healer claim Gabe's death would come from on high. Countless late-night chats and wine-soaked conversations have done little to ease Gabe's unfounded fears, mere superstitions planted by a wackadoodle medium when he was barely six. That must be it—Gabe didn't want to share his phobia with the old neighbors. An uneasy feeling settles at the bottom of my stomach. No matter how I explain his absence, something still feels off. Gabe never leaves me without explanation. We'll speak about it later, no doubt. Right now, the group is moving forward.

The others begin the climb as Griff closes the door once more. He explains to Kathryn and Frank that they can come and go as they please through the unlocked door and to let the others know when they return that they are welcome to follow if they wish. I stand aside to let Griff go ahead, but he insists that he bring up the rear. Conceding, holding firmly to the rail, I take the first step. I wish Gabe had shared his intentions with me; I would happily have considered joining him, especially considering how daunting this staircase looks.

Step after step, winding, twisting up, the walls growing more and more narrow the higher we ascend. Behind me, Griff continues to spout the tour information, his booming baritone easily carrying upward throughout the structure.

"Charles mentioned our lighthouse is the second oldest working lighthouse in the states, but let's talk dimensions. Lighthouses must stand strong to weather any storm and bring ships safely to the harbor. Our structure here is solid brick rising seventy-five feet into the sky. At the base, the diameter measures twenty-five feet and narrows to twelve feet at the crown, where we'll view the octagonal lantern that houses the lens."

Only about twenty steps up, we make it to the second landing. I stop briefly to refill my lungs, drawing in a big breath. None of our old group would be considered spry these days, but at least they aren't carrying the extra pounds I've put on over the years. Threatening to slim down does little to motivate me, though I wouldn't need a diet if I had to perform this trek often. The others continue to trudge upwards. Above me, their footfalls land heavily on the metal staircase. Griff stands three steps below me, waiting for me to continue forward, leaving me no way to turn and sneak back downstairs with Frank and Kathryn. But I can't do that—I got the gang into this excursion by being the first to agree to the tour, and now I must follow through.

Resuming the climb, I work to calm my thoughts. One step at a time, Carmen. Nice and slow, I tell myself. Breathe. In through the nose, out through the mouth. A tickle begins at the back of my neck. I slide my free hand under the length of my hair to rub away the irritation, feeling something move along my fingers, crawling up my arm. I jerk my hand from my neck to see spiders. Long, spindly legs attached to full red sacks at the center of their body. Several spiders scurry over the flesh of my uncovered forearm. My scream reverberates throughout the structure as I brush furiously at my arm to rid myself of these creatures. The screaming continues, no matter that I know how irrational and unhelpful it is. Griff closes his three-step gap, coming up behind me, catching me with both hands as I fall backward.

"Ms. Carmen, you okay? What's wrong? What happened?"

"Get them off. Get them off," I beg Griff. "Sp… Spi-ders," I manage to relay, holding out my arms for help. Griff holds a wrist, brushing at my arm, then does the same with the other, ridding me of the eight-legged monsters.

"What in tarnation is going on down there?" Patrick bellows from above.

Ignoring Patrick, I plead with Griff. "Under my hair. Please. Please look under my hair." I motion to the back of my neck.

Griff lifts my long hair. "Nothing back here, Ms. Carmen. Think they're all gone."

"Someone die down there?" Patrick calls out again.

I feel them scuttling over my skin. The prick of their legs digging into the bare flesh of my back. "I need you to lift my shirt and check my back. Lift my shirt, Griff. Lift my shirt!"

"But Ms. Carmen, I don't think me going up your shirt…"

Patrick impatiently calls out again. "Someone needs to answer me down there."

"Just do it, Griff," I manage over the sob at the back of my throat.

Griff lifts the back of my shirt as he answers Patrick. "All's well down here—just some baby spiders. Keep climbing and wait for us at the first room you find—the watch room. We'll be there soon."

I feel Griff's rough hands brush over the length of my backbone, cautiously moving over the straps of my bra. Though I can't see him, I can feel him flick the creatures away. "S'cuse me for this," he says quickly and quietly before running his hand inside the waistband of my jeans. "Okay. Think you're all clear." Griff lowers my shirt, patting it flat.

The pounding in my chest slows; my breathing lengthens. I hold to the stairwell railing for support as my body systems return to normal functioning mode.

"Do you want to go back down?" Griff asks.

Yes, I want to answer, but I won't. I made up my mind earlier to help Alyce learn about her mother. If not for my hasty decision to participate in this tour, the rest of the group would be at Dune Dweller, continuing to pickle themselves with drinks. "No. I want to continue to the top."

"All right then." Griff stands aside, waiting for me to begin the upward trek once more.

At the next landing, I rest briefly, listening for the others climbing above me. I hear snippets of conversation—it's so dark I can't see anything; how much farther; remind me why we're do...; oh, stop whining; talk about claustrophobia.

From his place behind me, Griff shouts upward, "Not much farther now, folks. Next level, you should be at the watch room entrance. Just hold there."

With each step higher, I think of the descent, how difficult it will be in this poorly lit environment where the dampness seeps into my skin, chilling me to the bone. And though Griff has assured me I'm all clear, I can't help but feel the sensation of something crawling over my body and through my hair. Not to mention, under the strain of the activity, I have now begun to perspire. Without realizing it, I've stepped up the pace and am face-to-face with the others at the watch room landing. Hand to forehead, I wipe away the light sheen of sweat.

The couples stand on opposite ends of the landing, away from the watch room entrance. Even through the dimly lit space, I can tell something has happened to shake them. Jude holds Alyce in an embrace. Melanie's proximity to Patrick is far closer than typical.

"What's going on?" I ask, the question presents breathy and a bit terse.

Griff comes up behind me, his eyes roaming over the group, assessing the situation. "Y'all doing okay? Ready to go on?"

"There's someone in there." Alyce barely gets the words out of her mouth. Jude pulls her tighter.

Griff's head tilts to one side, a question marking his face. He walks toward the door and turns the handle, pushing the door open slowly, cautiously. I step forward, coming up behind him to see what the others have seen, to look for myself. In the corner, a man sits at a desk, a book open in front of him. The man's back is to us, hair held back from his bearded face by a piece of string.

"Is that?" I whisper. Gooseflesh covers my arms once more, but this time in reaction to the drop in temperature, the scent of salt and decay.

"Yes," Griff says, his voice low, careful not to disturb the apparition. Something seems to catch the man's attention as his head slowly begins to swivel.

Patrick moves fast in our direction. "You're telling me...."

"Shhh," Griff says quickly, but the man disappears. Griff shakes his head and moves to the spot the man has vacated. He looks down at the open book, then at the rest of us as we pile into the room.

"Who was that?" Patrick thunders. "You got some actor up here, making us all think we're seeing ghosts?" Patrick looks at Melanie, then Jude. "This is horse manure. Come on. We're getting out of here."

"Mr. Perkins," Alyce starts, holding firmly to Jude's hand. "This is a ghost tour. We came to see ghosts."

"No. No. I did not come to see ghosts. I came because I got wrangled into this bull crap."

"That there was the lighthouse keeper. Charles spoke about him outside," Griff explains, his voice calm and steady. "He's harmless. Just thinks he still has a job to do. This room was where the logs were kept. The keepers logged weather conditions and various events that occurred daily. A journaling area, if you will."

"Give me a break. You all are buying this?" Patrick crosses the room to look in the small space behind the desk. He tosses a few of the loose papers around and moves the chair. "I don't know how you did it or where that person is hiding," Patrick says, pointing a finger at Griff's chest, "but there's no way that was a ghost. This man is taking us for fools." Patrick huffs, throws his hands into the air, then exits the cramped quarters of the room. Melanie shakes her head, then hurriedly follows Patrick to the landing outside the room.

The rest of us leave the watch room, and Griff pulls the door shut. "You all ready to continue? Service room is up next. Only one more stop after that, the lantern room."

"We're going to go on?" Patrick asks, his voice booming through the structure. "I don't want to go any further. I'm done with this."

"Well, we're not," Jude says to his father. "You all go on back down. Alyce and I will meet you down there when we're done."

"Oh, hell no. I'm not leaving you two up here alone. No. You both will come right back down with us."

Jude tugs Alyce's arm, and the two begin climbing again. Hands-on hips, Patrick watches them go, a dark look crossing his face. He says nothing more, rather turning to ascend the stairs behind his son and future daughter-in-law. Melanie follows without fuss. I draw a deep breath, take hold of the railing, and pull myself up and forward, following the others. Admittedly, part of me was hoping Patrick's tantrum would bring a conclusion to this jaunt, and we could all head back down. After all, we did see a ghost, didn't we? Maybe Patrick has a point. Perhaps this is all a show for the tourists—no truth to spirits and hauntings. Nevertheless, I try and keep up, but the others have pulled far ahead again.

We make it to the service room. I stop and look back, waiting for Griff to join me at the landing outside the door.

"Where are the others?" He asks breathily.

I shrug in reply, then add, "Maybe they're inside?"

Griff tries the door handle. It's unlocked. He shakes his head, saying, "We keep these doors locked. This is the second one that hasn't been secure." Griff pushes through the entryway to scan the room. "They're not in here," he says, looking back at me.

I move forward and peek inside for myself. As I step forward, I hear screams coming from ahead of me, above me, around me— I've no sense of direction at the moment. Griff looks upward, helping me to understand the chaos is happening above our heads. Screams continue while someone else yells for help. It sounds as if something horrific has happened. But then again, I just wigged out over spiders—supposedly baby spiders at that.

Griff grabs hold of my shoulders, bracing me as he moves around me and steps to the foothold ahead of me. "Go on ahead, down," he instructs. "Hold tight to this railing all the way down, and be sure your feet hit every step." Griff bolts upward and out of sight.

I stand alone on the landing, listening. The yelling, screeching —is that flapping?—I've no idea what to make of it, but I do as I've been told and begin the descent. As Griff instructed me to do, I grab hold of the handrail and lower one shaky foot the step below and then the other foot. My heart races, prodding me to go faster. My head spins as my breathing grows shallow and stuttered. I trip and stumble. Above me, the noise of mayhem continues, the screams reverberating off the cylindrical walls, each one sounding more frantic, urgent. Is there another ghost? Can't be. They didn't react like that to the lighthouse keeper's ghost. More spiders? The thought of spiders reinvigorates the sensation of them scurrying over my back and through my scalp. No. No spiders. Oh God, I hope it's not bats up there. If it is, I doubt they would fly down the staircase, right?

I round the staircase, coming to the landing where the watch room is located. Knowing the ghost of the lighthouse keeper frequents this room, I hurry to bypass the area. A sharp cramp travels along my right side, the exertion of the activity more than I've engaged in since I was in my twenties.

At the bottom, I fold in the middle, using my knees to support myself while I catch my breath, try to slow my heartbeat. The moment is surreal. It seems I've lost time, as I have no recollection of how I came to be standing at this very spot. The last detail I can see in my mind's eye with any clarity is viewing the door of the watch room, wondering if the ghost of the lighthouse keeper was behind it as I hurried downward.

The foundation floor is empty, Frank and Kathryn nowhere in sight. The screams from above have ceased, replaced by the sounds of footsteps descending the staircase echoing through the round chamber. I wipe away the cold sweat dripping from my brow.

The lighthouse entrance door flings open, a whoosh of wind banging it against the block wall. Kathryn enters, hurrying to my side.

"Oh, Carmen," Kathryn cries. "I'm so sorry. Are you okay?"

I lift to view the concern on Kathryn's face, readying to explain what happened. Why is she looking at me like that, and when did Kate learn to express compassion? I've never known her to practice the emotion.

"I'm fine. Where's Frank? Did we lose him too?"

"No. He's outside with the others. Charles is handling everything. Nothing for you to do right now except process this needless..."

"Kathryn, what in the hell are you talking about?"

The others have reached ground level now. Griff rushes around the group, racing out the door of the lighthouse.

"Where's Griff going now?" I ask. "No more surprise side tours tonight, I hope?" I pose the question to Alyce. She shakes her head, tears trailing over her young face.

I look at the faces of the others, all watching me, waiting for what I will do or say next. "What?"

Frank comes to stand in front of me. "It's Gabe, Carmen. Gabe is dead."

fourteen

OBLIGATIONS AND PRECARIOUS SITUATIONS

Rosey

Oh, Alyce, my love, what is this you've gotten everyone into? In the privacy of my room, I settle in, pull a few things from my bag, change into something more forgiving before heading downstairs to join the others in the recreation room. Outside, the wind continues to come and go, each gust ushering in more anxiety. This group invites tragedy of one kind or another to join them every time they get together. We may not be protected from one another, but at least, as of now, we are all unharmed and comfortably spread out inside the safe harbor of this house. It is indeed thoughtfully refurbished and roomy enough for all twelve of us—well, eleven now.

I contemplate the senselessness of Gabe's death, how on earth something so tragic could have occurred. Alyce will surely blame herself for this. How can she not? How can all the other guests she's wrangled to this island not place culpability at Alyce's feet? Clearly, this isn't her fault. It's not as if she pushed Gabe from the top of the Ocracoke lighthouse, but Alyce does bear some responsibility. That fact can't be glossed over.

You try, as a parent, a grandparent, to steer your children in the direction of less pain and little heartache. But they buck and carry on and sneak off to do whatever they've deemed vitally important, leaving mess after mess to be cleared away. Admittedly, after a point, a parent must let it happen. Mistakes have to be made before lessons can be fully understood, but I can't imagine what punishment my father would have served me had I behaved in the manner Alyce has.

As long as I'm serving up blame, I might as well ladle a bit out for myself. Alyce would never have put this weekend together in the first place if I had just shared a bit of information, a few details at least, about her parents (talk about a mess). The timing was always off, though. Alyce was too young, or we were heading out of the country, or Pops—my Henry—was ill. After a while, I determined Alyce was better off not knowing all the facts, and she seemed fine with what little knowledge she had.

I was wrong.

To think my grandchild, whom I've raised since infancy, has gone off, fallen in love, and chosen the person she's determined to spend the rest of her life with...and I was never introduced to the young man? Well, it's difficult to come to terms with, and it's not all about my pride.

I wanted to be the one Alyce confided in, came to for advice. God knows I mishandled my relationship with Alyce's mother, Amber, but I thought Alyce was my second chance at getting motherhood right. Instead, I wake up one morning and realize I've been tossed into another bin, and I've been in this bin, box, position, what have you—the one labeled old, stuffy, insignificant, opinion is too aged to count.

That's where I made my mistake with Amber. I wouldn't stay in that bin—I couldn't—it's not who I am. Since that point in time, however, I've succeeded in wrangling a bit more knowledge —with age comes wisdom and all that—and I am aware this is simply the natural progression of life. These bins are all part of nature's way of nudging us to let our children go, grow, become adults. You wake one morning knowing that any day, you're child will take leave of their childhood home to make a life of their own. And just when you think you'll never be able to live without them, that you can't possibly allow them to leave the 'nest,' they commit some heinous act or spout atrocities at you, none of which are true, heinous, or atrocious. But still, you deem those acts and words as such and understand perhaps a bit of a break is indeed needed to help sustain a healthy relationship between parent and child.

Wounds aren't the only thing time is good for healing. Time lends perspective and insight. It helps to resolve issues, to harmonize the ties and connections between people so that one day, all that was so detrimental is nothing but a memory of a difficult period overcome and withstood.

What happened tonight at that lighthouse, though, can't be smoothed over, swept away, or overcome necessarily. A man is dead. Hot chocolate and kisses certainly can't fix that.

Knocking sounds on the other side of my door. "Ms. Rosey?" Griff's voice calls from the hallway.

I open the door and look up at Griff. The others see a brusque man fiercely loyal to the island and its inhabitants. There's more to this man than he is letting on to the others, though.

"Sorry I didn't make it to the ferry terminal to pick you up this evening, ma'am."

"Don't be silly, Griff. You had other things to do. Besides, I managed to find my way just fine," I assure him as we stand in the doorway.

"Still, I wanted to check in—see if there's anything you need, make sure your room's up to snuff before I head back out."

I turn away to let the smile play across my lips; such a considerate man he is. "Everything's perfect, Griff. You've done a wonderful job on the house, quite tasteful. Dune Dweller welcomes guests once more."

"Thank you, Ms. Rosey," Griff replies uncomfortably from the entryway.

I pick up a cardigan from the suitcase and toss it onto the bed, then turn to ask Griff. "How's Alyce?"

"Not sure. She's not downstairs with the others," Griff stuffs his hands into his pant pockets. "Would guess she's off with Jude somewhere. He's not down there with the rest of them either."

"What about Carmen? Is she in her room?"

"Nah, she's down there with the rest of 'em. Surprised me. Kind of thought she'd want to be alone."

"Death works that way. Can't ever predict how someone will choose to deal with grief," I say, then recall Griff's earlier statement. "You mentioned you're heading back out. Is there a problem? I was under the impression we were all settled for the evening."

Griff steps through the doorway into the room, lowers his voice, points to the walkie-talkie on his belt. "Charles and I got a call earlier about a medical emergency with one of the locals. Their spouse was trying to make the last ferry to the mainland before the storm arrived."

"And they need your assistance to get to the ferry?" I ask.

"Nope. No," Griff mumbles, shaking his head. "Didn't make it on time."

"Didn't make the ferry or didn't make it?"

"The husband—he didn't make it. Charles called a few minutes ago to let me know they had an accident en route to the ferry. They think he had a heart attack and ran into one of the dunes on NC 12. Honestly, his wife is lucky to be alive. Course, she might argue that—they were close. Had been married forty-plus years."

"Oh no. So much death tonight."

Hands resting on his hips, Griff looks to the floor. "And I'm afraid there could be more with this storm coming in."

"Is it getting bad out there?"

"No, not yet. But Pamlico Sound is getting high; won't be long before it spills over, and we already got overwash on NC 12."

"Overwash?" I ask.

"Ocean has breached the dune barrier along the highway. Your ferry came in from the north side, so you passed by them on your way in."

"Those sand dunes along the side of the road? They must be ten to fifteen feet high. The ocean is coming through them now?"

"We try to keep them built up to twenty feet, but Mother Nature has other ideas. They require constant maintenance. But yeah, they've been breached, and the storm isn't even here yet."

I zip up my suitcase and move to lift it from the bed. "Here," Griff says, "let me get that."

"So you're leaving now to help out with that situation?"

"Yes, ma'am. Shouldn't be long. Need to get that car off the road 'fore the ocean takes it, make sure we take care of the deceased."

"Not to be crass, but since you brought it up…, what did you and Charles do with Gabe?"

"Well, can't get him to the mainland until this storm blows through, so we've made accommodations the best we can until that time. It's an island… well, we have our protocols."

I hold up my hand to stop any further explanations. "I don't need the nitty-gritty details, and for that matter, neither do the others."

Griff nods in agreement.

"I guess I should head on downstairs, see if I can be of any comfort to the others."

"I'll walk with you. Couple of the others asked about the hot tub. Need to make sure it's ready to go before I leave."

"Griff?" I pause, trying to decide the best way to word my inquiry. "When you saw Carmen with the women downstairs, how did she seem to be handling Gabe's passing?"

"Honestly, like I said before, I didn't expect to see her again until I drove everyone back to the ferry. Just figured she'd spend the rest of her time on the island in her bedroom, dealing with the loss. Don't get me wrong, Carmen seems to be pretty broken up about it, but not to the extent I thought a woman would be after having witnessed her partner's death."

I grab my cardigan from the bed, making my way to exit the room. "Well, I suspect there's a reason for that."

Frank

Behind the bar, Kathryn glugs vodka into a shaker as I sit on the other side of the counter, watching her. Across the room, Patrick paces the floor in front of the pool table, closely eyeing Kathryn's every move. "Don't you think you've had enough to drink?" he asks Kathryn.

I stand and walk around the bar, taking the vodka from her. "Let me do that for you, honey." I take the shaker from her unsteady hand, daring Patrick to continue chastising her.

"Actually, no." Kathryn's voice squeaks with the comment as she hands over the chore to me. "No, I actually think I need more to drink. Someone died tonight."

"Not someone. Gabe." Carmen wipes the corners of her eyes.

Gabe and I were never close. Obviously, none of us is anymore —but even back in our Perishing Hill days, we never had much in common. This situation, though… makes a person wonder what went through Gabe's mind as his body fell through the sky and drew closer and closer to the ground. Kathryn says I'm being morbid. "Don't you dare ask her that, Frank," she hissed at me in the privacy of our room. "I was only thinking to myself, Kathryn. I'd never ask something like that." She'd headed straight to our en suite bathroom. "You don't ask questions like that of a woman who has just lost the man she loves," Kathryn chided before slamming the bathroom door. And I wouldn't, but I can't get the thought to leave my head.

If I hadn't gone running out of the lighthouse, if I hadn't been the first one there to witness Gabe's lifeless, broken body, perhaps I could shake these ghastly thoughts and images. Instead, I shake Kathryn's martini more aggressively than necessary and pour it into a glass for her. Maybe she has the right idea—get drunk, forget, fall asleep, go home tomorrow, and leave all this madness behind.

Politeness dictates. "Sure you don't want a beer or something, Pat?" Not that I want to be this man's friend, but Jesus, after what we've all been through tonight, you never know when the last time you speak to someone might be. I can at least be cordial while we all share this uncomfortable space.

"Yeah, I'll take one." Patrick takes the beer I pass across the bar to him, twists the cap, and takes a long draft. Melanie cuts her eyes at him as she sees he's finished three-quarters of the bottle in one pull. She turns her attention back to Carmen, sitting beside her on the sofa.

"I'm so sorry, Carmen. We don't mean to seem insensitive with all the booze and bickering and mindless chatter. I guess we're all trying to make some sort of sense of this, but...," Melanie tries.

Carmen nods, easing back into the cushions of the couch. "None of this makes sense."

Yvonne pulls her feet underneath her sitting form. She sips the drink in her grasp and asks, "I understand if you all don't want to go into this right now, but what happened up there?"

"I couldn't tell you," Carmen says. "Gabe was nowhere to be found once inside the lighthouse, and I never made it all the way to the top."

This whole situation is simply implausible. "I don't understand," I start, stepping from behind the bar to lean on a nearby barstool. "We were all standing right there while Griff was talking at the base of the stairs. How could Gabe have made it all the way up to the widow's walk and lantern room without any of us knowing he was climbing the lighthouse staircase?" I take inventory of the faces around the room, reading what they offer up and what they try to conceal. "You were positioned closest to the bottom of the stairs," I say to Patrick. "Did you see him go up alone?"

"What are you trying to say, Frank? Are you accusing me now? Accusing me of somehow being responsible for Gabe's death?"

"God no, man. What is wrong with you?" Yvonne speaks out on my behalf. "Not everyone is out to get you, Patrick."

"There you go again, taking the Lord's name in vain," Patrick chastises.

Yvonne unfolds her legs to place her feet on the floor and scoots to the edge of the sofa, situating herself to stand quickly should she feel it necessary to battle Patrick. "Do not treat me as if I'm one of your lost sheep, Patty. I don't follow bullshit, especially not from a master bullshitter."

"What are you all squabbling about now?" Rosey asks, rounding the corner of the staircase. Griff follows behind, his gaze roving the room, eyes narrowing.

"I don't believe anyone called for a mediator." Patrick continues to lash out at anyone in his line of sight. What is it with this guy? Patrick always did have a chip on his shoulder, but he is particularly belligerent this weekend. Rosey has never been my favorite person either, but Patrick's son is hellbent on marrying Rosey's granddaughter. At some point, the two of them will have to learn to tolerate one another.

"It'll take more than a mediator to exorcise what's eating you, Pastor Perkins," Rosey says, then looks at me. "Frank, while you're pouring over there..."

That woman never did have a problem ordering us around. I remove myself from the barstool and step back to the bar, looking around for the ingredients to put together an old-fashioned. All the fixings, including an unopened bottle of Maker's Mark, are readily accessible. "Anyone else want an old-fashioned or a bourbon while I'm pouring?" A chorus of no thank you(s) and I don't do bourbon(s) sounds throughout the room. Alyce must have had some sort of idea of what we all drink. According to Griff, it was Alyce who made the selections to stock the bar. And as far as I can tell, each of our favorites has found its way to the shelves of this bar.

I finish preparing Rosey's drink and step around the bar to deliver the concoction, stopping to take in the show outside the windows. Through the wall of glass, lightning flashes in the distance, thunder rumbles. Rosey accepts her drink, sips, and nods approval as she keeps her gaze focused on Griff, who is fixated on the windows as well. Glancing around the room, I note the others also wear looks of apprehension but none quite as tense as the posture Yvonne has taken on. Terry moves closer to his wife, his hand rubbing circles on her back. The wind gusts yet again.

"Must be getting up to thirty-mile gusts out there now," Terry says to Griff.

"Yep," Griff agrees. "Sounds like it."

"How long do you think the storm will last, Griff?" Yvonne asks, trying to mask the unsure quiver in her tone. I've missed something. What the hell happened to shake Yvonne in the last five minutes? She's uptight at best.

Griff answers without pause. "Well, I can tell you they're predicting that it will hit full steam tomorrow mid-morning, then exit quickly, but don't set your sights on it."

"What is that supposed to mean? How are we to make plans for our departure?" Melanie demands.

"Forecasters claim we're in for a heck of an event. Not a hurricane, mind you, but tropical storm force is what they're saying. Regardless, we'll get rain, wind, storm surge—everyone on Ocracoke knows how to handle that, though. It's the aftermath that can't be calculated. The roads flood. Dune barriers get washed out to sea. Power goes out."

"I did not sign up for this. We can't leave the island. Gabe is dead. The storm is going to flood the roads, and now, we're going to lose power?" Melanie interrupts.

"These storms most often blow out our electricity, yes, ma'am. But that said, I installed a top-of-the-line generator. Best on the market. Power goes off, generator kicks on." Griff reassures the group.

Across the room, Yvonne murmurs to Terry. The muted tone of her voice provides little clarity on what she says, but I am sure I make out the words, *another fucking generator*. I scan the room to see if anyone else has heard Yvonne make this comment or if I am somehow mistaken, but everyone is listening to Griff.

Griff continues. "Nothing to worry about. But like I was saying, when the wind gets going, it's unpredictable. Wind gusts pick up objects and relocate them, sometimes on top of other structures or blocking roadways. We never know. We just play with the hand lying on the table when the storm finally takes its exit. Then, we can get out and take a look at what we're dealing with. A word of warning here, though. It's best not to get too antsy about taking that initial look around. You never know what might come flying at you or if a live electrical wire has fallen in your path."

As if on cue, Dune Dweller's front door swings open, slamming against the wall, the bell dinging wildly. Wind howls fiercely through the house, blowing sand across the floors, knocking over lightweight decor scattered throughout the room. Alyce and Jude stumble inside, clinging tightly to one another, laughing as if this outrageous situation doesn't include them.

Griff assists the incoming pair, securing the room from the outside elements. "You two okay?" he asks. The pair nods, straightening wind-blown clothing and flyaway hair.

Rosey addresses the disheveled couple. "Where have you two been?"

"We needed a walk on the beach," Jude answers for them. "Been kind of a heavy night, you know."

"Every one of us knows very well what you *needed*," Kathryn says with a smirk. She sips from her martini. "To be young again..."

"What the hell is that supposed to mean, Kate?" Patrick howls over the noise of the wind outside. "Are you insinuating that my son was out taking advantage of this girl? My son is a gentleman, a godly man."

Kathryn cackles. "Oh, Patty, are you really that daft? You act like these two aren't boinking. Look at them. They can barely keep their hands off one another."

Patrick shuffles weight between feet. "You need to keep your thoughts and accusations to..."

Alyce steps forward. "There was nothing nefarious about our walk." Alyce turns to address Patrick. "Jude is indeed a gentleman, Mr. Perkins. I wanted some fresh air, and Jude would not hear of me going out alone. Not after all that happened earlier."

"Yes, one hundred percent," Terry agrees. "It is definitely best we all use the buddy system from here on out."

"He's right," Griff says. "Besides the fact we've got a bona fide storm blowing up, there's a lot you all don't know about this island, and I don't have time to explain. Now, if you all will excuse me, I'm just going to make sure the hot tub is all set before I head back out. Someone asked me about a soak, and I'd say as long as the lightning stays clear and you can handle the wind, you should be fine to use it this evening."

"You said you're headed out," I begin. "If this storm is so bad, how come you're going back out in it, and exactly where are you going? You're just going to leave us here to fend for ourselves?"

"There's been a fatality, one of the O'cokers," Griff begins, only to be talked over.

"What?"

"Another death?"

"What the... who died now?"

"No need to worry yourselves. The man was ill, but with the ferry not running right now, we can't get him to the mainland. I gotta go help out. I'll be back before the storm hits."

Griff grabs the sliding glass door handle leading to the beach-side deck, pulling it open just wide enough to slip out. Before he steps through the threshold, however, he turns and addresses Carmen.

"Just want to say, ma'am, Ms. Carmen, I'm sorry for your loss. Your brother was a good man."

sixteen

AND THE NIGHT GOES ON

Alyce

Carmen wears a look of shock, though the reason behind her astonished expression isn't discernible. Is it one of a woman whose secret has just been exposed? Or rather, is the suggestion so preposterous, Carmen can't grasp what she's been accused of? I look at Jude, mouthing, "Did you know?" Jude shrugs his shoulders—"No idea," he mouths back. We stand in silence, watching the others around the room, waiting for what comes next, listening for who will offer the follow-up barb.

Griff has slipped outside. Dropped his little bombshell and exited stage right.

Kathryn, wide-eyed, a hand daintily covering her mouth, remains at Frank's side. He is the first to lobby for clarification, asking, "What the hell was Griff talking about?"

Yvonne twists to look Carmen in the eye. "Carmen, is that true? Gabe was your brother?" Yvonne asks carefully, her head tilting to one side.

"We weren't purposely trying to obscure our relationship, but yes. The lie was easier on both of us."

Kathryn looks at Frank for an explanation. "I don't understand," she says to her husband.

"Drink you another, Kathryn. Maybe you'll understand then," Patrick says, tacking on a *phish* as he walks to peer out the back door.

"Don't be an asshole, Patrick," Kathryn snaps. "I wasn't talking to you."

Yvonne pats Carmen's hand, encouraging her to ignore Patrick, to share her story.

"Gabe and I are—well, were—siblings. He was my best friend." Carmen silences, wipes her nose, then continues. "And before you all start bashing me for something you don't understand, let me say, I believe we had a better, stronger relationship than most of the couples in this room."

"But he was your brother," Melanie says. "I thought it was illegal to marry your sibling."

"Not only illegal, it's immoral, it's blasphemous and disgusting." Patrick paces back and forth. "What you all did goes against the teachings of God."

"Give it a rest, Patrick," Yvonne says, then turns her attention back to Carmen, taking the grieving woman's hands into her own. "Did your marriage have something to do with your family dynamics, or religion perhaps? I'm not judging, honey. We're only trying to make sense of this tragedy, to come to terms with something so horrific, and now to learn after all these years that you all were brother and sister... to be truthful, it's a bit shocking."

Carmen nods and sniffles. "We never followed through with the formality of marriage. As Patrick said, it is against the laws of the United States to marry a sibling. You all just assumed that we had taken vows." Carmen shrugs.

"But why?" I ask. Jude squeezes my hand supportively. "Wasn't that difficult on both of you? Pretending to be something you weren't? Never being able to confide in friends about the true nature of your feelings or your relationship? I realize I'm the youngest and therefore quite possibly the most naive of our crowd, but I thought, think, marriage is something you should be proud of, something to be celebrated."

"What the holy hellfire?" Patrick's voice booms through the downstairs recreation area. "You mean like how you and lover boy over there told your families that you're getting hitched?" His facial features contort and twist into ugly, scary expressions, conveying the intensity of his anger. "Because the both of you felt such immense pleasure about your decision to wed, you couldn't wait to keep it a secret from your parents?"

Melanie delivers a look to her husband. "You need to take it down a notch, sit down, and calm down. Your behavior isn't helping anyone."

Patrick moves to the corner of the room, hands on hips, refusing to comply with the direction of sitting, but at least offering the rest of us a reprieve from his hostile demeanor.

"I apologize for Patrick's behavior," Melanie starts, then quickly turns to give Patrick another glare, daring him to contradict her. "This must be so difficult for you, and here we are, demanding the details of your private affairs. But honestly, Carmen, I think we are only trying, as Yvonne said earlier, to make sense of this tragedy."

Carmen nods, then looks at Alyce. "To answer your question about withholding our marital status, it was more complicated than you might think," Carmen says through tears. "You see, our parents planned my marriage."

"I call bullshit," Patrick steps from the corner. "Mexico doesn't do arranged marriages."

"Patrick," Melanie threatens.

"I didn't say arranged. I said planned," Carmen replies. "My father owed money, a lot of money to a.... You know what, Patrick, this isn't any of your business, and I don't have to explain anything to you."

The room goes quiet. Only the wind dares to make a sound. This night has taken a turn I never could have anticipated. Did Rosey know about Carmen and Gabe? Across the room, she lifts her left leg to cross over the right, the sleek gray bob perfectly coifed. Rosey never presents as anything but perfectly put together—I learned from a maestro how to always put your best face forward, as Rosey likes to say. She holds her glass with both hands—her signature piece of jewelry on full display, the ring Rosey never removes. The six-carat round jade stone, worn to complement her green eyes, is set in yellow gold and encircled by a halo of diamonds.

Sipping from the old-fashioned in her grasp, Rosey's eyes roam the space, falling upon mine as I watch her. She pulls a tight smile and winks. Anyone observing might assume Rosey's actions are nefarious, but I know the look.

We've shared it on many occasions throughout my upbringing. Often, when we traveled, I was the only child among a crowd of retired tourists, all of whom had recently hugged their younger family members goodbye in anticipation of a quiet, child-free vacation. My presence would be ignored by most of our travel companions, but then there were a few who made their ire known via dirty looks or snide remarks. The silent smile and wink from Rosey told me I was safe. I was wanted, and I had every bit as much right to be on those trips as any one of the 'curmudgeonly old farts' in our company—Rosey's words, not mine.

While the exchange with my grandmother does bring me some comfort, I can't help but think Rosey knows more than she is letting on as she sits by and takes in the various altercations among these people. At the moment, those dissensions have turned to wordless contempt, communicated through sharp, piercing stares.

None of those hateful glares have fallen upon me—yet. I'm sure in time, they will all come to understand that, ultimately, I am at fault for what happened to Gabe. At this moment, however, everyone is simply seeking answers to such a senseless loss. They want to know what happened and how, what I saw and heard, where I was when the accident occurred. I've been questioned a multitude of times already: by my weekend guests, by the nearby locals who came out of their homes to view all the commotion at the lighthouse, by the local captain-sheriff, whatever he called himself. I've been as forthright about my part in this ordeal as I can be.

My story has remained the same for each account provided. I never saw Gabe ascend those stairs. When we began the climb, Patrick led, followed by Melanie, Jude, and me. Carmen was behind me, with Griff bringing up the rear.

Then, the order changed. I don't recall the reason why; I only remember Jude dropping my hand and rushing ahead, mumbling something about his dad. The next thing I know, Melanie pushed me aside, insisting she had to get to Mr. Perkins before…, and that's where it all gets terribly fuzzy.

Maybe it was the wine with dinner, but I haven't been able to retrieve a vivid picture or a distinct snippet of sound from that moment. All that surfaces are screams and hysteria, the urgent winding descent, the narrow stairwell, the fear of knowing something awful has happened but being in the dark—quite literally in the dark—about what transpired.

Yvonne scoots to the edge of the sofa and places her drink on the table in front of her. "At the risk of sounding nosey or pushy, can I ask why? I mean, besides the 'the lie was easier' explanation, which none of us seem to fully comprehend as to why living that fabrication would make life easier on either of you—why? Why would you let everyone think Gabe was your husband and not convey the truth that he was actually your brother?"

Carmen gazes out the windows at the black of night, emotions unreadable. She takes a deep breath and sniffles again. She begins, her words barely a whisper. "Because we did love one another and not the brotherly/sisterly kind of love. We grew up as siblings, but we only share the surname, not blood. My parents wanted a child, but their prayers went unanswered. After many years of trying to conceive, my father took the situation into his own hands. The adoption, my adoption, was not handled legally."

"So then, was Gabe also adopted?" Kathryn asks.

"No. Funnily enough, as it often happens, as soon as the

transaction for my adoption was completed, my mother learned she was pregnant with Gabe."

"And Gabe had a planned marriage as well?" Jude asks.

Carmen shakes her head, "No. Like Patrick was saying, forced marriages are unlawful in Mexico. The only reason for mine had to do with a deal made prior to the agreement of my adoption."

Terry clears his throat and asks, "You don't suppose this had anything to do with Gabe's job, do you, Carmen? I realize the question is a bit off-topic. But is it possible that someone at Gabe's work could have learned about the true nature of his relationship with you, his sisterly relationship, as opposed to you being his legal wife?"

Carmen's face wears a look of confusion. "I don't understand. What does Gabe's work have to do with whether or not we were married?"

"Gabe and I saw each other from time to time," Terry tells the group.

"You did?" Carmen sniffs. "I had no idea. Gabe never told me the two of you stayed in touch."

"Gabe and I didn't see a reason to publicize it; we simply enjoyed one another's company. We found it beneficial to have someone we could confide in. Someone who was not part of our daily lives. So yes, we'd meet for an afternoon meal every so often," Terry says. "I think Gabe appreciated that he could share the issues he was having in his work without having to worry that I would pass along the information to someone who knew him."

"Issues with his work?" Carmen tries out the words for herself. "And these meetings the two of you had, you've had them all these years?"

"Yes. In fact, we had one only a couple of months ago."

Yvonne rises and walks to stand behind the sofa next to her husband. "And how did Gabe seem during that last lunch?" She asks Terry.

"I must say, after that meet-up, I was concerned. Gabe didn't seem quite himself."

"How so?" Carmen asks, straightening herself to sit taller.

"During that lunch, Gabe was subdued. He looked... he appeared defeated. Sometimes that's what life does to people though, sucks all the energy, the fight right out of them."

"You and these word jumbles. Spit it out, man," Patrick growls. "Don't be a dickwad."

Yvonne turns in Patrick's direction. "Using your big words now, huh, Patrick?"

"What I'm saying," Terry begins again, "is that Gabe told me he'd been fired from his job with the city. He hadn't worked in over nine months."

"Nine months," Carmen repeats in a whisper. "He never told me." She wipes away the tears trailing her cheeks. "I could have helped him."

Patrick steps to the center of the room. "Sounds to me like Gabe was suicidal."

seventeen

EMOTIONS RUN HIGH

Melanie

"How could you be so callous?" I ask Patrick as he follows me through the door of our room. "You claim to be a man of God, but really you're just a huge asshole."

Many years have come and gone since the beginning of our union, and in all that time, I've never known Patrick to be so cruel. Yes, Patrick has been a buffoon for most of our marriage, but we've learned to manage the best ways to handle our feelings about one another. Yet to suggest Gabe committed suicide, placing the blame for Gabe's death on Gabe himself without any proof or indication of such, is heartless and difficult for me to justify. Carmen doesn't need to hear that when she has just lost her brother, her life companion, her lover. Carmen and Gabe have been cohorts in this obscure life they've built—left their home country, their family. To suggest Gabe took his own life without having all the facts or any consideration for his life partner's feelings is merciless, regardless of whether Gabe's death was intentional or accidental.

"I will not have my wife calling me such vile names." Patrick turns, checks the hallway, then closes the door. "Those people out there are trying to pin a murder on me."

"Paranoid much, Pat?" I sort through the drawer where I placed all of my clothing when we unpacked before dinner.

"They think I pushed him from the top of that lighthouse, Melanie."

I pull out the bathing suit I'm looking for and lay it on the bed. "Well, did you?"

"How can you even ask me such a question? 'Thou shalt not kill' — it's the sixth commandment, for Christ's sake."

"Um-hmm," I turn my back to remove my blouse and bra, replacing them with a bathing suit top. If I were feeling up to the fight, I'd call him out for using the Lord's name in vain, yada, yada, yada—one of Pat's favorite patronizing lectures to preach.

"What the hell is that supposed to mean?" Patrick asks, pacing the short distance in the room.

"Nothing. I'm just agreeing with you." Truth is, I don't know what to believe when it comes to this man anymore. It used to be I could read every heinous thought, but it seems Patrick has been perfecting his tactics of deception.

"Yeah, right. Since when. You've never agreed with me on anything."

"Well, as I recollect, we agreed on at least one thing, even if it was over twenty years ago. Perhaps you'll recall that's the major reason we agreed to attend this warped reunion." I head into the en suite bath to change into my swimming bottoms.

"Why would you bring that up now?" Patrick says on the other side of the bathroom door. He knows exactly why I broached that topic now. There's little more to be said on that issue.

I pull up the bottoms and grab my discarded clothing. Patrick steps aside as I walk through the door and back to the bureau to look for something warm to wear over my suit.

"What are you doing? Why are you wearing your bathing suit?"

I button my jeans and pull a sweater over my head. "Griff

warmed up the hot tub, and some of us would like to relax. Have you seen a robe in here by chance?"

Patrick huffs, ignoring my question to grumble, "Griff."

"What now? What do you hold against, Griff?"

"It's the weird way he's always lurking around. Seems to know everything and everyone. One minute he's a golf cart driver, the next a caretaker—one minute he's tracking the weather and the next, he's running a neighbor's dead husband to a makeshift morgue. And have you noticed he and Rosey are in cahoots?"

"Patrick, you are never going to live a fulfilled life if you distrust everyone you come in contact with."

"Think what you like, but that Griff fellow is hiding more information than he is letting on. And so are a few of the others in this house."

"In case you haven't noticed, desirable attributes are few and far between with this gang. Or should I say reputable characteristics are difficult to identify with these folks?" Either way, I can't help but wonder what the hell we've gotten ourselves into.

I turn to exit, looking back at Patrick standing alone in the middle of the room. One might predict that I feel nothing but contempt for this man, but the truth is, I am shrouded in guilt. He's not the same man I married all those years ago when we shared dreams and ideals. Pat may have become a different man over the years, but the truth, if told, would show that I share fault in that transformation.

Kathryn

"What in the hell did we just witness?" Frank says, following me into our bedroom and locking the door behind him.

"If this were a story I was covering for the station, I'd be up for an Emmy." I remove the heavy earrings weighing on my earlobes, tossing them onto the dresser.

"This situation is heavy with drama and intrigue. I'll give you that."

"Don't forget the subterfuge," I add, thinking of the looks I saw exchanged between Gabe and Patrick during cocktail hour and again during dinner. Terry and Gabe may have been friends outside our group gatherings, but it was obvious from the barbs and side eyes shared between Patrick and Gabe that they most definitely weren't comrades of any type.

Frank sits on the end of the bed. "How does Griff fit in with all this, do you think?"

"I've been giving that some thought." I join him to sit on the end of the bed. "And I definitely find it curious the way he dotes on Rosey."

"At this stage of her life, she is an old woman. Maybe he is simply respecting his elders." Frank tosses the theory out into the room.

"I suppose, but it seems like something more than good manners. And then there's Terry."

"What about him?" Frank asks, slipping out of his loafers and bending to remove his socks.

"All night, he kept lurking close to Rosey. He was the doting one, in my opinion: pulling out chairs, making sure she had a drink, helping her into and out of the van. And then, it just so happens, the three of them need a private restroom break—together."

Frank scrunches his face in consideration. "I guess I didn't think much of it at the time, but now that you point it out, it does seem odd."

"Odd? I suppose, but I find this whole event bizarre—letting the world believe your brother is your husband. Or what about dating a person for a year and a half, getting engaged, and keeping it hidden from your family?"

"Don't forget Rosey showing up out of nowhere, then somehow knowing exactly where to find us," Frank adds. "Talk about odd, or curious, or bizarre—what have you. It's downright suspicious."

"That's exactly what I'm saying and the way she watches us."

Frank twists to look at me. "Who are we talking about?"

"Rosey, of course. And then all the little barbs she tosses out. Did you notice she didn't even seem too surprised to find us all in one spot—on an island twenty-plus miles out to sea? I find that quite peculiar."

I push myself from the bed and move to open the suitcase I have yet to unpack as we plan to leave tomorrow when the ferry to the mainland resumes. I throw the lid open and rummage about for my bathing suit.

Frank eyes me. "Going for a midnight swim?"

"Hot tub. I heard some of the others talking about a soak later."

"I thought the last thing you wanted was to be around this group any more than necessary."

"Well, as true as that may be, we need to understand exactly what is happening here. How are we to protect ourselves if we don't know what we're up against? I might be able to learn something, get some more information. Maybe one of the others knows more about what's at play here than we do." I close the case and return it to the floor.

Frank lifts his wrist, checking the time. "Still early, I suppose. Guess a soak in the bubble maker wouldn't be the worst thing in the world." Frank lowers his arm. "It's strange, though, that here we are talking about duplicitous behavior and hot tubs when a man died tonight."

He's right. That seems to be the way of the world anymore, though. As sad as it is to admit, we have become a country that witnesses horrific tragedies and unthinkable acts of violence more regularly than we care to admit. Then we turn away, forgetting what's happened to someone else. It's awful, yes, but it didn't happen to us. Journalism hardens the heart, I suppose. One minute, you're reporting the horrors of war, and the next, you're expected to plaster on a smile for a fluff piece about animal babies. That may be my rationale, but what excuse does everyone else have?

Lost in puzzling thoughts, I fall to the bed to sit beside Frank again. "I'm going to figure this out. Journalism. I'm a journalist, for Christ's sake. That's what I do: figure stuff out, get to the crux of the story."

Frank's facial features take on a look of confusion. "I thought you said you report the news now, that some other pee-on has to find and investigate the stories for you."

"I know what I said, Frank, and thanks for throwing that comment back in my face. You know I had to work hard to get where I am. I was a damned good investigator in my day."

"I was just saying... sorry, Kathryn. I didn't mean to upset you. I just thought you were out of practice, is all."

"Well, my investigative skills may be a bit rusty, but I'm willing to try. It's okay," I say, patting his hand. "We're both under an incredible amount of stress, but we need to figure this out, Frank. We have a lot at stake here—our professional lives, our standing in the Norfolk community."

Frank nods, pursing his lips as he blankly stares my way.

"We need to understand what is happening here," I tell him. "Before Alyce starts digging too deep into the days of yore."

Terry

"It's so much easier to work with the dead." Back inside the safe harbor of our room, I drop to sit on the bed.

Yvonne sits beside me. "Terry," she shakes her head, bending over her knees to remove her boots. "You know I hate it when you talk like that."

"What? It is. So much easier, I mean. I don't have to worry about what they're thinking, if they're lying, if I've upset them or hurt them in some way."

A heavy sigh, "That makes sense, I guess," Yvonne says, slipping off her socks. "Did you know Gabe and Carmen were brother and sister? You all did spend all those lunch hours together."

"I had no idea. Gabe never let on anything untoward about their relationship."

"It's weird, right? We assumed their relationship began and flourished because of their shared ethnicity. It never occurred to me that they were somehow related. All our lives, we've been victims of racism in one manner or another simply because of skin color, and here I am, a racist."

"I'm not sure believing the deceit presented to you by another makes you racist, honey." Though relaying the confidence a man has entrusted you with makes one a weasel, and I can't help but feel I've betrayed Gabe. If he had wanted Carmen to know he had lost his job with the city, he would have told her. It wasn't my position to break that confidence, and now all of the old Perishing Hill gang is in the know.

"This has turned out to be some weekend," Yvonne says, pairing her socks together, turning one ankle over the other to hold them securely.

"Indeed. And that young woman, Alyce, I have a hunch she's not going to get the answers she's out for."

"If only Alyce had an idea of who she would be dealing with, perhaps she would have reconsidered putting this reunion together. You know, I feel for Alyce. You realize she's Trina's age?" Yvonne holds. Clearly, her mind is on our youngest daughter. "Can you imagine if Trina came home one Monday and said she had thrown a weekend get-together such as this so she could meet our friends from yesteryear? Because she wanted to know what we were like at her age?"

I nod. I hadn't thought about it like that—like I said, Yvonne has a unique perspective. "Do you remember Alyce or, I guess, Elizabeth during those days, from our time in Perishing Hill?"

"Oh yes. The girls were babies, but Amber and I got them together for playdates and socialization time. I admit, I've wondered about the girl, the young woman, over the years. Though I never once imagined a scenario like the one we all witnessed tonight."

"That was some showdown at dinner between the two of them, Rosey and Alyce. And now that you've brought up Trina, it's difficult to think what I would do if our daughter spoke about our private family history like that in front of mere acquaintances."

"Those two have a lot to work out, it seems. Makes me thankful we have a better relationship with our three girls."

"Mmmm," I agree. "Worrisome though, how quickly relationships can sour, isn't it?" If one of the parties involved feels slighted in any way, alliances and loyalties mean nothing in the end.

"You piss somebody off, baby?" Yvonne asks, her insights on my words hit closer than she knows.

"You know me. I don't care for confrontation, is all."

"I know, honey." She grabs her bathing suit from the chest of drawers.

"Where are you going? Is that your bathing suit?"

"Thought we might take a dip in the hot tub," she says, working to remove her clothing.

"But the storm..., you aren't bothered by all the weather elements out there?"

"Right now, it's still fairly calm, only heat lightning. I'm hoping it stays that way."

I glance at her bedside table to view the amber medication bottle, a soldier inside, waiting to be called to duty.

"Just let me know if you need help, okay? The last thing we need is for you to lose your reserve over this storm, especially amongst this group."

"Are you kidding me? Show the wolves I bleed? No, thank you."

Carmen

The bed is colder without Gabe lying next to me. I run my hand over the empty space, knowing it will never hold the shape of his sleeping form again. At the center of my chest, the pressure, the weight of understanding-of finality—crushes me, numbs me. The hand around my heart squeezes, wringing tighter, more than I can bear, taking my breath away. Tears fall freely in the privacy of the bedroom, where Gabe and I were to share this weekend. How can it be that I will never hold him again? That I will never feel the touch of his hand on my skin? That I will never feel his lips on mine? That I will never know the comfort of his embrace again? I've never known a life without Gabe.

How do I move forward now that he is no longer by my side? I don't think I have it in me. I'm not strong enough to do this by myself. Oh God, please. Please take it away, make it leave, this pain. Gabe is gone. My Gabe, my brother, my best friend, my one confidant.

Our secret is no longer a secret—one we managed to keep for over twenty-five years—I don't even have that to lean on. They all know. The looks on their faces, the disgust, the judgment, the disapproval in their eyes. It wasn't as if we planned to let the charade go on as long as it did. But it was working, and so we let it roll. That's the way life works, isn't it? Each day leads to the next, and then you wake up one morning to realize you've been living a life you never intended. Can you call it a farce if it's been your truth throughout the many years?

We never should have attended this reunion. Why did we come here? Who does that to a person they love—sign them up for a lighthouse ghost tour, knowing their fear of heights? If we hadn't come to Ocracoke, if I hadn't said yes to the lighthouse tour, Gabe would be alive, wouldn't he? Or was it just a matter of time? Did Gabe take his own life as Pat suggested? Or is it possible someone took him from me? We should have stepped right back on that ferry and returned to the mainland the minute we determined what this manipulation was all about.

In my mind's eye, I see the knowing look Gabe and I shared when we learned of Alyce's intentions just a few hours ago, when he was still with me, still beside me—warm and breathing and alive. We didn't have to put words behind our thoughts—we never did. We always knew what the other was thinking just by looking into one another's eyes, or so I thought. Regardless, I will never look into those eyes again.

Alyce is young and naive and under the impression that she can control what happens in her life. Once upon a time, Gabe and I thought the very same way, and look at what happened to us. Of course, it's only natural for a person to want to take command of their happiness. I cannot hold Alyce to blame for wanting to steer her destiny in the manner she sees fit. However, I can say it didn't take long for Gabe and me to understand that while we may have been at the helm, we never had full control. Outside forces will always continue to chip away at even the most carefully laid plans.

Terry was right in his observation. Gabe did exhibit signs of depression. I'd witnessed them myself, believing, hoping they were nothing more than a midlife crisis of sorts. No, Gabe did not confide in me about losing his job, but I wish he had. Now that he is gone, I will never be able to understand what made those circumstances so different that the one partner I've had all my life felt he couldn't share the burden with me. And what else did he keep hidden away? The question brings even more pain.

How am I to break this news to our parents, and should I even bother, given our history? Two children, one girl, one boy, whittled down to one offspring, who couldn't manage to keep the other from harm. After my adoption and Gabe's surprise arrival, our parents tried again for another child. But none of our mother's pregnancies were viable, and the cost of another adoption was more than the two could afford. Their dream of a bustling family gathered around the kitchen table was lost. The blame was readily placed on Gabe and me. If my adoption hadn't been so complicated and expensive, if Gabe hadn't been breech when he was born—leaving our mother in a state unconducive to another viable childbirth—a gaggle of children would have been theirs.

Our parents were devastated by the fact that my mother would never be able to bear the large brood they had planned. The two assumed Gabe and I would produce enough grandchildren between the two of us to keep their dream alive, albeit with spouses they approved. This infuriated Gabe—if I wasn't going to be allowed to live freely, choose my life freely, then our parents should never live out their warped fantasy. Now in their seventies, both have accepted that our immediate family is set and will not grow any larger in numbers. A disturbing theory tumbles into my thoughts. Is Gabe's death some sort of horrendous retribution we must pay karma for our role in this vendetta against our parents? Was Gabe's early death our punishment?

Right or wrong, fate or destiny, ill-timing or, in fact, karma, we always placed the blame for our deceit on our parents. The more our parents lashed out over their frustrations, the further they pushed us away—and together, if that makes sense. Gabe and I turned to one another for support and comfort—us against them, against the world—never realizing we were falling in love. So, when it came time for my parents to pay the remainder of their debt for my adoption, we left. Stole away in the darkest moment of a Tuesday night during the early nineties and made our way to the United States, never looking back or returning, even for a brief visit.

Gabe and I didn't run or hide out of fear; rather, we left because we wanted to live without constraint. What I told the others is true. My marital union was arranged as a portion of the adoption fee. While a fair amount of currency was exchanged in the transaction, so too was my hand in marriage to a suitor of the seller's choice.

My mother began to express her concerns about the arrangement as the time for my engagement drew near. She wasn't comfortable turning her daughter over to a man she didn't know, much less approve. But my mother had no weight in the matter as my father had set the whole transaction up eighteen years prior.

To my parents' credit, however, they never hid the information from Gabe and me or our extended family. My genealogy was common knowledge amongst the many aunts, uncles, and cousins. While there was no secret to keep, it didn't make the fact any easier to live with. Especially not when in the company of my young cousins. They often thought I was some sort of strange specimen, never a full-blooded member of the clan.

As we grew older, our parents chatted more openly and frequently about my future. Gabe and I already shared an unbreakable bond. The conversations about me having to wed a man I didn't know or love made Gabe furious and scared me to the point that Gabe and I began to devise our plan. We would leave for America after finishing preparatoria, or high school as it is in the States. The two of us worked to save money, gathered all the necessary documents required, applied to postsecondary schools, and squirreled away everything we would need to make the move. It was no small feat, but together we did it.

Most believe we acted impulsively, but that was far from the fact. Gabe and I had gone over the potential outcomes time and again. We weighed the risks of staying in our home country to carry out the plans laid out for us. We also considered how diffi-cult it would be to start over in another country.

I think that's when we first realized the extent of our feelings for one another, though we didn't act on them until a few years later. Gabe and I both tried dating other people while we completed our degrees at university, but we never made a connec-tion like the one we shared with each other. After many unsuc-cessful attempts at relationships with other people, we finally succumbed to our love for one another. We were tired of feeling 'less than,' of being made to believe we were vile and deplorable because of who we loved, and so the lie became our truth.

Gabe didn't want either of us to have contact with the family we left behind. I couldn't bear the thought of leaving Mamá in such a state as not to know what happened to her only two chil-dren, though. She never wanted this for us. We speak occasionally, Mamá and I, though I'm not sure my father knows. Gabe didn't know. I never told him—I guess we both had our secrets to keep. Every so often, I reached out to our mother, let her know we were doing well, but never where we were and how we lived.

So yes, Gabe and I did choose our own path, one where we stripped away the exterior, shellacked it, made it presentable to the outside world. As for the Perishing Hill gang, there was no reason we could unearth as to why the others should know the tangled situation Gabe and I were a part of. But that's the way of the world, isn't it? Just when you think you have it all figured out, when everything is running smoothly, here comes the boom.

Boom. No—really. That was an actual boom I just heard. What was that? Something from outside the house, or did I dream that? It sounded so real. A loud pop. A flash of light outside the window. I prop myself up on elbows, scanning the room, realizing the light I left on in the bathroom has gone dark. What was that?

Throwing back the covers, I swing my legs over the side of the bed and stand to walk to the door of the room. I ease the door open, checking both directions of the hallway for signs of the others. Nothing. No lights. No people milling about. No noises. Even the wind has died. Is the storm over? I don't even think it has rained yet. Suddenly, I realize I have no idea when this weather event is due to arrive and exit. My mind has been with Gabe.

I close the door and twist toward the balcony doors. Beyond the sliding glass, a flash of light darts across the sky. Footsteps sound above my head. One footfall—the second comes slow and measured, followed by a careful third and fourth. I lift my head to the ceiling, waiting for the noise above to sound again, trying to determine the direction in which the person travels.

After a moment, I lower my gaze from the ceiling, the noise above my head having ceased. Tip-toeing across the room to the sliding glass door, I ease it open, only to close it immediately as the wind whistles loudly through the opening. The racket will wake up the whole floor. I stare out at the ocean. Griff's promise of a glorious sunrise from this particular vantage point is what prompted Gabe and me to choose this room. Now, Gabe will never witness another sunrise. My breath catches, and I gulp for air, swallowing back a sob.

Outside the window, the sea churns. Frothy white waves break angrily as they trudge inland. A clap of thunder in the distance sends a jolt of nervous energy through my midsection. Far-off bolts of zig-zagging lines spread across the sky, the electricity lighting the starless night. My focus narrows, squinting to view the unidentifiable object at ocean's edge. Is that someone on the beach? I wait again for a flash of light—the growl of thunder gives way to the streaking lights. There. Someone is standing, looking out at the water. Who in their right mind would go out in the elements as they are? Griff was adamant that the islanders do not take these weathermakers lightly, making it difficult to believe that a local would be out seaside right now.

It appears to be a woman, her long hair blowing wildly in the wind. Is that Alyce? No. The person isn't tall enough to be Alyce. The woman turns, looking in the direction of the house, then back at the ocean. She points in my direction, then slowly turns and begins to walk, her long white dress flowing behind her. Breath caught in the back of my throat, I watch to see where she intends to go. And then, she's gone. Up and down the shoreline, I scan to learn where the woman is heading, but I can't locate her. It's like she just vanished. Another flash of heat lightning followed quickly by two more.

A creaking noise. Behind me, in the direction of the hallway. I twist quickly to listen, struggling to hear over the pounding in my chest. It is the undeniable sound of someone walking the long passageway between our rooms. Kathryn and Frank took the room nearest the stairwell, while Patrick and Melanie designated theirs as the last room on the oceanside. Yvonne and Terry are staying across the hallway. Rosey is in one of the bedrooms on the top floor where Alyce and Jude are staying. Even given all I know, it's still impossible to determine who might be up and roaming the hallways at this late hour. I vaguely recall someone saying the hot tub was ready for use, but that was a while ago. Surely, everyone has retired by now.

I pad lightly toward the door again, twisting the doorknob slowly, quietly, pulling it open with care so as not to make noise. There's no one there—no one making their way to or from a bedroom. The sounds I heard came from the hallway. I'm certain of it.

A door slams. My head whips left following the bang. How is it that none of the others have been disturbed by these noises? Barefoot, the soles of my feet absorb the shock of the cold flooring that runs the length of the hall. The black of night thickens, smothering my night vision to the point of no visibility. With darkness pressing in, I reach out to the wall, fingers gliding over the surface as I creep toward the staircase. Heel, toe, heel, toe, every move concentrated and quiet. Underneath the middle of my foot, I feel something sharp—it feels to be an uneven pebble. The pain takes my breath away as I grimace and unwillingly put sound behind the throbbing sensation. I clamp down the cry at the back of my throat and continue to make my way toward the stairs.

Behind me, hinges squeak. I halt, flattening myself against the wall, waiting to see who appears through the doorway. A head leads, surveying the area outside the room. The long, dark hair clues me in on who has emerged—it can only be either Melanie or Alyce. Rosey is fully gray, and Kathryn has that god-awful pixie she thinks looks edgy and professional. Yvonne has styled her hair in a classic no-nonsense bob, stacked in the back, falling at sharp angles along her jawline, leaving no doubt the shadowed figure can't be her. I think of the woman at the oceanside, the way she seemed to beckon me.

Then, the head swivels slowly, stopping when it spots me.

Alyce

The figure in the hallway startles me. She steps away from the wall to the middle of the passageway, waiting to be acknowledged. It's Carmen. What on earth is she doing up at this hour?

I hurry toward her, whispering. "Did you hear that loud boom?"

Carmen nods in affirmation. "What do you think it was?"

"I've no idea. But I do think whatever it was, the noise didn't come from inside the house. It was most definitely from outside."

"I saw a woman on the beach a few minutes ago," Carmen says, her voice low and quivery.

"Who was it? Do you think she might have had something to do with the boom we heard?" I whisper, trying not to disturb the occupants behind the closed bedroom doors.

"No. I don't think so. But I do know she isn't part of our group. I could tell that much. She looked older somehow—maybe it's an islander, someone who lives nearby."

"That's odd. Griff said Dune Dweller was situated inside the National Seashore. It's the only house around here. Someone would have to walk a good distance to get to this part of the beach."

"I don't know. Maybe I'm imagining things," Carmen shakes

her head as if trying to jar her senses. "Wait. Why are you coming out of that room? I thought the room you and Jude were in was one of the top-floor bedrooms."

"It is—I mean, we are on the top floor. I only came down here when I heard the blast outside. At first, I thought perhaps it was the lightning, but it appears we've lost power," I relay.

"How is that possible? Griff said the generator kicks on when the power goes out."

"I'm going to see if I can find him," I tell her. "Griff said something about having a list of items that the generator will power should the electricity go out, but I was only half listening. It was something like, 'emergency electrical units list,' maybe? I didn't figure we would have an issue. Why don't you go back to bed? Get some rest."

"No," Carmen rushes. "I can't sleep, and now, not knowing what's going on, I'll never be able to close my eyes."

"Okay, let's see if we can figure out what's happening." I take her hand (as much for my reassurance as for hers) as we move to find answers elsewhere in the house. The ordeal Carmen has been through tonight is unimaginable to me. Earlier in the evening, I was certain I was at least somehow responsible for Gabe's death and all that happened to put Carmen in the throes of grief. However, in light of the information following Gabe's tragic end to life, I don't think I can be held accountable for what has befallen us. But the way these people feel about one another, I am beginning to wonder if someone else in this house can.

nineteen

THINGS THAT GO BUMP IN THE NIGHT

Terry

The storm is percolating, warming up, if you will, before the big show. The heat lightning provides a prequel of what's to come, streaking the night sky with erratic bursts of light. Thunder grumbling, readying for a raucous, roaring performance. The wind, however, is the most pronounced of the weather elements this evening, the forlorn howls announcing the storm's imminent arrival. The only element yet to arrive is the rain.

There is no way I could sleep with the noises of the impending event just outside the window, even if sleep issues did not mar my nightly restoration process. It bothers Yvonne when I lament about the lack of rest I receive during the prone hours of the night. "If only I could sleep like the dead," I often iterate, thereby inciting Yvonne's lash of reprimands. "I've no intentions of sleeping with a dead man, Terrance Marshall. Take a sleeping pill like the rest of the world." Neither here nor there at the moment, I suppose.

The real dilemma of the moment is locating my wife. Last we spoke, Yvonne was off to soak in the hot tub, console Carmen, and make sure the others didn't put too much pressure on her about the secret of her salacious relationship with Gabe. That was more than an hour ago. Atmospheric conditions are deteriorating as are, I'm certain, Yvonne's grasp on her irrational fears. I know my wife.

I throw my legs over the bed. The cool flooring sends a chill up my spine, or is it a...? I'm sure it is only my imagination, all this talk of otherworldly apparitions earlier at the lighthouse. That said, I'm not one to dismiss chatter regarding (nor am I disturbed by) specters and spirits from another realm. You can't work in a mortuary and not give credence to messages from the other side. The number of strange occurrences I've experienced would curdle the stomachs of most individuals, but I've been in this line of work as long as I can remember.

The funeral home was started by my great-grandfather, so most of my childhood was spent running in and out of my family's private embalming and preparation facilities. The things I've seen over the years would give the average man nightmares, but I am quite attuned to the behavior of a decomposing body. A corpse placed in one position, only to be found hours later in another, is admittedly disconcerting yet explainable. The presence of a spirit though, is not so easily discounted, and we have had some spirited ones over the many years, to be sure. In the dark of the night, I chuckle at the pun. Yvonne would chuckle, but only after she called me a loon.

The chill has dissipated as quickly as it came—another sign of a looming apparition. Gabe comes to mind, and I wonder if there is some unfinished business he has to attend to before moving on.

I push myself from the bed to a standing position, then reach for the bedside lamp. Did this lamp illuminate earlier? I'm almost positive it did, though now the twisting action applied to the knob does not trigger the requested function. Using the bed as a guide, I run one hand along the perimeter, making my way to the other side of the bed where the matching lamp awaits to display a glowing beacon. It would be a bizarre coincidence to find that both of these lamps are unplugged, but I find it more disturbing as I come to the understanding that we have lost power. Is the rest of the house without electricity as well, or have I simply blown a fuse in our room somehow?

Hushed voices speak on the other side of our chamber's door. I make my way to the doorway, hurrying to find out who is up and roaming the house at this late hour. Ear to the door, I attempt to identify who whispers, yet no information is forthcoming. I turn the door handle and hastily pull open the door, startling the two women in the hallway.

"Terry?"

"In fact, it is," I answer Carmen, noting Alyce by her side. "What are you two doing up at this hour?"

"We heard a loud boom outside," Alyce whispers. "Did it wake you too?"

"Uh, well, no. Actually, I've yet to engage in even a light doze —I have issues sleeping, you see—but I didn't hear anything out of the ordinary."

Carmen gives a slight shake of her head, a puzzled look crossing her features. "Maybe because you're on the other side of the house? Which side of the house is your room on, Alyce?"

"On the oceanside like you," Alyce answers Carmen, then turns to me. "And you and Yvonne are on the opposite side overlooking the driveway. That would make sense."

"I think maybe the storm has taken our electricity," Carmen theorizes.

"Yes, but," I start.

Alyce interrupts. "I know—it doesn't make sense to me either. Griff assured me we would never be without power, no matter how bad the storm got."

"Because of the generator," I add, the thought spoken aloud as I think back on Griff's tour of Dune Dweller only hours earlier, when the comment had seemed like a bad omen.

"Right, the generator," Alyce says. "It was one of Griff's

biggest talking points when I chose the house for the weekend reunion. He assured me on multiple occasions that if the power were to go out for any reason, we would have a backup system to rely upon. He did mention something about how the generator wouldn't power the whole house though, only certain parts of it. Honestly, I didn't pay that much attention because I didn't foresee an issue, but I do recall there's supposed to be a master list of what rooms and appliances the generator powers when in use."

Even in the dark, I can see the look of concern that crosses Carmen's face. "Was," she starts, holds, then continues, "was that all he said about it?"

"Yeah, I think so, besides the fact that the one he selected was the most expensive, highly-rated, reliable, and safest brand on the market. He said that several times, come to think of it, that it was the safest," Alyce says.

"Good to know Griff is focused on our safety. Unfortunately, that information doesn't help us out right now," I toss out to the women, tucking the generator information away until later. Right now, I need to find Yvonne before conditions deteriorate any further. "Have either of you seen my wife or any of the others? She told me she was going to talk to you, Carmen."

Heads shake in the negative. Carmen backs up her claim with a verbal no, telling me she hasn't seen Yvonne since we all took leave of the recreation room and went our separate ways. Where is everyone, I wonder? When we all dispersed after post-dinner cocktails, I was under the impression we were retiring for the evening. It wasn't until Yvonne made her announcement regarding her hot tub intentions that I realized my assumptions were ill-conceived. Of course, Carmen wouldn't know where the others have gotten off to—she's in a state of grief and shock. However, given that Alyce is the host of this weekend soirée, the obvious conclusion would be that she knows what everyone is up to at this hour. And where is Jude? Wasn't he staying with Alyce, despite Patrick bellowing that it could not be permitted to happen?

"I haven't seen any of the others, and I'm starting to get concerned," Alyce's voice catches with worry as she utters the statement. "Shortly after everyone adjourned to private quarters, Mr. Perkins dragged Jude out of our room, and I haven't seen him since either. I tried to text him, only to realize he had left his phone in our room when his father took him away. I came downstairs to see if maybe Jude was in his parents' room, but nobody answered their door."

"It seems plausible to me that they could very well be deep in slumber and, therefore, didn't hear your request for entrance." I use the calm, measured cadence I typically reserve for the funeral home's bereaved clientele. Though, in my defense, this situation calls for a bit of de-escalation before we all let our fears run amok. One person has died this evening. It's bound to be taking a toll on all of us, and anxiety does tend to run higher in the long, dark hours of the night.

Carmen picks up on my de-escalation tactic and takes the baton. "The room Pat and Melanie are in is also on the ocean side of the house. I can't imagine that the booming noise we heard earlier wouldn't wake them. Maybe they're also somewhere in the house trying to determine what happened."

Alyce nods and breathes deeply. "Perhaps," she says softly, not quite accepting Carmen's explanation. "I guess Jude could be with them. Maybe? As soon as I heard the boom though, I came right down here to see if I could find Jude, anyone, for that matter —Kathryn and Frank didn't answer their door either. It just seems that I would have passed someone in the hallway if that were the case."

The calm, put-together demeanor Alyce has been exhibiting since our arrival earlier in the day is falling away. Given the level of maturity Alyce displays, it is difficult to remember she is the same age as our youngest daughter. I place my arm over Alyce's shoulders, hoping to be of some comfort to the young woman.

"Come," I address Alyce. "I'll go with you. We'll find them."

"I'm going too," Carmen says. "From what I gather, we're the only three on this floor of the house, and I'm not staying here by myself."

"All right then." I begin to move down the hallway. At the staircase, I turn to look at the women for consensus on whether we go up or down first.

"We know Jude isn't up there and Griff's room is on the ground floor," Alyce offers by way of aiding in the decision.

"What about Rosey?" Carmen asks. "I thought she was staying on the top floor with you and Jude?"

"She is, but I didn't check her room. I didn't want to wake her, especially not to ask about my fiancé, who she only just found out about," Alyce says, then adds, "I'm not sure she'll ever let me forget this one...."

"So then down first?" I ask.

All agree, and we begin the descent, carefully maneuvering the staircase in the dark of night. A loud whistling noise sounds from the direction we travel toward. A crash. Glass breaking. The three of us halt, barely breathing, waiting for what happens next. As quickly as the jarring discord presents, it ends, leaving us in loud silence, followed by the tinkling noise of a bell.

I halt, abruptly turning to address the women. "What was that?"

Carmen says, "It sounded like a bell."

"Griff's bell, on the door downstairs, maybe," Alyce speculates. "Someone's been outside?"

"Who is going to go out there at this time of night?" Carmen asks.

"Griff if I had to guess, but maybe some of the others were in the hot tub and couldn't get in the sliding door leading to the recreation room," I offer, grasping for a reasonable explanation.

"At this time of night?" Alyce asks. Then, "What was the whistling and the crash?"

"Alyce is right. It's a bit late for a soak in the hot tub, and that sounded like something big was broken downstairs, Terry."

"I'll go check it out," I say, turning to continue the descent.

"Wait, Terry, I'll go," Alyce says. "I'm the host of this week-end. It's my responsibility."

"While I appreciate that you are holding yourself accountable for your guests, I have a daughter your age, and there is no way I would let her go in search of things that go bump in the night. If you must go, then we will both venture forth."

"Again, I'm not staying by myself. Let's go." Carmen says, taking a step forward.

The night is blindingly dark as the three of us move down the staircase, falling into a single-file line, holding firmly to the handrail for guidance as I lead the way. Footsteps sound. I halt, holding out an arm to signal the women to stop. Carmen moves to stand on the stair step beside me, Alyce hovering over our shoulders.

Alyce whispers, "Is that someone else you think?"

Carmen nods, placing a single finger to her lips, motioning for us to remain silent, to listen for more movement, some tell-tale sign of what is happening on the floor below us.

A jangling noise cuts through the darkness.

"Was that a key ring?" Alyce asks, her words barely audible. "Maybe it's just Griff? Locking up?"

"That sounds rational," I say to my companions. I wave my arm in a gesture that we should keep moving, searching. Carmen falls behind me once more as we step to the landing to turn the corner and continue the descent to the bottom floor of Dune Dweller.

Carmen missteps, falling forward, catching herself on my back. I twist without a second thought and take her shoulders into my hands, stabilizing her, using signs to check she is okay to keep going. Carmen nods, and I turn quickly to continue down-ward. At the landing, I make another glance over my shoulder to check on Alyce and Carmen, then turn for the final descent, only to find myself stopped as I run straight into another evening prowler.

· · ·

Patrick

"What the hell?" I've hit something. A person. Male. At chest level. I lift my gaze to take in the group blocking the stairwell. It's Terry, along with Carmen and that little girl, who is to blame for having gotten us all stranded here on this godforsaken island.

"Patrick?"

"What are you all doing down here? Everyone is supposed to be in bed," I remind the three pairs of eyes peering back at me.

"Perhaps it is we who should be asking you that question, Patrick," Carmen says. "Seems you're down here making a right bit of noise. What are you doing up and out of your room?"

"I'm not responsible for all that commotion."

"So you heard it too?" Alyce asks for confirmation. "The loud boom? The glass breaking? Did you whistle?"

"Of course, I heard it. I'm not deaf," I say.

"Come on, Pat, there's no reason to be caustic."

"Knock it off with the mortuary blather, Terry. We all know how well-spoken you are. You're wasting your breath on me."

"Hmmph, yeah, that becomes clearer each time we speak," Terry says sarcastically. "The question remains, what are you doing roaming the house at this hour, Pat?"

"I'm looking for my wife, if you must know. She's not in our bed where she belongs. Next to her husband."

"Is that what the bible says, Pat? That the little woman should lie with her husband at his command?" Carmen asks.

"You're going to lecture me?" The nerve of this woman. Talk about double standards. "You've been living a life of sin with your brother, as his wife, lying with your brother and then lying to all those you associate with."

Terry turns to Carmen, reaching out to rub her arm in comfort. "Don't listen to his hateful rhetoric, Carmen. The rest of us understand the situation you and Gabe were immersed in."

"I don't need you to speak for me, Terry. I'm fully aware of what I'm saying, and I meant every word I just said. Now I'm going to find my wife and head to our legitimate marital bed."

"I highly doubt coital reverie is at the top of Melanie's mind right now," Terry lobs. Alyce giggles in response, then quickly places a hand over her mouth when she realizes just who she's laughing at.

"You smug bastard. I'm not listening to this." I reach out to push Terry aside. Terry grabs my hand.

"Hang on now, Patrick," Terry coaxes. "Wait," he says, stopping and turning my palm over. "Are those Griff's keys you've got there?"

I shove the massive ring of keys into my pocket. "Yeah, they're Griff's. Said I could use them. Now get the hell out of my way."

"No, you haven't answered me yet. What are you doing with those keys?"

"Stop this nonsense right now," Carmen sounds every bit the middle school teacher she is. "One of you is going to get hurt, pushing each other around on this stairwell. Something is going on in this house, and we're on our way to figure it out. Now, would you like to join us, Patrick, or would you rather set out on your own? Regardless of your decision, this biting chatter is ceasing right here."

I do not bother responding. I refuse to acknowledge Carmen's chiding me as if I'm some child who will do her bidding.

Alyce steps to Carmen's side. "Did you hear the loud boom, Mr. Perkins? Is that why you're up at this hour?" I understand she is trying in her own way to lighten this conversation by changing the topic.

"I'm up because—as I said before—I can't find my wife. Or my son, and neither of them seem to find it necessary to answer their damn phones."

"Jude's not with you?" Alyce's voice warbles with concern. "But you demanded he go with you earlier. What did you do with him? Where did he go?"

"I didn't do anything with him, and I don't know where he or Melanie went. That's why I'm looking for them. They were in the room when I went to the restroom and were gone when I returned." I finish with Alyce, then angle to address Terry and Carmen. "Don't suppose either of you could bother to let me know if you've seen them on your late-night escapade?"

"What if something has happened to Jude, too?" The girl starts to panic. "We have to find him." Alyce steps to descend the staircase as Carmen reaches out to comfort her.

"We are staying together," Terry speaks sternly to the young woman. "I'm sure Jude is fine. He's probably with Melanie, trying to figure out what has happened to the electricity."

"At least he's not with you," I mumble.

Alyce draws a sharp breath. I've rattled her. Good. The girl needs to be jolted, to have some sense knocked into her. What was she thinking bringing all of us out here to this practically deserted island, locking all of us in this house, and demanding we tell her stories about her dead mommy and daddy? I've got news for her; Alyce needs to be careful what she commands of others—they just might give her what she's asking for.

"That was uncalled for," Terry says.

"And it is none of your business. I don't see her vying to be your daughter-in-law."

"You're being unreasonable, Patrick, and we are wasting time. Either go on your way or join us, but we are not going to allow you to harass Alyce simply because she loves your son," Carmen says.

I'm not about to justify Carmen's last statements. These people think they're so smart, think they know everything. Let them believe whatever they like. But I know the truth, and I'm hoping to keep it to myself.

"Did you see anyone else downstairs, Mr. Perkins?" Alyce asks.

"If I had, I'd be down there now convincing them to go back to bed. Maybe I'd have more luck with that person than I've had with you all."

"We, too, are on the hunt for missing loved ones, Patrick. You can't expect that we are going to sit solo in our beds and wait for them to return with all the strange noises and occurrences that are transpiring outside our bedrooms," Terry speaks for the trio.

"Yeah, well, I went through the recreation room, and there was no one there. So now I'm heading upstairs to see if anyone is on that floor. Why are you all going down? Did you check the second and third floors already? Go room to room? Check all the bathrooms and closets?"

"Come on, Patrick. Of course, we haven't conducted a thorough search; we had no idea it was necessary," Carmen relays. "Did you?"

"Did I what?"

"Go through all the closets and rooms downstairs." That flippant attitude Carmen likes to throw off is going to get her in trouble. I don't care if she lost a spouse, lover, brother, what have you —partner in sin is more appropriate, but I don't say any of those things. See, I can be compassionate, no matter what they all think about me.

"Of course not. I went outside to look for Jude and Melanie."

"So that was you coming through the basement door downstairs, the door with the bell on it?"

"Yeah, so," I answer. What are these three up to with all the questions? We need to get moving.

"Did you break something, Mr. Perkins?" Alyce asks.

"Break something? No, young lady, I did not, and I will not be footing the bill for broken items. You brought all of us here, and that expense will be on you, just like everything else that happens this weekend will be on you."

"I was just asking..." The girl's voice squeaks with emotion.

"Let's go," Carmen quickly grabs Alyce's hand and moves to step around me. "There is no reasoning with the unreasonable." Terry steps forward to lead the women down the stairs.

I hurry after the three of them. If they think they're going to leave me behind and blame me for whatever they find, they have another think coming.

. . .

Alyce

When I find Jude Saches—Saches-Perkins—Perkins—whatever the hell it is I'm supposed to call him, we are going to have a long, serious discussion about his family. When we first became a couple and decided to leave the talk of families for future conversations, I assumed that Jude was merely going along with my wishes. I now know, however, that Jude had his own selfish agenda for prolonging the exchange. Now that I've met them, though, how can I blame him?

Rosey has always been somewhat difficult to deal with. She can be quite controlling and opinionated. But Jude's father is downright mean. At what point in our relationship was Jude going to share that his father is impossible to win over, to have a civilized conversation with? While that statement may sound like hyperbole, let's think for a moment about the fact that Jude is twenty-five years old. He has two bachelor's degrees as well as a master's degree, a job with excellent growth potential, and yet STILL hasn't won the approval of his father. I suppose that alone should tell me why Jude never let on about his life growing up.

As disconcerting as meeting Jude's parents has been, I find it even more unsettling that these people were once friends of my parents. Who would want to spend their free time with Patrick Perkins? Does the man even know the definition of the term fun? Of party?

Mr. Perkins leads our search group down the remaining stairs, heading back the way he came. I'm uncertain as to why he wants to join us if he has indeed already searched the bottom floor of the house, but here we are—Mr. Perkins followed by Terry, then Carmen, and me in the dead of night. I hold firmly to Carmen's hand, not because I'm scared but because it's nice to have someone to lean on, to count on. I like knowing that Carmen and my mother were close. If my mother trusted her, then maybe I can trust Carmen too. Maybe?

At the bottom of the staircase, we halt. Mr. Perkins seems to be moving on, but stops when he hears Terry whisper to Carmen and me, "Where should we check first? The back hallway of rooms or the recreation room?"

"Isn't Griff's room in that hallway?" Carmen asks.

"Yes. He told me his room was the last door at the end of the hall," I answer. "Griff said if we needed anything, that is where we could find him."

"Then let's start there," Terry says.

"I've already been down there," Mr. Perkins says as he rejoins our group. "Nobody answered when I knocked on the door."

"Then how did you get the keys?" Carmen asks.

"Not that I owe any of you an explanation for my actions," Jude's dad begins as he shuffles between feet, hands on hips. "But in order to get this charade moving along, I borrowed them."

"What do you mean you borrowed them?" Terry asks.

"I opened the door. No one was in the room. The keys were lying on the dresser. I took them. Shoot me."

"Okay, looks like we have a starting point," Carmen states, tugging me in the direction of Griff's room. The men follow behind us.

"Why? We know he's not in there," Mr. Perkins says.

"We're going to put Griff's keys back where you found them," Carmen says, striding forward through the hallway. "Which one of the commandments is it that addresses thievery? I'd think you'd have that one committed to memory, or do the commandments not apply to you?"

"It's not like I intended to keep them; that would be stealing. Stealing is a sin. We might need these keys," Mr. Perkins continues. "You have no idea what door might be locked that we will need access to."

"Then we'll come back and get them, but we are not taking this man's things simply because he is out of his bedroom in the wee hours of the morning," Carmen says. She stops outside the last door in the hallway.

Carmen drops my hand and raps softly on Griff's bedroom door. We wait for permission to enter. Carmen tries again—still, no answer or sounds of life from the other side of the door. "Griff, it's Carmen. I'm with Alyce and Terry."

"And Patrick," Mr. Perkins says loudly. Mrs. Perkins must have handled Jude's upbringing solo.

"Griff, we're opening the door now." Carmen twists the door knob to push through the entryway.

Like the rest of the house, there is no electricity. We step inside the room, scanning, finding Griff's bed undisturbed, a jacket tossed across the bottom near the footboard. No attempt at sleep seems to have been made, not even a pillow ruffled.

Terry turns, asking Mr. Perkins, "Where did you find Griff's keys?"

Mr. Perkins points to the dresser near the window. "Over there. Don't see why we need to put them back right now."

"Well, if we should find ourselves in a situation that requires the need for such an instrument, then we will know where to find them." Terry holds out his hand to take the keys. Mr. Perkins pulls them from his pocket and passes them over to Terry. Terry starts toward the far side of the room, where he places the keys on the dresser. He picks up an object, inspects it. Though my eyes have adjusted to the inky dark we've been thrown into, I can't make out what it is in Terry's hand. He returns to join us beside the bed.

Holding up the long tube, Terry says, "Flashlight. We might need this."

"What? Are you kidding me?" Mr. Perkins shuffles between feet, hands flying in synchronicity with his words. "It's okay for you to take Griff's flashlight, but I can't hold onto his keys? Who's the thief now?"

"This is a different situation, Patrick. Those keys are Griff's personal property, and as soon as we find Griff, we'll give him his flashlight and ask where we might locate another," Carmen says, taking up for Terry.

"It's not like I took his damn diary, Carmen."

"Look, I won't even switch it on unless we absolutely have to. We need to preserve the life of the batteries in case of an emergency anyway," Terry tries.

"Let's just get out of here and look for the others," I say. "Please." The bickering is starting to get to me. I've never been around so much fighting. It isn't as if I had siblings growing up or even the chance to make a friend I would be close enough to argue with.

"Yes, let's proceed," Terry agrees. He turns and starts for the bedroom door. Carmen and I follow. Mr. Perkins lingers.

At the doorway, I twist to look over my shoulder as I exit the room. Where did he go? Mr. Perkins was right behind me. I was sure of it. The black of night swallows the objects in the room. Visibility is nil. If Mr. Perkins were somewhere in the room at the moment, I would never be able to discern his position. He had to have left Griff's room first, and I missed it. I turn back to follow Carmen and Terry, checking for Mr. Perkins in the hallway.

I pull the door of Griff's bedroom closed, careful not to slam it. Turning to rejoin the quasi-search party, I understand the others have moved on without me. Using sound for direction and proximity of the others, I stand at Griff's door and listen. It isn't possible they've vanished into the dark of night, though if I hadn't been in their company only seconds ago, I'd think I imagined the entire exchange.

Hands outstretched, I run fingertips along both walls for guidance. Rustling of clothing—it's behind me. Impossible, Alyce. There is no one there, and I refuse to give more credit to the implausible by turning to take a look.

Again. Someone is there, someone trying to remain unheard. Unseen? Why? Who? Carmen wouldn't allow either of the men (not that Terry would pull this kind of stunt) to play such a cruel trick after all that has happened tonight. Still, the presence of another cannot be denied. There is most definitely someone behind me. My heart races, outpacing the chill running the length of my spine. I muster courage—set intentions. Twist quickly. Confront whoever is behind you. Don't give them the opportunity to have the upper hand. Go fast.

I draw in a deep breath and turn quickly to face the person. At the same moment, a hand covers my mouth, muffling the scream at the back of my throat.

twenty

LATE NIGHT GAMES

Kathryn

The ocean laps at my bare feet—a cloud drifts across the surface of the moon while the squiggly flashes of electricity dance across the sky. 'Hic.' The water whooshes over the sand, dragging any loose objects back into the sea as it returns to the basin. I awkwardly work the sash of the thick robe, pulling it tighter around my midsection—not an easy task when your hands are full.

A round of hot flashes drove the women out of the hot tub and down to the water's edge to cool off. A good idea at the time, but it's cooler out here than we thought it would be. Thank goodness for the plush robes we found in the cabinet near the hot tub. Griff thought of everything. 'Hic.' I sip from the glass in my hand. Finding it dry, I pull the bottle I hold in my opposite hand to my mouth and swig.

"You have the hiccups." Melanie laughs, joining me water side. She drains the last dregs of wine from her glass. "I'm empty," she says, holding it out for me to refill.

"I don't have—hic—the hiccups. I just swallowed air," I tell her, though I do have the hiccups—maybe from air, maybe from overconsumption. But I don't know and don't care, and I laugh at myself, and at Melanie, and at this ridiculous, precarious, absurd, bizarre situation we find ourselves in the middle of.

Wine sloshes over the lip of the glass as I pour. "Hold your hand steady."

"Tell me again why we're drinking wine out of martini glasses," Melanie sips to catch the overflow.

I run my finger up the side of the bottle to swipe up the wine dripping down the neck, pop the finger into my mouth, and suck away the Chardonnay. "Because Frank couldn't find the wine glasses, and now, I can't find Frank."

"We just left him at the house. Remember? He got us another bottle of wine because you said we had to have more wine if we were going to play a game," Melanie says, swaying with the beat of the ocean waves.

Feels like a storm might be coming in. Someone said something about rain earlier, I think. 'Hic.' At least the wind has died down.

"Where is old Francis? I thought he was right behind us," Melanie lifts the glass to her lips.

"Don't call him that."

"What, old?"

"No, Francis. He hates it."

"Now, Katy," Melanie starts.

"Unh, unh, unh." I wave my finger in a no-no-no motion. "It's Kathryn now."

"Why is that?"

"Why is what?"

"Why did y'all change your names? Seems suspicious to me." Melanie hops back to keep her feet dry as the water rolls toward her.

"You've been working for lawyers too long. You think everything is duplicitous, a deception."

"You've decided to go by Kathryn. Both you and Frank have dropped Carrickfergus and now use your middle names as your last names. There must be some story behind those decisions."

Melanie always had a way of getting straight to the point, asking difficult questions.

"Carrickfergus is a mouthful. You try saying that name multiple times throughout a news broadcast," I try side-stepping the inquiry.

"Twice? At most, you have to spout your name two times. Two times," she repeats, holding up two fingers for emphasis. "You can't fool me; I watch the news. You give your name once at the beginning of the broadcast and sometimes at the end."

"Fine. If we must go into this…. Surely, after what happened, you and Patrick thought about changing your names. Patrick did. As I recall, we used to refer to him as Pat. I mean, seriously, Melanie. The man changed careers. Car salesman turned preacher? Jesus, you all moved thirty miles up the road to get away from it. Hic. You can't say you all didn't react in a more extreme manner than we did."

"You all could have moved too," Melanie says, holding her glass out for another splash of wine.

I refill her. "We had careers, Melanie. Car salesmen can work from anywhere. And lawyers are always looking for decent legal assistants."

"Paralegal."

"What?"

"You said, legal assistant. I'm a paralegal. There's a difference."

"Okay, fine, that too. Lawyers are forever in search of paralegals."

Melanie shakes her head, an exasperated look marking her features. "I commute, by the way, which totally dispels your theory. We moved so Patrick could be closer to his congregation."

Laughter rolls from my middle. "How hysterical is it that Patty has a flock?"

"Yeah, well," Melanie says with an exaggerated eye roll. "They all squawk around him like he's some sort of alpha chicken."

I find it hard to believe anyone would follow Patrick for spiritual enlightenment but decide to move on. "My point is—Hic—

is that we each had choices. You all chose to leave Norfolk. Frank and I chose to stay. One night and our names were plastered all throughout the news cycles for days. I'm lucky to still have my career after all the fallacies and theories, all the conjecture. Carmen and Gabe weren't as affected by the events of that time. Who cares if a middle school teacher and a city accountant are mixed up in a 'compromising incident?'"

"Is that what we're calling it now?"

"Don't be flippant, Melanie. You know exactly what I'm saying. I still don't know how Terry and Yvonne kept the funeral home going after all that went down twenty-two years ago."

"Because the dead don't care what kind of scandal you're a part of."

This strikes me as funny. I throw my head back and laugh and laugh—for all of us, for the absurdity of the situation in which we all now find ourselves.

"What's so funny?" Melanie asks, but I can't answer over the uncontrollable fit of giggles.

The laughter fades, giving way to the seriousness of the moment. "Nothing. None of it," I shout to the churning ocean. "Nothing about this weekend is freaking funny," I scream.

One girl. One girl is about to wreak havoc on my life's work.

Melanie

"Should we go skinny dipping?" I toss it out to Kathryn.

"You can't be serious," Kathryn says, curbing her laughter.

"You're the one who said you were too hot in the hot tub, that we should go swimming and cool off."

"Hic. I remember having a hell of a hot flash, but I don't believe I ever said anything about skinny dipping. Frank might have come with us if I'd suggested that." Kathryn giggles at her joke.

"Why didn't he come with us, your great protector who can't leave your side without your explicit permission?"

"Saltwater and Frank don't mingle well. Why are you grilling me? Where did your sexy son sneak off to? Does he want to go skinny dipping? Wait. Aren't we supposed to be playing hide-and-seek?"

"Oh my God, you're right," I recall, and then it suddenly dawns on me. "Wait, where is Jude? He said he was going to check on her—I mean Alyce—and then come out and hang with us."

"Unh, unh, unh," Kathryn wags her finger again.

"This name game is getting old. I didn't even say your name this time, Kathryn."

"It's not that. You used the Lord's name in vain," she teases. "Patrick would stroke."

"Jesus. Fucking. Christ," I yell to the ocean, taking a cue from the woman standing next to me. "Take that, Patty." Kathryn doubles in laughter as I too, am overcome by the preposterousness of the situation. How did we get here?

My peripheral vision picks up movement in the distance. I tap, tap, tap, Kathryn, then punch her upper arm to get her attention. "Oww."

"Who is that?" I whisper, pointing. A woman in a long flowing dress draws nearer. "Who was that ghost woman they told us about at the lighthouse? Do you think it's her?"

"The Aaron Burr daughter? No, it couldn't be."

Behind us, a woman's raised voice startles us. Immediately, we move closer, clinging to one another without thinking of who it is we're holding onto.

"What are you two doing down there? That isn't a great hiding place," Yvonne yells, stumbling and sliding down the face of a quasi-sand dune.

"Yvonne," I say, releasing Kathryn, letting out the breath trapped at the back of my throat.

"Yvonne," Kathryn repeats. "Hic." She laughs again.

"Where have you been? Are you better now? We were looking for you," I yell over the increasing wind.

Kathryn turns to me. "We were?"

"Doesn't look like either of you overexerted yourselves," Yvonne says, her words slurring. Funny, I don't recall her drinking that much tonight. I guess if I'm comparing Yvonne's drinks to Kathryn's, then it's not a fair comparison. "The point of hide-and-seek is for one person to hide while another seeks," she finishes.

"I forgot how smart you are, but you're still a scaredy-cat," Kathryn says, cackling at her cattiness.

"You jumped when the bolt of lightning hit too, Kathryn," Yvonne says. "Don't act like it didn't startle you."

"I admit it frayed some nerves, but I didn't go into hiding. Maybe you should be drinking. Why haven't you been drinking? I'm not wrong, right, Melanie? Yvonne hasn't been drinking. Hic."

Yvonne comes to my side. "Well, I am now. Give me that." She reaches to take the wine bottle from Kathryn. "I have a bit of catching up to do." Yvonne drinks from the bottle, then passes it back to me. I fill my glass, then Kathryn's, looking to fill Yvonne's.

"Where's your glass?" I ask Yvonne.

"I don't have one." Yvonne shakes her head from side to side. "I wasn't supposed to drink."

"You were drinking earlier," I remind, trying to understand what seems to have gotten Yvonne so loopy if she isn't drinking.

"I wasn't on medication earlier either, but I am now, maybe not the prescribed dose, but I'm med-i-cated," Yvonne singsongs, then, "Do you have an extra glass?"

Before I can question Yvonne further, Kathryn begins rambling more thoughts. "Hic—we've lost husbands, a son, wine glasses, and one nosey little brat that wants to know all about her heavenly parents' pasts." Kathryn makes no effort to hide her disdain. "Like either one of those two was issued a pair of wings at the gates of eternity."

"Alyce isn't that bad," Yvonne says on our host's behalf, ignoring the disparaging comment about Amber and Shane. "Alyce is just curious. It's perfectly natural for a young woman to want to have her mother's wisdom and support as she stands at the precipice of starting her adult life."

"Dear God, you've been living with that mortician too long," I say, unable to deny just how much Yvonne sounds like her husband right now.

"Okay, okay. I hear what you're saying." Yvonne throws her hands up, surrender style. "But listen, Terry and I have three girls—I should say, young women. I happen to know a thing or two about this age bracket."

"We all do. We were all that age once. We were all about that age when we bought into that hellish neighborhood, Perishing Hill," Kathryn says, pulling her lip into a snarl.

"Perishing," I can't help but laugh at the irony.

"It's not funny, Melanie. Shane and Amber did perish in that neighborhood," Yvonne says. Then, "If I were Alyce, I would want to know about them too." Yvonne always was the diplomatic one.

"Oh, come on, Yvonne," Kathryn spouts. "Say what you mean, not some tactful bullshit that none of us here are going to buy into. You have freedom; you're not a celebrity. I have to keep my thoughts and opinions hidden from the public, but you have the liberty to say exactly how you feel."

"Of course, they perished—it's why we've all been roped into this weekend," I agree with Kathryn. "And it is NOT our responsibility to fill Alyce in on their untimely deaths," I add to hone my point.

"How can you be so callous, Melanie?" Yvonne asks. "Alyce is engaged to your son. She will be your daughter-in-law in the not-so-distant future."

Not if I can help it, she won't. And based on Patrick's actions throughout this shindig, he will be siding with me on this one, which, I might add, is a rarity. "You do remember Amber, right, Yvonne? The kind of person she was? You want me to fill Alyce in on Amber?" I ask.

"Your views of people, in general, are warped, Melanie," Yvonne answers. "If they're not fuckable, they're not likable."

"Wasn't it you that accused me of being crass earlier in the evening because it sounds to me as if you have that title secured?"

"Girls—hic," Kathryn tries for our attention. The wind has changed direction, a current of electricity buzzing through the night air. "We need to stick together on this. We made a pact over twenty years ago, and we need to keep it. Our lives, our livelihoods, our relationships all rely on us keeping this pact."

"Do you think we can count on Carmen?" I ask.

"She just lost the love of her life, and we just learned that Carmen has never had a family she could fully count on. I'd say she's definitely questionable," Yvonne surmises.

"But you're with us?" Kathryn asks for confirmation.

"Whatever comes out this weekend won't come from me," Yvonne says. "But whoever coined, 'dead men tell no tales,' was dead ass wrong."

Yvonne

"How can you say that...about the dead and the secrets?" Melanie asks me.

"Because I watch too many soap operas," I tell her. "Because my husband works with the dead and their very alive families. Because secrets always have a way of coming out. Because—and this is my biggest reason—when you have a precocious, tenacious young woman who has tasked herself with seeking out answers, she will eventually find them."

"You're right, Yvonne," Kathryn agrees with me. "And you all may have forgotten what Amber was like, but I certainly have not."

"What is that supposed to mean?" Melanie asks.

"Let's just say Amber was a free spirit," Kathryn replies.

"Sounds to me like you're calling Amber a slut," I say, hating myself for using that word. The girls and I have banned that term in our house. "Surely, you're not shaming a woman for enjoying sex, Kathryn."

"I enjoy sex as much as the next person, just generally with my husband, that's all," Kathryn cryptically replies.

"I gotta sit down for a minute," I tell the women, my head spinning with the banter, the meds, the alcohol, the barometric pressure. I should have waited to take my pill. Did I take one or two? The medication usually doesn't get to me like this. I generally just get loopy on the stuff—say crazy crap, carry out ridiculous actions. I head toward the softer, drier sand and sit. Kathryn and Melanie move in my direction, passing the wine bottle between the two of them, no longer bothering to fill their martini glasses. The two move to sit on either side of me.

"I'd offer you some more wine, but we finished it," Melanie says. I wave off the non-apology, not bothering to tell her I wouldn't have accepted it anyway, not sure what I was thinking when I grabbed the bottle from Kathryn before.

Kathryn nods. "Hic. I should probably stop drinking. It's that damn Rosey. Hic. She's making me do this. That woman gets my nerves tangled up tighter than a string of Christmas lights."

The three of us sit close together to help block the wind, each lost in our own thoughts, watching the sea churn. It looks angrier with each set that rolls ashore.

"I wasn't speaking ill of Amber," Kathryn slurs, attempting to correct her 'free spirit' comment. "I was remembering how she was always such a flirt. That's all."

"Well, I'm a flirt, too," Melanie offers.

"All women are flirts to one degree or another," I add.

"So then you think Alyce is—will be—a flirt?" Melanie asks. "I don't want my Jude mixed up with a woman who is going to run around—sorry, flirt around—on him regularly."

"Melanie, that boy is good-looking and well-mannered and intelligent. I doubt any woman would run around on him,"

Kathryn says, her pixie cut standing on end with the humidity and wind of the night. Perhaps it's the loopiness, but I can't help laughing at the effect it gives her.

"What's so funny, Yvonne?" Melanie asks. "You think Kathryn's wrong about Jude?"

"No," I say through laughter I can't control. "It's Kathryn. She's so tiny, and that hair is standing on end. She looks like one of those troll dolls the girls used to play with," I say through laughter, wiping at the corners of my eyes. "You know, the ones with the blue hair?" Melanie sees it, too, doubling over.

Kathryn pats furiously at the top of her head, trying to beat the hair down. Never one to laugh at herself, I await Kathryn's tyrannical reply. Instead, she plays out the scene for extra laughs.

"Can I just say this is nice?" Kathryn says as the laughter dies away.

"What? Being out here in the middle of the night, waiting for some huge storm—be it literal or figurative—is fun?" I ask for clarification, my head spinning, but I think I know what Kathryn is trying to say, and I have to agree with her. It has been a long time since we all enjoyed one another's company.

"You know what I mean, Yvonne." Kathryn continues. "Why did we all quit hanging out together?"

"Because people died," Melanie bluntly states the obvious fact.

"And here the three of us are, trying to get the dead people's daughter to leave the secrets buried," Kathryn laments.

"Why do you think Rosey changed Amber's daughter's name?" I ask the others. "I mean, Rosey didn't just change Alyce's last name. She changed the whole thing. Why? Did Rosey think we were going to try and locate the girl, even after each of us signed those statements?"

"I'm sure Rosey had her reasons. I just wish I knew what happened between Rosey and Amber," Kathryn says. "Carmen knew that they were at odds, probably had all the details, and kept the facts to herself all this time."

"At odds?" Melanie huffs. "That's putting it mildly. Amber refused to answer any questions about her mother. As I understood it, Amber couldn't tolerate her mother. I can't speak for Rosey except to say that she didn't have any involvement with her daughter during the time I knew Amber. But if you recall the period right after Amber and Shane died, when Rosey came into town to settle their estate, Rosey never had any kind words for Amber, and she certainly didn't conceal her feelings about Shane."

"Remind me," Kathryn drawls. "Why did Rosey handle all of the details and logistics of Amber and Shane's estate? Where were Shane's parents? Did we meet them at any point?"

"No, you never met them because Shane was in the foster care system growing up. He was constantly being transferred from one home to another, never had any stable family to fall back on," Melanie explains.

"Oh, I remember now," I say, wrapping my arms around my legs, leaning on my knees. "So then that was why Amber didn't take Shane's last name. God, I can't believe how much I've forgotten. But tell me this. What is it with you, white women?"

"You're going to make this a race thing?" Melanie says, wearing a scowl.

"No. I'm talking about how y'all don't take your man's name. Kathryn and Frank use middle names as their last names, and you opted to take a hyphen instead of taking Patrick's last name. When Terry and I jumped that broom, I became Mrs. Terrance Marshall and never looked back. Like I was saying, Amber didn't take Shane's surname either. The only way I ever knew her was as Amber Fischer, not Fischer-Thompson like Alyce claims her mom's name was."

"Carmen has Gabe's last name. Hic." Kathryn tries disproving my observation.

"Carmen and Gabe were sister and brother. They weren't married," I remind her. "No more wine for you tonight."

Kathryn bats her hand at me as if to shoo away the comment, saying, "Yeah, well, Amber and Shane weren't married either."

"What? Since when?"

"They were never married. That's why Amber was always fooling around with other men," Kathryn continues. "And Shane had his fair share of outside entertainment, too, from what I heard."

I shake my head. "You've had too much to drink, Kathryn. We need to cease this conversation before someone overhears and gets the wrong idea." I place my hands into the sand and prepare myself to stand, get these two back inside before the others start wondering where the three of us went.

Kathryn follows my cues and stands as well. Taking an argumentative stance, she moves her hands to her hips. "I haven't had too much to drink. I'm telling you the truth. I remember. You may not, but I do. I can't tell you how many different times I had to pull Amber off Frank."

"Like you would care if Frank saw action somewhere else."

"My marriage and what happens or doesn't happen in it is none of your business, Yvonne Marshall—Miss I'm So Proud to Have my Husband's Last Name."

"All right, ladies." Melanie stands, positioning herself between the two of us. "Let's call this tête-à-tête off."

"Hardly," I mumble, ready to drop this conversation and head back inside.

"Hardly, what?" Melanie asks.

"You used the wrong word. Just forget it. Let's go," I take a step, but Kathryn pulls me back.

"Let go of me. We really need to end this discussion before you and Melanie start making more false claims."

"You can pretend you're better than us," Kathryn starts, "bury your head in the proverbial sand if you like. But you don't know what you're talking about, and I do. "Amber slept around, and she wasn't particular about who she was with either. You don't believe me? Ask Carmen."

"Carmen just experienced a horrible loss. I'm not bothering her with your crazy ass shit, Kathryn."

"Tell her, Melanie," Kathryn whines. "Tell her that Amber and Gabe slept together."

twenty-one

STOLEN OBJECTS AND HIDDEN AGENDAS

Griff

This group's gonna break me in good. First rental property I have a stake in—first renters. Got more than I bargained for. Certainly didn't plan on having people in my bedroom, going through my things.

Now, I realize most folks don't stay on property with their renters. Heck, most of these owners don't even live on the island, much less stick around to hang out with the folks staying in their vacation homes. Wasn't supposed to happen like this for me either. I was prepared to bunk up with a friend this weekend, but Alyce wouldn't hear of it. Still, this experience is a first for me, and it never occurred to me that I would need to lock my bedroom when I stepped outside my personal quarters. Call me naive, but I assumed people to be respectful of others' space. Then again, I now have some understanding of these people and have seen for myself how self-absorbed they all are. Instead of going through my things, they need to focus on their own misdeeds. They've got more to hide than I do.

Who was in here is what I want to know. I've been trying to keep up with this crew, but between me running around to help out neighboring O'cokers and these people sneaking around on one another, it isn't easy. Jude was snatched into his parents' room earlier. The hysterics were too much for me, and I left them to it. Not long after that, I saw Jude and his mama leave out toward the beach, then Jude disappeared. No idea if Patrick is still in their room or not. Kathryn and Frank went to the hot tub, then were joined by Yvonne and Melanie, but the women all left Frank there to soak and took off to the beach. Seemed they were hitting the wine bottle hard. Guess their game of hide-and-seek fizzled out before it ever got started.

Speaking of seeking out the hidden, where the hell is my flashlight? I put it right here on the dresser next to my keys, which also seem to be missing—she's going to owe me for this. Long time ago, I got the good advice to make sure I have a backup set for instances such as this, and there's another flashlight under the kitchen sink. I'll have to head upstairs to get it before I can get back to the generator. Won't be long before the rain starts, and I won't be able to fix anything if it comes down the way they are predicting. Luckily, we've had as much time to prepare as we have. Living on this island these last many years, I've learned to take the early warnings seriously. I sure can't say that for Dune Dweller's first guests—well, first guests after her remodel.

She was in quite a state when I got hold of her. Opportunity fell right into my lap, too good to be true, but she's mine no matter the details of how I came to be her owner. The renovations took me right at two years to complete. If nothing else, at least this whiny group respects the hard work and craftsmanship I've put into Dune Dweller's rebirth. They've been nothing but complimentary on that front, even if nothing else is getting through to them.

This gang is under the impression I will be driving them to catch the ferry back to the mainland in the morning. Thinking they're all going to get through this weekend unscathed, their secrets still under lock and key. It won't happen. Ferry isn't running 'til this storm has cleared. Didn't see any reason to go into it earlier. They all think they're smarter than me, and I see no reason to try and argue with them. But the fact is, I've been getting text alerts all afternoon about the cancellation of ferry routes. Hell, on a normal weekend, we typically have cancellations and reschedulings due to mechanical issues, routing difficulties, and various small weather events. This is a storm, and I do mean a storm, coming in on both sides—weather maker arriving from the west and King Tides coming in from the ocean. We may not be in for a hurricane this weekend, but being twenty-some-odd miles off the mainland and surrounded by water, you learn to stay put, preferably up somewhere high.

Storm won't last long, thank goodness, and we can all be rid of one another. They won't have to listen, and I won't have to keep repeating myself. Good news, too, 'cause none of 'em pay attention to a dang thing I tell them. They all see me as the 'shit-doer' with sand for brains, and I'm fine with that for the time being. The way they're acting, they'll be doing good to make it to morning, never mind the storm. Can't believe we already lost one. Charles sure wasn't happy about a leaper taking a jump from his lighthouse.

I pull out my smartphone and activate the flashlight app to search for the misplaced items. Neither of them is here. Dammit, they took my stuff. I check the battery display on the phone to learn that the battery is at half capacity. I close out all apps to save as much juice as possible. Wind took out the power line down the street already, which shouldn't be a problem with my new generator ready to go, but it's not going. Need that flashlight to figure out what's happened to it.

In the distance, muffled thunder rolls, faint streaks of lightning follow. It's not here yet, but it sure ain't too far off now. Hopefully, they all got out of that hot tub. Sure, most of the flashes have been heat lightning, but you never know when or where a bolt will strike. My top priority at this moment is getting that generator back up and running again. Being a caretaker for all the rentals has taught me a lot, but the biggest lesson I've learned is that people get wacky when the lights go out. Act like they don't have the good sense God gave 'em. These folks are already prone to that behavior, as far as I can tell.

I walk outside, moving along Dune Dweller's lowest deck. The wind gusts. Not been too bad—yet. I scan the beach for the women. Three of them down there now. Looks like Yvonne, Kathryn, and Melanie. Where did Jude go after he left Melanie? Maybe he's with Alyce. Knocked on her door a bit earlier to let her know the power was out and the generator took a hit, but she didn't answer her door. This isn't going to sit well with Alyce. She's a planner—got everything scheduled out to the last detail for this weekend—meticulous and used to getting her way, it seems. I don't say that with contempt. Nah. Alyce is a nice young woman. Makes me wonder if she's anything like her mother.

twenty-two

LATE NIGHT RENDEZVOUS

Rosey

Where in the hell has everyone gotten off to at this hour of the morning, the darkest point of the day? No one is answering their doors. No one is in the recreation room playing games or drinking. At some point during my search for the others, I expected Griff to materialize, but he too, seems to have disappeared. Holding to the railing, ascending the staircase, back to the kitchen, I go. Maybe someone is preparing a late-night snack, getting a drink of water perhaps.

I began my search by knocking at Alyce's door, hoping we could have a more in-depth discussion about her plans for this weekend, about exactly what information she hopes to pull out of this group. Alyce believes these people hold the answers to who her parents were, the type of people they were, the way they lived their lives. Placing her trust in this gang, though, is ill-advised. Alyce isn't going to take my word for it, and why would she? We've never discussed the relationships I have with these couples or even the fact that I know who they are. Old acquaintances or not, Alyce wasn't the only one wearing a look of shock when I popped into dinner unexpectedly. The faces may be more deeply etched than years prior. The circumstances may be different this time around. But they all still wear that cloak of duplicity—and wear it well, I might add.

When I showed up after the untimely deaths of my daughter and Shane Thompson, they didn't know me, or of the status my family name carried, but I knew them. I'd been keeping tabs on Amber, along with anyone she had close contact with, for years. Twenty-somethings taking their first steps into adulthood, the youngest homeowners in the shoddily named neighborhood formed an alliance. They called themselves the Perishing Hill Gang, eager to lend support and aid during my time of loss. Hogwash. Their stories glistened; all speaking so highly of Amber and Shane, of how close they all were, trying to console me while protecting their own interests. I didn't buy it then, and I can tell they aren't honest and forthright now, either. The only people they intend to help are themselves. All of them so disingenuous, so insincere—if I hadn't known Amber the way I did, I would have assumed I read them wrong. But Amber was never one to hang with a reputable crowd.

That girl gave me fits from the moment she filled her lungs with air. Amber started her life fighting me and, in the end, devastated me with her complete departure from my world. The only good thing to come from Amber's death was Alyce. I was granted another opportunity to raise a daughter, to get right all that I got terribly wrong the first time around. Alyce may be hard-headed at times, but she is nothing like her mother, and I've never wanted her to be. All these years, I've tried to protect my granddaughter from the truth. I wish Alyce could understand she is better off not knowing what all happened in that godforsaken neighborhood they all call Perishing Hill.

At the top of the staircase, I pause to catch my breath. It's getting harder and harder to get around these days. I start for the kitchen to find a glass, quench my thirst. Behind me, I hear heavy footsteps traveling upward, heading in the direction of the kitchen. My chest tightens in response. I twist from the cabinet to see if I can determine who is approaching, but it's too dark.

"Who's there?" I ask.

"Just me, Ms. Rosey," Griff says, rounding the corner.

"What are you doing up?"

"Same as you, I 'spect."

"You got your eye out for them then? Where have they all gotten to?"

Griff answers as he pulls a glass from the cabinet. "Got three of them on the beach; one of 'em, Frank, was in the hot tub earlier, but I haven't checked to see if he's still in there."

"Well, I haven't run into him. He must have returned to bed. Where's Kathryn?"

"She's on the beach with Melanie and Yvonne. You can see 'em out that window over there. Been keeping an eye on them, making sure they aren't so drunk they go running off into the ocean." Griff reaches for my empty glass and moves to fill both glasses with water from the kitchen sink.

He returns to stand next to me at the counter, offering me the water. "Sorry, it's not cold. No power to work the spout on the refrigerator."

I reach out to accept the glass. Even in the dark, with his facial features obscured by the lack of lighting, Griff is a formidable figure. His stature alone states he is not a man to be messed with.

"Have you seen Alyce anywhere? I can't find her." I sip from the glass of water.

Griff shakes his head. "Nope, haven't seen her. My guess is she's off with that fiancé—haven't found him yet either."

"He's probably hiding from Patrick. I can't imagine what that boy went through during his childhood with a parent like Pat Perkins. Speaking of Pastor Perkins...."

"Not sure of his whereabouts either," Griff anticipates, shaking his head. "Just know he's not with his wife."

"Well, if Alyce and Jude are together, they're not in her bedroom."

"Could be they're on the beach as well, and I just didn't see them." Griff pauses, eyeing the cell phone in my hand. "Are you recording us?"

I look down to see the light on my phone indeed displays the recording in process. "Goodness, I didn't realize. I've gotten into the habit of recording conversations to play back later." Griff continues to study me with a distrustful eye. "Disturbingly, my memory just isn't what it used to be."

I turn away from his scrutiny to place my glass on the counter. "Any news on the weather? This crew going to be able to pull out of here in the morning?"

"Nah," he says, his posturing easing as he turns to place his glass on the side of the sink next to mine. "Ferries aren't running 'til this thing moves through."

"Well, then, I'd say there's work to be done."

"Ma'am?"

I think for a moment about the best possible way to phrase this. "We need to try the best we can to circumvent some old storylines that might arise. This group has quite a bit of history. No telling what they're going to say or do to one another next," I explain.

"They seem to be getting along pretty well," Griff says, stooping, searching the cabinet compartment under the sink.

"Take my word for it; they're just getting warmed up. We'll need to monitor them closely." Griff continues to rifle through the contents of the cabinet. "What are you looking for down there?"

"Flashlight. Had one in my room, but it's gone, along with my keys. Can't imagine which one of your friends took them from my bedroom."

"I did say they were reprehensible, and they're not my friends. We share unpleasant history, is all." I watch Griff press the button on the flashlight. When nothing happens, he beats the handle against his open palm and tries again. This time, a spotlight appears on the far wall.

"Why the flashlight drama? What has happened to the electricity?"

Griff sweeps the light source across the room. "Gone. Lost the generator, too."

"You assured me you had it under control, Griff. You said we wouldn't be without power this weekend."

"I know, Ms. Rosey. Don't worry. Probably something got knocked off-line, is all. I'll fix it. Just have to get out there and figure out what went wrong." Griff uses the flashlight to peer inside a drawer, rummage through its contents, and pull out a pack of new batteries. He shoves them into his jacket pocket.

"You think it was the storm? Lightning hit it?"

"No, ma'am. We ain't had no lightning to speak of yet. Just some heat lightning going on out there right now, but it won't be long. We'll be dealing with the real thing 'fore you know it."

"So, no idea how long we could be down?"

"I'll have a better idea as soon as I get a good look at it. I'm headed outside right now to see what kind of damage we got going on. Just had to find a flashlight. Before I do, I want to check one more time on the women. They're tying one on down there near the water's edge."

"You're going down to the beach now?"

"Not if I can help it. I can see them from here. Just gonna take a look out of the window over there, make sure they aren't doing anything stupid."

Griff points the light at the floor and begins moving toward the other side of the room. I follow behind, staying close to make use of the light while it's available. Griff slows a bit, turning to check that I'm still behind him. We come to a stop in front of the wall of windows. The ocean beyond is black and ominous. No beams from the moon to cast a shimmering light over the vast sea.

"Do you see them?" I ask.

Griff points. "Over there. See. Wait a second. What is she doing?"

"Looks like she's undressing to me."

Griff looks at me. "The preacher's wife? Oh, hell. What is she thinking? Surely, she's not going into that water with this storm on the way." Lightning flashes on cue, lighting up the sky, briefly illuminating the scene on the beach. "That's only heat lightning," Griff says, nodding slightly at the scene outside the windows. "But like I said, won't be long 'til the real thing arrives."

From the safety of the house, I watch Kathryn and Yvonne pull Melanie away from the ocean's edge, picking up Melanie's discarded clothing as they drag her back toward the house. The three laugh, their heads thrown back, hair whipping in the wind. While Yvonne works to get Melanie back into her robe, I glance farther down the beach.

Griff moves to start toward the stairs. "Guess I'm gonna have to go down there and bring those three back inside."

"Griff?" I call out, halting his progress.

"Ma'am?"

"Come back," I say, never taking my eyes from the scene outside the window. "Do you see that?"

"What you got there?"

I motion for him to look away from the horizon and down the beach. "That way. There. To the right."

Griff shifts closer, peering out.

"See. Just there. It looks like a man." But I've lost sight of him."Where did he go? He was there."

"I don't see anyone, Ms. Rosey. Could be the lack of light and the cloud formations messing with your eyes."

"I don't think so, Griff. I know I saw a man. He was there." Griff scans the beach, but the man is gone.

"Maybe it was one of your neighbors. You did say you all are always looking out for one another. Someone saw the women seaside and decided to check on them?"

"Doubtful. O'cokers don't fool with these weathermakers. No one gets out unless it's an emergency. Could you tell what the man looked like? Maybe it was Terry or Frank; could've been Patrick. 'Course he's probably gonna be about ripe if it is him.

Pastor's wife is out there performing a striptease on the beach. Probably be in for a pretty good sermon, if I had to guess."

"Patrick has no choice but to accept his wife's promiscuous behavior. And believe me, he's had plenty of time to come to terms with it. But I don't think it was Patrick or any of the other men in our group. This man looked older somehow."

"Regardless, I still need to go get them and bring them back inside before someone else gets hurt," Griff states as he watches me. He must surely think I'm crazy, seeing strange men in the dead of night. But I know what I saw and continue to scan the beach for the man.

"There! Right there. See him. He's wearing a long gray coat. Wait, that man doesn't have any legs."

"Oh hell," Griff exclaims, twisting quickly to view outside again. "It's the Gray Man."

"The who?"

"I gotta get down there now. He's going to scare the daylights out of those women."

"Griff," I call, following as fast as I can go in the dark without falling and risking a break. "Are they in danger? Should I call someone for help?"

Griff turns, halting suddenly. "Stay here, Ms. Rosey. I'll take care of this."

"But are you...."

"He can't hurt them. It's mostly just local folklore. The Gray Man is a ghost. He shows up to warn islanders of an approaching storm."

Alyce

My eyes flutter open, taking in the dimly lit room. Recall sluggish after the late night, it takes a moment to pinpoint where I am. Dune Dweller. Gabe died at the lighthouse. The power went out; I went looking for Jude only to find his father.

What time is it? Tell me I haven't overslept. Dull gray light fills the room. I look at the sliding glass door across the way. Dark clouds skirt by, wind fiercely serenading them along. Rain falls steadily. I guess the storm has arrived. Hopefully, this will be the worst of it.

Sounds of soft snoring fill the room. I turn toward the noise, finding Jude asleep next to me. Dammit. Mr. Perkins is going to throw one heck of a fit when he finds out.

I push myself to a sitting position. "Jude," I whisper, tapping his arm. Shaking his shoulder, "Wake up."

Jude's eyes open, meeting mine. "Hey there, gorgeous." He gives me that smile, the one that makes me forget the rest of the world.

"Don't do that," I say, trying to mask the grin working its way up my face.

"Do what?" Jude pulls me into his arms, kissing me deeply. The feeling is delicious.

I reluctantly push him away. "Act all endearing and innocent. You fell asleep. You promised you would leave once I dozed off last night."

"I know. I just crashed. I can't believe how tired I was. Besides, I love waking up next to you."

"Okay, but you've got to get up and get out of here," I say, pushing him toward the other side of the bed. "Your dad..."

Jude rolls toward me, grabs hold of me, pulling me down on top of him. "You're kicking me out? I just woke up," he pleads through soft kisses.

"Jude, ugh, seriously. Everyone will be up... and moving about... and looking for us—if they aren't already." I push away quickly, twisting toward the edge of the bed.

Jude proves faster, pulling me back down and throwing the covers over our heads. I look at him under the tented sheet. There's something extremely romantic about this action, and I wish again it was just the two of us. "I would stay in this bed with you all day if I could. But the truth is, your father will lose his shit if he finds out you spent the night in my bed."

"Look at what a quick understudy you are," Jude claims, giving me that mischievous, boyish grin that gets me every time. "Don't worry. I'm used to daddy-o's tantrums. And besides, I've spent lots of nights in your bed." Jude wrestles an arm around my waist, tugging me closer. "I know what I'm doing and how to do it." Another wicked grin. "I'm armed and dangerous." I giggle. Oh, this man.

"That may very well be the case, but your daddy isn't aware of all those fun-filled, dangerous evenings." And I don't want him to know about last night either, especially since I disappeared on the rest of my late-night hunting party during the wee hours of the morning—and without explanation.

"He'll never know what happened. Dad thought I was with Mom. Mom was drunk and assumed I went to bed."

"I know. I was there. And you," I poke at his chest in a teasing manner. "You run around snatching women away from their search parties while they're out trying to see to everyone's safety. They're probably still wondering where I went."

"Come on now. Admit it. You weren't too worried about finding anybody but me," Jude says, holding firmly to my middle, keeping me forcefully pressed close to him—well, not too forcefully. The pleasurable sigh escapes before I can squelch it.

"I'll admit I had a much better time in bed with you than I did tromping through a dark, creepy house, looking for the others. I wonder if they found everyone."

"If who found what?" Jude asks, moving to kiss the spot under my earlobe.

"That is totally unfair, and you know it."

"Um," Jude moans, ignoring my pleas.

"What am I going to do with you?" I ask, giving in to the kiss Jude offers.

"I've got plenty of ideas."

"We have to stop." Truth be told, I'm not fighting him off with any real resistance, though.

"I need a better reason than appeasing my dad."

"Where's my phone? What time is it?"

"Time for you to lighten up, my love."

"Jude. I have guests to attend to." I pull away from him, throwing the sheet off and checking my phone on the nightstand. "It's eight o'clock." I run my fingers through my hair. "I can NOT believe we slept so late. There's no signal strength on my phone. Do you have cell service?"

"Service, schmervice. Griff said we'd be lucky to keep cell service this weekend, especially with this storm moving in. Come back to bed. I'll show you some service," Jude says playfully.

"I can't. It's late, Jude."

"It's not that late," Jude says, pulling me back down into the bed.

I sit up and pull away from Jude's embrace, though it's the

only place I want to be. "Someone has got to keep things under control."

"I think we've long passed the opportunity for control," Jude says, slipping his hand under my nightshirt.

I smack his hand away but can't suppress the giggle at the back of my throat. Jude takes this as a sign of consent and moves in for a deeper kiss.

His lips touch mine gently as his tongue moves—BOOM. BOOM. BOOM. Someone pounds on the other side of my bedroom door.

"Alyce," a man's voice calls. "Are you in there? Open this door, missy."

"It's my dad." Jude flips to his back in defeat.

"What do we do? Should you hide?"

Jude looks at me, cutting his eyes and dragging his top lip into a snarl. It's a look that says quite definitively, hell no.

From the hallway, Patrick calls out, "Is my son in there with you? I hope you're decent. I'm coming in."

Patrick

On the other side of the door, I hear muffled voices—giggling. That girl is in there, and she's got my son with her. I knew it. All that nonsense last night—nothing but a ruse to throw me off track. No doubt about what they've been up to. I was once a young man myself.

"What the hell is going on in there?" I pound on the door. "That's it. Time's up; I'm coming in." I move to grab the doorknob.

The door swings open. Jude stands in front of me, boxers gaping open.

"Jesus, son. For the love of God, put on some pants."

"I don't need pants for what I'm doing, Dad."

"Don't be flippant with me, boy."

"Good morning, Mr. Perkins," Alyce says as she sashays to

stand next to Jude, tying up her robe, tossing that long hair over one shoulder.

"That's debatable," I reply. "Let's go, Jude."

"Go where? I just got up."

"We're leaving. I'm heading to round up Griff next; get him to fire up the van. It's time to go." I step aside, motioning for Jude to come through the threshold.

Jude stays planted next to Alyce. Whether it's the light of day or the act of finally allowing myself to get a good look at this girl, the resemblance to her mother is uncanny. I can't believe I didn't notice it when we met yesterday.

"Come on. You need to get your things together," I command my bull-headed, horny son. My gaze finds Alyce again. And her mannerisms—my God—how did I not see it? Incredible. I'd forgotten.

"Dad," Jude says, pulling me from reverie. "Are you listening?"

"Of course. What was it you were saying?"

Jude shakes his head and begins again. "Number one, my things are in this room, our room. Number two, I'm not leaving. This weekend is important to Alyce, and Alyce is important to me. So, if you need help with your bags, I'll be right there to give you a hand. Just let me get dressed, and I'll meet you in your room."

"Dammit, Jude. This isn't negotiable."

"You're right, Dad. It isn't." This boy may have Melanie beat in the arena of stubbornness. I'm going to have to appeal to the one person he can't deny, and while it may be underhanded, it's for his own good.

"If you insist on staying, then I can't stop you, son. But listen, we don't know how bad this storm is going to get. We're right here at the edge of the ocean, Jude. This is dangerous for both you and Alyce. We need to get going, to get out of here while we still can. The others are in agreement as well. None of us wants to get stuck on this island. So you see, Alyce isn't going to get the answers she's looking for anyway. Even if everyone decided to stay, to ride out this storm, to take their chance, think about it, Alyce. As it is, one of your guests is already dead. You don't want another tragedy on your hands."

"Christ, Dad. You act like Alyce is responsible for Gabe's death."

"Boy."

"Don't start your bible sermon bullshit. It no longer works on me. You can shame me, chastise me, threaten me, but from now on, all my decisions are made with my partner, my future wife, and when we're ready, I'll let you know what we decide."

"That storm has done all of us a huge favor by moving so slowly. God has done us a favor. It should be sitting on top of us right now, but we still have time." I look from Jude to Alyce and add, "Before anyone else gets hurt or worse."

Alyce looks at Jude, her nerves on display.

"Well, then. I'm going to find Griff, grab a cup of coffee. I'm sure I'll see you both before we leave for the ferry." I turn slowly and pad down the hallway toward the staircase. Behind me, a flurry of hushed words fly through the air—and then the door closes.

twenty-four

TIME TO GO

Carmen

The empty suitcase lies atop the unmade bed. Only yesterday, Gabe and I had been unpacking this very bag, anxious and apprehensive about what this mysterious weekend event had in store for us. Gabe was still alive then. We had one another to lean on, to count on, to go through the experiences of life together. Now, I am alone. I must face what comes next solo—all those plans we made for our future ripped from the spiral notebook, leaving nothing behind but messy shreds and jagged edges. I just can't believe that Gabe did this because Gabe wouldn't do this. He wouldn't leave me.

And I wouldn't be leaving Gabe right now either, if not for Terry. Terry pulled me to the side last night after we found the other women on the beach. He escorted me back to my room and offered to arrange for Gabe's body to be transported back to Norfolk. Terry assured me I wouldn't be alone throughout the process and that he and Yvonne would handle all the burial arrangements through their funeral home. While I appreciate their kindness more than I can relay, it doesn't change the fact I've lost the love of my life and now have to figure out a way to carry on.

I begin transferring items from the dresser to the suitcase, but Gabe's things give me pause. My throat thickens, closing off my airway. Warm wetness bathes my cheeks. Not right now; I slam the case closed and plop down on the bed beside it. I can't.

Last night, Yvonne offered to pack up our things if I found it too much to handle. Maybe later, I will find the strength to do so, or I will allow myself to lean on those who want to help. Honestly, I don't have the energy to shrug off the offers, much less to accomplish the simple tasks of getting through a day without Gabe.

I stand from the bed, take a tissue from the box, dry my face, and go in search of a friend.

Terry

Yvonne offers me a towel as I step out of the shower. "Thanks, hon."

"Mmm," she replies.

"You feeling okay this morning? Late night," I say, waiting for her to pick up the conversation. Yvonne continues her makeup routine, staring silently at her reflection. I try again. "Stormy night; bit of lightning and thunder."

"Yes, husband, you are correct." She pulls a tissue from the holder and blots her lips.

"You disappeared for a while."

"I told you I was down at the beach with the other women." Yvonne searches the contents of her makeup bag, dodging the inquiry.

"I'm talking about after that. I was worried. Did you take your medication?"

She clears the counter, tossing everything into her bag, zipping it closed. "You know I did, Terry; otherwise, I wouldn't have been good company to anyone. I only took half a pill, if you must know."

"I worry, is all. Thought you might blackout again. Like last time."

Yvonne ignores my last statement, effectively ending the topic. "I'm going to finish throwing my toiletries into the suitcase and head upstairs for coffee. You want me to bring you some, or do you want to go up with me?"

"Give me a minute to put on some clothes?"

"Of course," she says, leaving the bathroom, her arms full of toiletries she intends to repack for the journey home.

Dressed and ready for travel, Yvonne and I traverse the staircase, making our way upward to the kitchen. "I was hoping it would be warmer up here," I say, rounding the corner for the top floor of Dune Dweller. "I guess we should just be thankful for the power we do have, huh? Without that generator, we wouldn't have had a semi-warm shower and chargers for our electronics—not that I am getting any signal on my phone."

Yvonne follows behind. "Let's not talk about generators. You know how I feel about them."

"I know, but without this one in particular, your daily caffeine fix would suffer greatly. And, thereby, so would I," I say, turning to plant a teasing kiss on her nose. Then I think of Griff's list, the one Alyce mentioned last night, and hope that the coffee maker did indeed make the list of 'emergency electrical items,' or we're all going to experience malaise.

Carmen stands at the kitchen counter, staring out the window at the ocean. Hearing our approach, she turns. "I can see why Griff likes this island. It's peaceful," she says, stepping away from the window. Carmen busies herself, opening cabinets, searching for coffee mugs, sugar, and spoons, gathering all the items for the morning brew, and situating them on the countertop. "Coffee's almost ready. Terry, will you see if there is any creamer in the fridge?"

Thank goodness for small caffeinated favors, I think, and turn toward the fridge.

"I made sure to have Griff pick some up as part of the ordered provisions," Alyce says, stepping into the room, Jude following close behind her.

"Good morning, Alyce," Yvonne says politely. It isn't until this moment that I realize I didn't offer Carmen the ritual of a morning greeting.

I nod at Alyce and Jude, glad to see Alyce is fine and well after abandoning our search last night. "Good morning, you two." I head toward the refrigerator, hoping to be of some help. "You all sleep okay after last evening's late escapades?"

Carmen looks at Alyce and says, "You left us last night. We didn't know where you went." Her words hint at accusation mixed with flustered worry.

"I'm so sorry," Alyce starts. "I do hope you all didn't worry about me too much. This one," she turns to punch Jude's arm, "abducted me, quite literally, and dragged me off to bed."

"Lucky you," Yvonne teases.

"Depends on who you ask," Patrick says by way of announcing his arrival, Melanie bypassing him and moving in Carmen's direction. We all watch as Melanie walks to Carmen and pulls her into an embrace.

"Good morning, all," Melanie says, releasing Carmen from her hold.

"Oh good, there's coffee." Patrick maneuvers around the others, takes a cup from the counter, and heads directly to the coffee pot. He pours a cup and moves into the other room, where he positions himself in front of the floor-to-ceiling wall of windows, looking out, slurping obnoxiously.

"I guess the coffee's ready," Carmen announces, looking in Patrick's direction, his rude actions recognized by all and ignored by the same.

Melanie rubs her hand over Carmen's back once more, then turns to address the rest of us. "Anyone for coffee?" The group all speaks in the affirmative while Melanie doles out coffee mugs. The last mug she passes to Jude before placing a kiss on his cheek and inquiring about his sleep.

. . .

Rosey

The group huddles in the kitchen; spoons tink against cups, muffled conversations fill the open space.

Alyce spots me before the others realize I've stepped into the room and hurries to my side. "Morning, Rosey," she says, kissing my cheek. "Can I get you a cup of coffee?"

"That would be fabulous, love. Thank you." Alyce scurries away, leaving me to survey the group. Melanie and Jude hold a private conversation while Terry and Yvonne stand with Carmen, heads close, serious.

"Good to see everyone getting along," I say, approaching the trio.

"Morning, Rosey," Terry says. "I trust your sleep was gratifying; if not, then I hope at the very least it was satisfying?"

"Yes, thank you, Terry. It's nice to know a few members of this group understand the art of politeness." I look toward the wall of windows at the far end of the room. "What's up with Patrick this morning? He's behaving?"

"So far, so good," Yvonne answers. "He's been rather tame, actually."

"Don't get too excited," Melanie says as she comes to stand next to Yvonne. "His coffee hasn't kicked in yet," her disparaging tone more bitter than the substance she sips.

Alyce approaches Jude at her side. "Are Kathryn and Frank up yet?" Alyce asks, passing over the full coffee mug to me. "Here you go, Rosey."

"I haven't seen Kathryn or Frank yet," Melanie says. "I'm sure it's going to take Kathryn a bit to pull herself together this morning. A: She doesn't have her make-up team to glamorize her, and B: She drank a lot of vodka last night, which she washed down with wine beachside."

"Terry, Patrick, and I ran into Frank last night when we were looking for Griff, but I've not seen Frank since then," Carmen relays, looking to Terry for confirmation.

Terry nods, sipping from his cup, then adds, "He was headed to find Kathryn. That was after you ladies had that fright surfside."

"What happened?" Alyce asks, alarm marking her features. "Is everyone okay?"

Melanie places her empty mug on the counter. "We found a ghost."

"What? You did? On the beach?" Alyce cannot veil her intrigue. All of her short life, she has been fascinated with ghost stories and tales of ghoulish folklore.

"I never saw it," Yvonne says.

"He was there," Melanie insists. "I'm not lying or embellishing, even though some might say so."

"You saw a ghost on the beach?" Jude asks.

"Careful, honey," Melanie addresses Jude. "You're starting to sound like your father. He didn't believe me either."

"Sorry, Mom. Of course, I believe you. Just shocking to hear you string those words together."

"It's true," I say, feeling the need to back up Melanie's story. "We saw him from the very window Patrick stands in front of. Griff called him the Gray Man."

"The Gray Man. Wait, I read about him while researching this area," Alyce says. She looks at Jude. "Remember? I told you locals report seeing him right before a bad storm is due. They say he appears as a warning for people to take shelter."

"The scariest part of the experience was the man's look—one minute, he had legs; the next, they were gone. He never got near anyone, not from my vantage point," I tell them. "By the time Griff got down to the beach to warn the ladies, the figure had disappeared."

"Yeah, along with Kathryn," Yvonne says. "Maybe that's why she ran off so quickly," she says to Melanie.

"Kathryn told me she was going to find Frank," Melanie

relays. "I was exhausted and went straight to bed. I didn't see her after that. Come to think of it, I saw no one after returning from the beach last night—not even you," she says to Pat as he rejoins the group around the counter. "Where were you, Patrick?"

"Where was I what?" Pat asks.

"You weren't in our bedroom last night when I returned from the beach."

"I told you last night—I was looking for you and Jude," Patrick says.

"Figures," Melanie drawls. "Never around when I need a man."

Patrick lays both hands on the countertop. "And what did you need a man for at two o'clock in the morning, Melanie?"

Melanie laughs maniacally, then says, "To protect me from the Gray Man, of course. What other purpose could you possibly serve at that hour?"

Patrick misses the diss Melanie has delivered, instead retorting, "A ghost? You want me to save you from some ridiculous child's story, some make-believe nonsense Griff and this girl have put into your head?"

"Now Patrick, according to studies, these urban legends all have some semblance of truth to them," Terry contributes. "As a matter of fact, I also read about the Gray Man prior to our arrival. Multiple accounts have been relayed, all attributing credit to this apparition for saving their lives with his advanced warning of these storm systems moving into the area."

"Well, I don't see any storm. Just a bit wet out," Patrick says. "Sounds like a bunch of hogwash to me."

"Try not to use all your fancy talk in one place." Yvonne delivers a cutting glare at the man.

"Has anyone seen Griff this morning?" I ask, deflecting.

"He was outside earlier," Carmen says. "I happened to catch a glimpse of him from the window while I was waiting for the coffee to brew."

"Probably out there with his prize generator," Patrick spews.

"Don't be so hateful. At least we have partial power. I, for one, am grateful to have had a hot shower and my morning coffee, especially given how cold our room was this morning." Melanie says.

"Yes," I confirm. "Griff said something about losing the heating units for the first and second floor but that the third-floor HVAC unit was working. However, the generator can't handle powering the HVAC unit and all the other items pulling energy, so it has to run on its own."

"Lots of stipulations..." Yvonne says absently.

"It has something to do with having enough fuel and juice to keep the heat running," I reply. "From what I gathered, the heating unit is only on Griff's 'emergency electrical units list' to warm up the top floor this morning, and then he was going to have to cut it."

Yvonne looks at Terry and shrugs. "Layer up then, I guess."

"Can I get anyone some breakfast?" Alyce changes the subject. "The kitchen is stocked, and we have power to these appliances. I'm happy to cook."

"Nope. No time to eat," Patrick says, draining the last dregs from his mug and slamming it down onto the countertop. Time to get going," he says. Hands on hips, he looks at Melanie and Jude. "Y'all go get your things. I'll go find Griff."

"I thought Griff said the ferries weren't going to be running," I relay. Patrick has never listened to reason. I don't know why I would suspect that man might start now.

"That was last night, this is this morning. I don't see a storm. Do you see a storm? It's just raining, people. 'Fraid of getting wet?" Patrick patronizes. "I'm sure we can hire a boat at the marina to take us back to the mainland."

Carmen steps closer. "I don't know about that. Have you looked west, on the sound side, back toward the mainland? It may look like only rain outside the window, but there's a different story being told in that direction."

"All the more reason to get moving," Patrick continues his

rant. He grabs Jude's mug, yanking. The liquid sloshes over the lip of the cup.

"Jesus, Dad. Calm down," Jude exclaims, jumping back to avoid the staining substance from marring his crisply pressed khakis. He walks to retrieve a paper towel from the other side of the kitchen. "I already told you I'm staying with Alyce."

Jude

Griff blows in as I clean up the coffee mess Dad made, top off my cup. He hovers behind me, waiting. A crackling noise sounds from the walkie-talkie clipped to his belt—nothing audible, however.

"Better get settled in 'cause you're all staying with Alyce—and me." Griff takes the coffee pot from me, busies himself with the task of preparing his drink, slurps, then turns to face the group.

We all watch and wait. Next to me, I feel Dad bow up again, readying for battle.

"What the hell are you talking about, man? Settle in for what? A trip to the funny farm?"

"Oh, don't be so dramatic, darling," Mom retorts.

"You mean cliché, I'm sure," Yvonne says.

"That too," Mom mumbles under her breath, sipping again from her mug.

Griff swallows and wipes his beard. "Storm's here. Told y'all last night it was on the way."

"Like a damn broken record…," Dad starts.

"And there go the clichés again," Yvonne counters.

"There's not a cloud in the sky," Dad waves his arm erratically in the direction of the windows. "I'm not buying this storm malarkey."

Yvonne continues to spar. "You're on a roll this morning, Pat. Careful, don't want you to 'strain the brain' too early out of bed now."

Dad ignores Yvonne and continues to berate Griff. "I've had it with your crappy weather reports. You said last night that the storm was blowing in, and no storm was seen. And here you go again with this bull crap when look," Dad motions toward the wall of windows once more. "Do any of you see a storm cloud in the sky?"

Outside the windows, gloomy gray clouds continue to multiply, stitching together to block the sun.

"Nope, none out there," Griff concurs. "It's coming from the west. Forecasters have us under a tornado watch right now."

"Griff is telling you like it is, Patrick. I pulled the weather forecast when I awoke this morning." Rosey tries to talk some sense into Dad. "The storm slowed significantly overnight, releasing a deluge of rain. Evidently, several communities in the path of the storm are now suffering severe flooding."

"So then, let's move it out before the storm gets here. Griff, get the van. Take us to the marina. We're packed. I'm not waiting on the rest of y'all. We're getting out of here."

Griff shakes his head without replying. I get it. As the man's son, it is impossible even for me to get through to him. Come to think of it, I don't know if I've ever witnessed anyone make him understand or accept an alternate viewpoint.

"The ferries aren't running, and no one is going to take a boat out in this, Dad."

"I've had enough of your mouth, young man. Contradicting everything I say. Melanie, talk some sense into your son and meet me outside at the van. I'll get the bags."

Patrick storms off.

"He'll figure it out," Melanie says. "In the meantime, I'm going to make more coffee. Anybody else want another cup?"

twenty-five

THE STORM IS HERE BUT WHERE IS EVERYONE

Melanie

"Did you all hear that? I'm fairly certain that was thunder," Alyce says. Before any of us can respond, the crack of lightning rings through the house. The sound startles me, and I jump involuntarily.

Yvonne teases. "You know what they say, Melanie. It's the menopausal women who frighten easily." Her comment is nothing more than a deflection technique. Yvonne can make light all she likes, but I remember. Does Yvonne really think we've all forgotten? How many times did we witness her toss back one of her 'chill-pill cocktails' and forget what happened the rest of the evening? Every time there was storm potential, that's when—too many times to count. She can't fool me. Admittedly, she held it together last night when we were all on the beach, but that was just a tiny precursor of the storm compared to what is happening outside right now.

"I guess we're quite the pair then," I toss back. "Jokes aside, that was really close."

"'Pert near now," Griff agrees.

"Griff," Rosey calls from the other side of the room. "Will you run downstairs and make sure Melanie's husband doesn't get himself struck by lightning with this foolish agenda he insists on following?"

"'Course, Ms. Rosey," Griff says obediently, then runs off downstairs, doing as he's told. There's an interesting dynamic between those two. I don't know that the others have witnessed it, but I certainly have.

Jude and Alyce step aside, heads close in whispered conversation. I glance in Rosey's direction to see she is also watching the exchange. Alyce seems to be a lovely young woman. Creds to Rosey, I suppose. Jude has had plenty of girlfriends in the past, though he has never exhibited the depth of feelings for any of them that he displays for Alyce. The truth is neither of them can keep their hands to themselves. They. Can't. Stop. Touching. One. Another. Must a body part be connected somehow during every waking moment? If the two of them display this much affection in public, I can only imagine what they do in private... oh, ew, stop that, Melanie. A mother shouldn't think such thoughts about her child. Patrick maintains they aren't sleeping together, saying that Jude has been raised in a God-fearing home and knows the importance of a woman's virtue. My husband seems to forget that when he was Jude's age, he frequently reminded me that he was in his sexual prime and had no intentions of wasting it. Jude and Alyce would make beautiful babies, no doubt—provided they are Jude's, of course. I shouldn't say that about my kid, but hey, I'm not. I'm saying it about Amber's kid. One does have to wonder how far the apple fell. I shudder thinking of my own use of a cliché. Yvonne would be ever so disappointed in me.

Seriously though, if this engagement holds after this weekend, I'm going to have to try harder to like the girl, at the very least, get to know her. And then there's the whole Rosey thing—she'll be an in-law. I can't imagine Patrick welcoming either of the women into our family. Amber and I got along fine back in the day, but that doesn't mean I'm eager to have her daughter marry my son. Yes, I admit it. A piece of me is hoping they don't make it through this weekend. I'm rooting for Patrick's success in breaking them apart. Although I'm not sure what Patrick's reasoning is for wanting their separation, mine, of course, is wholly selfish. Jude is my son, my only child, and I am not ready to give up my status as the most important woman in his life.

"Careful, Melanie," Rosey says in a hushed voice, approaching me at the counter. "Your thoughts are written all over your face."

"Okay, I'll play. Give it your best shot. What's on my mind, Rosey?"

"Jealousy, of course, my dear. It's only natural. A mother's son, choosing his life partner, leaving behind the one female confidant he's kept all throughout his upbringing."

I consider Rosey's words. She's right. That was always the thing with Rosey. She always had to be right. The more concerning piece of knowledge, however, is that she usually was—she always saw what the rest of us never saw coming.

Terry

Boom—the volume of nature's boisterous tune performs at one of its highest decibels. Windows rattle, and the floor under our feet vibrates. The raucous storm startles everyone around the kitchen counter this time. I walk toward the wall of windows to view the weather outside Dune Dweller. At water's edge, sand swirls into mini funnels racing over and around the dunes. Blam. A long streak of white lightning cuts a hole through the darkening sky—the entire house rattling with the proximity of the strike as it hits the sand right outside the window. Thunder follows closely behind, announcing that this storm means business.

"Come away from that window," Rosey says forcefully.

Jude yanks Alyce by the wrist, pulling her away from the scene beyond the glass.

"It's fine, babe. We're inside. The storm is outside," Alyce says to Jude, softly stroking his arm.

Rosey counters. "Lightning can break windows. It may not be common, but it does happen."

Beside me, Yvonne trembles. She's cocooned herself inside her own embrace, making herself small. I run a hand along her back, draw her in closer to me, placing my arm around her, worrying over how much more of this she can handle. For as long as I've known my wife, she has experienced irrational fears during these weather makers. Throw a snake in her path, put her in a cave of bats, let spiders scurry through a dark, damp basement—Yvonne is bothered by none of it. Yvonne has come a long way in over-coming the phobia she's lived with all her life, but the big weather-making events still get to her.

"Everyone up here, okay?" Griff says, rounding the staircase once more. The man returns solo, without Patrick in tow per Rosey's previous instructions.

"Where's Patrick?" Melanie asks.

"Didn't see him," Griff returns. "Thought he gave up on his nonsense and came back up here with you all. Took a look around outside. He wasn't loading the luggage or anything. Went and checked the bedrooms. He wasn't in any of them either."

"Well, where did he go?" Jude asks. "He couldn't have gotten far without a vehicle."

Behind Jude and Alyce, outside the window, lightning flashes again. Though the proximity of this strike is nowhere near as close as the last bolt, I hold tighter to Yvonne, knowing the growl of thunder will follow.

"Maybe he went looking for a car or a way to get to the ferry?" Carmen theorizes.

"We're the only house on the beach. He'd be in for a heck of a trek. There aren't any homes nearby, and ain't nobody going out right now. O'cokers know better than to get out in a mess like the one brewing up out there," Griff relays.

"I wouldn't worry too much about Patrick," Melanie says. "He's probably off sulking somewhere because he didn't get his way."

"Griff," Alyce steps forward, pausing to collect her thoughts. "You said you checked the bedrooms?"

"I did," the man replies.

"Did you speak to Kathryn or Frank while you were searching? Are they still insisting on leaving today, as well?"

"No. I mean, no, I didn't find anyone in the bedrooms. I figured the two of them had made their way upstairs while I was outside looking for Patrick. They're not up here either?" Griff asks.

Alyce shakes her head, apprehension crinkling her forehead.

"Do you think they're out there in this storm?" Yvonne asks.

"I know you all think I'm overdoing it about how close-knit this community is, but most of the islanders knew you all would be here this weekend. If one of them spots a stranger out in this weather, rest assured that resident will reach out for me to come collect my guest before any harm comes."

"Perhaps Kathryn and Frank left under the cover of night," I suggest.

"I doubt that," Griff says. "Like I said, there's nowhere to go if the ferries aren't running, and they shut down routes last night. Besides that, when I opened the bedroom door to check for Patrick's whereabouts, Frank and Kathryn's things were scattered about the room." It's become difficult to ascertain if Griff is physically agitated by the current situation or perhaps is growing impatient, having to repeat himself. Nevertheless, the man appears disconcerted by the recent turn of circumstances.

In an effort to give Griff a moment to regroup, I address the others. "We should set up some ground rules before this storm really gets going."

"Then we'll need to gather the rest of the group first so that we have complete buy-in from everyone," Rosey announces. She's right, of course. Patrick will never go along with a plan for which he has no input, and if memory serves, Kathryn and Frank will most likely feel the same.

Another boom of thunder from outside. The room grows

dark, the sun completely obscured by ominous clouds settling over Dune Dweller. The temperature in the room drops in response. A crack of lightning rings through the silence. Yvonne audibly gasps this time. The others turn toward her in response.

"That sounds closer than before," Alyce says.

Thunder roars overhead.

"It is," I say to the rest of the crew. "We need to find the other three so that we...," I begin, my statement cut short by a loud banging noise from downstairs.

"What was that?" Carmen asks.

A male voice carries up the staircase. Immediate assessment does little to determine if the voice belongs to Patrick or Frank.

"Hurry. Come quick. Down here."

Jude asks, "Is that Dad?"

"Sure sounds like him," Melanie answers, rushing toward the staircase. Jude follows closely behind his mother as Alyce hurries to catch up to the pair making their descent. Temptation is too much for the group as we all follow suit, heading downstairs to learn the reason behind Patrick's urgent summons.

In the center of the recreation room, Patrick stands, one hand on the edge of the pool table to brace himself—bent at the waist, breathing heavily as the rest of our gang arrives.

"Out there," Patrick points to the outside patio area leading to the beach. "That door," he says, making little to no sense.

Alyce steps closer, asking, "Is there another ghost out there? Is the Gray Man back again?"

"No. I didn't see any damn ghosts," Patrick says breathlessly.

"Patrick, there is no reason to be confrontational," Melanie chides. "Alyce only asked a question."

Griff heads to the back door. I drop Yvonne's hand to follow, see if I can help somehow. Yvonne grabs my hand again, hurrying behind me, insisting she's coming too.

Outside, we hurry down the staircase, taking cover underneath the stilted house. Griff points to the right, indicating we should look in that direction while he takes the opposite side of the house. The wind has picked up significantly. Sand flies around our faces, attacking our eyes and noses, rooting into our scalps. The gusts catch us off guard and swerve us off our intended path. Yvonne fights to keep hair out of her eyes. The storm wastes no time settling in.

Rosey stands at the bottom of the staircase, head down, shielding her face from the flying sand. "Go back indoors," I shout, waving her back inside Dune Dweller. "The wind is too strong."

Rosey yells in response, but her words are picked up and carried away by the wind. She's pointing in the direction Griff followed moments ago. I shout back, shaking my head to indicate we can't hear what she is saying. Peppered syllables ride the wind, but I'm still unable to make any sense of her words. She continues to motion in the direction Griff took furiously.

"I think Rosey is trying to tell us to follow Griff," I say, tugging Yvonne closer. "Let's head over that way and take a look." Yvonne nods her understanding, and we begin to move back toward Dune Dweller.

"Can you hear what she's saying?" Yvonne asks. I shake my head in response.

As we approach, I see the others crowded underneath Dune Dweller near the alcove housing the hot tub.

I halt suddenly, causing Yvonne to bump me from behind. My gaze locks on what the others view.

"Oh my God," Yvonne says, placing a hand over her mouth. A sob escapes as she turns her head into my chest to obscure the sight of Kathryn and Frank floating in the hot tub.

Yvonne

"What in the hell is going on with this house?" Patrick rants, pacing the length of the recreation room. "First, Gabe falls to his death, and now Frank and Kathryn boil to death in the hot tub."

"Jesus, Patrick." I can no longer hold my tongue. "Don't be so callous, so graphic, so morbid. Watch your words, man."

Patrick continues to stride across the room, his hands cutting the air wildly to accentuate his points. "Be careful, Yvonne. The way people are dying around here, you should think twice before committing blasphemy."

"Oh, good grief. Can we move past this man's temper tantrum and discuss the fact that Frank and Kathryn are dead?" Carmen, who has barely said a word, finds her voice. It's hard to imagine how these new deaths must be affecting her.

"This isn't some tantrum." Patrick raises his voice another couple of decibels. "I'm trying to come up with a solution to get us out of here."

"Stop being so damned obstinate, Patrick," Rosey says from across the room. "Griff has explained multiple times that there is no way off this island until the storm passes."

"People are dropping left and right, and that ogre tells me I can't leave? Nope. Unh-unh. This doesn't work for me. There must be a car service for hire somewhere."

"And how do you propose to get across Pamlico Sound, Dad? Are you going to swim? Is there some amphibious vehicle dealership here on the island we haven't been made aware of?" Jude asks Patrick.

"Don't start that smart-ass shit with me, boy." We watch as the father and son stand face to face, bowed up, ready to go at one another.

"First of all, I'm not a child anymore, Dad. More to the point, however, is that you are the one acting incredibly immature. Griff has already explained to us that the ferries can't run during these storms."

"I'm the only one thinking around here," Patrick says, then turns to address Griff. "You claim to know everyone on the whole damn island. You must know someone with a boat. The ferries might not be able to get into their ports, but surely one of the fishing boats we passed on the way to the house yesterday can be hired to take us off this godforsaken island."

"On a good day, yes, I could ask one of my buddies to run you to the mainland. But newsflash, Pastor Perkins, we're in the middle of a tropical storm."

"Exactly. A tropical storm, not a goddamn hurricane," Patrick continues his rant.

"I'm curious, Patrick, in this blasphemous situation, which do you prefer to be, the pot or the kettle?" I ask. The man has lost it. I'm doing all I can to control my anxiety, but Patrick Perkins is pushing me way beyond my limits.

Terry tries reasoning with Patrick. "The bickering, this blatant disregard for Griff's knowledge of the situation, is doing none of us any service, Pat. We must come together in a cohesive manner now, in this time of grief and death."

"This isn't one of your cheap funeral speeches, Terry." Patrick paces the floor in front of the pool table.

Melanie uses the other side of the room for pacing, her arms crossed over her midsection, holding firmly to her body. "Patrick, stop being such an asshole."

"Amen," Terry says under his breath.

"I've had enough—of all of you," Rosey announces, her sleek gray bob smoothed back into place. She turns to address Griff. "We need a plan for the bodies, aside from allowing them to lie in the elements."

"Yes, ma'am. I've got one. Might need a bit of muscle to help me out though," Griff answers.

Jude steps away from Alyce's side. "I'll help."

I tug at Terry's arm. "You go ahead, honey. Help them out. You're the one who knows what to do, how to care for the bodies."

"You're sure you're okay?" I nod in response. Terry squeezes my hand, then follows Griff and Jude outside.

Melanie stops pacing. "You're not going to give them a hand?" She asks Patrick.

"I plan on it. I was just about to ask the ladies if they all feel safe enough for me to leave you all alone."

"Ever the gentleman," Rosey scoffs.

"Thank you, Mr. Perkins. I think we'll be fine to look after ourselves," Alyce announces. "I'm sure the others would appreciate your assistance." Patrick huffs and makes his exit.

Carmen sits on the sofa, head down, nervously picking at her fingernails and cuticles. Alyce stares out the window—though there's nothing to see, with the massive dunes blocking the view of the ocean—while Rosey watches her protectively from a stool at the bar. I walk toward Melanie, pulling her away from the path she has worn on the floor underneath her. We step together to take a seat on either side of Carmen and wait in silence with our thoughts. The weather outside grows more ominous by the second. The wind howls. The skies darken. Rain begins to pound at the dunes.

Alyce turns away from the window to address us. "What happened to them?" She asks, her voice catching with emotion.

"They drowned, darling," Rosey answers.

"I'm not five, Rosey. You all saw their bodies. They were bloated and blistered, discolored. I realize this sounds naive, especially given my declaration of being older than a toddler, but do you think they really boiled to death?" Alyce silences as she takes in each of us. "Like Mr. Perkins suggested? Could that be true? I mean, it's just too awful to think about."

"No darling," Melanie offers, softening towards Alyce, sounding almost motherly. "I have a feeling Kathryn and Frank were dead, long before the chemical burns occurred to their skin," Melanie says.

"Then how exactly did they die?" Carmen asks.

Carmen

No one has an answer to the question I posed. We sit in quiet contemplation, mulling over personal theories, feelings, our grief.

The other women are so consumed by their private thoughts, none seem to notice I study their expressions, their postures, looking for any signs of duplicity. It's the only thing I can do right now. If I think too hard about what has happened, I will fall into a very deep, dark, bottomless hole that I may never claw out of.

No one seems to have any idea of what happened to Frank and Kathryn—why it happened. Of course, I care about the what and why of their deaths. Their demise gives me pause, but it's Gabe's exit from this plane that I must know the answers to. During the long hours of the previous night, I thumbed through all the possibilities. He lost his footing. His fear of heights pulled him to the edge. Perhaps Gabe left me, took his own life for reasons I can't fathom. Or was he pushed?

I dismissed the last awful thought, squashing it before it had time to worm its way into my mind and secure itself to my already frail psyche. Gabe was the kindest, gentlest man I've ever known. I can't imagine anyone harming him, much less shoving him to his death. But the horrific discovery of Frank and Kathryn's bodies in the hot tub has my mind reeling straight back to that dark possibility.

I'm careful with what thoughts to give time to—there's always someone watching, especially in this group. I've gone over all the general reasons why a person would take another's life. Anger, fear, envy, and vengeance are the obvious explanations. But do any of them apply to the given situation? I mean, what did Gabe ever do to anyone to elicit such an action taken against him? Setting courtesy aside, Kathryn was bitchy, and Frank could be condescending. Did someone take their lives due to their personality flaws?

Melanie leaves the sofa to resume her act of pacing at the far side of the room. She's poised to head directly out the door should a situation arise that requires such action. Her face is etched with worry and apprehension, but who is she worried for? Herself? Jude? Maybe she has concerns about Patrick. Besides the fact that there are now three unexplained deaths, that man is a ticking time bomb. He spouts off without consideration for anyone's feelings. He's selfish, rude, and hostile. Perhaps Patrick is more volatile than any of us perceive. But volatile enough to kill? The man is a pastor, after all.

Alyce has curled her long limbs into the corner of the sofa across the room. She flicks her fingernails, deep in introspection. Such a striking young woman, it's no wonder Melanie's son is so taken with her. Alyce's ease of self-possession is something to be envied. Women spend their lives trying to achieve the stature that only a handful ever accomplish. Looking at Alyce now, it's difficult to surmise what is on her mind. It is clear she is fretting over something, but the manner in which she holds herself suggests that she could be pondering what to serve for lunch, not which of my weekend houseguests killed the others.

Rosey has one eye on Alyce and the other on the door to the back patio. Is she watching for the men? Wondering what they will do with the bodies, perhaps? I'm sure that thought has crossed all of our minds, though none of us wants to be the one to put the voice behind the question.

I think back now to the days when Amber and I were friends. Our friendship was inevitable. We were both teachers, having taught the same children, living in the same neighborhood, sharing the same friend group. When Amber was pregnant with Alyce, I was more than envious. I wanted a child too, but it wasn't meant to be for Gabe and me. Still, I was determined to be there for my friend, excited to share Amber's elation and apprehension about motherhood, all the plans and dreams she had for her baby. During moments of shared confidence, Amber made it clear she did not trust her mother and wanted Rosey to have nothing to do with the child she called Elizabeth. Ironic was the word that came to mind over and over during the days after Amber and Shane's deaths. Not only would Rosey know her grandchild, she would end up raising the baby girl as her own.

Yvonne's lovely features are chiseled with anxiety. Each time the sky lights up and the heavens boom, her body tenses in response. Is it the brewing storm that has her on edge, or is something more sinister on her mind? Yvonne has always suffered from astraphobia, so I've no doubt this weathermaker is wreaking havoc on her sanity, and I do worry for her; yet, I can't shake the unease I continue to feel after witnessing a moment between her and Kathryn last night.

After we lost Alyce and Patrick, Terry and I continued along the rooms of the bottom floor—the area of the house Patrick had claimed to have come from. Once there, we found nothing and no one. It was Terry's idea to check the beach and around the front of the house. Terry went to the front while I went to check out the beach.

Finally, I thought, spotting Kathryn, Melanie, and Yvonne at the ocean's edge. I started toward the trio, who all appeared to be stumbling, laughing. But as I neared them, I heard their voices carrying over the wind. At first, I wasn't sure of what I was witnessing and hearing, but then I saw Kathryn grab Yvonne's wrist, yanking Yvonne back toward her. The two appeared to be in some sort of altercation. Melanie stepped forward to break them up, but not before I heard Kathryn spew her filthy accusation about my Gabe and Amber.

twenty-six

LET'S GIVE THANKS

Griff

Morning turned afternoon real quick like after we found the bodies of the news lady and her preppy husband. Shame they had to die in such a way. There may be worse ways to go, but even still, hope my last breaths don't come in that manner.

The full force of the storm arrived while the other fellows helped move the bodies of Frank and Kathryn to a place where they could rest until the time we are able to get them back to the mainland. I've been around my share of the dead, but never knew as much about the recently deceased as I do now. Terry knows his stuff—chatterbox, that one—could probably use his expertise on the island. Creepy crap though. Preacher man barely kept his coffee down.

Back inside Dune Dweller, we climb the stairs to the top floor. The winds howl, rattling the windows. The skies, darkened by clouds, release rain by the bucketfuls, showering the wall of glass overlooking the ocean one minute, pelting at it the next.

The women crowd around the island in the kitchen, working to put out the lunch spread Alyce instructed me to pick up in town yesterday: sandwiches, wraps, a bunch of salads, chips, and cookies. The amount of food is obscene, particularly now that three members of the party are no longer around for this meal or any other—ever again. Alyce explains that she had initially planned on everyone picnicking on the beach this afternoon. I'm surprised any of this crew has an appetite—finding two more dead, the stress of the storm, being trapped with people who are clearly no longer friends and definitely don't trust one another. Yet, they're all anxious to get the food to the table and ready themselves to eat. I suppose it makes sense. No one has eaten since last night's meal at the Red Lion Pub.

The daylight grows darker; the storm grows louder—rain pings at the windows, the roof, the siding on the house. Voices rise to be heard over the noise of the storm—Where are the napkins? Will you get the drinks from the fridge? Where did I see silverware? Alyce asks what I would like to drink with my meal. I try declining the invitation to join them at the table, but Alyce, Rosey, and a couple of the others insist. It's then I realize I've been so busy running about gathering up bodies that I haven't eaten either and decide to take them up on their offer.

They've set the big table. I renovated the sunroom across from the kitchen into a dining room. Put in a long rectangular table seating sixteen guests comfortably (twenty if you've got a couple of small ones), a single bench on one side, chairs along the other, and at the ends. This is the first time a meal has been placed on this piece of furniture. As a matter of fact, this is a weekend of firsts for Dune Dweller, though not the type of firsts I anticipated. If news of this weekend's disaster gets out, I doubt I'll have any future renters. Can't worry about that now, gotta get through the rest of this weekend without losing any more guests.

Everything out and on the table, we linger about hemming and hawing over the seating arrangement, trying to determine who sits next to whom. Did I just say that? Good Lord, that Alyce is rubbing off on me—who, whom, next thing you know, I'll be using thee and thou. I gotta admit, there are a few of them I don't feel comfortable sitting next to, but I button up and take my seat next to Rosey, who has chosen the head of the table. Across from me is Alyce, Jude right next to her. On my right is Yvonne, Terry next to her, and Carmen on his right. Patrick takes the other head of the table position at the far end, then insists Melanie take the seat on his right side, separating them from the rest of the group. As we all sit, it dawns on me that I should've pulled a few of the extra chairs away from the table so we could spread out a bit, not draw attention to the loss of lives.

Platters and bowls are passed back and forth. Everyone is polite and cordial with one another. Pleases and thank yous are murmured all around, to the point I'm beginning to wonder if this is some sort of survival tactic I'm not aware of. Plates piled high, we prepare to dig in, but not before Patrick prays over the food.

"Should we join hands?" Terry asks.

"I suppose those of us at this end of the table could fulfill that request. Patrick and Melanie are going to have a difficult time being that far down the table though," Rosey states, a snide edge to her tone.

"Here," Alyce says, extending one hand to Rosey and the other to Jude. "We'll do what we can at our end while Mr. and Mrs. Perkins take care of themselves at the other end."

I offer one rough hand to Rosey and another to Yvonne, ready to get on with this meal. Hand in hand, heads bowed, we sit and wait for Patrick to say grace.

"Bless us, O Lord, for the bountiful meal placed before us. Amen."

"That's it?" Carmen asks. There's no mistaking her scoff. "That's all you could come up with? We've lost three people in less than eight hours, and that's your prayer?"

"Fine," Patrick says. "You want more? We thank you, Dear God, for the sustenance you have provided to nourish our *living* bodies. Amen."

Mumbling amens, we begin to eat. While I chew, I stare out the window (although I can see no details other than a wall of gray sky) to avoid eye contact and the need for conversation. This tactic is one the others also seem to employ as voices around the table quieten. A bolt of lightning brightens the sky, cutting through the gray. Thunder immediately follows. Next to me, Yvonne jumps. I should have suggested she sit on the opposite side of the table so her back would be to the windows. She uses her napkin to dab the corners of her eyes. This is not the place to be if you're scared of a storm. Terry rubs his wife's hair, her back, encouraging her to take deep breaths.

"Yvonne," Alyce begins, "I have some Xanax if you want. Do you think that might help?"

Rosey's attention snaps to Alyce. "What are you doing with Xanax? Did Dr. Wentz prescribe that for you? He never said anything about it to me."

"And why would he, Rosey?" Alyce lays her fork aside.

"Because I am your caregiver."

"No. You were my legal guardian, but now I'm an adult, and as such, I decide whom my medical information is shared with."

Uh oh. I didn't see these two stepping into the ring today. Thought they got it all worked out last night.

"I just don't understand what it is with the younger generations and their love of drugs," Rosey says absently, raking her fork through the remaining potato salad on her plate.

"And what is that supposed to mean, Rosey?" Alyce asks. "You know as well as I do, I have never been one to partake in recreational substances other than alcohol."

"Well, darling. If you had listened more carefully to my words, you would understand I wasn't only speaking about your generation."

I scan the faces around the table, staring at Rosey as she talks in riddles.

"And, quite obviously, I don't know much about you anymore, Alyce," Rosey continues. "For instance, you assembled this weekend, gathering your parents' old neighbors without my knowledge, though I know quite well that I'm funding it. You have a fiancé for God knows how long, and I am only now meeting him—much less hearing about him—for the first time this weekend. And now, I find out you're popping pills."

Alyce shakes her head and rolls her eyes, not bothering to reply to Rosey's observations. Rosey lets her last judgments fall away while Alyce continues to pick at her food.

Yvonne sets her fork aside. "Thank you for the offer, Alyce. I actually have some Xanax in my room, but I've been avoiding taking it due to the side effects I sometimes experience when I use it."

Terry looks at his wife. "I know you want to be in control of all your faculties, my love. However, it might be helpful for you to take your medication, given the reactions you're experiencing to this storm—the full dose this time. You may have been able to get away with a partial dose last evening, but the severity of what's going on out there is much more significant than what we witnessed last night. It may be several hours before the thunder and lightning die down." Yvonne looks unsure about this proposal. "I'll be here with you every moment to help you stay in control," Terry encourages in a quiet voice. If I weren't sitting right beside Yvonne, I don't know that I would have heard Terry's last urging. Judging by the expressions around the table, none of the others heard Terry's whispered promise.

Yvonne gives her husband a slight nod of assent, and Terry hurries downstairs to get the medication for his wife.

"Terry's right, Mrs. Marshall," I confirm. If Yvonne is this afraid now, the storm will have her pretzeled before it blows over. "We're in store for a lot more clashes and crashes. This thing isn't supposed to be all the way outta here until tomorrow morning."

"Are you telling me we are all stuck together until tomorrow?" Patrick bellows from the other end of the table.

I shake my head, not bothering to respond. Doesn't matter how many times I tell this man or how many different ways I deliver it; nothing gets through to him.

"Speaking of being with each other all weekend, I think it might be a good idea for us to stick together—as in one room,"

Jude says. "You know, so that we can all keep an eye on one another." The implication couldn't be any clearer. The boy has the right idea if you ask me.

"Good idea, son." Patrick slams his napkin down on the tabletop. "You, your mother, and I can hang out in our room until this thing blows through. Get the hell out of here tomorrow; put this whole ridiculous weekend behind us."

"I'm sorry you feel that way, Mr. Perkins," Alyce says, her voice catching with emotion. "This weekend has gone so terribly wrong."

"Oh, baby," Jude says, pulling Alyce into his embrace. The table watches as he whispers to her, offers her his napkin. She nods and wipes her eyes. Rosey watches her granddaughter, never allowing her gaze to veer away.

Jude turns to address his father. "There's no reason to be an asshole, Dad. We all have to be here…"

Patrick cuts Jude's statement short. "We all have to be here because that little twit tricked us into coming here. Her big plan, some brilliant idea to collect us all in one remote place so we can tell her bedtime stories about her mommy and daddy. If she had been forthright about her intentions, maybe the others would still be alive."

"Patrick," Melanie warns.

Patrick's outburst silences the others, their attention turning to finish lunch. The noise of fork tines hitting ceramic plates and the occasional rattle of ice in a glass sound between the grumbles of thunder. Even Pastor Perkins manages to keep his thoughts to himself for a few moments.

Terry returns, slips into his chair, and then places the medication into Yvonne's hand. She tosses it into her mouth and sips from her glass.

"Everything is great, Alyce," Carmen says politely, breaking the silence. "Thank you for lunch."

"Really?" Patrick spouts from the other end. "How is everything so great? Seems to me you should be the first to say everything is not great, considering you just lost your fornicating sibling."

Mouths fall open around the table. Yvonne quickly reaches across Terry to place her hand atop Carmen's and gives a reassuring squeeze.

"Patrick!" Melanie chastises. "Shut your filthy mouth."

Terry sets his sandwich aside and wipes his mouth while he finishes chewing and swallowing. "You know, Patrick, I would think you might choose your words a bit more carefully, especially given that you believe one of us around this table is a killer."

"Did I piss you off, Terry? Sorry to offend."

"No, you're not apologetic. As a matter of fact, none of your expressions of regret, what few you've offered, have been genuine," Terry says. "You're going to spew those repugnant utterances about the wrong person one day, Pat."

"Is that a threat? Are you threatening me, Terry? Is that what that was? Did Gabe offend you too, and then he didn't heed warnings? You make sure he toppled off the top of the lighthouse for hurting your feelings?"

"I wasn't even in the lighthouse, much less at the top, to push anybody over, you imbecile." Terry's losing patience.

Carmen pushes her chair back and stands, her hand flying to cover her mouth as she rushes from the room and down the staircase.

"Now look at what you've done," Melanie accuses her husband.

"I didn't say anything that wasn't true. Every person around this table knows that."

"Dad," Jude tries. "Please, let's just eat. Maybe have a peaceful meal; think about the ones we've lost."

It's all over her face. Ms. Rosey has had enough. She has no intention of letting this go. Not yet. "We should talk about some of your bright ideas of yesteryear, Patrick. I think some of the others might find them interesting."

"Don't threaten me, Rosey."

"Why is it you think everyone is threatening you, Pat? Sounds to me like you've got a guilty conscience on your hands," Rosey counters.

"I don't have to sit here and take this malarky." Patrick rises from his chair, shoving it under the table in a manner that rattles all the glasses around the tabletop. He stands looking at Melanie, the command written clearly across his features. You will be backing me up, right?

Melanie remains planted in her chair, staring up at her husband. "We just spoke about all staying together, Patrick. I think Jude is right. I realize you're upset, but for the sake of what is best for the group, we should all remain in one place. Collectively."

"If for nothing else, to prove innocence," Yvonne says.

"What the hell is that supposed to mean? You're accusing me of killing the others?" Patrick's hands fly through the air, his anger distorting his facial features into something monstrous. After having witnessed her future father-in-law, I have to wonder if Alyce will want to go through with her nuptials to Jude. This Patrick Perkins dude is a piece of work. I wouldn't want him as my family.

"We may have agreed to stay together, but someone needs to check on Carmen," Yvonne says.

"I'll go with you," Terry says, pushing back from the table.

"No, honey. You stay. Finish your lunch. I'll be right back. I just want to be sure she's okay, see if I can get her to rejoin the group," Yvonne says, then gives Patrick a scathing look.

"You're sure? You just dosed, honey," Terry reminds her.

"I'll be fine. It won't kick in for a bit. I'll be back before then."

"Don't be too long," Terry suggests.

Yvonne leaves the room. Alyce stands, making her way to the kitchen. She returns to clear away dirty items, announcing, "Griff picked up an assortment of cookies at the local bakery yesterday. Would anyone like coffee to go with dessert?" A round of yeses and thank yous reply. Melanie pushes away from the table and starts for the kitchen to help Alyce with the coffee.

Rosey pushes her plate forward, checks her phone, taps the display a couple of times, then turns the display side down and pushes it aside. Placing her elbows on the table in front of her, she clasps her hands and addresses me. "What are we really in for here, Griff? I sense there is something you're not saying." That Ms. Rosey sure is good at reading people, even if her memory is failing her. I doubt anyone else noticed, but she's been recording us since preacher's god-awful saying of grace.

"The worst of the storm is due to arrive late, possibly in the overnight hours," I say, then pause to turn down the crackling of the walkie-talkie on my belt. "Sorry about that. That thing has a mind of its own sometimes. Yeah, I'd say this storm is moving slower than anyone expected or predicted—what have you."

"Okay, but that doesn't explain what has you so worried," Rosey says.

"Salty Dayz is already standing in it."

"What is Salty Dayz?" Jude asks. "Isn't that some sort of wetsuit?"

"It's the name of a house I oversee for the Mastersons. A couple of streets toward the center of the island," I say.

"What's it standing in?" Terry asks, wiping the crumbs from his mouth. By all accounts, he is a methodical, careful man with his food. Once again, he is the last one in the group to finish eating.

"Water," I tell them.

"Isn't that why they build all these places on stilts? Pretty commonplace if you ask me," Patrick says. "But then everyone in this house wants to make mountains out of molehills."

I explain quickly before any other quips are tossed out. "Locals use Salty Dayz as a gauge."

"But like Dad said, they're on stilts, right?" Jude pipes in again. "How high do they typically build the houses up?"

"Around four feet is the general rule of thumb."

"Then we should be fine, right? You never hear of the water rising that high, do you?" Patrick's voice registers a hint of panic.

"It's okay, Dad. You're going to be fine. No one is going to make you get out in the water," Jude assures Patrick, then explains his statement to the table. "Dad can't swim."

"You never learned to swim, Pat?" Terry asks.

"No, I didn't. Not that it's any of your business, but the opportunity never arose."

Ms. Rosey sits silently, taking in the conversation, mulling over the information, twirling her jade ring. She sits back in her chair and folds her arms over her chest. "Let's get to the crux of this conversation, Griff. What does the standing water at Salty Dayz mean to you? Why is it so concerning?"

"If water builds up under that house, you can bet it's coming for the rest of the structures on the island. And the way it's raining out there right now," I motion toward the window wall, "It won't take long t'all before it's in the house."

Alyce

Jude's mother and I have finished cleaning up the lunch items, packing away leftovers, and now work to brew fresh coffee and get it into mugs. The activity almost feels normal. A mother and daughter-in-law working side by side to accomplish a caring task for the ones they love. I have to remind myself this is far from a normal situation.

Yvonne rounds the staircase and stumbles as she returns to the kitchen area. "How's Carmen? Resting?" I ask her.

"Can you believe," Yvonne pauses for a breath. "Carmen was about to walk out the door?" Yvonne's speech is slower and starting to slur since taking the medication Terry brought her during lunch. Is this one of the side effects she spoke about?

"What?" Melanie exclaims. "In this weather? Does she have a death wish?" Melanie asks, then immediately follows with, "Oh, I shouldn't have said that."

"Well, it's out there now," Yvonne says. "Honestly, though, that was the first thought that ran through my head, too."

"Then you were able to talk some sense into her?" I ask.

"Ummmm hmmm," Yvonne draws out. "Convinced her to take a nap instead."

We work in silence, each pondering recent events, the current situation. The storm has quieted for the time being, no doubt building momentum for the next round, given what we've experienced thus far. Maybe Yvonne should have let Carmen get her air now while we're in a lull. What if Carmen decides to go out later, and we don't hear her? The bell, I recall—Griff's signal for letting him know someone has entered the house. No reason it can't work to tell us who is exiting as well.

"Jude, honey," I call across to the dining area. "Would you mind running to the bottom floor and making sure that bell Griff attached to the door is still there?"

Jude responds, "Sure thing," while Melanie tosses out, "Good idea."

"Do you think Carmen will be okay?" I ask the women. "I mean, losing Gabe so tragically, not having any answers as to why."

Yvonne struggles to string together a response. Melanie jumps in, taking the question.

"Carmen was always a strong woman. That said, it's been a long time, and I don't really know her anymore."

"Your mom was closer to Carmen than the rest of us, maybe because they worked together. At least, that's what we all assumed," Yvonne manages.

"Yeah, well, we all assumed Gabe and her were a regular couple too," Melanie tosses out.

"Correct me if I'm wrong, but didn't Carmen say she and my mother taught at the same school?" I ask, transferring cookies from the bakery box to a couple of platters I found in the cabinet.

"No, Amber taught high school—English, if I'm not mistaken—Carmen was at the middle school next door as an ESL teacher," Melanie says, then adds, "English as a second language."

"So maybe they would have had some of the same students then?" I ask her.

"Perhaps," Melanie says passively.

The topic falls away; no further questions to be answered at this time. I'm beginning to wonder if there will ever be such a time when all of my questions have answers.

"Yvonne, will you grab the creamer from the fridge, please?" Melanie asks. In reply, Yvonne makes her way to the fridge, a slight wobble to her step.

I turn my attention back to the task at hand, placing coffee mugs from the cabinet on the tray, then grabbing the sugar. Yvonne approaches from behind, reaching around me and slamming a bottle of white wine on the granite countertop next to the coffee tray. Instinct spurs me to grab the bottle, sure that the force has cracked the glass container, and move it quickly to the sink. Fortunately, the bottle remains in one piece.

"What in the wor...?" Melanie exclaims, then understands what has happened. "Yvonne, honey, why don't you go and have a seat with Terry?" She walks to stand beside Yvonne. "We'll finish up here. There's not that much left to do. Right, Alyce?"

"Absolutely, we've got the rest of this," I agree. "You go have a seat with your hubby and relax. We're almost finished with everything in here. We'll be right behind you with the coffee and cookies."

Melanie takes Yvonne's elbow, steering her toward the table, situating her in the seat next to Terry.

"Is she okay, you think?" I ask as Melanie returns.

"I wouldn't worry too much. It's the Xanax."

"Really? I don't ever recall having such a reaction."

"Medication hits everyone differently. Guess it makes Yvonne a bit loopy. I doubt she'll remember any of this afternoon. At least, that's how it used to go. Give Yvonne a dose of Xanax and she can't tell you what she did, when she did it, or who she did what to."

Rosey

Melanie and Alyce traipse back and forth from the kitchen, placing mugs of coffee around the table, platters of assorted cookies set at both ends. Yvonne slides her cup in front of her, sloshing some of the liquid over the top of the cup, quickly flicking her hand to cool the coffee burn. Terry reaches over her and uses his napkin to wipe away the mess, then proceeds to prepare Yvonne's coffee with cream and sugar.

"Where did Mr. Perkins go?" Alyce asks the group sitting around the table. "Does he still want coffee, you think?"

Griff spoons sugar into his mug. "Said he was going to make sure Jude didn't do anything stupid."

Alyce tilts her head, a look crossing her face that tells me she is quite over the pastor's quips. Still, she keeps quiet as she works to deliver coffee to her weekend guests. As Alyce twists to return to the kitchen, she runs into Patrick.

"Pardon me, Mr. Perkins. I didn't realize you were behind me."

"Hmmph."

"Where's Jude?" Melanie asks Patrick. "Thought you were giving him a hand."

"Nope. He's still off somewhere doing that little girl's bidding." Patrick waves a dismissive hand in Alyce's direction, taking his seat at the end of the table.

"You didn't find him?" Melanie tries again.

Patrick reaches across the table to grab a cookie from the plate. "Nope. Don't know where he went."

"But Griff said you went to check on him." Melanie's voice rises an octave. I can't blame her for reacting in such a manner—her only child, with all this death happening around us in the past eighteen hours.

"For God's sake, can't a man go to the bathroom without being interrogated?"

Melanie sets a mug of coffee in front of Patrick, clearly making an effort to do so with force, yet not so much as to spill the hot beverage. "He should be back by now. Jude only went to check the door on the bottom floor, Pat. We're worried Carmen might try to leave the house without telling anyone. Silly me thought you were working in pairs."

"Shh," Yvonne says, placing a coffee spoon to her lips. "Carmen's sleeping."

Terry strokes the back of Yvonne's head, soothing her. We watch the pair as Alyce and Melanie take their seats at the table once more.

Approaching footsteps sound from the direction of the staircase. Heads around the table turn in attention, anxious to view who will round the corner. A smile crawls across Alyce's young face as she sees Jude enter the room.

"Made sure the bell is on the door and the lock is secure." He saunters across the room, settles next to Alyce, and nuzzles his head against her ear to whisper something the rest of us can't hear. I pretend to be lost in thought, my gaze on an item across the room, but instead study the two of them in my peripheral vision —their careful actions, the silent language they speak using only their eyes. The moment over, Jude pulls Alyce's seated form closer to him, casually hooking an arm around her waist.

My eyes roam to the end of the table, where I see Patrick keeping a close eye on the young couple as well. Melanie holds her mug with both hands, gently blowing over the top of her mug while she, too, takes in the actions of her son and his fiancée.

I turn my attention back to Griff. "Before our conversation got sidetracked, you were saying the water is already rising around Salty Dayz. How long, then, do you think we have before the water starts to rise here at Dune Dweller?" The question pulls Patrick's attention away from the kids and into the weather discussion, the fear in his eyes unmistakable.

"Not long," Griff answers, tugging at the corner of his eye, nodding toward the view outside the wall of windows. "Helps that the rain has eased up a bit. Just don't know when the rain will start again and how much we're going to get in total." As if Mother Nature heard Griff's challenge, the rain begins to pound the side of the house again. A gust of wind slaps a sheet of water against the wall of windows, startling Yvonne. Griff nods toward the storm happening outside, saying, "Them forecasters can make predictions till all their spit runs dry, but no one knows for sure what the final outcome will be. It's hard to predict out here."

"Well, I can't get a weather report now, can I? No damn cell service. What happened to that assurance, Griff?" Pat asks accusingly.

"If you recall, Griff told us earlier we'd probably end up losing cell service as the storm made its way here. You should probably try listening every now and then, Pat," I relay, watching the man bow up at the other end of the table.

Terry speaks up before Patrick can start again. "Forgive my naivety on the matter, Griff," Terry says, twisting, turning his mug in circles. "You mentioned King Tides yesterday. I assume this is the same phenomenon we experience in Norfolk. How concerned should we be about them this far out to sea?"

"Sorry to interrupt. What are King Tides? I'm not familiar with the term?" Alyce asks.

At the end of the table, Patrick smacks his forehead with the palm of his hand in a show of frustration. I glance around the table and see that everyone is ignoring this current dramatic display of juvenility. Instead, all have turned their attention to Griff, waiting for him to answer.

"King Tides are nothing more than the most extreme tide that occurs—high or low, though most people only refer to them when they're high. That's when they do the most damage. Raise the water levels, cause flooding, particularly in low-lying areas," Griff explains.

"And you said earlier there are King Tides forecasted this weekend? Is that due to the storm?" Alyce asks.

"No, they happen a few times a year. Without going into a long explanation, it basically has to do with the positioning of the moon and sun, how they line up, and such."

Having started the conversation, Terry now appears pensive,

concerned. "That can't be good, given this tropical storm sitting on top of us right now."

"Nope," the one-word reply is punctuated by a rumble of thunder outside. "Not good at all," Griff agrees, taking another cookie from the platter in the center of the table. "Just means the water rises faster, higher," he adds, biting off half of an oatmeal raisin cookie.

"How can you sit down there eating cookies? You just told us this place is going to flood." Patrick is losing control of his composure—if he ever had any.

Griff chomps on the cookie. His mouth full and working to chew, I take care of the reply. "Griff never said there was a certainty of flooding, Patrick."

I watch Griff, see that little spark in his eye. "That's true. Don't know nothing for certain. Besides, it's the storm surge you really need to worry about," he says, then pops the rest of the cookie into his mouth. That's when I know Griff's enjoying this —toying with Patrick. The problem is that Griff doesn't know who he's playing with. When Patrick Perkins feels cornered, one would do best to get the hell out of his way.

Jude

Dad hurls himself from his seat and stands. In true Pastor Perkins' dramatic flair, his chair topples with a loud thud. Next to him, Mom jolts at the noise. She takes hold of Dad's hand, tugging his arm in an effort to reseat him, calm him. Dad jerks away, looking out the window as the rain falls with vengeful purpose. From the look on my father's reddening face, one would think Griff's comment was a personal attack on him and not a comment about the inaccuracy of a weather forecaster.

"Please, Patrick," Mom tries.

"Take a breath, Dad."

"Do not treat me like an old man," Patrick bellows. "We're stuck here in this godforsaken house. Three people have died, and now the rest of us are in danger of losing our lives to rising water. This is all her fault. Little slut. Just like her mama."

Next to me, Alyce gasps. Rosey shoots daggers in Dad's direction. Griff shoves another cookie into his mouth. Yvonne bursts into a fit of giggles. Terry turns all attention on his wife, trying to calm her, make her understand the intensity of the comment, the moment.

Mom slams her hands on the tabletop, her face a shade so red, it tinges purple. "How dare you say that about an old friend, our son's fiancée's mother, Rosey's daughter. How many lectures have I heard you dole out about speaking ill of the dead? Amber meant something to everyone around this table... except Griff, of course. Regardless, I have had it with your rude, abhorrent manners, Patrick. You need to apologize this minute."

I cannot believe these two picked this occasion to have one of their feuds. Alyce is getting the full familial welcome this weekend. But stepping in at this point would be a mistake. The best thing I can do now is be here for Alyce. My right arm still snaked around her waist, I pull her closer to my side, taking her hand into my left hand, lacing our fingers.

"I will do no such thing. That woman was never faithful to her husband. You know that as well as I do," Dad yells at Mom.

"Well, she wouldn't have been, would she, especially since the two of them weren't married in the first place."

"Bah, haha," Yvonne laughs, pointing at Patrick. All heads whip from watching the end of the table to where Yvonne and Terry sit. "Where's Kathryn?" Yvonne slurs. "She's gonna luuuve this."

Alyce yanks her hand from my grasp to cover her gaping mouth. I feel like we're in the middle of something we shouldn't be. But then again, Alyce wanted answers; she wanted to know what kind of people her parents were. We couldn't have discerned the information would come out in this manner, all the bickering and finger-pointing.

"Yvonne, honey. Let's give these people some space. We'll go to our room. Come now." Terry gently tugs at Yvonne, trying to pull her from the bench, but Yvonne is not having it.

"What? Kathryn was just saying last night that Amber and Shane weren't married. I didn't know that, but Melanie did." Yvonne points an accusatory finger in Mom's direction.

Next to me, Alyce shakes her head, confusion and disbelief marking her features. "I don't understand. I thought my mother and father were married. You all have known this whole time and haven't bothered to tell me?" Alyce asks the table, then swivels to confront Rosey. "You knew about this? That they weren't even married? How could you keep something like that from me?"

Rosey does not respond, her silence all but outright claiming culpability for the deceit Alyce accuses her of.

Mom looks at Dad. "Do you see what you have started?"

"How is this my fault?" Dad counters without hesitation. "I spoke the truth. Little girl over there wanted to know about her parents. Well, now she knows. They weren't married, and her mama got around."

"Jesus, Dad."

"Don't start that blasphemy stuff with me, boy."

Outside, the wind howls its own chorus of disapproval. I can't help shaking my head, rolling my eyes, mumbling under my breath, "Only you can do that."

"What did you say to me? You will not disrespect me like that."

"Patrick!" Mom shouts above Dad's tirade. "Give it a rest. Everyone around this table is over your bullshit." Their voices rise to be heard over the wind.

"Are you kidding me right now? Whether you like it or not, you're my wife, Melanie. You don't talk to me like that." Dad is practically spitting his words at this point. "'Wives, submit your-selves unto your own husbands, as unto the Lord. For the husband is the head of the wife, even as Christ is the head of the church,' – Ephesians 5:22-23."

And now he's quoting scriptures. I draw in a deep breath,

deliberate and slow with the release. Forget the production going on outside the windows. We're in for a show. No telling what is coming next.

"'Marriage should be honored by all, and the marriage bed kept pure, for God will judge the adulterer and all the sexually immoral.' – Hebrews 13:4." Sounds like Mom has been brushing up on her bible.

"What the hell is that supposed to mean? Do I need to remind you, Mel, that you're the one always sleeping with other people?"

"Don't act like you aren't guilty of screwing around, Pastor Pat," Mom gives it back.

"Um, guys, do you really want to do this right now?" I try, but they're wound up. It's doubtful either of them even heard me. Alyce grabs my hand this time, trying to comfort me, but this is not a new argument for me. Having my parents' sex lives tossed out onto the middle of this dining room table for all the others to peruse at will, however, is not something I'm readily willing to endure.

"I've had enough," I push away from the table. "You two are embarrassing me. Do you really need to do this in front of my fiancée, her grandmother, our weekend guests—your old friends, I might add?"

"You're right, Jude." Mom agrees. "My apologies to all of you for making this situation more uncomfortable than it already is. And Alyce, I'd like to apologize for having you find out about your parents' marital status the way you did. We had every intention of telling you this weekend, but the right moment has yet to arrive. And, please, disregard Patrick's outbursts. They have nothing to do with you but rather Patrick's insecurities."

"I do not appreciate you speaking on my behalf, Melanie." Dad starts again. "And this has everything to do with that one down there," Dad says, pointing at Alyce. He twists his glare from Alyce to me. "And you, young man, would do best to mind your own business and cut that one loose. While you're at it, I'd get that ring back if I were you."

"Good God. Really, Patrick. I'm just as upset as you are that we didn't know about this union, but let's get to know her a bit. Give this young woman a chance."

"A chance, Melanie? You want to give those two a chance to marry, to be intimate, to have babies? Over my dead body."

"Be careful, Patrick. Someone might take you up on that," Mom warns.

From the opposite end of the table, Rosey speaks. "I'm curious myself, Patrick. While I'm not particularly thrilled by the prospect of sharing grandchildren with you, I don't dislike your son enough to threaten Alyce about marrying him. So, what exactly is it that you have against Alyce?"

"I don't have anything against the girl."

"Seriously, Patrick? All you've done is disparage this young woman all weekend," Mom counters.

"I might add, Melanie, you're not crazy about this union either. You told me so yourself, but you never said why. Is that perhaps because you slept with Shane? Because you think Jude might be his son?" Dad waves his pointer finger back and forth at Alyce and me. "You think those two might be brother and sister like that twisted relationship Gabe and Carmen had? That... that... incestuous... perversion. I can't even think about it."

What in the holy hell... God, what I wouldn't give for a drink right now. A quick jaunt across the room to grab a beer from the fridge would fix that ail, but I can't possibly leave Alyce right now. And as probably the only person in the room who can get through to these two, I need to be present. How much worse can it get, though? Both parents have already called out the other's extramarital activities. But worse than that, Dad just claimed Mom had an affair with Alyce's father, potentially making the two of us siblings. That beer is sounding better and better.

"Dad, come on now. Don't be ridiculous. Alyce and I aren't brother and sister."

"You're insane, Pat. I never slept with Shane," Mom counters.

Dad returns. "You're on a roll, Mel. Pissing God off every

time you open that mouth. Breaking all the commandments today, are you? Just ticking 'em off, one by one." Mom shakes her head, an exasperated look settling over her face. "Don't lie to me, Melanie. Have you forgotten how you two were all over one another at every get-together the group had? It was embarrassing the way you threw yourself at Shane."

Someone clears their throat for attention. Heads turn to the opposite end of the table where Rosey sits, waiting to comment. "Isn't it about time you came clean, Patrick? Go on. Tell us what you know and what you're really worried about."

"Oh, don't play coy, Rosey Fischer. I don't know what you're talking about. You have something to add? Go right ahead."

"You sure, Pat? You know I never speak without proof to back up what I say," Rosey returns.

"Oh, Rosey, please don't start something," Alyce begs.

"The way I view the situation, young missy, Patrick down there has thrown out quite a tangled mess for the rest of us to unravel. I'm simply trying to determine if what he's saying is the fact that he is worried you might be his daughter, or if Patrick might have other information he believes the rest of us are unaware of."

"Wait. What?" Alyce looks from Rosey to Patrick, back at me. I've no clue how to comfort her through this accusation. We've actively been seeking answers about family and have found a few, entertained a couple of hypotheticals, even acquired information that was difficult to accept. But never did we presume something as outrageous as Rosey's last pronouncement.

Rosey pulls the coffee mug to her mouth, sipping carefully. Her gaze is on Dad, challenging him to get back up, return the next jab.

It's Mom who takes care of the follow-up blow, however. "Is that what you're worried about, Patty?" Mom's voice carries a high ring of false concern. "I had no idea you believed Alyce might actually be your daughter and not Shane's. Well, that makes perfect sense."

"Now, hold on here a minute," Yvonne slurs. Terry delivers his wife a look that says, are you sure you want to get in the middle of this. Yvonne doesn't catch Terry's warning and continues. "Let me get this straight. Pat was sleeping with Amber. Amber was sleeping with Gabe. But now Melanie, you say you weren't sleeping with Shane? So, who was sleeping with Shane? Carmen, were you... Now, where is Carmen?" Yvonne looks up and down both sides of the table, then behind her in the kitchen area. "Carmen," she singsongs. "Come out, come out wherever you are." Yvonne turns her attention back to Terry. "Am I it again? I thought it was my turn to hide. Where did Carmen go? Wasn't she just here?"

"She's sleeping," Terry says in a hushed voice. "Shh," he soothes. Yvonne nods, reaching across for a cookie.

"Is that true?" Alyce asks the table. "Were Carmen and my father sleeping together?" Alyce asks no one in particular. Although at this point, I'm not sure who here could be counted on as a credible witness to the happenings of twenty-five years ago.

"No," Rosey answers, sipping again from her coffee mug. "Shane Thompson was your father, and Carmen was not sleeping with him."

"So, my mother is my mother, and she wasn't sleeping with Patrick?" Alyce asks for clarification.

Rosey shakes her head. "I didn't say that."

"You mean..." Alyce lets her statement fall away.

"Yes, dear. That's exactly what I mean."

Alyce turns to me, her eyes filled with shock, confusion, disgust, disbelief—I can't put my finger on it. "How can this...? Your father and my mother?" Alyce's voice catches, and she cuts herself short, unwilling to let the others see how upset she is by this new information. I doubt this is a scenario she saw coming— definitely didn't prepare for it anyway. She breathes in deeply and sits taller, pulling her back fully upright.

"It's just a little kink, baby. It's going to be fine," I console.

Alyce nods, though not with much conviction. "We didn't plan on this, but it doesn't change anything," I assure her.

Alyce draws another big breath. My girl is strong, and she will proceed accordingly; no matter the curves and hairpin turns, she must maneuver. Alyce twists once more toward Rosey. "Then how can you be certain Shane was my father and that Patrick is not?"

Rosey's eyes shift left and upward as she, too, takes in a big breath, reluctant, it seems, to move forward with explaining her declaration.

"Because," Mom says, "Patrick is sterile."

Melanie

As if God himself is proclaiming, 'Enough is ENOUGH,' a loud clap of thunder rings through the room, startling everyone around the table. Another follows immediately. This one announces the lightning bolt that streaks the sky and sounds as if it delivers a direct blow to Dune Dweller. Alarms begin to sound from various areas in the house. Griff jumps to his feet, hurrying in the direction of the high-pitched chirping noises. Terry looks uncertainly at Yvonne, whispering something to her that I can't hear, given my position at the far end of the table, not to mention the racket. Terry stands, places a reassuring hand on the back of Yvonne's neck, bends to kiss her forehead, then hurries out of the room, following Griff. Jude tells Alyce to wait where she is. He is going to go with Griff and Terry to make sure everything is okay.

"Well, I'm not going to be the only male sitting at the table with a bunch of women. I'm going to help out." Patrick stands and rushes to follow Jude down the staircase.

As I watch my husband leave the room, I can't help but wonder if God was indeed trying to strike me down, as Patrick always threatens will happen to me if I continue to run my mouth. The truth. That's what I told everyone, and surely God doesn't strike a person down for telling the truth.

"Everyone okay?" Rosey asks, raising her voice over the high-pitched beeping noises.

Alyce nods her affirmation. Yvonne's eyes search the room, darting about. For Terry? For the source of the noise? For more sights and sounds of the storm? I take Alyce's lead and nod, unwilling to give the power of speech to any more of my thoughts. I've already said too much. Is it possible the violence of the storm will cause the others to forget my revelation, words spoken out of my own wrath? It would be beneficial, for me at least. Patrick will never let me forget, however. I will pay for my indiscretion one way or another.

We wait. The minutes carry the awkwardness of unspoken thoughts. Though, in our defense, none of us could possibly carry on a conversation with the ear-piercing trills blaring through the house.

Alyce pushes herself to stand. The three of us left sitting, watch her turn toward the wall of windows to take in the sights of the storm. With practiced elegance, she uses two fingers to drag her long, thick hair over her shoulder. It's a move Alyce has repeated several times over the weekend. What must she be thinking, mulling over? The claims her mother-in-law has made that her fiancé's father is sterile, possibly? Or perhaps it's her future in-laws' sexual indiscretions? Patrick and I may get what we have hoped for since learning of their engagement. After this weekend wraps, will Alyce and Jude still want to carry through with their wedding plans? And if not, will Jude ever forgive us?

Rosey

More thunder, desperate to be heard. This time, it rolls over the sky as if traveling, drawing nearer with every dooming rumble. The ominous silence that follows is more troubling, however.

Moment by moment, the trilling noises die away then cease completely. The skies take the cue and go quiet as well.

Coffee, long gone cold and nervous energy surging, turns Alyce away from the windows. She begins to collect the dirty mugs, walking them to the kitchen, placing them in the sink. The dishwasher did not make it onto Griff's generator 'emergency electrical units' list. As such, Alyce begins the process of handwashing the used items.

Yvonne stands, turning, stepping with deliberate purpose toward the staircase.

"Yvonne, dear," I call to her. "Why don't you come back and sit down? Terry and the others will be right back."

"I'm going to check on Carmen," Yvonne says in a convincing, level-headed manner. Given her demeanor over the last hour, it doesn't seem a good idea for Yvonne to go galavanting about the house on her own. I've never known Xanax to make a person act in such a way—if that was indeed what she took. Whatever the case, Yvonne is clearly not in her right mind, as they say.

Alyce sets a clean mug on the dish drainer, then offers, "I can go with her."

"That won't be necessary," I tell Alyce. "We don't need to split up any more than we already are."

Melanie pipes in from her end. "I'm sure the fellas checked in on Carmen. She's probably on her way back up here now. I can't imagine anyone could have slept through all that ruckus."

Stopping in her tracks, Yvonne nods. Presumably, having gotten through to her, Alyce turns back to her cleaning tasks, drying coffee mugs and wiping down countertops. Melanie picks at a hangnail while I keep an eye on Yvonne. She turns now to head in the direction of the kitchen. Alyce, her face taut with apprehension, steps aside, allowing Yvonne space. Yvonne walks past Alyce toward the back counter, where the knife block sits.

Yvonne grabs a butcher knife by the handle and pulls it free from the storage block. The sound of metal on metal sends a chill running the length of my spine.

"What are you doing with the knife, Yvonne?" Alyce asks carefully.

Yvonne holds the knife up, the steel of the blade glinting in the light of the overhead lamp. "Well, I don't have my gun, and this seemed the next best thing."

"Gun?" Alyce asks, her eyes searching my face for direction.

I ask, "Did you bring a gun with you, Yvonne? Are you sure you didn't leave it at home in Norfolk?" If we can keep her talking, Terry may have time to get back to her and handle this situation.

"Yeah, it's in our room downstairs," she says nonchalantly.

"Yvonne," I pause before issuing the obvious. "Why do you need a gun?"

"Protection, of course." The blade cuts through the air as Yvonne waves it carelessly. "But now that I think about it, the knife will definitely be less messy."

From the other end of the table, Melanie mouths to me, "What in the hell is she talking about?"

I shrug in reply.

"Now, where are the chickens?" Yvonne says as she begins her trek toward the staircase once more.

WATER RISING

Terry

The lightning set off every smoke detector in the house. The four of us—Griff, Patrick, Jude, and I—started on the top floor, then split up, and have now managed to reset them so that the grating noise has ceased and some sense of balance has been restored. I hear a couple more of the alarms chirping somewhere in the house, but here on the bottom floor of Dune Dweller, I've double-checked all of them. Not that we discussed it, but I've also gone through to be certain all the doors and windows are secure as the wind picks up.

I scan the room to verify again that I've done what I can before heading back upstairs. Darkening skies have left the room with little light to see by, given the absence of electricity. Nothing on this floor made Griff's infamous 'emergency electrical units list.' I glance at the sliding glass door across the way. The scene outside doesn't look to be improving, causing me to think of Yvonne. I hope her meds are evening off a bit.

The bell on Dune Dweller's front door dings behind me. A door slams shut, heavy footfalls follow. I turn to see Griff enter the recreation room. "You get all the detectors silenced?" He asks.

"Everything's all set down in here," I say. "Did you all finish up the second floor?"

Griff appears uneasy. "Left Patrick and Jude to handle those rooms. I took outside. Checked on the water levels, had to see where we're at, and moved the van to the end of the driveway, highest ground we've got. At least I got it started. It's right temperamental. Hates the wet weather. Old electrical system has been waterlogged one too many times, and now it won't make it around the block in this kind of weather. Just hope I got it pulled far enough inland, especially since it belongs to a buddy."

"How is it looking out there?" Based on Griff's appearance, conditions can't be great. His jeans are soaked through up to his thighs. The shirt he wears clings to his torso, while that mass of hair is plastered to his head and dripping.

"Not great. Tide's rolled up underneath the house already, mid-calf. And these slow-moving downpours we keep getting hit with aren't helping the situation." Griff says, tugging at the corner of his eye. "Won't be long before this floor starts taking on some water," he adds.

"Really?" I ask. The prospect seems preposterous, though to say so would be placing me in the box with Patrick.

"Yep. Know so. Seen it happen. That's why I laid these floors down here in tile."

"And you think the water will rise all the way up here?" The threat is difficult to comprehend. The house is situated on four-foot stilts, after all.

"Yeah, unfortunately. Didn't figure on this happening with my first set of house guests, though. It's the storm surge. Sure, in the best-case scenario, we could sit and watch the water come in around us, not be bothered. But we've no idea what the wind and waves are going to do, how far they'll push the water in and up. Gotta be ready for the worst."

"Should we move some of the chairs and tables? Maybe get them to a higher level? Salvage what's possible?" I offer.

"That's my plan. Thought I'd change out of these wet things

and start moving some stuff upward once all the smoke detectors were reset."

"Why don't you take care of changing and grabbing some of your personal items? I'll go get Jude and Patrick to help me take some of the furniture upstairs."

It seems I have surprised him with my offer of assistance. "Yeah. Um. That'd be great, man. I appreciate that," Griff says. He turns to head down the back hallway, stopping suddenly and turning back to address me. "You're not like the others, are you?"

Now it's my turn for surprise. "No," I say, shaking my head.

"She said you weren't," Griff says, then turns to make his way to his bedroom.

As Griff disappears down the back hallway, I grab a small side table and lamp to carry with me on my hunt for Patrick and Jude. Two at a time, I take the stairs, pondering Griff's last comment. Who might he have been referring to when he used the pronoun she? *"She said you weren't."* Yvonne? Alyce? I can't think for a moment that Melanie would vouch for me in such a way. Rosey, maybe? I've witnessed her and Griff in hushed conversations. Is it possible Rosey has been sharing details of our group's history with Griff? What would Rosey say about our actions, and how much would she dare to share with Griff? I doubt Rosey's commentary on any one of us would be glowing. Rosey has never cared for any members of our Perishing Hill gang.

On the second-floor landing, I look at the items in my hands. What should I do with these? I glance down the hallway, assessing the most out-of-the-way location. This floor is all bedrooms, doors lining both sides of the long passageway. Kathryn and Frank won't be using their room. Their deaths still ring surreal, shocking. Going into the room they occupied would be disrespectful, not to mention it could also be perceived as tampering should an investigation be required. Finding their bodies floating in a closed hot tub struck me as suspicious. No doubt, the authorities will draw the same conclusion and will want answers as to the specifics of their deaths. Determining their manner of death will be necessary. Working with the dead may be something I do on a daily basis, but I am no medical examiner. Moving Frank and Kathryn out of the hot tub without informing the appropriate authorities was bad enough, albeit warranted by the circumstances. That said, I certainly don't want to muck up an investigation more than what we have done already. No, I think, looking down at my haul. These will fit just fine in our room. I'll store them in there, then look for Pat and Jude.

I place the table on the floor, freeing a hand to twist the doorknob. As the door swings open, I grab the table and step through the threshold, then startle, almost dropping the lamp. Jude and Patrick stand together on the far side of the bedroom near the en-suite bathroom. I perform a cursory glance around the bedroom, looking for anything out of place. All seems to be in order, other than my uninvited guests.

"Might there be a plausible reason as to why the two of you are in our bedroom?"

"We were checking all the smoke detectors, same as you are," Pat says caustically as if I've accused him of something sinister. It may have slipped Patrick's mind, but I have not forgotten that during last night's escapades, we caught this man taking Griff's things from his private quarters.

"Well, this one seems as if it's all good," I say, making a point to look at the ceiling above my head, where the smoke detector light blinks silently once more.

"We were just checking to see if another detector was in the bathroom as well," Jude rushes to say, then looks at his father. "This room checks out. We get them all, Dad?"

"Yep, everything's copasetic in here," Patrick says. "We're all set. What are you doing there?" Patrick nods at the items in my hands. "With those things? You redecorating?"

Ready to get these two out of our bedroom, I explain Griff's rising water scenario and ask for their help moving the other items to higher floors.

"We're four feet off the ground," Patrick barks, putting the edgy bounce between his feet back into motion. "Griff thinks the water is going to come inside the house? Inside? And he's okay with that? And then... And then, you're rearranging furniture like everything's just hunky-dory?"

"Dad, take a breath."

Patrick does as Jude instructs, then turns to the window to right himself.

"There are two other floors and a roof," Jude says by way of calming.

"A roof? What, we're all going to set up camp on the roof?" Patrick shrills.

"Only if the situation calls for it, Dad. Seriously, calm down. If Griff's not worried about it, we shouldn't either. Griff's lived on this island for a long time. He's the expert. Everything's going to work out just fine. You'll see."

"I don't understand why the hell we don't move inland. Has anyone thought about that idea? You've got transport. Let's load 'em up and get to higher ground somewhere," Pat's practically dancing and has the look of a rabid animal.

I shake my head sympathetically and drop my voice a notch to explain that the van has electrical issues and won't get far in this weather, as Griff explained to me earlier. As I continue to attempt de-escalation of the discussion, Griff enters the room, almost as if he were summoned. "Griff goes through storms like this one all the time. Right, Griff?"

Griff eyes each of us in turn, his face marked in question.

"I'm not a toddler, Terry. Stop your coddling," Pat says.

The man can't be reasoned with. My temper gets the better of me as I snap back. "Then perhaps you'd like to head on out of our personal space and help Griff and me get this furniture to higher ground." I've had it with Patrick's tantrums. His mannerisms verge on bullying, and I'm too old and too tired to allow this man any authority over me.

"It's coming in faster than I anticipated," Griff looks at me as he speaks. "Whatever this is, I ain't got time for it. High tide is at 5:41 this afternoon, so conditions aren't going to get any better. I've got to get moving."

I think back on Griff's explanation of King Tides and understand that this high tide will be notably higher than the typical incoming high tide. No sense in riling Patrick up any more than necessary. I decide not to put this subject back out there for rehashing and instead toss out a plan of action. "We'll head back downstairs, grab some more items, and take them to the top floor. I'm sure we can solicit some help from the ladies."

Griff nods. Patrick and Jude step toward the door, following Griff out of the room without further comments. I'm not sure what to make of their silence, but I don't have time to ruminate, either. I take one last look around the room and pull the door shut behind me.

thirty

SECRETS AND LIES AND MISUNDERSTANDINGS

Patrick

Not much room to speak of here on the top floor now that we've brought all the movable items from the bottom level, bypassed the second floor, and jam-packed them into the available spaces on the top level. Rosey observes the comings and goings as we work, arms folded over her chest, assessing the chaos at hand. Griff drags a rather large, bulky chair to the perimeter of the room. Terry keeps Yvonne busy working to sweep up the mess of a spilled potted plant that took a hit during the move. Alyce and Jude work to make a clear trail in and out of the kitchen, clearing a passageway to the nearest bathroom. Melanie runs around rearranging the extra furniture items, trying to make some organizational sense of their placement.

"It's pointless, Mel. Leave it," I say to her. "There's too much stuff to fit comfortably in this room."

"He's right, Ms. Melanie," Griff agrees with me. "This situation is all temporary anyway. Storm'll be over soon," he says, placing another lamp onto the only clear space left on the kitchen counter.

My shin finds the edge of a squatty table crammed into what used to be a walking path leading to one of the two sofas in the sitting room. The club chair catches me from the fall. Holy hell, that hurt. I was just trying to make it to the damn window to see what's going on outside.

I hold onto the back of the chair, catching my breath from the exertion of moving furniture, traversing stairs, and wait for patience so that I can continue dealing with fools. Across the room, Yvonne pulls a feather duster from a cleaning closet in the kitchen area. "What the hell is she doing over there?" I ask no one in particular. "She's not really going to dust right now?" I swear, I heard her clucking.

Terry hurries over to Yvonne, taking the duster from her hand, explaining the current situation. Again.

"But I need this to check on Carmen," Yvonne babbles, waving the duster in the air as if she's conducting an assembly through some damn silent symphony. Good God.

"Oh no, we forgot about Carmen," Melanie says, looking first at Alyce, then Rosey. She turns to me, asking, "Did you all look in on her while you were resetting the smoke detectors?"

"Is that what this is about?" Terry asks Yvonne. Yvonne bobs her head up and down, looking like one of those bobblehead things.

"I'm sorry, honey. I didn't understand," Terry says, holding firmly to Yvonne's upper arms, stroking. "Yes, Jude and Patrick looked in on Carmen. She was sleeping, and there were still other detectors chirping. So they left her to rest while they went to reset the other alarms," Terry explains.

Melanie moves to take a seat on one of the sofas. "I can't believe she slept through all that noise."

"It's probably for the best," Rosey says, making her way to one of the club chairs, flanking either end of the coffee table.

Working cautiously through the maze of furniture, I head again to check on the current weather. Outside the wall of windows, the rain continues to fall in sheets. Wind gusts slap the water mercilessly against the glass. Current conditions make it impossible to view the ocean, to see how far up the tide has made it. I glance at my watch. Griff's call for high tide is fast approaching. From my pocket, I pull out the useless cell phone to check the signal strength. Still nothing, a big 'ole 'NO SERVICE' tauntingly displayed at the top of the screen. If purgatory is anything like this, I've got to work on being a better person.

"You getting a signal over there near the windows, Pat?" Rosey asks.

"Nope." I run a hand over my forehead and wipe it down the leg of my jeans.

"How can you be sweating?" Melanie asks. "It's freezing in here," she says, rubbing furiously at her arms.

"Sorry about that, Ms. Melanie," Griff jumps in. "Wish I could get the heater going, but we need to conserve the fuel since we don't know how long we'll be without power."

"Everyone understands that you're only doing what's in our best interest, Griff," Rosey says to the man. Did Rosey just give Griff a pass? What the hell is going on with those two? She's never been one to empathize, sympathize, or condone excuses, much less inadequacies.

"Yeah, well, we were promised a state-of-the-art generator," I remind the group. "Power all weekend long, you said. Wi-Fi guaranteed, you said. Right, Griff?"

"Dad, give the man a break. Griff can't control the elements."

"He can control his mouth, can't he? He's the one who lied to us. Promised us this safe-storm-proof house. Never said squat about the loss of heat, the possibility of being without Wi-Fi, and now, although you can't see it through the blanket of gray, we have a freaking ocean of water coming for us."

Griff walks toward where I stand in front of the windows, purpose in his stride. He's big, got at least six inches on me, but I can take him. I just have to be a smarter fighter, keep a low center of gravity. Fists form at my sides as I draw in a breath, preparing.

But Griff isn't coming for me. He stands at the other end of the window wall. He reaches inside a cabinet on his left and pulls out a pair of binoculars. I unclench my fists, watching as he lifts them to his eyes.

"You're not going to see anything out there, not through that soupy mess." I motion toward the thick gray skies.

"Unlike you, I know what I'm looking for," Griff says, holding the binoculars to his eyes.

"What the hell is that supposed to mean?"

"Just what I said." Griff twists the center knob to sharpen the view.

"And you see something out there?" I ask.

"I do." Griff lowers the binoculars, squinting as he peers out the window, then lifts them to his eyes again. "Water."

"Oh." I turn to address the others, who have now ceased all activity and keep a close watch on Griff and me. "Did you hear that, everybody? Magellan here found water."

"Patrick, please. We can't do this right now," Melanie whines.

"Where's the water line, Griff?" Rosey asks.

Griff continues to hold the binoculars to his eyes as he pulls in a deep breath. "Rushing the barrier dunes."

"You mean the ones at the back door of Dune Dweller?" Alyce squeaks.

Griff nods. "Yeah, it's filling in under the house right now. With any luck, it won't get much higher, but I can't guarantee what the surge will do."

"Do you think the water will breach the second floor?" Rosey asks.

Griff lowers the binoculars, twisting to face the group as he speaks. "Not likely, but it all depends on the storm surge. Typically, the island averages anywhere from three to eight feet of surge depending on the event and when high tide happens."

"Eight feet! That's well into the house. And you said this is a King tide—a higher tide. Does that mean a higher surge?" A ringing noise runs through my head, blurring my vision. I turn to face the window, my back to the others. Pull it together, man.

Griff ignores my question. "To answer that, Ms. Rosey, it

might be a good idea to grab any medications or necessities from the rooms on the midlevel just in case we all need to stay up here and ride this thing out."

Alyce speaks. "I think that should be our plan—to ride the storm out up here on the third floor, all together. We did talk about staying together earlier—given all the unexpected deaths—that way we can be certain everyone stays safe."

"You want to know what I think, Alyce? I think you need to stop making plans for us. Your plans are what got all of us into this situation."

"Alyce is not to blame for this storm, Patrick," Terry says.

"Three people are dead, Terry. The way I see it, those deaths are on her. She may not have ordered up a storm, but none of us would be here right now if it weren't for that girl."

"Dad," Jude warns, holding firmly to Alyce's hand.

"Let me ask you, Patrick," Rosey says. "What do you think the group should do?"

"I don't give two shakes what y'all decide to do, but I intend to gather my family and get to the highest ground we can find," I say, wiping my forehead again. It's a sauna in here.

"Then Alyce will come too. We may not be married yet, but she's family now, Dad."

"No, she's not." I step away from the window wall. "There's no ring on her finger, no vows, no marriage certificate. And let me tell you something, boy. You should be glad you haven't made that mistake. There's still time to re-correct and get the hell out."

"Are we back on the brother/sister thing again? We already discussed this, Dad. Mom did not sleep with Alyce's father. I'm not Alyce's brother." Jude shakes his head, turning his back to me.

"Alyce could still be your sister, Jude." Everything else has come out this weekend. I've no doubt this information will find its way into the discussion sooner or later. I might as well get it out there now.

Melanie rubs at the lines crinkling her forehead, closing her eyes. "We went over this earlier, Patrick."

"That's not what Patrick is talking about this time around," Rosey jumps in, always trying to show me up. Old hag can't even give me the courtesy to share my own indiscretions. "He's trying to explain to you all about the affair, the paternity questions he…"

"You think I didn't know that, Pat?" Melanie jumps in before Rosey can continue. "Of course I knew you slept with Amber. I figured all the men in the group had been with Amber," Melanie says nonchalantly, then realizes what she has said. "Oh, I'm sorry, Alyce. I don't mean to speak ill of your mother, but it was no secret Amber loved the company of the opposite sex." Melanie finishes her apology and places her focus back on me. "Besides that—we just talked about it—you're sterile, Patrick."

"I had that vasectomy after I had my lapse in judgment with Amber, Melanie. So, you might think you know everything, but you don't. Alyce could very well be my daughter."

"You didn't need that procedure back then any more than you would need it now."

"What the hell are you talking about, Melanie?" I'm over all these people treating me like I know nothing.

"Do I need to spell it out in front of all these people, Patrick? Don't tell me you've forgotten the fertility test you took when we were trying to conceive Jude."

"That test came back fine."

"Did you see the results? No. I gave you the results because you didn't want to go to the doctor. You claimed the whole process was emasculating and pointless," my wife shares with everyone.

"But you got pregnant with Jude right after we did all those fertility tests," I point out.

"I did," Melanie says matter-of-factly. "Right before the results of your analysis came back negative. So I lied, let you believe you were fertile and that Jude was yours."

Hands on hips, I turn my attention to Jude. He seems

unfazed by this topic of conversation. Jude's face shows no signs of surprise or shock. "And you knew?"

"I did, Dad," he says, standing by Alyce's side at the kitchen counter.

"I can't believe both you and your mother have kept this from me all these years."

"First, I thought you knew, but more than that, Dad, I didn't think it mattered." Alyce wraps her hands around Jude's upper arm, holding him close.

I twist to look Rosey in the eye. "That's what you were trying to tell me earlier, wasn't it?" The anger wells deep in my chest, tightening, squeezing the air from my lungs. "You old bitty."

"Patrick!" Melanie's on me again. Can't she see Rosey is manipulating all of us?

"Who is it, Melanie? If I'm not Jude's father, who is?" I rub the back of my neck where the sweat has begun to pool.

"You're really going to make me say this in front of all these people, Mr. It's-Nobody's-Business-but-our-Family's?"

"I want to know. This minute. Who is it?"

"Patrick, you seriously don't know?" Melanie asks, softening. Her eyes search my face, looking for deception, I assume. "Have you ever looked at Jude? He's the spitting image of Grant."

"Grant Genard? As in, the lead lawyer of the group you work for? Jesus Christ, Melanie. And you've continued to work with the man all these years later? Are you still fucking him—some sort of perquisite of the job?"

"A-hem," Terry interjects. "I suggest we all take a break from this conversation."

"Yes, I agree, Terry," Melanie says, then turns back to me. "I'm sorry you didn't know, Pat. We need to work this out, and we will, but not right now. I will say, however, I always believed you knew."

thirty-one

NOT AGAIN...

Griff

The rain continues to fall by the bucketloads. To Ms. Yvonne's benefit, the lightning and thunder have died down a bit, but the water is coming inland fast, faster than I've ever seen it do before. As the rest of the group retreats to their bedrooms to collect personal items needed to get them through the evening, I head to the first-floor level to assess the situation again.

The front door is first on my list: the bell is still attached, and the floor is dry—both good signs. Through the window, I see the van at the end of the long driveway. Thankfully, the water hasn't risen far enough to threaten the borrowed transportation, but it won't be long before it does, given our location on the island. Truth be told though, it's the back of the house I'm worried about. The ocean is coming and coming fast. Out of earshot from this crew, I radioed into the station, let them know our location and status. From the way this storm is behaving, though, we're going to need some help getting out of here, cause I don't know any way of getting these folks to higher ground without assistance at this point. That old van won't make it to the station through all this rising water.

Long strides take me through the recreation/bar area to the

back door. The view beyond the sliding glass door is more of what we've seen most of the day—a sunless gray wall. Before I open the door, I take the hair tie from my pocket and pull my hair into it.

Working quickly, I slide the door open and shut—the wind attacks immediately and without regard or remorse. I lean over the balcony of the deck to look below. The water is under the house as it was earlier. Hard to tell from this vantage point if it is higher than it was at last check, though. Oh hell. There goes the top to the hot tub. It's made to fold in half at the center point and is as heavy as it is awkward to fit onto the top of the hot tub. Looks like in our rush to get Kathryn and Frank out of the shallow pool, we didn't fit the topper back on and secure it. I've got to get it. Otherwise, it will either blow inland and rip to shreds, possibly hurt someone, or it'll get washed out to sea.

The stairs are wet and slick. I step cautiously downward, holding to the handrail. The rain lets up a bit, but the wind is relentless. At the bottom of the staircase, I step into the ocean, wading slowly toward the cover, floating back and forth with the motion of the tide. The lid is unwieldy in good weather, but mix in forty-mile wind gusts, and it becomes a parasail. It takes all my might to get it to fit securely back into place and the snaps locked.

With the last corner battened down, I turn to head back inside Dune Dweller. I lean forward into the wind, trudging through the water. A wave pushes forward as a forceful wind gust pushes me back, causing me to lose balance. Shit. I hurry to push myself up, my hands and wrists sinking into the sand, the strong surf working against my center of gravity. Saltwater rushes up my nose, into my eyes. The ocean calls the water back, and I use the moment to right myself. I move to the house in a crouched position, ducking my head against the wind, watching my legs forge through the ocean.

From the base of the staircase, I grab the handrail, using it to pull myself forward. The water measures three steps up as the tide rolls inland. It's going to make it into the bottom level of the house. It's not even high tide yet. At this point, there isn't much else I can do to prepare. All the movable furniture is out of harm's way, and the bottom floor is constructed to withstand this type of flooding. If it gets too high, rising to the second floor, then we're going to have some problems. Nothing else I can do except wait and see what happens.

I continue my climb. A voice in the distance rides the wind, but when I survey the surroundings, I find no one who could have made the noise. I'd believe it was my imagination, but then I hear it again. This time, I lift my head. There, on one of the second-floor balconies, is a woman. She hangs over the railing, waving frantically, shouting hysterically. Is that Yvonne? What's she doing up there, and why is she leaning so far over? Where is Terry? Thought he was watching her. Looks like she's trying to get someone's attention. Who? And where? There's nobody out here. Yvonne's arms flail about as she continues to yell. Oh hell, she's going to fall over if she's not careful.

Pushing forward against the wind, I slide open the doors and hurry inside. Dripping water all the way across the length of the recreation room, I haul myself up the staircase, yelling Yvonne's name as I go. At the second-floor landing, I raise my voice, calling out for Yvonne, then Terry. Doors open along the hallway. Melanie's head is the first to show through her and Patrick's threshold, and then I see Terry pop out of another door.

"Where's Yvonne?" I shout at Terry.

"I don't know. She was just in our room. She was going to lie down while I gathered our things together. She must have slipped out while I was packing my toiletries."

"What's going on?" Melanie joins us in the hallway, Patrick on her heels.

"Yvonne's on one of these balconies." My voice is loud and booms in my ears. "The backside of the house. Leaning way too far over it. We need to find her ASAP. The wind gusts are strong. One good blast, and she could fall."

We each take a door. Even Patrick joins the effort. The only room left unchecked is Carmen's. Asleep or awake, we'll have to disturb Carmen. Yvonne is not in her right mind. Melanie raps gently at her door, calling to her softly, but no one answers.

"You're going to have to knock harder if she's sleeping," Patrick says, actually making some sense for once. He reaches around his wife and pounds the door with force. Still no answer.

"Ms. Melanie, open the door. See if Carmen's decent so we can go in," I press.

"Hurry, Melanie," Terry says anxiously.

"Carmen," Melanie calls, walking into the room. "She's clothed but sleeping."

Terry is first inside Carmen's room. I follow—Patrick right behind me.

"I see her. There." Melanie points toward the balcony door.

Terry slides open the balcony door and hurries out to coax Yvonne back inside the house. As we wait, watching the two of them, more voices arrive in the hallway behind us. I turn to see Alyce, Jude, and Rosey at the bedroom entrance.

"What's going on down here?" Rosey asks. "We heard the shouting all the way upstairs."

On the other side of the room, Terry speaks to Yvonne. "That's good. It's much better in here, right?" Yvonne nods in response. She's rain-soaked and windblown. "What were you doing out there, honey?"

"I saw Gabe," she says, shivering, folding herself inside her arms. Melanie pulls a blanket from the closet and hurries to wrap it around Yvonne's shoulders.

"Yvonne, honey, that's not possible," Terry explains, drawing the blanket tighter around his wife. "Remember? Gabe died last night."

"I know, but he was here. Well, down there," Yvonne says, pointing in the direction outside the balcony door. "That way, further down the beach where the water is just starting to rush through the dunes."

Terry shakes his head and gives the rest of us standing by a slight shrug of his shoulder.

Melanie tries. "What did Gabe want?"

Yvonne pushes the hair from her eyes. "He's looking for Carmen."

Melanie glances at the group standing around her, then turns her eyes back on Yvonne. "So Gabe was on the beach…,"

Yvonne interrupts her to say, "With the Gray Man."

"Gabe was with the Gray Man?" Melanie asks.

"Yeah, remember the guy we saw by the water last night? The one Griff told us about…he was showing Gabe where to go," Yvonne claims. We exchange glances of disbelief, brows rising into hairlines, doubtful shrugs.

Patrick throws his arms up. "All right, this is bull crap. What the hell? Now, we have ghosts that give directions in addition to warning us about storms and running lighthouses. Surely, to God, at least one of you gets how ridiculous this is?"

Yvonne breaks free of Terry's hold, the blanket falling to the ground at her feet. "It's not ridiculous! I know what I saw. Gabe was here for Carmen. And he got her," she says, breaking down, turning to cry into Terry's chest.

Terry consoles Yvonne. "Honey, Carmen's right here. Look, she's on her bed right there."

"Yeah, and how in the hell is she sleeping through all this commotion?" Patrick asks. "What'd y'all drug her with this time?"

Melanie turns, easing herself down onto the bed. Carmen lies on her side, her head tucked down into the crook of her arm. Melanie gently shakes Carmen's shoulder to stir her. When Carmen doesn't respond, Melanie tries again, but still, there is no response from Carmen.

"I told you," Yvonne says through tears. "I told you he took her. Gabe took Carmen with him."

"Oh my God. Is she saying what I think she's saying? Carmen's dead?" Alyce asks, searching the faces of those around her for answers.

"Now, wait a second. Nobody is dead here—well, besides the other three," Patrick says. "You all gave Carmen something, something to calm her down. One of those pills you all are always yabbering about. Xanax? Right? That's what's making her so crazy," Pat says, pointing at Yvonne. "Maybe it made Carmen sleep," he says, twisting back to eye Alyce. "Weren't you the one passing out drugs earlier? How many did you give Carmen?"

"I didn't give her any of my Xanax," says Alyce. She turns to Yvonne. "Did you give her one of your pills?"

Yvonne shakes her head in the negative, holding tightly to Terry. Terry bends to retrieve the discarded blanket. He stops mid-hunch, cocking his head to one side, something catching his eye. He gently pushes Yvonne away from him and bends to the floor beneath the bed. We all watch as he squats, then gets on hands and knees. "Oh no."

"Oh no, what? You can't say that and not tell us what you're talking about," Patrick says.

Terry sits back on his knees, holding up a collection of prescription vials to inspect, letting them fall to the floor as he grabs an empty vodka bottle as well. Rosey shakes her head. Alyce turns into Jude's arms. Melanie lifts her hands to cover her face.

Yvonne folds her arms across her body, saying, "She's with Gabe now."

Jude

"Move. Move over, Mom. I've got this." I push her aside, taking Mom's place beside Carmen. Rolling Carmen to her back to assess signs of life, I lay an ear to Carmen's chest, listening for a heartbeat. A finger to her neck finds no pulse. I double-check Carmen's airway.

"Is there a pulse? Is she breathing?" Alyce asks.

"No, nothing, but we have to try. Terry, help me," I say, hoping we're not too late. There could still be a chance to save Carmen if we can get her breathing, maybe get her to vomit. Terry moves to the end of the bed, taking Carmen's feet while I grip under her arms. The two of us work to get her body carefully to the floor. I begin the chest compressions and follow with two breaths.

Terry hurries to the other side of Carmen to help with the compressions. The two of us work, trying to pump and breathe life back into Carmen. The others gather around, watching, waiting.

I hear Mom ask Alyce, "What time was it when Carmen came down here to rest?"

"I don't remember exactly, but I know we hadn't yet finished lunch. Mr. Perkins said something about Gabe's death—that one of us tried to murder Gabe, that was it—and then Carmen ran from the room."

"Don't start this crap again," Dad shouts. "I didn't kill Gabe, and I'm sure as hell not responsible for that one," he says, pointing to Carmen's lifeless body.

"Dad, please. This isn't helping. We're trying to save her."

Alyce tries to give Mom a more definitive answer. "We sat down to lunch right around noon, I think." She sounds doubtful about her recall. "I only remember that it was before twelve."

Rosey adds, "And you all were putting coffee and dessert out when Yvonne left to check on Carmen. It was right after that Yvonne told us Carmen was trying to leave the house."

"That's right," Mom says.

Silence fills the room again as Terry and I continue our efforts, taking turns with compressions. The others look on as we work until our arms can do no more.

"It's too late," Terry calls it. "It's no use. She's gone."

thirty-two

UNPACKING THE BAGGAGE

Alyce

Roaring and hissing, wind works into Dune Dweller through the eaves and cracks. The noise is ominous and unsettling, as if it's trying to make entry. To make matters worse, the sun is sinking quickly into the horizon. It's that time of year when it barely feels like you're getting a full day's worth of light, but today, we really got cheated. An occasional lightning streak brightens the sky, but in practical terms, night will be here sooner than any of us would prefer.

At the risk of sounding like Mr. Perkins, I am ready to leave this island as well. Nothing about this weekend has gone as planned, and that is putting it mildly. Four people are dead. Four. Dead. I would ask, how can that be, but I know how each one of them died. Worse, I'm responsible. Those four people would still have their lives at this moment if I hadn't insisted they participate in this reunion.

Heavy footfalls ascend the staircase. Griff steps into the great room, where we all sit, pondering silently—each of us coming to terms with another death.

"You found some dry clothes?" Rosey asks Griff as he enters the room. The poor man was soaked through when he came barrelling in earlier to save Yvonne from falling over the balcony. Thank God he got there when he did. We might have been facing another group member gone too soon.

Griff pushes his damp hair behind his ears and offers a slight nod. He looks in the direction of the Marshalls and Jude's parents. "Did y'all get everything you needed from the second floor?"

From their perches on the parallel sofas in the middle of the room, the two couples nod silently. Rosey watches them from her chosen spot in one of the club chairs. She knows more than she is saying. But about what? About who?

Melanie uses a tissue, dabbing her eyes, wiping her nose. "I don't know how much more of this I can handle," she says under her breath. We all watch as she turns her focus on Mr. Perkins. "You were right. We should have left yesterday when you wanted."

Mr. Perkins places his arm around Melanie's shoulders and pulls her into his side. It's the first sign of affection I've witnessed between the two—I didn't think it possible.

Melanie pulls herself upright and away from Mr. Perkins. She looks at Terry, sitting with Yvonne across from her and Mr. Perkins. "Did you check to see who those prescription bottles belonged to, Terry?"

Terry pulls himself to sit on the edge of the sofa, placing elbows on his knees, then teepees his hands in prayer. "Well, there was Yvonne's empty Xanax vial. Kathryn's oxycodone and some sort of sleep aid—gone. Frank had Xanax and Ambien—also both depleted, and then there was a bottle that appeared to have been recently refilled by Gabe for Trazodone. I assume it was close to full, given the date of the bottle."

"And you think she swallowed all of whatever was in them?" I ask.

"I do," Terry says. Then, "And the empty bottle of vodka suggests she swallowed them down with that. Hard to reconcile with what I knew of Carmen, but yes, I believe she ingested everything she could find."

I consider Terry's account and realize something about it seems off. "If she was hell-bent on taking her life, why wouldn't she have rummaged through everyone's medications? Carmen didn't take my Xanax prescription, and she was at the table when I offered it to Yvonne at lunch. Carmen had to have known I had a vial. Why didn't she take my vial too? And for that matter, why not go through Rosey's prescriptions as well?"

Standing at the wall of windows, Griff shifts his weight between feet. "Probably 'cause all those vials were upstairs where we were having lunch. Carmen couldn't risk going through yours, Ms. Rosey, and Jude's things. She'd be heard. We were all right out here in this room and would have seen her coming and going."

"Good point, Griff," Terry agrees.

Melanie scoots nervously to the edge of the sofa, putting more distance between her and Mr. Perkins. "You don't suppose someone could have forced Carmen to take all those pills, do you, Terry?"

"It would take quite a bit of coercion, but I suppose someone could force all of them into another person," Terry says. "But who here would do that? Besides, we were all sitting around the table."

"Not all of us," Rosey says.

Rosey

"Are you kidding me right now? Here she goes again." Patrick sticks that finger in my direction. Jab. Jab. Jab. That man is incorrigible. "Can't you all see it?" He's practically shouting over the noise of the storm. "She's constantly lobbing these little innuendos and then leaving us to fight it out."

"I simply stated a fact, Patrick. Nothing more, nothing less."

"Yeah, and there were a lot of insinuations in that fact," Patrick tosses back.

"Jesus, don't you ever get tired of bickering with people all the time?" Terry asks, falling back into the sofa cushions. "It's got to be exhausting."

"Quite the opposite, Terry. Patrick thrives on the conflict," I say. "He's an antagonist. The art of the argument is how Patrick has made his living all these years—first as a car salesman, then as the leader of a congregation."

"I'm not sure what that's supposed to mean, Rosey. Yes, I was a vehicle sales specialist. People needed a car, I sold them a car. Now, I deliver the word of the Lord. I hardly see how either of those callings is antagonistic."

"He's right, Rosey. Neither of those professions is hostile or aggressive." Alyce sides with her father-in-law-to-be.

"Dear girl, I must differ with your ideals about these jobs," I begin. "You see, some people come in looking for a vehicle because they want one. They might even convince themselves they need one. Though let's face it, most people have public transportation available to them in some form or fashion. But by the time Patrick finished with them, those prospective buyers didn't see a life in which they could live without a car. Interestingly enough, many of those buyers arrived at the car lot where Patrick was employed, driving a dependable and reliable auto. Before they left, however, that car ended up having an extensive list of dire repairs. Signing on the dotted line for a four to five-year loan payment was much more logical and cost-effective than trying to piece their old jalopy back together."

"This is bullshit."

"Now I'm not finished, Pat. Indulge me for a moment while I paint you unethical. Besides, where else do you have to be?" I pause and then start again. "You see, Patrick was a fabulous car salesman," I tell the others, taking a moment to look him in the eye. "I'm not sure why you quit, Pat. Oh, that's right. I remember now."

"Come on, Rosey." Patrick slumps back into the sofa cushion.

"No. No. It's time."

"What's going on here?" Jude asks his father.

Patrick ever so slightly shakes his head at Jude. Those arms folded over his middle, holding tight.

"You didn't quit, did you, Pat? No, they fired you, and not because of your performance—top salesman of the year five years in a row, is that right?—and not because of your less-than-gentlemanly behavior with the female staffers. Nope, it was that last DUI that got you, not all the ones that came prior, of course, because you didn't inform your employer about those. No, wait, that's not right—the priors didn't land you in jail."

Jude turns to his father. "Jail, Dad? How long were you in jail? Was this before or after I was born?"

"Jude, one day I'll sit down and tell you everything, but now isn't the right time."

"Rosey, these people are my guests. I've invited them here for a reunion that has gone horribly wrong, to state the very least. Needless to say, I don't think pulling out ugly secrets on top of everything else that has happened this weekend screams hospitality," Alyce says.

My granddaughter believes I'm clueless about her ambitions and intentions. The only thing I'm questioning is how much longer she's going to let this disastrous weekend continue. Nevertheless, I've put 'ole Pat in his place, and now I'm done. Let Alyce take the win.

"Your grandmother wouldn't know hospitality if it slapped her in the face," Yvonne says.

Well, it seems we're not done after all.

Yvonne

"Yvonne," Terry cautions as thunder rolls ominously across the clouds. I've surprised him, but I don't know why. He knows who Rosey is just as well as I do.

"What?" I ask the seven pairs of eyes watching me closely for what I will say and do next. "She wouldn't—Rosey's never done anything for any of us that was remotely hospitable." Their eyes never waver—waiting, expecting a show. No, telling what I did or said earlier, I can't recall, but the worst effects of the Xanax have passed. Now, I can float by without all the anxiety, better yet, without the loss of my mental faculties. However, I confess that I do tend to be a bit more forward in putting words to my thoughts while in this twilight phase. Terry knows all the stages of my Xanax stupors. He scoots closer, grabbing my hand, squeezing, warning. "The only thing Rosey knows is blackmail," I say.

"Uh-oh," Melanie says under her breath. Behind her, beyond the wall of windows, lightning illuminates the dark skies, but I'm calm, calmer anyway.

"Oh, stop fretting, Mel. She already got a hold of y'all," I say.

"Yvonne," Terry warns again.

"I'm so tired of living with the fear that one day, Rosey is going to publicize everything she knows. Maybe if we just face it, we'll all be free to move forward."

Terry continues to hold onto my hand, applying the warning pressure again. "I don't think this is a good idea, Yvonne."

"Whatever happens from here on out, we'll be free, Terry. I'm doing us a favor." My husband hangs his head, shaking it. He pulls his hand away and begins wringing both in the manner he does when something has him stressed. "Look at it this way, honey; we're alive. Kathryn and Frank died, never knowing the feeling of being free from Rosey's grasp. We've all lived by her rules and that stupid non-disclosure agreement for over twenty years now, and I'm done. We've held up our end of the deal."

"Oh my God, Rosey. Frank and Kathryn, too? Is there anyone here this weekend who hasn't been coerced by you?" Alyce asks as if seeing her grandmother for the first time. That girl was raised by Rosey. I'm not buying that she doesn't know the type of person Rosey is and has always been.

"So you want in on this, Yvonne?" Rosey threatens.

"I do. I'm done. We're done. Let's get on with it." I'm so ready to be rid of this woman and her hold over us. "Should I tell the room, or do you want that honor since you've been holding so tightly to the information all these years?"

Rosey looks relaxed and calm, cocooned in the club chair. A smug smile plays on her lips. "Oh, I'm quite curious about what you have to say, Yvonne. Go ahead."

"As Melanie and Patrick may recall, the funeral home is a family business. It's been in Terry's family since the late 1800s—it's an institution. It's what his family has always done. Successfully, I might add. But like even the most successful businesses often do, ours fell on some hard times.

"We had undergone extensive renovations both aesthetically and technologically that would carry the family business into the next generation. We made big plans for our One Century in Business re-opening event. How proud were we that our family's funeral home was the only Black-owned business in Norfolk that could make that claim? Terry's father could barely hold his pride. There was a lot riding on the event, most importantly, our family's reputation.

"But people weren't dying fast enough for us to cover the renovation expenses, and the bank came down on us. Threatened to take all that Terry's family had worked so hard for. About the same time, Rosey came into our lives—that's another story with a nightmare plot I won't go into right now. For the sake of time, I'll just leave it at this; for our silence, Rosey lent us the money to keep the bank off our backs until business picked back up again. All we had to do was sign one of her non-disclosure agreements. In return for our cooperation, Rosey paid the bank, and we paid Rosey back. No one was ever the wiser about our financial issues. However, we are now debt-free—no obligations to the bank or Rosey." I turn to Rosey. "And as far as I'm concerned, I can't imagine what reason you could give for requiring our silence at this point in our lives. It's not as if what happened twenty years ago is going to ruin your stature as you've always claimed. That said, I've no intention of breaking that agreement."

I smile, placing a hand on Terry's forearm. I've freed us, so why does Terry look as if he is still beholden to Rosey?

One knee crossed over the other, Rosey flicks her foot. "Should I elaborate on Yvonne's simplistic anecdote, Terry, or would you prefer to inform her yourself? Given all we've learned this weekend, it seems you, too, have been keeping secrets of your own, Terry. Perhaps you'd like to share yours with Yvonne now?"

Terry leans over, planting elbows on his knees, hands twisting. "Rosey was responsible for keeping the funeral home out of bankruptcy. That is true. But there's more to the story, I'm afraid." I watch as he brings his hand to his furrowed brow, rubbing his forehead back and forth in procrastination. "Back in the nineties, we had this fellow working for us. His name was Earl." Terry turns to look at me. "Remember Earl?" I nod in reply. Terry hangs his head as he begins again. "Earl was hired by my father years before I ever took over the business. I had no reason not to trust him—until I did."

Terry looks at Alyce. "I doubt you are aware, but my funeral home handled the farewells of your parents. It was my deepest privilege to celebrate their lives and honor them with the most respectful of ceremonies for their crossing over."

"Jesus, you've slipped into the funeral home babble again. Just get to the point, Terry," Pat fumes.

Terry ignores Patrick's outburst and continues. "Rosey and I had been through the complete process of making the arrangements regarding details of their remains, the celebration of their lives. We determined a time for her to drop off the personal clothing items she chose for the two of them at the funeral home. Unbeknownst to the staff and me, Rosey arrived early. When she couldn't find anyone to leave the attire with, she searched for someone to assist her. As it turns out, Rosey found Earl. And as it also turned out, Earl was a necrophiliac."

"Oh please, no!" Alyce, eyes wide her hands fly to her mouth in horror. Her actions confuse me, but Terry clarifies quickly.

"No. No. No. He wasn't attending to your mother. It was someone unrelated to this story."

Terry draws a breath. "The point is, Rosey learned of Earl's disturbing proclivities and threatened to expose them to all of Norfolk. While I had no idea about Earl, my father had known for years and turned a blind eye to Earl's perverse ways. Finding people willing to work with the dead is not particularly easy. The pair had an unspoken deal. Earl kept his mouth shut, and my father never saw anything nefarious. The information that this had been going on for years would have ruined my family's business. We were coming up on our big celebration of a century in business. Our reputation was sparkling. But yet, we were still facing bankruptcy. If Earl's vile and disgusting actions had been made known to the public at large, we would have, for certain, had to close the mortuary."

All these years, my husband has carried this burden alone. "Why didn't you tell me?" I ask Terry.

"I was embarrassed and scared. Even though I fired Earl, I feared Rosey would move forward with her threat if I said anything. And too, I couldn't believe I was so oblivious as not to see what was going on when Rosey walked in and, five minutes later, knew all the dirty secrets of my family's business."

"Oh, honey. I wish you'd have said something. We could have worked through it together."

"It makes perfect sense to me now," Alyce says, stepping forward. "No wonder you all didn't want to share stories and memories from the time you spent with my parents." Alyce turns to her grandmother. "You knew that Carmen and Gabe were siblings, didn't you? That's what you were holding over them, wasn't it?"

Rosey gives her head a slight tilt as if to say, so.

"And Kathryn and Frank? What were you holding over them?" Alyce asks.

Melanie takes a deep breath and says, "I actually know this one. Kathryn shared…, well, shared might be strong. Let's say a few drinks loosened our tongues. Frank and Kathryn had a life-style that completely contradicted their professional personalities. Kathryn confided it was in both of their best interests to play by Rosey's stipulations if they intended to climb ladders socially, professionally, and ethically.

"Frank and Kathryn were a few years older than the rest of our group. Not much, mind you, but a mere four to five years seems like a lot when you're in your twenties. When we all first became acquainted, each of us put heavy weight into whatever the two of them said, advice they gave, or suggestions about how to handle precarious situations. We deemed the pair had more life experience than the rest of us. They would know better. But, after a few months, we began to realize the two of them were not the mature older couple we labeled them as. Those two could out-drink an elephant, and of course, there were the drugs." Melanie pauses for a minute to address her son. "Sorry, Judey. Your parents did partake back in the day, but that does not mean I'm advocating on behalf of narcotics or experimentation. Quite the opposite, actually. Your father and I understand firsthand what can happen to a life when using these substances. They're illegal for a reason.

"But Frank and Kathryn knew how and where to find these substances," Melanie says.

Alyce sees an opening and asks for clarification. "So, Rosey, is that what you were holding over Kathryn and Frank?" Alyce doesn't give Rosey an opportunity to answer her question, instead imploring Melanie. "Was that it, Melanie? The drug use?"

"No," Melanie says. "Drug use can be explained and over-come. Check yourself into rehab, and the world believes you've recovered. No, Rosey had something more damning. Frank and Kathryn were part of a group... well, let's just say they all shared sexual desires that went beyond the parameters acceptable to soci-etal standards: bondage, submission, voyeurism, spanking, hair pulling, biting—you name it, they'd do it. There's a term for it, an acronym I can never remember."

"BDSM," Terry offers. I look at my husband. Terry was aware of Gabe's issues but never shared that information with me. Then this thing with the funeral home... Did he know about Kathryn and Frank's sexual penchants as well? His face doesn't show any signs of knowing about our old neighbors' sordid actions, but it's not something we've ever experimented with in our marriage or even discussed, so how does he know about bondage and the like? Before I can attract Terry's attention, Alyce probes deeper.

"But those are personal preferences, intimate acts that aren't being forced on another. Are acquaintances and employers really going to hold what you do in your private time against you? Most people live by the philosophy of 'that's not for me, but you do you.' Right?" I'm not sure whose case Alyce is pleading. Rosey's or Kathryn and Frank's? It must be difficult for this young woman to reconcile all that she has learned this weekend about her family, about the woman who raised her.

My eye finally catches Terry's. The confusion wrinkling his brow, the tiny lift of his shoulder, let me know he was not privy to this information either. I breathe easier. He's not lying to me, as Rosey alluded to earlier. Reaching for his hand, I let him know I'm there for him, that I will not allow Rosey to come between the two of us.

"The people in the group were influential and connected," Melanie continues. "Frank and Kathryn couldn't risk being exposed because it would put the rest of their fetish group members in jeopardy, members who had helped to build both Kathryn and Frank's careers. But you see, it was more than just their careers and livelihoods on the line. Allowing that secret to surface would have put some formidable people in an ugly spotlight. For that reason alone, it was crucial that Frank and Kathryn make sure that knowledge never seeped out."

Next to Melanie, Patrick shakes his head in disbelief, his body rigid, the anger visible. "You old hag. You've been holding this shit over our heads for years. Manipulating us into thinking we couldn't trust one another when, all along, it was only you we should have been leery of."

"Dad, let's give Rosey a chance to explain. I'm sure there's more to this story," Jude says.

"We may have raised you to be diplomatic, but that woman does not deserve the benefit of the doubt, Jude," Patrick says, and though we don't share many of these moments, I agree with him. "She's been holding this information over all of us, using it against us, for well over twenty years. The real question is, why let go of it now?"

"Because I don't need it anymore," Rosey says. "The information has served its purpose."

"So then, you openly admit that you've been actively extorting these people?" Alyce shakes her head in disbelief. "There's so much wrong with this, Rosey. So much more I want to know. But foremost, how did you come by all of this information?"

"I can answer this one," I speak out, "and will gladly do so. Rosey has her private investigator on speed dial. Her informant was so efficient at locating your mother and father that Rosey put her PI on the rest of us. If I had to guess, I'd say she's had you followed all along, Alyce. Hell, I'd even go so far as to say that's how she found you this weekend, on this island, in this house."

thirty-three

POPS SAID SO

Melanie

Yvonne's accusation shuts down the conversation. Only the wind dares to make a sound—whistling, searching, seeking entry through whatever small opening Dune Dweller might have overlooked. Each of us commits to our private thoughts. I can only speak of my own, but if I could read the minds of the others, I'd most definitely pop in for a peek. There are far too many unanswered questions at this moment. Who knows what? What do I not know? Did Carmen take her own life? Did Gabe? Or is one of the people in this room capable of murder? We've had so much death in the last twenty-four hours. The deaths of Gabe and Carmen may have been accidental or at their own hand, but the demise of Kathryn and Frank seems something more sinister—drowning in the hot tub like that.... Convincing me otherwise will prove difficult. And then, what will happen when darkness settles? Sure, part of the house has electricity—for now. How long will that last? One more good lightning bolt to the generator, and we're completely in the dark.

That's what is going through my mind.

The remaining eight of us sit, feeding anxiety and pondering away, the shadows and silhouettes of my companions looming and menacing. The room we occupy is dimly lit by the one lamp that made the cut for Griff's emergency appliance log, or whatever we're calling it. In the kitchen, on the other side of the open room, the overhead light seems positively glaring in comparison.

Across the way, Yvonne scoots closer to Terry's side. He places an arm protectively around Yvonne's shoulders, pulling her to him, shielding her eyes from the lightning errantly dancing outside the windows. The thunder has grown more raucous this last hour, the building crescendo matching the intensity, blow for blow, of the prior discussion in the room. So far though, none of the weather elements have compared to Yvonne's last supposition.

We knew that somewhere in the background of our days, Rosey was watching. That's what she was always best at—that and using what she saw to her advantage. Rosey also made it clear to each of us how well-connected she and her husband were—the people they knew, their knowledge about the 'ins and outs of the system.'

I think back on all her veiled threats, on the overt ones. We all knew to keep our mouths shut, or Rosey would make us regret speaking out. At this very moment, as she rolls that big ass jade ring around her finger, Rosey has her eye on my son, and it scares the crap out of me. The look she dons is not one of compassion and understanding. What does Rosey have planned for Alyce and Jude? Patrick has handled Jude's engagement horrifically, but to Patrick's credit, our son has no idea of the family he is marrying into. Jude may have gotten a small taste of Rosey and her capabilities these last few hours, but my son is ill-equipped to handle a woman of Rosey's stature.

Alyce and Jude have stepped into the kitchen while I've been lost in my inner debate. The two of them huddle together, whispering animatedly. Beside me, Patrick inches to the edge of the sofa again. He's watching them as well.

What must he be feeling, having just learned Jude isn't his son? I never meant for Patrick to learn of something so private in such a public manner. But then again, I would have bet my life that Patrick was aware Jude was Grant Genard's son. Honestly, I'd figured Patrick knew he was sterile but didn't want to tell me, knowing how much I wanted a baby and feeling less like a man for his inability to provide me with what I wanted. And it was no secret we both had relations with others early on in our marriage. When I learned I was pregnant with Jude, I considered it meant to be. Patrick seemed happy enough about it, not that I really gave two cares about how Patrick felt at the time. Believe it or not, he's not always been the easiest man to be married to. "Ha," I say aloud, putting unintended sound behind the word.

Patrick turns his gaze on me, deep frown lines forming over his brow. I shake my head slightly to signal it's nothing. He drags his focus back to Alyce and Jude. "Something's going on over there," he whispers, lifting his chin toward the kitchen, at the pair. I nod, knowing he's right, wondering, cringing at what he might do next.

Here it comes.

"What's going on with you two?" Patrick asks them. Why must every word out of his mouth sound so antagonistic?

Jude meets his father's gaze. Alyce turns her head, swiping a finger from the corner of her eye to the outer edge. Is she crying?

"Nothing. This has nothing to do with you, Dad." Oh, Jude. Why? Why did you have to say that?

"There's a lot going on in this room, Jude. And by God, it involves all of us. She. Her." Patrick points heatedly at Alyce. "Invited all of us into this house of torment. People are dying. For all intents and purposes, we're sitting in the middle of the damn Atlantic Ocean during a storm that is throwing out major—deadly—weather elements. But you're right, son. None of my business. None of my business that my only son has decided to get married. None of my business that your bride-to-be is the granddaughter of a woman who has been blackmailing the lot of us over the past twenty-odd years, all to protect her reputation. None of my business that four people from your mother's and my past are dead during a weekend reunion that Alyce, whom you profess to love, orchestrated." Patrick pulls his hand to his face, rubbing the heavy shadow of growth that has appeared over the long hours of this day.

"Mr. Perkins," Alyce begins, stepping away from Jude and into the sitting room. "As you have pointed out several times these last many hours, yes, I organized this weekend. I own that. So, if you could please stop with the same banal, overworked comments, I would be most appreciative. If you must know, Jude is trying to talk me out of confronting my grandmother in the midst of you all."

Alyce's remarks stun me and leave Patrick speechless—momentarily, of course.

"Well, then," Rosey pipes up, continuing to roll that ring around her bony finger, "Patrick would be correct, and Jude would be wrong. By all means, Alyce, confront away."

"Have it your way," Alyce says, folding her arms across her body. "Do you have a private investigator that you employ regularly?"

"Yes," Rosey says without further elaboration. She's going to make Alyce work for it.

I drag my watch from the granddaughter/grandmother quarrel to the other sofa. Yvonne meets my stare, pulling her lips taut as she raises her brows.

"Has this investigator been keeping tabs on my parents' old friend group?" Alyce hammers again.

"Yes."

Alyce takes a deep breath, frustration contorting her lovely features. "Has that investigator been reporting to you on my actions?"

"Yes," Rosey gives a nod of her head, punctuating her affirmative answer.

Huffing, Alyce tosses her hands into the air. "Is that how you found out about this weekend?" Rosey looks up at Alyce, withholding comment on Alyce's last question, and glances briefly at Griff standing by the window wall. I check the faces in the room to see if any of the others have seen the exchange as I have, but their looks are fixed on Alyce, waiting for what she will say and do next.

Alyce moves to stand in front of her grandmother's chair, leaving Jude's side for what seems to be the first time this weekend.

Rosey looks up at Alyce. "You've had your fun, Elizabeth Alyce. You've gathered all your parents' old friends, inconvenienced them, not to mention put them in danger. They've told you all they know. Now, can we please move forward? I think I speak for everyone here when I say, we want this weekend over and checked off the books."

"You may not speak for me," Patrick says, then under his breath, "regardless of how bad I want off this island."

"I already knew," Alyce says somewhat cryptically, leaving the rest of us to wonder exactly what she is referring to. "Pops told me about my mother even though you told him not to."

"Wait just a minute," Patrick commands. "You already knew? Knew what? Are you saying there was no point in any of us being here this weekend? That this whole disaster wasn't necessary?"

"Dad, this is between Alyce and her grandmother."

"She dragged us into this, Jude. I can put my two cents in if I so wish."

Alyce ignores Patrick, continuing. "Pops told me what he could and then swore me to secrecy. He knew Rosey would be furious if she found out he had gone against her wishes and told me about my mother." Alyce moves to the opposite end of the sitting room. She turns to face the group again. "Pops believed that a young woman should know the mother who gave her life. He disagreed with you, Rosey. Amber was his daughter, too, and regardless of how you felt about her, Pops was proud of my mother."

"Your grandfather was an old fool. Honestly, if not for my father, your great-grandfather, we'd have been living off a district attorney's salary. My father understood my affection for your

Pops and saw to it that my Henry was given a position in the political arena, that we continued to hold our place in society. It was up to me, however, to uphold our social position—i.e., clean up the messes he and Amber were always creating. I loved your Pops dearly, but he fell short in the area of common sense."

"What's nonsensical about loving your own child?" Alyce asks.

"Amber had..." Rosey pauses. "Amber had issues."

"You don't throw people away because they don't fit your preferred mold, because they have issues." Speaking of sense, Alyce has a great perspective. I do hope my husband, her father-in-law-to-be, is listening. Patrick could use a bit of that insight.

"I don't throw people away," Rosey says, shaking her head, that white bob swishing with the action.

"Don't you? Pops told me you kicked Amber out and that you never even talked to him about it. An argument, an ultimatum, and you're done?"

Rosey studies her hands, caresses her fingers.

"At least he didn't listen to you," Alyce seethes.

"And what does that comment mean?" Rosey picks lint from her pant leg, then folds her hands together in her lap, waiting.

"Pops defied you. He kept seeing Amber. He knew about her life, about her career, and Shane. How do you think I was able to pull this weekend together? How do you think I found all of their old neighbors?"

Across the room, Yvonne leans into Terry's ear. The two exchange whispers, then turn back to the scene playing before them. I can only imagine what Yvonne must be remembering, surmising. It's all going through my mind, too. Rosey has been following us our whole adult lives. Well, practically. We were all first-time home buyers living in Perishing Hill, beginning new marriages, and having babies. If Rosey had been following Amber even prior to that time, then she must have been keeping an eye on the rest of us since we all met in Perishing Hill.

"Your grandfather would have told me if he had continued

seeing Amber. He knew how devastated I was when Amber walked out of our lives."

"You mean your life. She walked away from you, Rosey, not Pops."

Even in the last dregs of the day's light, I can see Rosey's eyes burn with fury. Her husband, daughter, and granddaughter have all acted against Rosey's command and spoken of Rosey's inadequacies and flaws without her knowledge. How must that make her feel? "Amber made her decisions, and one of those was emancipating from what little family she had," Rosey says, venom gurgling beneath her words.

"Have you ever stopped to ask yourself why she felt it necessary to take such drastic actions?" Alyce flings back. "You and I both know the term emancipate is too strong a word in this particular situation, but the estrangement was, indeed, my mother's decision—according to my grandfather, anyway."

"Unlike you, my dear, I happen to know the full story; and unlike your grandfather, I was present for the full sordid tale."

thirty-four

THE NIGHT THE LIGHTS WENT OUT

Terry

I find it interesting that bearing witness to an ugly family argument is far more uncomfortable than being one of the participants in the said altercation. This exchange between Alyce and Rosey has most definitely reached the ugly factor. If the two of them continue, there'll be nothing of their relationship to rebuild on. Perhaps, if I can help mediate.... "The quips, the barbs, the duplicity. This is no way to conduct family affairs," I say, with a modicum of diplomacy.

"Oh, mind your own business, Terry," Rosey snaps. Perhaps more than a modicum was necessary in this situation. I proceed with care.

"Now, Rosey, I thought we were on good terms. I am only trying to offer my assistance. Yvonne and I have three daughters. If this discussion were being held among our familial unit, I would want someone to step in to remind us that emotions have a tendency to take over even the most meaningful and well-intended discussions."

"I appreciate your thoughtful offer, Terry," Alyce says. "However, I am not in the market for discussions. Maybe before, but now, I want the truth. I want to know what really happened to my parents."

"Is that what we're all doing here? Filling in the missing pieces of your little Nancy Drew mystery?" Patrick quips.

Jude saunters across the room to stand near Alyce again. "Dad, this is important to Alyce. She's been looking for answers all of her life." He grabs Alyce's hand. There has hardly been a moment this weekend when those two haven't been touching. If Rosey and Patrick are harboring hope for these two to split, they ought to redirect it to something more attainable.

Patrick looks up at Jude, standing to the left of the sofa Patrick and Melanie have claimed. "Being a bit dramatic there, son. She's what, twenty-three, twenty-five tops?"

"Why must you belittle what others consider important?" Yvonne asks. "This has nothing to do with us, Patrick." Yvonne is pushing for Alyce's agenda, but then again, she could be playing the contrary simply to goad 'ole Pat—he's never been her favorite person. Ordinarily, I'd cheer her on, but something about this exchange feels highly volatile.

"Are you kidding me?" Pat retorts. "Of course this is about us, all of us—and the dead ones too. They just aren't here to speak on their own behalf because someone took them out before they even had a chance to explain their roles in this shitshow."

Alyce steps forward, placing both hands on the back of the club chair, fixing her eyes on Pat. "What exactly are you alluding to here, Mr. Perkins? Please. Please tell me what you know." Jude stands close to Alyce, one hand firmly on her lower back.

"What is it you're looking for, Alyce? Specifically," Yvonne tries. "You've made it clear all weekend that you want to know more about your parents, but it seems to me you've learned quite a bit from your grandfather."

"You're right, Yvonne. I haven't been completely forthcoming. I apologize for that," Alyce says.

"Finally," Patrick huffs. Melanie jabs a pointy elbow into Pat's side, scowling all the while.

Alyce eyes Patrick. She lifts one hand, using two fingers to draw her long, dark hair away from her face, tossing it lightly over her shoulder. "I admit, I was aware that my parents were unmarried. Pops informed me. He said my mother was reluctant to commit herself to someone when she couldn't connect, much less maintain a relationship, with the one person in the world who was supposed to love you unconditionally. From what Pops relayed to me, I know that my mother was terrified while awaiting my impending arrival. She was scared she wouldn't be able to love, to nurture the way a mother should. I know that she was in love with me from the moment I was placed in her arms. What I'm specifically looking for are the circumstances behind their deaths. Pops provided me with the death certificates, so I know that the official cause of death was carbon monoxide poisoning, leading to asphyxiation. I know that autopsies were performed and that several drugs, as well as alcohol, were listed in their toxicology reports. I know that you all were with them on that fateful night. But what no one can, or rather will, tell me is of the events leading up to their deaths."

Alyce's lovely eyes pool to the point of spilling, wetting her young face. Once again, I think of our girls, how I would feel if this were one of them standing before us pleading for truth. Yvonne must be thinking much the same. "Well, if none of you will tell her, then I will," Yvonne says.

"Yvonne," Rosey states simply. I take my wife's hand into mine, knowing what she is about to do, applying a bit of pressure, striving to convey a warning. We've kept this secret at Rosey's directive all these years. But if Yvonne understands my signal for caution, she certainly isn't taking my counsel.

Despite Rosey's glare, Yvonne begins. "Perhaps you've taken a drive through the old 'hood to see where your parents lived when they brought you home, but maybe not. Regardless, it was small. There were no more than forty, maybe forty-five houses, positioned along two cul-de-sacs. The homes were tightly clustered on small lots, smaller in size and more affordable for those of us starting out. That said, it wasn't just a starter neighborhood. We lived among some retirees and empty nesters, but most of us congregated with others who were at the same stage of life. Our gang was the rowdy group of the community." Yvonne takes a breath.

All eyes in the room watch my beautiful, brave partner. I note Melanie nodding her head in agreement, Rosey viewing the account through narrowed gaze.

Yvonne continues. "Those few years, we would gather at one another's homes at least every other week, sometimes more. It was so much easier than scheduling sitters, hiring car services, or going out on the town. Baby monitors lined the kitchen counters, then were pushed aside when the shot glasses came out. We never claimed to be the best parents, and truth be told, I've had plenty more parenting fails under my name since. The thing is, we were all about the age of you and Jude when everyone met and began spending time together. I don't know what you two like to do for fun or to let off some steam, but that's what our group was doing when we all got together. The point I'm trying to make is that we were still trying to maintain some piece of our youth. Letting loose, acting crazy. Drinking, dancing, and experimenting with different drugs became something we all looked forward to."

"Let's not forget sleeping with one another's partners," Rosey says snidely.

"Not all of us participated in those activities, Rosey," I remind her, matching her snarky tone. I'm not going to judge anyone for their actions, but Yvonne and I have remained faithfully committed to one another throughout our marriage, even in our younger years. Rosey will not make such disparaging remarks about the union Yvonne and I have worked so hard to cultivate. Yvonne looks at me, offering a thin smile of solidarity, then continues with the story of what happened the night Alyce's parents perished.

"On the night your parents died, it was Shane and Amber's turn to host the get-together. I'm not sure how much you know about their relationship, but I want to stop here for a moment and tell you how they were when they were around one another.

"I realize now that you've known all along they were never married. But I tell you, you would never have known it. We could go round and round about the two of them sleeping with other people, but I don't think it diluted their feelings for one another. Terry and I didn't understand it, but it wasn't for us to understand. As I was saying, we all thought they were married when our group started spending time together. The way Shane looked at Amber... it was almost like he was pining for her. Maybe he was. She wasn't officially his wife. Amber looked at him just the same, though. They were very much in love, and when you came along, Lord, you would have thought no other baby in the history of mankind had ever been born before. Anyway, I thought you'd like to know."

"Yes. Thank you, Yvonne," Alyce says, quickly adding, "That means a lot. I hope you'll continue, though. Please."

"Of course. Like I was saying, it was your parents' turn to host. There were no baby monitors on the countertop that night. We had a big night planned. And not that we didn't love them dearly, but we didn't want the responsibility of children that night. As it happened, my mother and sister volunteered to watch the kids at our house. We only lived two doors down from Shane and Amber, so all the kids were nearby in case something happened."

Yvonne turns her attention to Jude. "You were there too, Jude, not that you'd remember. You were far too young, but you used to love to play with our girls when you all were little." She stops again to look at me. "Remember how they used to love to play house? Kendra—our oldest—and Jude were mommy and daddy to the other girls. Edie was their nanny, watching after the babies, Dionne, our youngest, and Elizabeth Alyce. I'd forgotten all about those sweet little games. Probably because that was the last night any of them ever played together."

"I'm sorry," Alyce interrupts. "But, can we go back to the 'big night?' I want to be sure I'm understanding correctly. What does that mean exactly—big night?"

"Should I say blowout instead, maybe? Does your generation use that term? Anyway. The gist of the evening was that each couple was tasked to bring something for the group, and that would be the narcotics that showed up in your parents' autopsy reports. The night went as you might expect—lots of joshing and dancing. I think we played a game at one point—maybe charades. Then, the storm rolled in. Not metaphorically, but as in a literal weather event. Mind you, it was nothing like the storm we are experiencing right now, but we lost electricity, which was a common occurrence for the residents of Perishing Hill.

"That neighborhood should have remained Perishing Hill—they've since changed it to the name initially planned for the development, Pershing Hill, if you weren't aware. What I'm trying to convey is that the neighborhood had multiple issues, pre-development issues, electricity lines being one of them. Every time a light gust blew through, half the neighborhood would lose power. It became the thing to own a generator. So when the storm came through and took out the electricity, we went on as if nothing was out of the ordinary.

"Something was off, though, like we mixed the wrong things or something. You know that old saying they have for the inexperienced drinkers—beer before liquor, never sicker; liquor before beer, never fear—like that. We all started to experience odd side effects. I know, I know. We were on illicit substances. How could we tell, you ask? Once again, not proud of that time in my life, but the drugs we consumed that night weren't anything we hadn't tried before, and we were careful not to overindulge; we had responsibilities. The evening was already breaking up when the storm arrived. We'd had our fun. The next day was a Saturday. The children would be up early, chores were meant to be performed, errands to run. We waited until the brunt of the storm died down, chatting and cleaning up, feeling generally very icky. I recall several times we spoke of getting too old to have such events.

"I remember Amber talking about how exhausted she was. You were young, not even a year old, and had yet to sleep through the night. My mother and sister were staying the weekend with us, so I offered to keep you overnight. My girls played with you like you were their own living, breathing little doll, and there were four adults at my house, all of whom were much more rested than your mother. After a bit of convincing, Amber agreed. She would be over first thing the next morning to pick you up. Except that I never saw Amber or Shane again." Yvonne pauses for a moment, picking at her cuticles, collecting her thoughts. I consider taking over the recollection for her, but Yvonne looks up and begins again.

"Because our homes were small, with barely enough square footage for our families, we kept our portable generators in the garage. None of us could afford anything fancy, but the device kept power going to the small necessities. When the units were running, we made a point to keep our garage doors open. We were young and naive and didn't know any better. Countless times, we had run our generators with our garage doors open and never had a problem. But that night, somehow or other, the door on Shane and Amber's garage closed and never reopened.

"That was when we met Rosey." Yvonne pauses, tossing a glance at Rosey, then back to Alyce. "Unlike our precious friends, we still had breath in our lungs, but the lives we knew before that night were changed forever."

thirty-five

SCARED SENSELESS

Griff

It's quiet—too quiet, and the whole room feels like it's been vacuum-packed. The wind has died down. No flashes of lightning streak the sky, and the thunder seems to have been packed away. But for how long?

"Yvonne's right," Melanie says, her voice catching. "We counted ourselves fortunate to have been spared, but we had no idea of the guilt and hell we would be left to endure after your parents' passing. Given the events of that night, death could have come for any one of us, and yet it only took Amber and Shane. I'm sorry, Alyce." Melanie's voice is thick and strangled. She swallows back a breath and begins again. "You've no idea how many times I've thought of that night. How many times I have wished I had looked out our front window and realized the door on your parents' garage was closed.... We lived across the street. I could have popped over, made them aware of the error. But after the escapades of the night before, our blinds were shut tight."

"It was Carmen who found them unresponsive," Yvonne takes over for Melanie. "It was the opening day of our local farmers' market. Carmen and Amber had made plans to attend, to take you on your first trip to the market."

Alyce brings a hand to her mouth. Jude slides his hand from Alyce's lower back around her waist, pulling her closer. Rosey eyes the pair, one leg crossed over the other, her foot flicking back and forth. Jude whispers something to Alyce. She nods in reply. What are they up to now? Whatever it is, Rosey ain't going to like it—just glad that narrowed scrutiny isn't focused on me. From all I've seen and witnessed of this group, finding yourself on the other side of that woman's fury is not a place I wish to be.

Melanie begins once more. "We were all questioned about their deaths. Authorities wanted every detail from the night of our party and inquired about each of our histories with Shane and Amber. One by one, we were each interrogated, the process leaving us to feel culpable and guilty, but even worse, wary of our own friends. After that, none of us trusted one another again."

"So that's when you all fell out of touch?" Alyce asks.

"It is," Yvonne answers. "After the funerals were over and Rosey had collected you, the rest of us put our houses up for sale and moved forward the best we knew how."

Alyce sighs heavily, shaking her head. She's not buying that explanation. "But I don't understand. In most instances, following a tragedy or some unexpected disaster, the parties involved become closer. They've experienced something collectively and then together share a bond that others could never understand without having been through a similar situation. At the very least, you all had one another to lean on, to help each other through the grief. What happened to lead you all to believe you couldn't trust one another?"

Patrick sits up animatedly. "I can answer that. That one over there," he says, pointing at Rosey. "It was Rosey. Always Rosey, stirring up a mess, poking at the fire, putting everyone on the defensive. Telling one couple something about the other and vice versa. Nobody knew who to trust."

Melanie delivers her husband a warning look. "What Patrick's trying to relay is that we were scared. Amber and Shane were so young, as were we, and if they could so easily be erased from this life, then the rest of us could face the same outcome."

"Don't speak for me, Melanie. I know exactly what I meant. You tell me Rosey didn't turn you against Yvonne and Kate and Carmen with all her so-called 'confidences,' and if I had to guess, there wasn't a bit of truth to those disclosures. Manipulation, pure and simple—Rosey manipulated all of us. Every last one of us acted as that woman instructed us to do. Think about how differently our lives—all of us—would have been had Rosey not shown up that day."

On the other side of the windows, lightning returns with a fierce crash that brightens the sky, the bolt magnificently cutting through the heavy, dark shelf cloud—a photographer's gold shot. Behind it, the thunder, not to be outdone, cracks open the sky, and the rain begins once more. Act Two is here. Yvonne fixes her eyes on the glass wall, darting, searching for the next strike. That last one was intense; it'd give anybody the willies. She seems to be handling it okay, though. At least she's not trying to crawl under the table again. That pill she took earlier seems to be managing her irrational fears. Terry places his hand on her knee, rubbing back and forth.

Once Terry is sure Yvonne has settled, he addresses Patrick's last claim.

"Melanie's right, and Patrick's right. We were scared. Of Rosey, of death, of reputations ruined before they ever had a chance to be firmly established." Terry pauses and looks at Yvonne. "That night, that storm, that life-changing event—we were all transformed in one way or another. Each of us adjusted the best we could and without complaint because we were the fortunate ones. Up until that point, we considered ourselves to be invincible—nothing could hurt us. We'd been in extreme situations throughout our youth, our young lives, and had come out remarkably unscathed. But then, we found ourselves at the funerals of two dear friends who were leaving behind a baby girl they would never have the opportunity to see grow and thrive, become a young woman." Terry takes another moment to make eye contact with Melanie and Patrick, the only other survivors left from that night. "We couldn't, we wouldn't object or protest; we still had our lives and the promise, the hope, of seeing our children into adulthood." A tear rolls down the man's face. "So we did what we were told."

"You're exactly right, Terry," Patrick says in a stunning moment of agreement—with anyone. "Now, tell her exactly how, of exactly who we were so scared."

"Is it necessary to do so, Patrick? What good can come from the indelicate details?"

Patrick slaps the side of his thigh, throwing his hand up in Alyce's direction. "I'm not the one asking for *indelicate details*, but that one is. That's all she's done all weekend. Whine. Whine. Whine. Who was my mommy? What kind of person was my daddy?"

"Are you not listening to a word I've said, man?" Terry asks Patrick. "I just finished telling this young woman that we were grateful just to have our lives and raise our kids. Her parents never got that opportunity. Like it or not, good or bad, your son, Jude, knows all about you, about his mother. That's all Alyce is asking for. As her future father-in-law, I'd think you'd want to embrace a new daughter into your life, not do everything you can to turn her against you before she ever marries in."

"Fine. Alyce, I'm here to set the record straight, to tell you whatever I can about your parents, but if you want my opinion, Shane and Amber aren't the ones you should be asking about." Patrick sits back on the sofa, turning his glare on Rosey.

Not one to be outdone, Rosey holds her icy gaze on the man, taking up the spar. "Ever the dramatic one, aren't you, Pat? That's one characteristic you've clung to over the years. Just can't let go of it, huh?"

Melanie looks at her husband, his arms folded across his chest. Patrick holds his silence. "He's right. Patrick's right. It's Rosey's doing that we all split up, and it was hard," Melanie's voice is coated with sadness. "I would have liked to have had my friends to grieve with, to remember the friends we lost. The whole mess felt like a nasty divorce." Melanie looks at Yvonne across the room. "I can't tell you how many times I picked up the phone to call you, to tell you about something that happened during my day, some milestone Jude had reached. But it was part of the agreement—no communication with the group."

Yvonne nods. "I know. Me too, I was scared. I'm not afraid to say it; I did what I was told because I was fearful of what the consequences would be if I didn't."

Alyce steps closer. "What were you both so afraid of? Rosey?"

"Yes," Melanie answers. Yvonne nods again.

"Back then, my days were consumed with being a mom and a wife, running a household, and working part-time at the funeral home," Yvonne pauses. "Like we said before, we weren't much older than you two are now. Rosey was so much older than us—respect for your elders; yes, ma'am, no sir; they know better than you were phrases burned into the psyches of our generation. And then, Rosey knew everyone, from the local sheriff to the governor. Not only was Rosey older and wiser, she was connected, and that in itself scared the crap out of me. That's my excuse. I own it, and I'm not proud of it, but I don't think I could have come to that conclusion earlier in my life." Yvonne runs her fingers underneath her eyes, then continues. "We've all been living with the belief that we are responsible for your parents' deaths."

"But you just told me it was the generator?"

"It was," Yvonne says. "But remember, we were all on multiple substances, multiple illegal substances. Rosey found each of our weaknesses and used them against us."

Alyce shakes her head. Breaking from Jude's hold, she begins a shallow pace behind the club chair. Jude steps aside, giving her some room to move about. "I still don't understand," she says. "If you all didn't kill my parents, then why would you even bother to do what Rosey said?"

"The police ruled the tragedy an accident." Yvonne tries to

explain. Alyce pauses her pace to listen. "What was our story, Melanie? The one that was decided we would use?"

Patrick clears his throat, answering for Melanie. "That we all gathered at Shane and Amber's for our monthly dinner meeting —we had tacos and pizza, somebody brought beer and canned margaritas, a laid-back night, no one needing to cook. When the storm came in and we lost power, everyone went home. We told 'em that one," Patrick points at Alyce, "was asleep at Yvonne and Terry's place, so Shane and Amber let her stay the night instead of waking the baby."

"But why did you need a story?" Alyce asks, her voice rising with frustration. What was wrong with the truth?" she asks, placing both hands on the back of the chair, bracing for the next round.

"Think about..." Melanie lays her hand on Patrick's knee, as much to keep it from bouncing up and down as to stop him from expressing any more animosity. He takes her cue and sits back, both feet flat on the floor.

Melanie takes over. "We knew autopsies would be performed. Once the results were in, the authorities would know Amber and Shane had taken illegal drugs before they died. If any of us had admitted we frequently gathered to party, the investigators would have pried further into the events of the evening: who did what, who said what, who took what. By keeping our stories the same— a simple gathering of neighbors to enjoy a meal and conversation —we could avoid having child services brought in, digging into our pastime activities and child-rearing techniques."

"We weren't bad parents," Yvonne adds. "But we were young and foolish... and gullible."

Alyce tilts her head in question. "Why is that? What do you mean gullible?" Alyce keeps delving in, unsatisfied with the account.

"Because I told them what to say," Rosey says.

Alyce whips her gaze to meet her grandmother's eyes. "What do you mean you told them? I thought you were notified by the authorities of my parents' deaths. Are you saying you knew about their demise before the police informed you?"

"That's exactly what she's saying," Patrick booms.

"When Carmen went to meet up with Amber to go to the farmer's market that morning, she found Rosey at Amber's front door," Yvonne explains. "Carmen told me she knew exactly who Rosey was the minute she saw her on the doorstep. Nevertheless, Carmen was confused and surprised to find her there. Amber had shared photos of her mother with Carmen during a conversation they'd had about their families. Carmen knew Amber and Rosey were estranged, that Amber was adamant Rosey was to know nothing about her baby girl. Carmen confided to me that she had probed Amber on a couple of occasions as to why she didn't want the baby to know her grandmother, but the topic upset Amber, and she would shut down. So, Carmen dropped the discussion."

"Carmen told me that she was uncertain what to expect or think. After what Amber had shared about her relationship with her mother, Carmen wasn't sure whether to stay to support Amber or leave the mother/daughter pair to their privacy. Carmen decided to stick around and let Amber know she came by —she planned to offer to watch the baby while Amber and her mother talked. Except no one answered the door. Cellphones were new on the scene back then—some of us had one, others, not yet. Regardless, everyone still kept landlines. Rosey had a cell phone in her handbag and tried calling Shane and Amber's home phone. Carmen and Rosey could hear the ringing, ringing, ringing inside." Yvonne pauses, looking from Alyce to her hands, keeping her gaze down as she continues, her voice muffled by emotion.

"Carmen used Amber and Shane's hidden key to let herself and Rosey inside the house. An alarm beeped somewhere in the distance while a grumbling rattle came from the garage. It didn't take long to determine what had happened. Rosey and Carmen ran through the house, opening doors and windows, searching for Shane and Amber. They found them in the primary bathroom.

Shane and Amber's floor plan was such that their bedroom was located directly across from the garage. We concluded they decided to have a bath after our party broke up the prior night, closed their garage door by mistake, and fell asleep in the tub."

Yvonne holds, sniffling, dabbing at the corner of her eyes.

"Rosey called us all together. She instructed Carmen to go round up our group and meet back on the front porch. Rosey said that she would call emergency and told Carmen to hurry because Rosey wanted to talk to all of us before the officials showed up. Carmen came to me first because she knew Elizabeth... Alyce had stayed with us overnight, and then somehow or other, everyone was standing on Shane and Amber's front porch listening to Rosey give direction as to what we were going to do and say."

"Telling you what to do?" Alyce asks. "But you make it sound like you all are guilty of something?"

"And Rosey made us feel like we were," Patrick bellows.

Melanie explains. "We never would have thought about the drug use, about how the authorities would view that."

"At the time, we thought she was doing us a favor," Yvonne says. "The situation was so unbelievable—our friends were alive, and then they weren't. None of us was in control of our emotions or our wits, and were in no condition to make decisions. One minute, we've been gathered together to have this bombshell laid at our feet, and only seconds later, we're being interrogated by Rosey for every minute detail from the night before. We didn't have time to think about what we were saying, much less process what had happened and how our roles in the matter would look to the authorities. Everything Rosey said made so much sense when we could make no sense of what had happened inside our small piece of existence."

Terry takes over for Yvonne. "I was absent during these discussions. I had gone inside to assess the conditions of Shane and Amber, to be certain there was nothing we could do for them, but we were hours too late. By the time I joined the group again, the plan had been formed. We all had the same story, right down to the 'we knew that Amber's mother was coming for a visit, so we decided to cut the evening short when the power went out, even though we all had generators.' The officials determined Shane and Amber were enjoying a peaceful night without their baby. They resolved that drug use had impaired their faculties, leading them to close their garage door. Their deaths were ruled a tragic accident."

The two couples stare at one another, vacant looks in their eyes, mouths drawn down. Even from my position at the window wall, I can see the recount has etched new creases and ruts across their faces. That's a hell of a tale to have lived with your whole life. I understand why they were so reluctant to speak of it.

Did Alyce get what she wanted? She and Jude have turned their backs on the folks who finally did what she kept asking for. The two of 'em over there are in deep conversation again. I can only wonder about what now. Rosey keeps her eye on them too, as she casually lifts her phone to check the screen, then lowers it face down on the arm of the chair.

Under the pretense of seeming to check the weather—if for no one but myself—I turn to the window wall. The gray haze is shading dark as the last dregs of the sun's refracted rays slip away from this day. From what bit I can see of it in the distance, the ocean sure has a mean look about it. The waves are building, prepping, gearing up for a big push inland.

I hope Alyce is about done with this, cause we don't have much longer. We're going to be in the water real soon.

thirty-six

IS THERE AN ADULT IN THE ROOM?

Rosey

"Yvonne's right, you know," I lob from my seated position in the club chair, Alyce and Jude turning at the sound of my voice. Yes, it's the perfect vantage point, really. I've got a good view of each of their faces, a perfect spot for reading expressions (which I much prefer to reading minds). "I did all of you a favor by thinking ahead for you. The way I saw it, you all were indebted to me for keeping each of you out of the fray. The investigators never questioned your stories—no clarification was needed whatsoever. It all checked out."

"Yes, and it seems a bit too clean to me," Alyce says.

"Alyce, Alyce, Alyce. Everyone here has catered to your whims all weekend, so much so that we're all quite worn out with you. This petulant routine must end if you are ever to be treated as an adult." My patience for this activity has run dry.

"I suggest you stir up a second wind, because I'm not done with this." Alyce juts her hip out to the left, bringing her hands to rest on each side of her slender frame.

"What more could you possibly want, Alyce? These people have traveled all this way without an explanation as to why or what for, only to ride out a vicious tropical storm, share their darkest moments in life, and paint a lovely portrait of your parents. All on top of losing four more friends. Enough is enough, Elizabeth Alyce. It is time to call this what it is. A disaster."

Alyce brings the flat of her palm to her forehead, shaking her head back and forth. She removes her hand and looks at me. "This is what you do. You bully people into submission. Since I was just a child, I've watched you use this manipulation tactic. You dig, dig, dig, find a person's insecurity—flick it here, poke it there—play off their inhibitions, tell them how irrational they're being, and use that authoritative tone to convince them of your superiority. How could your victim possibly know more than you?"

What has gotten into this girl? Obviously, it has to do with this boy, Patrick Perkins's son, no less. "This isn't like you, Alyce. You're fraught with nerves and stress. This storm isn't helping any of us to stay centered."

"This isn't some freaking yoga retreat, Rosey. These people are here to help me find the truth once and for all," Alyce throws back at me.

"Yeah, and we've done our part," Patrick barks. "Melanie and I told you what we know. Jude helped you plan out this weekend, and now my family and I are done. I've said all I'm going to say, and so has my wife." Next to him, Melanie stares at her husband, rolling her eyes and sighing heavily.

Alyce turns to face Patrick. "I'm. Not. Done." Heat races up her neck and throat, coloring her face. Alyce turns her focus back on me. "What were you doing there in the first place?"

"Doing where, Alyce? You're going to have to be more specific with your requests."

"Perishing Hill, outside my mother and father's house. Why were you there? The two of you hadn't spoken in years, and the day your daughter dies, you just happen to be on her doorstep—some serendipitous act of fate?" She pauses, looking at the faces around the room, some dramatic effort to make a point with the others, I suppose. "Am I right?"

"The thought has crossed my mind a time or two," Yvonne says. "But posing that question would have put my family in danger." Terry looks at her and nods in agreement.

"I'm finding it difficult to believe you were there by sheer coincidence, Rosey," Alyce says, the sharp edge in her tone making her sound so much like her mother, Amber.

I reposition my legs, bringing the right one to sit on the left knee, straightening the crease that runs the length of my trousers. "That is correct," I answer. "It was not a coincidence." I continue, though I do not address Alyce. Her behavior is incorrigible, and I will not address such hatefulness from my own granddaughter; therefore, I speak to the remaining members of that ridiculous Perishing Hill gang Amber was a part of. "The fact that I had a private investigator following Amber has already been made known. Obviously, Amber didn't live in a bubble; therefore, my investigator reported on all those within Amber's orbit. He reported on the gatherings you all had—knew of the penchants for alcohol and drugs, and parties you all shared. Because of Amber and who she was, I was drawn into your lives, not by chance or choice.

"And then I learned Amber gave birth to a daughter, my granddaughter, and never bothered to inform me. There she was, same 'ole Amber, going on about her life like she was some sixteen-year-old girl without any responsibilities and not the mother of a defenseless infant. How could Amber raise a child when she conducted herself like a child? After Alyce was born, I put the investigator on her full-time." I pause, twisting to address the Marshalls and the Perkins. "Surely, you all can understand. You each have children. You know their strengths and weaknesses better than anyone else. I knew Amber wasn't capable of being a good mother. Amber was selfish—a terrible thing to call your own offspring, but it's the truth. Keeping Alyce out of my life corroborates that very point."

I give them a moment to gnaw on that thought before

proceeding. The concentrated looks on their faces tell me I have their complete attention.

"My investigator informed me that it was a party night. When the gathering broke up, the investigator let me know that Alyce didn't return home that evening. Eight months old, and Amber was already allowing the baby to sleep away from home so that she could party and carry on like some teenager. The fact only solidified the knowledge that Amber had no idea how to take care of a baby. I was on the doorstep because it was time for Amber to realize she had no business raising a child. My intentions that morning were to collect Alyce and take her home with me."

"Amber would not have allowed that," Yvonne says, pulling herself to sit on the edge of the sofa, placing elbows on her knees. "I'm not sure what all your P.I. told you, but Amber was a good mother. She was so devoted to Elizabeth. Sorry. Alyce."

"So you say. But let me ask you, Yvonne. Did you neglect to tell your mother about the births of your three children?" Yvonne lowers her gaze in defeat, not bothering to answer such a ridiculous query. "And since you've yet to be blessed with grandchildren, you cannot possibly understand how hurtful it is to be excluded from such a momentous life occasion."

"It's understandable such an oversight would be hurtful," Terry begins carefully. "However, I think you must consider your words, Rosey, your accusations. By claiming Amber an unfit mother simply for blowing off steam as a young woman with her friends one evening every couple of weeks, you've condemned the rest of us to the same odious declaration."

"You and that slick spiel of yours, Terry. You always did believe you could talk me down by pulling out the melodic baritone and using some big words. Well, I suppose it's high time you understand—that tactic never worked on me."

"Don't let it tear you up too badly, Terry," Alyce says. "No sense arguing with someone who is never wrong. Because even when she is wrong, Rosey tweaks her stories to make herself appear the victim. If you don't believe her tales of woe, if you question her, dare contradict her beliefs, Rosey will shut you out, and then she will make you believe you are at fault."

"For the life of me, I can't understand what has gotten into you, Alyce. I have a sneaky suspicion it's this boy you're dating. Has he been putting thoughts into your head? It wouldn't surprise me, given who he was reared by."

"Don't bring my family into your twisted, cynical scope, Rosey." I have Melanie's full attention now. "Jude is a good man. He is only trying to help Alyce find the truth you refuse to impart."

"Do you see what you have done, Alyce? By pushing these people for answers, you have turned them against you, against us. I'm not sure I see a path to a future for you and this young man. His family is far too combustible, and now you have gone and made it awkward for them. It will prove impossible for the Perkins to genuinely welcome you into the family after all that has happened and has been said this weekend."

"Jude is my future. We will be married, regardless of how you or his family feels about the matter. I planned this weekend for one reason only: to collect as many details as I could about my parents. The weekend may not have played out as I would have liked, definitely not as planned, but I have indeed learned more about them as people."

This weekend has brought about some clarity for me as well. I must ensure Alyce and Jude do not unite. I'm sure I'll have no issue obtaining Patrick's help with this matter. He is about as anxious for this union as I am. However, I'm going to have to play a card I hadn't intended to throw out.

Jude

Rosey's eyes narrow, though who her focus finds, I can't be certain. Of course, I don't know Rosey like Alyce does, but it doesn't take a family member to see she has something building, inching toward the surface. Rosey's head turns in slow concentration toward the wall of windows. Her focus lands on the scene out the window—or is it Griff she has her eye on?

Griff has had little to say during this lengthy exchange. What must he think of this group? His eyes shift back and forth between Rosey and Alyce. He must wonder what he's gotten into. It's evident to everyone here, though, that there is more to his relationship with Rosey than has been let on.

"Interestingly enough," Rosey starts, breaking through the silence that has fallen over the room. "I just recalled another piece of information about the night Amber and Shane died," she says coyly, tracing the outline of the cell phone perched on her knee.

All attention is back on Rosey. Alyce did say her grandmother enjoys the spotlight. My parents exchange a glance very much like the one Yvonne and Terry share—curiosity and apprehension about the chaotic disaster unfolding. Alyce is right. People are intimidated by this woman, and she loves it. Rosey has them where she wants and continues.

"As we've already established, the investigator was outside the house the night of the party. In the aftermath of my daughter's death and all the arrangements that required my regard, I failed to make the connection. However, it seems pertinent for me to mention this particular detail to you all now—it might even shed some new light on the events of that night." Rosey tosses a look at Dad. As odd as I find the newfound emotion, I understand I am worried for him. Dad must anticipate the chaos coming his way as well. The glare Dad fixes on Rosey, the expression he pulls—eyes piercing, lips slightly parted—is a sure sign his full wrath is on the way. Perhaps my concern is misplaced; maybe it's Rosey I should worry about.

If Rosey notices Dad's fury, she doesn't acknowledge it.

"After the funerals for Amber and Shane, I met with Tom, my private investigator. We'd barely had time to recount the facts as they had happened that fateful evening, much less get his insight on details that might seem insignificant to others. Tom is so good with details. There's a reason I've employed Tom all these years.

That man has quite the eye or eyes, I suppose. The thing is, Tom sees everything, and yet no one ever notices him lurking about. Nothing is considered minutiae in that man's estimation—his work is nothing short of impressive, really."

"Do you have a point to make, Rosey?" Dad interrupts.

"You're correct, Pat. I'm sure you're anxious to hear the details. I'll get right to it," Rosey says to Dad, an ominous aura shrouding her. "Tom noticed a man walking that night. Seems the fellow was out for an evening stroll; at least, that's what the man told Tom when they came in contact with one another. Tom acted as if he went on about his way, all the while paying careful attention to the minutiae. Like I said before, Tom is so good with minutiae, nothing too trivial, I tell you."

Dad stops her again. "Okay, Rosey. You've had your fun."

"But I haven't told you what else Tom saw." Rosey's stare cuts through Dad. Something's about to happen that can't be… unhappened. Dad must see it too, judging by the way he scoots around on the sofa, adjusting his positioning. Does this have something to do with him? "Tom said the lone fellow approached Amber and Shane's home. Obviously, Tom watched what this man did. After all, that's what Tom was being paid to do: watch my daughter and all those she had contact with."

"Rosey, this is ridiculous," Alyce says. "This is what I'm talking about. You craft these little narratives, and we're all supposed to hang on every word like you're the most interesting person we've ever encountered. And no doubt, when the story is over, you come out smelling like lilacs while some other poor bloke will walk away covered in shit."

"The use of such vulgarity is so unappealing. I did not raise you to use such language, Alyce. Now, I haven't finished my narrative, or anecdote, or whatever other derogatory label you're slapping on it at the moment."

Alyce clamps her hair in two fingers, running them down the long length and tossing it over her shoulder. "By all means, continue. Please, prove me right."

"I think we've heard enough," Dad tries to halt Rosey again. "I'm sure Alyce is right." What the hell was that? Dad agrees with Alyce? My dad doesn't allow others to be right, and very rarely does he agree with anyone but himself.

"Well, I think the others might like to hear the rest of what I have to say, regardless of Alyce's predictions."

Alyce steps aside, shaking her head. Rosey continues. "Tom observed this man as he walked inside the open garage. Tom thought it odd and stepped closer to the house, watching to see if the man had taken anything from Amber and Shane's garage. As he got a better look at the man's features, Tom realized the man was a member of the Perishing Hill group he'd been following under my employ. After more observation, he determined that the man going into and leaving Amber and Shane's garage was Patrick."

"Now, wait a minute," Dad says.

"What now, Patrick?" Rosey asks. "As I recall, I'm the one relaying the events of the evening. Was there something you wanted to add? Something you might be aware of that the others haven't been privy to?"

"You left out some minutiae, as you put it," Dad says, his words coated in sarcasm. "There was someone else there that night, not just me. A woman was also out walking that night. I thought it odd because we'd just had that storm blow through. I know your guy told you about the woman, Rosey, and you know it too. We talked about it. Hell, I even gave you both information on which direction she approached from and the route she took to make her exit."

Mom twists to address Dad. "What is this all about, Patrick? You never mentioned you went back out after the storm that night. Was this before or after we collected Jude from the Marshalls' house? Because once we had Jude settled in bed, I could have sworn we both retired as well."

"You went to bed; I needed air. After all the crap we had put into our bodies earlier that evening, I wasn't doing too well. I wish to God I hadn't gone back out that night, though."

"Okay, so fine, you went back out. What about the woman?" Mom asks for clarification.

Dad drops his head into his hands, concealing his eyes, fingertips massaging his brow, working into his hairline. "Like I said before, there was an older woman walking the neighborhood." His head hanging, the words drop to the floor. "She approached me. Asked if I knew the people in the house with the garage left open. Of course I said yes, that they were friends. She said I might ought to run up and shut their door for them, even went on to talk about how her home just up the street had been burglarized recently."

"Oh dear Lord! Patrick," Mom says, eyes wide with shock and fear. "Are you saying you closed the door on Amber and Shane's garage? It wasn't them that caused the carbon monoxide poisoning by closing that door, but that it was you?"

Dad slowly raises his gaze to find Alyce and nods. "It was me. I closed that door. If I'd left well enough alone, if I'd never listened to that woman, your parents might still be alive."

thirty-seven

YOU DID WHAT?

Yvonne

"Well, Alyce, it seems you're getting more answers than you bargained for," Rosey says snidely, adding, "and a confession, to boot."

"Now, before we all jump to conclusions..." Terry tries, only to be cut off by Rosey.

"It's a bit late for that, don't you think, Terry? Patrick here has just admitted to killing Alyce's parents." Rosey wears a smug look. Is it that she hates Patrick so much that she would want him found guilty of murder? Or is it that the wedding is surely off now that Alyce knows her father-in-law-to-be is her parents' killer? Either way, if I were Rosey, I'd be livid, having found out I'd just spent the weekend with the man responsible for the death of one of our girls. Poor Alyce, though; she stands in shock next to Jude, who is working to soothe her. He steps her back toward the corner of the room, away from the bickering.

"Hang on a minute," Pat scoots himself to the edge of the sofa, ready to pounce. "I didn't admit to killing anybody. The only thing I'm guilty of is doing what some old, busybody hag told me to do."

"You didn't have to go inside their home. No one threatened

you to close that door," Rosey says. Her tone is even and measured, careful. Conciliatory? Why is she not more upset about this? I can't understand. Rosey does not give the appearance of a woman devastated to have just learned the true way her daughter died. She has sparred with Patrick all weekend about far less critical topics, and now she has no emotion, nothing to say about this new knowledge regarding the death of her daughter. Something is off here. If Rosey won't get to the bottom of this, I'll handle it myself—for Alyce's sake, if nothing else.

"Let's take a step back for a moment and talk this through," I begin. "Who was this woman, Patrick? Our neighborhood wasn't that large, and Terry was on the homeowners' association committee. He knew everybody. Maybe if you describe the woman, Terry and I can help identify her. Then maybe we could locate the woman? Get her recollection of the events that took place that night? Ask her what she remembers from her time in the neighborhood."

"Over twenty years ago?" Rosey asks incredulously. "Come on, Yvonne. Surely, you have more sense than that. I couldn't tell you what happened two weeks ago on a random night. I think we're grasping for something that was settled over two decades ago. Let the dead rest in peace. I see no reason to exhume the past."

Why is it I'm more concerned about getting to the truth than Rosey is? "Seriously? You want to let it go? I would think you'd want as many details about Amber's death as you could hunt down."

"Patrick has readily admitted to his role in the deaths of my daughter and Alyce's father, so why would we need to go hunt down someone to corroborate his account? To make him look guiltier? He's basically admitted to committing murder. Think for a minute about who we are discussing." Rosey's fingers tap the arm of the club chair, one by one, as if she's pressing piano keys, that jade ring sliding along her finger.

"What the hell, Rosey? What was that jab? And I'm not a

murderer," Patrick's voice rises with intensity. "Murder is intentional. I didn't kill anybody in cold blood. Shane and Amber's deaths were accidents."

"It's called involuntary manslaughter," Melanie says.

"Jesus, Mel. Do you want me to go to prison?" Melanie tilts her head to one side, a signal of apology—sorry, I said what I said. What would I do if I had just found out Terry was responsible for another person's death? The possibility is so far out of my husband's character realm that I can't possibly place myself in Melanie's shoes.

In an effort to de-escalate the situation as much as to seek the truth, I try again. "Do you remember anything about the woman, Patrick? What about physical attributes?"

"I don't know. She was old. She had short hair. It was so dark —all the electricity was out and I was so messed up." Patrick runs hands through his hair.

I pull away from Terry's side, sitting up taller so as to look Pat in the eye."Was she short? Tall? Thin? Heavy-set?"

"No. I told you. I was screwed up," Pat drops his head into his hands again. "Can't remember what all I took and drank, but it was like I was having some out-of-body experience, like I was looking at everything from above. But here's the thing that's not adding up: Rosey knew about that woman, and she's acting like this is new knowledge." Pat lifts his head, his glare finding Rosey. "I know you remember that, Rosey, and I know you never said anything to the police about the woman."

"What makes you think Rosey knew about that woman, Dad? How can you be so sure Rosey knew about this woman if you were so messed up?" Jude asks. Next to him, Alyce watches the proceedings, her face drawn in confusion and focused concentration.

"Because I told her—that's how. After everything happened, Rosey brought her spy around and started asking all these questions." He's animated, arms flying, face contorted, desperate to make his side of the story known. "The two of 'em grilled me on every detail of that night, and I was completely sober for that conversation. So yeah, my memory's just fine about that woman, son—nice of you to question your old man, though; thanks for having my back." Pat leers at Jude, then continues.

"After I told them about what happened that night—including the meddling old woman—that's when Rosey laid the initial blackmail."

Patrick and Rosey's eyes meet, some silent communication happening between the two of them that the rest of us struggle to decipher.

"I stand corrected. We did speak about the woman," Rosey admits, slow and measured, a slight shrug of her pointy shoulders to punctuate her statement. "I forgot how persistent you can be, Pat."

"And again, what?" Alyce says. She turns her gaze on Rosey. "More blackmail? Good God, Rosey." Alyce starts to pace again and stops suddenly, spinning on her heel. "If Patrick told you about the woman initially, why didn't you say something to the police then?" Alyce looks from Pat to Rosey. "One of you knows more than you're saying."

"There is no reason to be so bossy, Alyce," Rosey chastises. "If memory serves, Patrick did speak to me about the woman to whom Tom verified his story, and I do, in fact, recall Pat telling me that the woman suggested he close the garage door. Forgive this old woman; my memory isn't what it used to be."

"And the blackmail, Rosey," Alyce charges.

"Hold on a second." Patrick suddenly pushes his body to the edge of the sofa again, leaning his body over his knees. "I never told you the woman said I should close that door. I never told anyone that old lady told me what I should do. I didn't tell anybody that I was the one who closed that door until this afternoon. Because you see, it didn't matter. I was too fucked up on God knows what to reason that we left it open for the goddamned generator. Hell, I was so messed up I didn't even hear the generator running when I went inside the garage and closed the door.

Here is what I do remember about that old bitty. She looked a lot like you, Rosey. I've never thought about what the woman looked like because, as I just said, what did it matter? But then, just now, when Yvonne was asking me what the woman looked like, I started thinking back on it, and yeah. She looked A LOT like you, Rosey."

Terry looks at me, shock and understanding registering. I can no longer hold my tongue. "You were there that night, weren't you, Rosey? That's how you got there so early the next morning." I shake my head, look at Terry, then back at Rosey. "We never thought to ask. It didn't occur to me what a coincidence it was that you were already in town, that no one needed to contact next of kin because next of kin had previously arrived. But you were there the night before. That's how you came to be on their doorstep that morning. You already knew what happened to Amber and Shane. My God. Your own daughter...."

Looking unsteady on her feet, Alyce holds to the back of the club chair. "Are you all saying what I think you're saying?" She slowly lifts her sight to Rosey. "You were there the night my mother and father died?"

Rosey sits in her chair, one leg still crossing the other, foot still flicking to and fro. "My intentions were to meet the grand-daughter I was not told about. So, yes, I was in Norfolk that night."

"Amber never mentioned you were in town on a visit," Melanie accuses. "I'm pretty sure that is a subject we would have discussed." Melanie looks my way for validation as I nod in the affirmative.

"She wouldn't have, as I didn't tell her," Rosey says. "And why would I announce my arrival? Amber had already kept Alyce's existence from me. Had I announced I was coming for a visit, do you really think she would have welcomed me back into her life after having gone to such lengths to keep me in the dark about her child, my grandchild?"

"So Patrick is right?" Melanie asks. "You were the woman that night who told him to close the door to Shane and Amber's garage?"

Terry jumps in. "Even if it was indeed Ms. Rosey who was in the neighborhood that night, and she did, in fact, suggest Patrick close their entryway, who's to say she knew the generator was running?" God love my husband, ever the one to dole out the benefit of the doubt. "Rosey didn't know about the issues in our neighborhood, about the electrical outages we oft experienced. Her suggestion that Patrick close the door was most likely to make sure that Amber and Shane weren't burglarized. Patrick did say the woman told him she'd been robbed recently. Surely Rosey was only looking out for her daughter's best interest."

"Give it a break, Terry. Don't you see, man? Haven't you been listening? Rosey was having us tailed for years prior. Her private investigator was watching every move we made so that she could keep tabs on Amber. Of course, she knew about the problems in Perishing Hill. There's no telling how long the PI had been following us up to that point. Hell, Alyce over there was eight months old when Amber and Shane died. My guess is that Rosey had us under surveillance well before Alyce was born. She probably knew every routine, every ritual we practiced. That's why we're all really here. Rosey didn't want us telling any of this to Alyce," Patrick says.

Rosey remains quiet as all eyes in the room swivel to take in her expression, her demeanor, waiting to see what she will say, whether she will admit to what she has been accused of.

Alyce finally breaks the long stretch of silence. "So that's it? What Mr. Perkins has revealed is the truth? You told him to close that door, knowing the generator was running?"

Still, Rosey refuses to claim innocence or to acknowledge guilt. She sits silently, twisting the jade ring around her finger.

"That's it!" Patrick shouts. His sudden movement startles Melanie.

She looks at Patrick, forehead wrinkling in confusion. "What has gotten into you?"

Pat's practically bobbing up and down with renewed dramatic flair, which none of us have the energy for after everything we've been through this weekend. "That ring. I remember that ring."

"What on heaven's green earth…?" Melanie asks.

"That night. The old woman. The one who told me about the garage door. When she pointed toward Amber and Shane's garage, there was a flash of green. It was that ring. I remember that ring," Pat insists.

"Is it true?" Alyce's voice breaks. Tears spill down her face. "What Mr. Perkins is implying—Is. It. TRUE?" Alyce asks, stepping toward Rosey. Rosey meets Alyce's eyes. "Tell me, Rosey. Did you tell Mr. Perkins to close their garage door? For decency's sake, be honest with me for once in my life," Alyce pleads.

Rosey levels her gaze. "They went peacefully, experienced no pain whatsoever. You want to know pain? I had pain every day of my life with that girl."

thirty-eight

THE FAMILY TREE

Melanie

The words swirl inside my head, lining up and rearranging to make some sense of the conversation. I think I heard correctly, but how can that be? How can a person be so blasé about killing two people? Moreover, how could a mother kill her own child? Immediately, my eyes find my child—just the sight of him swelling my heart. I can't imagine ever being so angry with Jude that I would personally see to his demise.

This version of events contains twists none of us so much as considered while living through the moment. We all believed that Rosey had turned up on Shane and Amber's doorstep in hopes of reconciling with her daughter, to meet her granddaughter, only to be delivered the horrific blow that she was hours too late. The thought of their relationship ending so tragically broke me. At the first opportunity, I remember ringing my mother to let her know I loved her, that I was grateful for our connection.

Sitting shoulder to shoulder with Patrick, he looks at me and asks quietly. "Did Rosey just admit to murdering Amber and Shane?" I offer a slight nod of affirmation, then train my eyes on Alyce, waiting to see how this poor girl will move forward with this new information.

Through tears, Alyce looks at Rosey—eyes narrowed, brow furrowed. "Oh dear God. You did it. I always believed you knew more than you were saying, but to know you killed them, and I could have died along with them." The realization is visible in Alyce's stature, her shoulders falling in dejection and sorrow. "What if I had been in that house, Rosey? I would be gone, too."

"I knew you weren't in the house," Rosey says matter-of-factly, no tinge of remorse detectable. "Tom informed me earlier that evening that you were at the Marshalls' house. He relayed that you didn't return home after everyone dispersed that night."

A disbelieving stupor drapes over Alyce. She stands rigid and silent, absorbing. *Well into my fifties, and I am having difficulty grasping this new information. How punishing must it be for this young woman, who has yet to begin her adult life, to learn of the cunning deceit that runs straight through her family?*

Yvonne takes the opportunity to jump in. "Alyce, please accept my apologies for speaking up right now. I know this is your ordeal to bear, and I don't want to be insensitive—but Jesus, Rosey. You deceived every last one of us. The grieving, the questions, the 'if I had just reached out sooner' bit. And then, when you took Alyce, that poor baby wanted nothing to do with you. She cried every time you came near her. We pitied you. Your daughter was dead, and her child wanted nothing to do with you. Then, to learn you killed your own daughter and her partner. Why? Because Amber didn't tell you about the birth of Elizabeth Alyce? Have you ever heard of therapy? My God, woman, there are therapists who specialize in rehabilitating familial relationships."

"No amount of counseling would have, could have repaired the fissure in our relationship," Rosey says. "The state of our mother/daughter bond was irreparable. I had long moved past ever thinking Amber and I might reconcile."

"Then why kill her? Why not live and let live?" I ask as Patrick takes my hand in an uncharacteristic show of support.

Rosey looks at her hands. As she ponders her answer, she

strokes a finger over the protruding vein running atop her aging hand. Without looking up, she says simply, "Alyce," no explanation to follow.

Alyce crosses her arms in frustration, huffing. "What is that supposed to mean? You're blaming me for the fact that you murdered my parents?"

"No, that's not what I'm saying," Rosey answers.

"Then please just fucking say it," Alyce yells over the raucousness of rain belaboring the roof, siding, and windows. I'm not sure which storm is more destructive: the one outside the walls of Dune Dweller or the one within. I do hope Rosey will forgo the lecture on language here. I don't know how much more of Rosey's chastising Alyce can handle in light of this incredible account.

"Your mother couldn't even get you named properly. Elizabeth Alyce, it should've been Alyce Elizabeth—flows better, sounds proper. She had no business being a mother in any fashion or form."

"And you did?" Alyce asks.

"I had done the job once prior," Rosey says—then, "I had far more experience than Amber did."

Alyce shakes her head in disbelief. "You never gave her a chance."

"That girl was always in trouble," Rosey snaps. "And always so contrary. Whatever I said, Amber did the opposite."

"That does not mean she would have been a bad mother," Terry states. "Before reaching adulthood, daughters are notoriously at odds with their mothers. Yvonne and I have three girls, and each one of them presented as iron-willed and uncompromising during their teen years," Yvonne nods along with Terry's shared knowledge.

"'Mother knows best,'" Rosey says. "Have you ever heard that expression? I raised that girl. I knew what she was capable of, as well as incapable of doing, of handling. And let me tell you, Amber was not mother material."

Patrick fidgets as I lean forward to speak. "I still don't understand how you can be so certain Amber would have been unable to fulfill such duties, particularly if you all were estranged during most of Amber's adult life." I try, drawing Rosey's animous in my direction.

"Because she had already proved she couldn't do the job," Rosey says, a slight knowing tilt to her head.

"How's that?" Alyce raises her hands to take her long hair into them and flings it over one shoulder in aggravation. "How could you possibly know what kind of mother she would have been?" Her voice rises with the noise of the rain, hammering relentlessly on the roof. "Pops told me Amber left when she graduated high school and that, as far as he knew, you two didn't speak after that occasion. Ten years. A lot can happen to a person in that amount of time. A lot of maturation can occur over ten years. Save those lies for yourself because no sane person would ever find truth in them."

"Oh Alyce, why can't you leave well enough alone? You have this misconceived, actually borderline delusional, ideal of the person Amber was. I realize your Pops filled your head with sugary sweet stories of Amber, but it seems he left out the *unpleasant* chronicles."

"What could possibly have been so unpleasant about my mother's actions that you would have nothing to do with your own daughter?" Alyce asks. She leaves Jude's side to begin pacing once more.

Rosey drops her gaze, picking at the sharp crease of her trousers. "Fine. You were not Amber's firstborn."

Alyce stops abruptly, twisting, turning, to get eyes on Rosey. We watch in stun-struck silence, careful not to breathe too loudly lest the pair understand they are being observed and quell the conversation.

Alyce's glare narrows. "What do you mean by that, Rosey?"

Rosey rests her elbows on the arms of the chair. She brings her hands together, matching fingertip to fingertip. "If I'm not mistaken, I just finished paying your tuition at a well-respected, reputable university. I should think, for all the money I've spent and the degrees you've earned, that you would know perfectly well what that statement means."

Alyce declines to address Rosey's clapback as she brings her hands to rest on her hips, waiting.

"Oh, for heaven's sake. Must we be so terribly dramatic? Amber had another child," Rosey says pragmatically, folding hands in her lap.

Alyce remains wordless, an unreadable look masking her features. No telling what comes next. I look at Yvonne sitting across from me to see if she has any knowledge of this secret. Eyes wide, she signals back with a slight shake of her head. This is news to her as well. Terry and Patrick have taken a vow of quietude, not that I blame them. If possible, I think we all would have taken an exit and let these two work this out privately. However, given the intensity of the storm outside, we must all witness the uncomfortable and awkward battle taking place between the two.

"That's it? That is all you have to say about that? You sit there, dropping little bombs—let's see first, it was that you instructed a private investigator to follow my parents and their friends. Then, you were blackmailing those same people with the information you gathered. Oh, and let's not leave out the part where you are responsible for seeing to the early demise of my parents. Now, you want to toss out there that I have a sibling? And that's it. No further explanation, no backup for your statement?"

"When I said Amber was a difficult child, it was not an exaggeration," Rosey says. "We did everything right with that girl, yet at every turn, she changed direction simply because she didn't want to take the paths we so carefully, so thoughtfully laid out for her. Amber wasn't only ungrateful for all that she had been given, she was spiteful. And to spite me, she got herself into a situation at the young age of fourteen." Rosey sits with her story for a moment, eyes cast down, drawing slow and steady breaths. "It broke your grandfather's heart. Daddy's good, little girl wasn't good, or little, or a girl anymore. Amber was a child with child." Rosey lifts her stare to Alyce, her head slightly tilted, lips tautly stretched across her face.

Rosey is compelled to continue as we all wait expectantly, silently, for the rest of the story. When she is ready, and only when Rosey is ready, does she oblige. "Amber kept the baby a secret as long as she possibly could—until she was showing, and I began questioning what was going on with her weight. By the time I understood what was happening, Amber was too far along for any option but to have the child. So your grandfather and I rented a condo in Florida, pulled Amber out of school, and hired private tutors to foster her education until the situation was resolved."

"Resolved? Does that mean she had the baby?" Alyce asks.

Nodding, Rosey answers, "She had the baby. As a family, Pops, Amber, and I came to the conclusion that the baby would be put up for adoption. Amber was on board with the plan initially. She understood that she was not ready to care for a child of her own. But as the end of her pregnancy drew closer, Amber changed her mind. Of course, all the plans were already in the works. Lawyers, documents, promises, monies spent—Amber pitched a fit. But that was to be expected from a fifteen-year-old girl, barely fifteen, I might add.

"Amber was furious, but we all knew it was in the child's best interest. Nevertheless, your mother never forgave me for that. You see, when I learned Amber was pregnant with you, I had to know for certain that she was ready for motherhood. Who could save Amber from herself except for her mother? And then, it came to light that Amber hadn't even bothered to marry your father, shamelessly sleeping around with anyone who tickled her libido. It was apparent to me that age had not matured your mother. Amber was quite clearly incapable of being a good role model for you."

"So that's it? That's the reason you killed your own daughter, my mother? Because she didn't meet your expectations?"

"Amber was unfit, Alyce. You are much better off for having been reared by your pops and me."

Alyce's chest expands as she draws air into her lungs, swallowing the ugly truth Rosey has imparted. She turns slowly toward the wall of windows, the storm raging outside no match for the one we've all just witnessed between grandmother and granddaughter.

Alyce wraps herself in her arms, chin jutting out defiantly. She looks at Griff. "Well, brother—you heard it from the horse's mouth."

thirty-nine

A KILLER AMONG US

Jude

"So you know," Rosey says. "Or more to the point, have known."

My Alyce is impressive, keeping her cool all the way through that intense grilling from Rosey. Damn, but that Rosey is evil. She's as conniving and diabolical as Alyce said she was. Casually tossing out that she killed Amber and Shane. 'They went peacefully, experienced no pain whatsoever.' Blackmailing these people for the last twenty years. Hiding away her grandson, Alyce's brother. No wonder Alyce was so adamant about doing it in this manner. She said Rosey prided herself on how people viewed her and her family, their stature in the community. Because of such, Alyce said Rosey would be mortified for anyone to know the true nature of her family. Alyce wanted Rosey to squirm, and I'd say she's practically floundering in that chair. Alyce coached me on the signs. You have to observe closely to catch those little twitches and tell-tells, but Alyce named them, told me what to look for, and I'll be damned if my girl wasn't right. Rosey, playing with her clothing, tapping her fingertips, spinning that big ass green rock on her finger. Yep, Alyce knows Rosey's game.

"You mean that Griff is my brother?" Alyce responds to

Rosey's last utterance. "Yes," Alyce says, turning in the direction of her brother. "A couple of years now, right, Griff?"

Still standing sentry at the windows, hands stuffed deep inside his pockets, Griff nods.

"Now that I think about it though, you could have another connotation in mind. If by have known, you mean know that Griff is my brother—well, yes, we've established that. But you could also be asking if I was aware that you have been grooming Griff, having him do all of your dirty deeds. In that case, yes, again. Griff and I have had plenty of opportunities to get to know one another. We've covered all the topics we missed throughout our lives: what our childhoods were like, our hobbies and interests, how we were raised, where, and by whom—that sort of thing.

"The exchanges I found most compelling, however, were the deets we shared about our families or, I should say, how and what we were told about our families. It was fascinating to compare notes and stories. We knew that we shared a mother and all of her maternal family members, but it was odd that we had come to the discussion with such dissimilar portraits of who the very same people were. For me, our mother was a teacher, a good girl who always wanted to make her mommy and daddy proud, and boy, did she—all those stories of her many accomplishments you rattled off. For Griff—let's see, what was it you told him? Oh yes, our mother was a reckless heathen, drugged up and sex-crazed, just shy of a whore—he had been so much better off for having been placed with a new family. You see, where I had no family other than Rosey and Pops, Griff had an adoptive family with all the cousins and extended relatives and such. But then, surprise! Griff got a bonus granny, and she had money to throw around.

"Of course, with that money came the exchange of services." Alyce holds for a moment, realizing her audience. "Don't worry y'all. Those services had nothing to do with any of you. The jobs Rosey assigned Griff would barely be of interest to any of you.

Except, Rosey did buy this house for Griff, paid for the entire remodel, as a gift for his silence and compliance."

Around the room, all eyes are on Alyce, waiting for her to continue. This is playing out exactly as my girl and I planned. They're hanging on Alyce's every word, looking to place blame on anyone but themselves—deny responsibility and run. I'd never let on with Alyce, but I was a bit worried that she had made more out of this situation with Rosey than what it really was. After all, the story itself is incomprehensible to the normal person. But if this weekend has proved anything, it's that Alyce was right about our families, about their secrets and cover-ups, their need for greed and notoriety.

"Someone needs to explain this to me," Dad spouts. Surprisingly, he's kept his mouth shut for as long as he has. There must be some condition my father suffers from that makes him believe he has to be in the middle of fucking everything. Everything, all my life, has been about that man. God knows why Mom has stayed with him, but she is just as blameworthy for his actions as Dad is. When it comes to families, the three of us—Alyce, Griff, and myself—we got screwed. What is it that Dad likes to throw out at me? 'God helps those who help themselves.' Well, here we are, and that's exactly what we intend to do. Help ourselves.

"Amber gave birth to Griff when she was fifteen," Yvonne explains to Dad. "Griff is Alyce's brother and Rosey's grandson."

"I got that much, Yvonne. I'm not an idiot," Dad says. He's gruff and anxious; there's fear there, too—not a good cocktail for my father.

Terry takes over for his wife. "So, did you understand the part about how these two have long known about our gang, about how they've worked to pull all of us together this weekend to exact their revenge on us?"

"What the hell have we done to deserve revenge? It's all that old hag," Dad shouts, his face reddening with fury. "If anyone deserves to take the fall, it's Rosey. Everything that happened has been at her hand, at her direction."

"You know, at first, Mr. Perkins..." Alyce stops abruptly, changing her mind mid-thought. "Why am I still offering you respect? You've not earned it. In fact, your part in all of this is so much larger than you've let on, isn't it?"

"What is that supposed to mean, little girl?" I have a lot of faith in my girl, but Alyce is not aware of who she's dealing with.

"Name-calling will get you nowhere with me. But just so the rest of the group understands, I'll explain myself." Alyce swivels to make eye contact with each member of the group as she says, "Pastor over there is responsible for killing Gabe."

Dad's face twists and pulls at the accusation. "Now, you listen here," he says, working up an excuse for what he's done.

"No," Alyce stops him short. "We've all listened to you far too much this weekend. Jude was right. There's not a lot of truth that comes out of your mouth, is there? Except that you were ultimately the one who closed the door on my parents' garage, thereby snuffing them out long before their time. I do appreciate your honesty. But you've gone and done it again, haven't you? They all know about what you did to my parents. Do you want to fill them in on how you did away with Gabe as well, or should I?"

"I didn't mean to kill your parents. I told you all that. Gabe's death was an accident, too. I haven't taken any life on purpose," Dad swivels in Mom's direction. "Melanie, tell them I'm not a killer." A tear streaks Mom's cheek. "I'm not, Melanie. I swear."

"You killed Gabe?" Terry asks. "Why?"

"It was an accident," Dad says to Terry, then turns to me, "Tell them, Jude. You were there. Jude was there; he knows it was an accident."

"Okay, let's give Pat a chance to explain," Yvonne says diplomatically. "What happened at the lighthouse, Patrick?"

"I don't really know, to be honest. When we started up all those stairs, I was in the lead. Melanie was right behind me. At some point during the climb, I understood someone else was in that stairwell, up ahead of us. As far as I knew, Melanie and I were leading the way. So I stopped and checked behind us to rule out anyone who was below us on the staircase. But it was so dark I couldn't see anything or anyone. Still, I knew someone was up there. After we all caught up to one another at the first level for that ridiculous, there's a ghost in the watch room charade, Jude and Alyce took the lead. Youth had the advantage, and those two took off. Mel and I couldn't keep up—breathing hard and wheezing. Melanie got a cramp and told me to go ahead without her; she'd catch up.

"When I got to the top, I found Alyce waiting inside the door that led to the ledge. She told me Jude was talking with Gabe. I had no idea Gabe was even in the lighthouse. Thought he'd disappeared along with the rest of them who went to the restroom. But there they were, Gabe and Jude, having some heated conversation. Gabe didn't know my son. He didn't have any business raising his voice to my boy, so I went over to see what the altercation was about." Dad takes a gulp of air.

"Well, what were they arguing about?" Terry asks impatiently.

"I still don't really know. I heard them say Griff's name and Alyce and Rosey's—something about you should have told her. Hell, it could have been about anything. All I know is that I didn't like the way Gabe was addressing Jude. So, I went over to settle the argument, but it got more heated. The next thing I know, they're in each other's faces. We were eighty feet above the ground. All I could imagine was a fistfight breaking out and someone going over the edge of the lighthouse. I tried to separate them, but when I did, I used too much force, and Gabe lost his balance. That's when he fell. I swear I didn't have malicious intent. Hand to God, I had no reason to want Gabe dead. He used to be my friend back in the day."

Rosey decides it is time for her to jump in. "Don't tell me you all are buying this story. First, Amber and Shane, then Gabe. Should we talk about the fact that Pat disappeared during lunch —right after Carmen went downstairs to nap? And that soon thereafter, we found Carmen as dead as her brother."

"Oh hell, Rosey. I had nothing to do with that either," Dad

says, the defeat in his voice ringing clearer than the defiance. "For God so loved the world, that he gave his only begotten Son..." Dad mumbles.

"What are you trying to say, Pat?" Yvonne asks.

"He's trying to keep from implicating me," I tell the group as their attention turns toward my way. "The man won't give me a minute to myself. I'd gone downstairs to confront Carmen, and here comes Dad, loping into the room, interrupting our conversation."

"What were you and Carmen talking about?" Mom asks.

"Griff, actually. You see, Carmen knew about Amber's first child. She was aware that Amber had a child and that Rosey had made her give him up at birth. That's how Gabe knew; Carmen was the one who filled him in on Amber's secret. All Carmen had to do was be truthful with Alyce about what she knew. But, like Gabe, Carmen was selfish. Keeping that information to herself. Not that Alyce didn't already know, but it was the injustice of the matter. Every last one of you has been complicit in keeping Rosey's secrets. A chosen alliance. Alyce has given every single person here a chance to 'fess up, and not one of you has taken it upon yourself to do the right thing."

"Jude, darling," Mom starts carefully. "Are you saying that you are responsible for Carmen's death?"

"No. I didn't kill her. When I found her this afternoon, she was coming out of Terry and Yvonne's room, headed toward Frank and Kathryn's bedroom. When I confronted her about it, she claimed she was only looking for the Xanax Yvonne offered her earlier. Even showed me the vial. I know now that she was searching for whatever drugs she could find from everyone. At the time, I figured she was snooping to see if any of you had something to do with Gabe's death. If I'm guilty of anything, it's not trying hard enough to get Carmen to come upstairs with everyone, but I honestly didn't think she was going to kill herself. Carmen was so damn adamant about not knowing anything in regard to Amber's first child though, I got frustrated and left. Dad saw us stepping into Carmen's room so we could talk in private, and took it upon himself to follow us. Didn't bother to get the whole story, did you, Dad? Instead, in true Pastor Perkins' form, he jumped to conclusions."

Mom's hands come to each side of her forehead, massaging. "Oh my God, Jude. You're policing these people? First, Gabe, then Carmen, and now they're both dead. What is going on here with you?" Mom asks.

"I could probably ask you the same question, Mom. You're the one who made a deal with the devil's mistress over there." I gesture in Rosey's direction.

"What the hell has gotten into you, boy?" Dad is up off the sofa, puffed up, readying to spar. I laugh at the sight of my old man thinking he has any sort of control over me, over Alyce, the situation at hand. "I tried to give you the benefit of the doubt. Told myself you were thinking with your dick—you'd eventually get your head together and realize what this little girl and her grandmother really are."

"The only conclusion I've come to, Dad, is that Alyce has been right about everything, including how incredibly hypocritical you are." Dad steps toward the kitchen, then back.

"Jude, that is no way to speak to your father," Mom's voice takes on the commanding tone so familiar during my upbringing.

"Really, Mom, you're one to talk. You've kept your fair share of secrets. Would you ever have come clean about the identity of my real father if I hadn't presented you with that genealogy report last year?" My mother keeps her words under her tongue. She understands she has no argument to make, reaching to wipe away the tear that rolls over her cheek.

Alyce inches closer to my side, taking my hand. "Jude and I understand love in a way our families never have." She gives me that smile, the one that swells my chest. I nod in agreement, watching her as she tells our families that our hearts are already fuller than any of theirs have ever been. "For the first time in our lives, we know what it is like to love and be loved unconditionally.

You see, we don't want anyone interfering with what we have. Once we made the connections between our families, about our upbringings, we knew that the two of us would never be allowed to carry on with our lives the way we saw fit. We understand our happiness is in our hands. Now that I have all the answers I was looking for, Jude and I are ready to start our married life, to begin our own family."

I nod at Alyce and smile. " Yep," I concur, turning to look my parents in the eye. "Now that we have the truth, you all can do as you see fit, knowing Alyce and I will have no part in it. We intend to move forward with our lives without the burden of familial obligations. Alyce and I have given a lot of thought to our decision, about what we want for ourselves, and the family we will build together. This weekend was to elicit your confessions so that you all would have a full understanding of why we will no longer allow any of you to be a part of our future. Surely after all that has come to light this weekend, you can understand why, as well as how we came to this decision." The devastated look on Mom's face almost gets me, but Alyce squeezes my hand in support, giving me the courage to stay strong.

"Jude," Mom says through tears, "Surely, you can't mean...."

Across the way, the kitchen lights flicker, dim, and extinguish, cutting short my mother's plea as the room grows darker. With the sun tucked away until morning, the loss is even more noticeable. Panic races over Dad's features. He may not be my biological father, but I know him better than most. We lose all power now, and it will put him over the edge.

Dad looks toward the wall of windows. "Griff? What's with the generator? Is it going to hold out?"

Griff offers a slight shrug. "It's doing what it can. Probably trying to pull too much out of it. All we can do at the moment is hope for the best."

"Hope? Is that what we're doing to save ourselves here? Hoping? You don't know if it will hold?" Dad's voice booms over the thunder.

"Should be fine," Griff says. "Should've been fine last night. I got no control over the lightning and where it strikes."

Terry twists his hands together, watching the exchange, gauging the situation. "Griff, have you heard from anybody on your talkie over there? I haven't heard it go off in a while. Maybe someone has been able to procure a weather report?"

Griff looks at the side of his body, the walkie-talkie hanging from his belt. His body tenses as he begins to twist the button at the top of the device, causing the familiar crackling noise to sound.

"Did you turn it off?" Yvonne is the first to pick up on Griff's actions. She looks at Terry, her eyes round with understanding.

"I didn't do it on purpose. Must've gotten switched off when we were bringing up the furniture pieces from the bottom floor," Griff says, yanking the cumbersome box from his belt, holding it to his mouth.

"This is Griff Munson, Dune Dweller. Do you read me? Over."

Heavy trepidation hangs from the faces around the room as we realize we have been on radio silence these last few hours. All the air in the room is sucked away, lodged deep inside the lungs of its occupants. A collective exhaling of breath as the crackle returns a response.

"Ocracoke Fire and Rescue, go ahead. Over."

"Lost comms. Back up now. Please advise as to storm status. Over."

"Got a bathtub out there, Griff. Water levels on both sides of the island are rising fast. Over."

"Any buildings in immediate danger? Over."

"Middle of the island still has some dry ground. All coastal areas flooded. Rescue team is working to evacuate residents along the sound. Over."

"Advise status of road conditions. Over."

"Debris and high water levels have rendered roads impassable. Evacuation by vehicle ill-advised. Over."

"Any change to the forecast? Over."

"Storm is on course as predicted. Heavy rain and damaging winds remain constant for another three to four hours. Advise location. Over."

"Dune Dweller—water rising, barrier dunes have been breached. Eight souls. Over."

"We'll dispatch the boat first chance. Move to higher ground, hold tight, and await instruction. Over and out."

"Roger that. Out."

forty

WHERE IS IT?

Melanie

"Did I just hear what I think I heard?" Pat punches out the question. "We're flooding, and there's no way out of this house?" Of course, we all heard the chatter, the status, but hearing the words spoken plainly, threateningly will push my husband's fear to a limit I'm afraid is dangerous for all of us. Patrick stands in front of the sofa, looking like a trapped animal. His stance, draped in defiance and aggression, Patrick is stuck, no space in the over-packed room for his signature pacing.

Not that he has addressed any one person in particular, but no one bothers to answer Pat's redundant, repetitive, ridiculous question. Perhaps everyone is weary of Patrick's tantrums, or maybe it's because we've all witnessed and heard the conversation on Griff's walkie-talkie and believe his inquisition to be rhetorical. Then again, maybe it's the exhaustion that has settled upon our shoulders after the revealing tell-all. Each of us is wearing a heavy cloak of guilt in one color or another, and now we learn the existential threat Pat keeps harping about is indeed credible. If the fire and rescue department can't get to us, if the boat doesn't make it in time, we may all float out to sea.

"Did I hear correctly, Griff? It's inevitable? We're going to flood?" Alyce asks.

Griff nods. "Now that the barrier dunes are breaking down, yeah. One good push of the surge and the ocean will be in the recreation room."

"But the water has quite a way to rise before it reaches us," Jude hurries to remind everyone.

"Are you hearing yourself, boy? Your mother and I didn't raise you to be a fool. All you've done this weekend is make excuses for that nightmare she-devil. That girl has turned you against your own family, not to mention the fact she turned your damn brain into mush. You better wise up, son, 'cause you can't talk your way out of this one. The ocean is coming for us."

Alyce speaks before Jude has a chance to respond to his father. "The water has to rise all the way to the widow's walk on top of the house before we succumb to the sea, Pastor Pat. You heard rescue. They'll be here as soon as they can, and the water hasn't yet reached the recreation room floor, four feet up. You've been an alarmist all weekend, and it's quite unbecoming." Oh, Alyce. What have you started? She's a smart, clever young woman, no doubt—but she is no match for my husband. Patrick, however, doesn't clap back. Yvonne has his full attention.

Across the way, on the other sofa, Yvonne has pulled her handbag into her lap. She digs furiously inside the dark hole. With no lighting from the room to aid her in the search, she begins removing the items from the bag. The action is frantic and urgent.

"Yvonne, is everything okay? Can I help you find something?" I ask.

Terry realizes Yvonne's alarm. "Honey?"

"It was here. I know it was here. I put it in here," Yvonne says.

"Put what?" Terry asks, running a hand over his brow. Terry, too, is losing his calm demeanor.

"My gun," she says, continuing to toss random objects from the designer tote.

"Are you sure you put it in your bag?" Terry tries.

"The better question is, why do you need a gun right now, Yvonne?" Rosey poses.

"I don't need my gun. I need the portable flashlight I keep in here. But the point is that someone in this house has taken my gun."

We watch as Yvonne dumps the contents of her bag onto the floor in front of her. As she rifles through the spill, one of two possibilities is made clear: Yvonne is still experiencing side effects of the Xanax she took, or Yvonne is quite lucid, and someone in this room is armed with Yvonne's weapon. Given her conduct these last couple of hours, it seems the wacky side effects are over, and sanity is now seated next to subdued anxiety. The thought yanks me back into an earlier conversation. Xanax and prescriptions, about Jude disappearing earlier and Patrick searching for him, only to come back upstairs solo.

Patrick shifts his weight from foot to foot, his eyes wild and dark. Is he thinking what I'm thinking? Careful not to swing my gaze too conspicuously, I look at Jude across the room, standing with Alyce, arms twisting together, hands clasping in solidarity. Does Jude have a gun on his person? Is that what he was searching for when he disappeared? Of course he would conceal it, but I don't see any shadow or silhouette that would suggest he's armed. Jude could have moved it somewhere safe, so no one else could mishandle it. I'd like to think that is what he would do, that I know my son, and that is definitely what he would do, but after this weekend.... I've come to understand that my son has been coerced into whatever scheme Alyce has going on and that eighteen years under your mother's roof falls quickly away when under the spell of a beguiling young woman.

"It's not here, Terry." Yvonne's voice registers on the verge of terror. The loss has triggered an attack. Her panic fills the room as Yvonne gasps for air. Tears fall freely. Terry speaks softly, trying to quieten her fears.

In a flash of movement I didn't anticipate, Patrick reaches behind his back. He whips out the gun Yvonne has been desperate to find and waves it erratically. "I've got the damn gun right here," he shouts, then begins to spout commands. "Get together. Everyone. Get closer together." Laughter rings through the room. I look for the source and then realize it's coming from me.

"This is not a joke," Pat rages. "Now," he orders. "Behind Rosey. Go." He points the gun at Yvonne and Terry. Terry pulls Yvonne to her feet, moving hesitantly toward the club chair where Rosey sits wordless, clutching her cell phone.

Following the others, Jude and Alyce tread tentatively toward Rosey's chair. They share an indecipherable look as they move to stand behind Alyce's grandmother. Patrick supervises the movement, keeping the gun aimed toward the group. Wondering if I am to join this gathering at Rosey's feet or if somehow I am exempt, I look at Patrick for direction. His eyes remain trained on the five people across the room. I realize Patrick has not given Griff the same command. But then, Griff is behind us at the window wall. Did Pat forget he was there? Should I say something? What if Griff does the hero thing, and Patrick somehow manages to fire a shot off? Does Pat even know how to use a gun?

What is Patrick doing? What is he thinking? I'll be the first to admit that Patrick and I don't have the closest bond, but I thought I knew him better than this. First, he tells everyone he drunkenly killed two people, then goes on to say he pushed a man off a lighthouse, and now he's shaking a gun in the air, threatening six people, one of whom is our son.

"Melanie, come over here," Pat commands. I try to work my face into an expression that is less suspicious than what I am feeling. "Come here," he orders again, impatient by my lack of urgency. I understand and hurry to follow instructions.

"Jude, come," Patrick demands. Jude stands motionless, holding firm to Alyce's hand.

"Jude, I said, come here. Now."

"I'm not going anywhere Alyce isn't going," Jude says, his voice managing an octave lower than typical.

"I'm not going to say it again, boy. Get your ass over here," Patrick points the gun at Alyce's chest.

Jude steps in front of Alyce, holding his fiancée behind his standing form. "I've told you. I'm not going anywhere Alyce doesn't go. You plan on killing her, then you're going to have to kill me first."

"Jude, please," I beg. "Please, baby, just do what Daddy says."

"Now he's daddy; that's convenient for you, Mom."

I step closer to Patrick, placing a hand on his arm, easy, gentle, so as not to cause an accidental discharge of the gun. We've never been gun people. Mace is the only type of weapon I've ever carried. Hell, as far as I know, Patrick's never even been hunting.

"Patty, please put the gun away. You don't have to give it back to Yvonne. Right, Yvonne?" Yvonne remains silent, holding tightly to Terry, her eyes pooling with fear.

"We're getting out of here," Pat says. "Nobody is going to stop us this time, or I will be forced to use this gun."

Jude inches forward. "Come on, Dad, get serious. You know you can't go out there in this storm. We've talked about this—REPEATEDLY. Jesus, you never listen."

"Don't test me, Jude. I know what I'm doing," Patrick says, waving the gun aimlessly through the air without caution or regard for the power of such a weapon. "We're twenty-some-odd miles out to sea, with the water coming for us on all sides of this island. You all heard it for yourselves. The inland roads haven't flooded yet, but the water is rising up to the bottom floor of this house as we speak. I'm not sitting here waiting around for the ocean to kick the stilts out from under us and wash this house out to sea."

"And where are you planning to go?" I ask Pat, trying to make him see some sense, to understand this idea of running is unrealistic and just as dangerous, if not more so, than staying in this house.

"Rescue's on the way," Terry reminds. "They'll get us all to the middle of the island, to higher ground."

"Yeah, and how long will that take? These rescuers, whoever they might be, are all busy saving the island residents. I'm pretty sure Melanie and I are not at the top of the list on this island full of O'cokers."

"I highly doubt they'll ask you for proof of Ocracoke citizenship before allowing you in the rescue boat, Pat," Rosey says snidely. For the life of me, I can't understand why Rosey feels the need to provoke Patrick while he has a gun trained on her and her granddaughter. "But, they may suggest that the women be moved to safety first," Rosey taunts.

"Patrick, the people on this island go through these storms all the time. The rescuers are professionals. We have to trust they know what they're doing," Terry says in his calming, consoling baritone. "Griff has spoken to them. They know where we are and of our situation."

Patrick's eyes scan the room frantically, holding aim at the group across from us. "Griff. What the hell are you doing over there? I said everyone, behind Rosey. Move it," Patrick snaps.

Griff remains motionless at the wall of windows.

"Patty, please." I try to pull Patrick's attention back on me. "We have to trust Griff. He knows this island, these storms, the rescue people."

"He's her brother." Patrick points the gun directly at Alyce. "And her grandson." Pat moves the gun to aim at Rosey. "Tell me you trust either of them with your life, my life, Jude's life, for God's sake. They'll be on that boat before we are. They'll leave us to drown, Mel."

I can't blame Patrick for seeing this situation in the manner that he does. He's been living for years with the knowledge that he unwittingly killed Shane and Amber, only to find out that Rosey orchestrated the whole thing, that she let him believe he was responsible. And I've no doubt that if the authorities had suspected foul play, Rosey would have found a way for Pat to take the fall for her actions. Of course he feels threatened by this situation. The real threat for all of us in this room is how volatile Patrick becomes when threatened.

In my peripheral vision, I note movement. Flattening himself, Griff steps sideways along the windows, easing further along the wall toward the sliding glass door leading out to one of Dune Dweller's many decks. The motion catches Jude's eye as well, his head jerking toward the action. Jude's sudden movement alerts Patrick, who turns hastily; the weapon moves with him this time. Pat fixes his stare and the gun on Griff. Terry and Jude share a look, a silent plan forming between them. Fear locks my body as I watch what is happening around me without any way to stop it.

The gun discharges. Given my proximity, the noise is deafening. I feel the scream at the back of my throat, yet I hear nothing but the ringing of gunfire. My God. Patrick shot the gun. Did he mean to shoot it? Griff?

Oh, dear Lord. What's happening? Griff falls to the ground. Someone screams—it's not me this time. Glass shatters. Wind whips through the room, screeching, blowing the rain inside, soaking the furniture, the floor. There is a scuffle somewhere, but I can't decipher who it is or where it takes place. Another shot slices the air. More screaming, howling. I fall to my knees, covering my ears with my hands, trying to make myself small. Tears wet my cheeks. The room goes in and out of focus as more gunshots fire. What is Patrick doing?

The gunfire stops. Tugging at my wrist, yanking on my arm, Patrick pulls me up from the floor, dragging me along with him. Our surroundings grow fainter with each step we take toward ground level. As we round the stairs to the bottom floor, I hear the water—I don't see it, but I know it's close. Patrick pulls me through the back hallway toward the front of the house.

Patrick wrenches the door leading out of the house, the wind blowing the tinkling bell mercilessly. "Watch your step. Don't trip us up," he yells over the storm's chaos. One hand holding firmly to my wrist, the pressure tight and uncomfortable; the other grasping the gun. "Let's go."

"Go where? There's so much water. We have to get Jude?" I try, knowing full well there will be no reasoning with this man.

Patrick's grip on my wrist tightens as we work our way down the outside staircase. The wind blows me off balance as the rain pelts my extremities with relentless fury. Somehow, we make it to the bottom of the stairs, water rushing, foaming around our knees.

Patrick trudges forward, forcing me along, awkwardly sloshing behind him. "What about the others?" I yell over the noise of the weather. My hair, stringy and wet, hangs heavy over my face, obstructing my view. "Patrick, I'm not leaving Jude?" I scream at him, anchoring my feet to the ground under the water and using my other hand to try and free myself from Patrick's grasp. He turns around, tossing off my escape efforts, ripping me from my stationed position. "Stop that. Let's go. Don't worry about the others."

"Patrick, please," I beg. "This is wrong. We should wait for rescue."

"Look, there's the van," he says over his shoulder.

"What? Now you know how to hot wire a car?" I yell over the noise of the storm.

"I've got Griff's keys. Come on," he says, marching toward the vehicle at the end of the long driveway. He jams the gun into his waistband to free up his other hand.

"It's not safe to drive in this, Pat. The roads are flooding." Maybe if I can appeal to his fear of water, Patrick will see that going back inside is our best and safest option. "The van won't make it through all the water. We'll drown."

Patrick continues to tug me by the wrist while stepping behind me to push me forward, but I lose my footing and fall into the water. The saltwater stings my eyes and nose. My vision is clouded with tears. Patrick yanks, and pulls, and tugs. "I'm not leaving our son," I yell in protest.

Patrick manages to get me to my feet. Pain shoots up my arm, brought on by the force he uses. With his free hand, he wipes away the water dripping into his eyes and looks dead into mine. "Your son is dead."

forty-one

THE RESCUE

Griff

Wind drives rain into the sitting room on the top floor of Dune Dweller. Shattered glass covers the floor. It takes a minute for me to wrap my mind around what happened, how I came to be sprawled out in front of the window wall. The information lurks about in the periphery of my memories but is cloudy beyond focus. I push to stand, conscious of the large shards scattered around me. Everything hurts—my head pounds, but all body parts seem to be working as designed. The ringing in my ears helps to trigger pertinent recall. Gunshots. Pat fired them with the weapon he took from Yvonne. My upper left arm is on fire. He got me. The wound is superficial—a few stitches at best, but it sure doesn't feel trivial. How many shots were in that gun? If I'd been coherent, I might've thought to count as he sprayed off bullets. S'pose I could round up the casings, but judging by the mess of the room, I understand that exercise would take longer than worthwhile.

Vision slowly honing, I glance around for the others. It quickly becomes clear there are no signs of activity from anyone other than me in this room. Terry, Yvonne, Rosey, Jude, and Alyce appear motionless, lifeless. I hurry over to check their vitals. Alyce and Rosey first, but the moment I look down at Rosey, I know there's no reason to check. I have to move Jude to get a check on Alyce, but it's too late for them too. Terry and Yvonne are clutched together next to Rosey's chair; neither displays any signs of life. I look back at Rosey and Alyce. A hitch in my heartbeat, my chest tightens with the knowledge that the only blood relatives I've ever known are now gone.

The damnedest thing... when Patrick started swinging that gun around, I would have bet my last pair of good socks that man had no idea how to handle a gun. He sure didn't act like a man intent on killing his friends and family, but then again, I guess what they say is true: you never really know what's in another's head and heart. He might not've come off like a marksman, but he sure did have a good aim. Thinking I got lucky—real lucky. If I hadn't fallen to the floor and knocked myself out, I feel certain I'd be lying in this heap with the others.

Makes me wonder why. Why would he want everyone here dead? His own son? I know Patrick wasn't Jude's biological dad, but I don't have one of those either, and my adoptive father, the man who raised me from birth, would never pull a gun on me. Did we piss Pat off, or did we all just know too much about Pastor Pat and his *accidental* killings?

Speaking of, where'd he and Melanie get to? I hurry across the sitting room, through the kitchen, and down the back hallway to the opposite end of the house. I reach the room Rosey used. Stepping through the threshold, I rush to the balcony door and heave it open. Outside, the rain pelts at my skin, plasters the hair to my head. I hold to the deck railing, bracing against the wind, searching the surroundings for Patrick and Melanie.

Look at that. They made it to the van. Don't know where he thinks he's going. The cabin light illuminates, and I see Patrick sitting behind the wheel of the borrowed passenger van. His face twisting and scrunching, his mouth moving as he tries to start the thing up—that's where my other set of keys went. Working the key with one hand, his other hand bangs against the steering wheel. That old van's got a little trick to getting it running. Won't start with the gear shift in the park position—only neutral. Yep, looks like it's starting to piss him off.

From the passenger seat, Melanie spies me watching from the top perch of Dune Dweller. She looks at Pat, then turns her attention back to me, pointing in my direction. Looks like he's yelling something at Melanie. Pat certainly doesn't agree with whatever she's saying. Melanie reaches across the space between her and Patrick. The scuffle appears to be Melanie grabbing for the keys. Patrick elbows her away, and I hear the engine crank over. They must've knocked the gear shift into neutral by accident. It got the van started, though.

Patrick manages to shift into reverse as I see him pilot the van backward down the chert drive and onto the street running in front of Dune Dweller. With the sun gone and the rain starting up again, it's hard to see. But the van's headlights and taillights give me some clarity on the direction they take.

From this vantage point, I just make out that most of the roads further inland are still in the clear. There's a long stretch along the east side of the island that is entirely underwater though. They won't make it through those rising waters, especially with the ocean rushing inland. I shake my head; I've got to do something. No matter how I feel about the man or what he's done, I can't stand here and watch this happen.

I step back inside the threshold and unclip the walkie from my belt. I'll do what I can for them.

"Ocracoke Fire and Rescue. Griff Munson. Dune Dweller. Do you read? Over."

"Ocracoke Fire and Rescue, go ahead, Griff. Over."

"Hey, Donnie. Gonna need some help. Got a runner. Over."

"Thought y'all were holding tight for rescue? Over."

"That was the plan. This one got anxious. Over."

"Rescue boats are working the low-lying areas on the sound side of the island. Can't get the helicopter from Hatteras until the brunt of this thing blows through. Over."

"They'll be out to sea before either of those units gets over here. You can't get a truck through there to this side of the island? Over."

"Water's rising fast from both sides of the island. Gonna have to wait till it subsides. Do you have their location? Over."

"Checking. Hold for report. Over."

I step back out into the storm. In the distance, I see the van has stopped making forward progress. Water must be higher than it looks from here. Van's flooded out already. Even though no good can come of it, I can't help but think of how many times I told that guy he was better off staying put. All the bad that man has done, I have to believe this is the poetic justice Alyce kept going on about. Patrick killed Alyce and Rosey. Regardless of how I feel about them—hell, even I don't know what I feel for the two of them right now—they were my family. Melanie doesn't deserve to be dragged down with that guy, but then neither did Terry and Yvonne. Still, I've no way of saving them, and if I did, I'd be signing my own death certificate in doing so. None of us would make it out alive.

I head back inside, lift the walkie-talkie, and press the button.

"Van stalled at the junction of Cedar Lane and Middle Road. Water rising rapidly. Over."

"Oh, man. Can't get out there from here right now. They take life jackets? Over."

"No. Over."

"Hope they're strong swimmers. We'll be that way as soon as the boats get back from the other side of the island. Maybe they'll be able to hold on till we get there. Over."

"Maybe," I say, stepping away from the window, the scene that's about to turn tragic. "Dune Dweller, out," I add, wondering what comes next. The water or the rescue?

epilogue

Ocracoke Island Voice

By Louann Baily

Last weekend's tropical storm proved unpredictable as it converged with a low-pressure system, wreaking havoc and deadly destruction on the tiny island of Ocracoke. Multiple structures on the island sustained damage, one home collapsed into the Atlantic Ocean, and twelve people reportedly lost their lives during the violent storm. According to local officials, however, not all of the deceased died as a direct result of the storm's wrath.

Ocracoke resident Gina Williams reported that her husband, Wayne, fell ill during the early hours of the storm prior to intensification. Wayne Williams was driving himself and his wife to the Hatteras Ferry Terminal in order to seek medical services on the mainland when a health emergency caused him to slam into the barrier dunes alongside NC12. Local health officials have stated Williams's death was cardiac-related.

Visitor Gabriel Torres was also lost during the early hours of the storm's entrance. According to a local resident and lighthouse tour guide, Charles MacDougal, Torres was touring the lighthouse Friday evening when an altercation with another sightseer turned heated. Torres lost his footing when he was pushed, causing him to fall to his death from the lighthouse observation deck.

Torres' sister, Carmen Torres, died Saturday, just hours after her brother's fatal fall from the lighthouse. The cause of Ms. Torres's death is being reported as an apparent suicide.

A prominent couple from Norfolk, VA, who were staying with a group of friends at the newly renovated Dune Dweller, also perished in the early hours of Saturday morning before the storm's recorded arrival. Frank Alan and his wife, Kathryn Caron Carrickfergus, were found dead in an enclosed hot tub Saturday morning after friends realized they were missing. Autopsies are being performed. At this time, foul play is not suspected.

Pastor Patrick Perkins and his wife, Melanie Saches, both of Carrolltown, VA, drowned trying to swim for assistance after their vehicle stalled in flood waters off Middle Road. The couple was staying at Dune Dweller while on a brief holiday with friends when the convergence of weather systems arrived.

Five other visitors were killed inside Dune Dweller by gunfire before the house was swept away by the ocean's fury early Sunday morning. The victims reportedly included Rosey Fischer, Alyce Fischer, and Jude Saches, all of Raleigh, NC, died from gunshot wounds. Yvonne and Terrance Marshall of Norfolk, VA, were also part of the group who were killed in the hail of gunfire at Dune Dweller late Saturday afternoon. While the investigation is ongoing, a victim's cellphone recording recounts Pastor Perkins seized Mrs. Marshall's personal firearm to open fire, fatally wounding the five visitors.

Dune Dweller, the only rental home on Seacoast Lane, collapsed into the Atlantic Ocean during the late-night hours of Saturday. The house was initially built in the 1950s but was recently purchased and renovated to provide the only beachfront rental option on Ocracoke Island.

The owners of Dune Dweller, Griff Munson and an undisclosed partner, found several loopholes in old laws and reconstructed the home despite warnings from commission advisors.

According to owner/caretaker Griff Munson, the eight-bedroom, six-bath home had just welcomed its first visitors. Preliminary reports point to structural integrity issues as the cause of the collapse. The official report is pending further investigation.

The National Park Service and the owner will be overseeing the clean-up process.

Griff

I push the article aside and try to focus on the day ahead. Lots of cleanup to get to. Lots of questions to be answered. Not looking forward to those. Hard to explain to people how the first eleven people to enjoy your rental property met their demise, yet you got out free and clear, barely a gunshot wound.

Me and Fortune had a good day—that bullet only grazed my left upper arm—a few stitches, and I was fine. Joshing aside, it was lucky I got shot. Sure did aid in explaining my side of things. Besides all those recordings Rosey was always making and what bit of security footage I managed to salvage, that wound verified my story.

It was Kathryn and Frank's deaths that almost took me down. If it weren't for that camera mounted under the deck near the hot tub, we'd have never known what happened to those two. As if I couldn't have guessed, the authorities now know why they were naked inside that tub. But good Lord—try using some of the common sense He gave you—trying to hide away under a weighted hot tub topper during your sexcapades is not a smart idea. Those two did put a hurtin' on the liquor cabinet, though. Just speculation on my part, but I'd say all that alcohol played a big part in their drownings—autopsies will let us know for sure. Yep, that's the best argument I ever lost 'cause I wanted nothing to do with putting that surveillance equipment into Dune Dweller.

At Rosey's (my undisclosed partner) insistence, I installed security cameras. We needed them for insurance purposes, or so she claimed. After all that came out during that tragic reunion, I now wonder if there weren't other reasons for her demand. Truth be told, I never had much say in how Dune Dweller was constructed or what went into the property. Rosey bankrolled the renovation. Hell, I would never have purchased that old house to refurbish it even if I could have afforded it. Rosey wanted her house to be oceanfront. I tried to explain to her that the old structure was only there because it preempted the National Park, that nobody would be building on that beach. But Rosey said the oceanfront status would ensure the house was in high demand, especially if it was the only one. I still don't understand Rosey's logic. That said, there's a lot I don't understand about all of it and all that went down. What I am certain about however, is that I was their pawn. First, Rosey's, then Alyce's.

When Rosey found me right after I graduated high school, she knew all about my adoptive family, where I lived and had gone to school, who my prom date had been. She appeared as a doting grandmother, upset that she had missed my formative years and was determined to be part of my life if only for a brief bit—given her advanced age, she had said. Rosey presented as a harmless old woman. She'd ask me to complete tasks for her, which I understood were not to be questioned. Some of the things she asked me to do weighed on my conscience, but I was thrilled to know my maternal grandmother. Until I met Alyce, I had no idea Rosey's intentions were ill-intended.

One of Rosey's assignments was to keep an eye on Alyce as she began her college education. Rosey said I should maintain a low profile, that Alyce was a distant family member who had never had to deal with life on her own. Rosey said Alyce, albeit not intentionally, was at risk of harming herself and her family. My bio grandmother kept the details on the cryptic side with little to no explanation. All Rosey offered on the matter was that my covert actions would be to the benefit of Alyce's well-being. I never knew the reasoning behind Rosey's lack of transparency, and like all else, I didn't question my grandmother or her directives.

When Rosey caught on that Alyce was looking into the deaths of her parents, Rosey approached me about going in as a mole to keep a closer eye on the situation. It was then Rosey sat me down and finally told me Alyce was my younger sister. Rosey also informed me that Alyce wasn't well and could be volatile in certain situations. In time, Rosey promised to introduce me to Alyce as her brother, but until then, I wasn't to let on who I was in relation to Alyce. Problem with that plan was that Alyce found me before Rosey had any inkling we were acquainted. Rosey had no idea that Alyce and I knew about one another and had already spent a fair amount of time together. Talk about a rock and an even bigger rock. I didn't know who to trust, but worse than that, I didn't feel very trustworthy myself, given I was keeping information from each of them at the other's demand.

Rosey and I had known one another for over fifteen years when Alyce found me. After Alyce's Pops told her about my existence, Alyce made it her mission to find her long-lost brother. All the time I was keeping tabs on Alyce, she was actually searching for me. When Alyce initially approached me, explaining that we were siblings, I didn't believe her. I mean, if what Alyce said was true, why hadn't Rosey told me I had a sister years ago? Especially since she had me tailing Alyce, looking out for Alyce's safety. Then Alyce and I started comparing notes, throwing in all that we had been told about our mother, sharing all that we experienced in our relationships with Rosey. Nothing correlated. It became clear we'd both been led to believe different versions of the same tale. From that point forward, I really had no idea where to place my allegiance. The accounts just weren't adding up, but I'd been raised by my adoptive family to weigh all I knew, to assess each situation fully before coming to conclusions.

What I did know was that I was far more surprised to find out about Alyce than I was about Rosey. Rosey, my biological grandmother, I had expected, but I had no idea about Alyce, and I couldn't find one reason Rosey would keep that information from me in all the years we'd known each other. Alyce and I had thirteen years between our birthdays, plenty of time for Rosey to tell me about my baby sister. All those years, I could have been an older sibling for Alyce, been there for her growing up. And then, to find out I had a grandfather that I could have known before he died... that was the information that gave me the greatest pause.

To give Rosey a bit of credit, it wasn't like we saw each other every week or, for that matter, every month. Although plenty of time had passed for Rosey to let me in on the fact that I had a sister. During the years before Alyce, I'd started to see a pattern in the assignments Rosey would put out there for me to complete. Something about all those random tasks always felt wrong, had an 'ick factor' as Alyce liked to put it.

After meeting Alyce, I knew right away that Alyce and Rosey were two different people. While Rosey had told me nothing about Alyce, Alyce sure had lots to say about Rosey. My sister had been doing a bit of digging into the past and had learned some disturbing information about the woman who raised her. Alyce was planning the reunion weekend so that she could verify what she already knew and see if there was more that she didn't. I know now it was more than that, but I sure didn't have any idea about her warped plans for justice then. I was just glad to have found more family.

While I was surprised to find out I had a sister, Alyce was surprised to learn I had long been in contact with our grandmother. And it may have stumped me why Rosey wouldn't have mentioned a sibling or a grandfather (who actually would have cared to know me—in direct opposition to what Rosey told me about the man), but it didn't surprise Alyce. She knew exactly what Rosey had been thinking. The only reasons I could come up with were A: Rosey was protecting Alyce, or B: Rosey was embarrassed by me. But then Alyce explained to me what Rosey was really like. Only a chosen few knew the real Rosey Fischer, Alyce said. The Rosey who hired private investigators to follow loved ones and their acquaintances, gathering dirt to blackmail them with, information to block or nudge along whatever they may be striving for in their lives. Honestly, when Alyce told me all that stuff, I didn't believe her—didn't want to, I 'spose. It wasn't until the plans were being made for this disastrous weekend that I understood the truth of what my sister had been claiming all along.

My grandmother instructed me to call her Ms. Rosey throughout the weekend, not to act like I knew her or let on to any of the others that we had any sort of relationship. I ain't too good at acting though, and Rosey let me know it a time or two. She was furious that I was giving away our connection, said I was terrible at keeping secrets. Well, I knew that wasn't true. I'd been keeping mine and Alyce's secret from Rosey for two years throughout the entire rebuild of Dune Dweller. And that wasn't the only secret Alyce and I shared. I'd never so much as hinted to Jude that Alyce and I had planned their meet-up or 'meet-cute,' as my sister called it. Got to say I'm glad it never got back to Rosey that I fixed those two up. There'd have been hell to pay.

The deeper Alyce got into planning the long weekend, though, the more I understood that this reunion was not about obtaining information or seeking out fond memories from her parents' old friends but more about exacting revenge. Now, I'm not into the revenge thing, and I've never been one to choose sides. But I didn't want to go muddying up the waters with my newfound sister, even though I'd known Rosey for much longer. Figured it best to keep my mouth shut and see how long I could ride the fence. It was harder than I thought it would be not to let Rosey know that Alyce and I had found one another. According to Alyce, it was crucial to her plan that Rosey was not privy to our new bond.

I suppose I felt like I owed Alyce, especially since she and Jude had put their confidence in me. Alyce said I was the only one who knew she and Jude were engaged, going on to express her intentions that I would be part of the wedding. Alyce wanted me to give her away. Made me feel like I was part of their team... until the ferry ride. One Alyce sent me to pick up that group of people, and a different Alyce met me when I delivered them at Dune Dweller's door, just the way my sister had commanded.

When she gave her initial spiel to the group upon meeting them, I thought to myself, what the hell game are we playing here? I didn't know that Alyce. In no way did she present herself to those people as she had to me over the last couple of years. Deep down, I think I knew there was more at play between Rosey and Alyce than I was aware of. Still, I did as I was told by both of them, figuring they knew more about their business than I did. I mean, really, who could I trust? Including myself. I was so busy keeping everybody's confidence that it was difficult to remember what I could say and what I was supposed to hold back. So, I just kept my mouth shut and tried to stay away as much as possible.

I can't help but wonder, now that all is said and done, if I hadn't kept from Alyce that Rosey was planning to show up for the reunion unannounced, would everyone still be breathing, enjoying their families, going on about their lives? But then, another part of me thinks Alyce had figured Rosey would show up unannounced–Alyce did seem to know exactly what Rosey would do before Rosey even acted. And again, I'm not sure what Alyce and Jude had planned in terms of their revenge scheme, so maybe all this back and forth is for nothing.

What I am sure about is that Alyce and Jude lied to all those people. The two of them had been busy, busy, gathering intel on each of the couples, including Jude's parents (Jude had told me what his father was like, so his brusque ways came as no shock to me). Those two were rather resourceful if you ask me. Their faces showed shock with regard to some of the information that came out during the reunion, but they had most of the details figured out well before the weekend rolled around. Alyce and Jude had been planning retribution against those people for what they had done as much as for what they had not done. How far the two of them would have taken action against these people was not shared with me, but I had an idea. A 'killer couple,' that's what I called my sister and her fiancé. Don't get me wrong, those two were like no other couple I'd ever met. Alyce and Jude were good together, but still terrible for one another, if that makes any sense. I can sit here and mull on this all I like, but the truth is I'm culpable, too. If I hadn't introduced Alyce and Jude, I doubt this weekend would have gone down.

I knew Jude through some projects Rosey had assigned to me. When Alyce told me about the private investigator thing, I sure didn't believe her. Rosey had me keeping an eye on the preacher and his wife, their son, on occasions—I was just supposed to observe and report. Why would Rosey have me do that if she had a PI in her back pocket? Guess I'll never know the reason behind that either.

I'd told Alyce about Jude, suggested he might know some information about the Perishing Hill gang, something from the inside, since his parents were a part of that group. Alyce had jumped on the idea of meeting Jude, but thought it should be on the sly. So, I arranged to meet Jude at that coffee shop the day he and Alyce met. I waited until I saw him go inside the shop to text and say I had to cancel. That's when Alyce made her move. To hear Alyce tell it, though, I had nothing to do with Jude and her meeting and becoming a couple. Neither here nor there at this point, but I can tell you, not once did I think getting those two together would turn into this, that eleven people would end up losing their lives. They were dangerous together, Alyce and Jude, and I've no idea what they really had planned. All I can say is that they took what they learned about their families and twisted it into something even uglier than it was, and that's hard to imagine. Nevertheless, they were determined that someone or someone(s) was going to pay for it. Only then could they start building their perfect life together. Perfect. That word has new meaning for me these days.

Seems to me everyone's always in search of perfection. Life is rarely perfect though, is it? Been a long time in the making for me to reach that conclusion. You'd have thought I'd learned that lesson sooner in life, given the way I entered this world. Used to watch people coming and going, wonder about how they spent their days. I saw an ease, a perfectness, if you will, in those people that I couldn't seem to find. Maybe it wasn't full-on perfection I was after, but I certainly envied the ease with which they carried on with their days simply because they knew who they were and how they fit into the world.

All those years I spent not knowing why my biological family gave me up or who that family was, what their days looked like, made me feel less than—I wasn't welcome in that family. I know it's not good to think such thoughts, but it was always there, lying just beneath the surface of all my relationships. Maybe if I had those answers... maybe I would have been more at ease; maybe I might at least teeter on that edge of perfection. Strange to think I now have those answers; I don't have to look anymore—for answers or family. They sure haven't done for me what I'd hoped they would. Think I had it wrong all along.

While I had hoped for a true sense of self, Alyce hoped that by avenging all the wrongs in her life, she'd somehow find her sense of perfection. Rosey hoped that by trying to control other people, her life would be presented as perfect. Hope's funny like that; means one thing to one person and something else to another.

It's difficult to reconcile my feelings for Rosey and Alyce. At best, they can only be labeled as confused. When you get right down to it, the two of them used me, and hell, yes, that pisses me off—at them and at me for allowing it. Still, I want to believe they felt something like affection for me. Can't say I came out empty-handed though, cause I learned a heck of a lesson from the two of them. Rosey and Alyce knew that hope doesn't change the world or bring perfection to it; only actions do that. Confused or clear-eyed, I do know I'll miss them, and Dune Dweller—got attached to that house.

Can't think about Dune Dweller unless I think about that wall of windows, my favorite part of the house. Standing, staring out over the horizon—a vastness of nothingness—was where I had my clearest thoughts. As I stood there that afternoon, in the hours before death, I looked out that wall of windows, and I thought about my family—my real family—and I was grateful. I realized then how thankful I am for where I'm from and who I've become, all thanks to the people, the family that wanted me.

Guess it's about time to realize I am enough—take a liking to myself.

never miss a book

Thank you, dear reader, for coming along on this ride. I hope you had as much fun reading this work as I did writing it. If so, please take a moment to post a review and, by all means, tell a friend!

If you'd like more information on Perishing Hill and receive notifications of new releases as well as special offers on my books, please join my email list by visiting my website, Leliaapiet.com.

Lelia A. Piet grew up in the shadowed woods of the deep South, where silence could stretch for miles and stories were born in the dark. Her obsession with secrets, consequences, and the complexities of human behavior began early—crafting twisted tales for her sisters as they explored the wilderness of Little River Canyon. A graduate of Florida State University, Lelia left a career in education to write full-time, exchanging lesson plans for layered plots and unsettling truths.

Now based in Tennessee, she spends her days penning psychological suspense, filled with storm-lashed coastlines, buried betrayals, and characters on the edge. When not writing, she walks her dog, plots her next escape, and awaits visits from her grown sons —she has so many stories to tell them...

9 798988 254539